W9-BEL-492

AN
UNQUIET
GRAVE

Also by P. J. Parrish
in Large Print:

Island of Bones

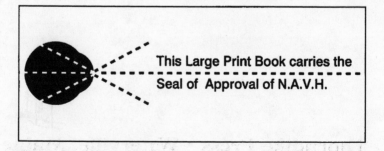

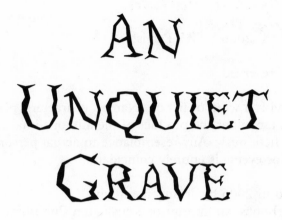

An Unquiet Grave

P. J. Parrish

Thorndike Press • Waterville, Maine

Published in 2006 by arrangement with
Pinnacle Books, an imprint of Kensington Publishing Corp.

Thorndike Press® Large Print Americana.

The tree indicium is a trademark of Thorndike Press.

The text of this Large Print edition is unabridged.
Other aspects of the book may vary from the original edition.

Set in 16 pt. Plantin by Ramona Watson.

Printed in the United States on permanent paper.

Library of Congress Cataloging-in-Publication Data

Parrish, P. J.
    An unquiet grave / by P. J. Parrish.
      p. cm. — (Thorndike Press large print Americana)
    ISBN 0-7862-8649-0 (lg. print : hc : alk. paper)
    1. Private investigators — Florida — Fiction. 2. Florida
— Fiction. 3. Serial murderers — Fiction. I. Title.
II. Thorndike Press large print Americana series.
PS3566.A7567U57 2006
  813′.54—dc22   2006006343

For all the mad housewives who weren't

As the Founder/CEO of NAVH, the only national health agency solely devoted to those who, although not totally blind, have an eye disease which could lead to serious visual impairment, I am pleased to recognize Thorndike Press* as one of the leading publishers in the large print field.

Founded in 1954 in San Francisco to prepare large print textbooks for partially seeing children, NAVH became the pioneer and standard setting agency in the preparation of large type.

Today, those publishers who meet our standards carry the prestigious "Seal of Approval" indicating high quality large print. We are delighted that Thorndike Press is one of the publishers whose titles meet these standards. We are also pleased to recognize the significant contribution Thorndike Press is making in this important and growing field.

Lorraine H. Marchi, L.H.D.
Founder/CEO
NAVH

* Thorndike Press encompasses the following imprints: Thorndike, Wheeler, Walker and Large Print Press.

The wind doth blow today, my love,
And a few small drops of rain;
I never had but one true-love;
In cold grave she was lain.

I'll do as much for my true-love
As any young man may;
I'll sit and mourn all at her grave
For a twelvemonth and a day.

The twelvemonth and a day being up,
The dead began to speak:
'Oh who sits weeping on my grave,
and will not let me sleep?'

— *The Unquiet Grave*
Arthur Quiller-Couch

Chapter 1

The Christmas lights were already up. He had the top down on the Mustang and he could see them as he drove up, a cluster of small white lights that someone had strung on the coconut palm in his yard. A stiff breeze was blowing in from the gulf, moving the fronds and sending the lights bobbing and dancing like fireflies on a hot summer night.

Louis Kincaid turned off the engine and just sat there, looking at the lights.

Fireflies. July Fourth. Michigan.

But there were no fireflies here. It was November, not July. And he was in South Florida.

His mind was playing tricks on him.

He reached over and popped the glove box, pulling out his Glock. Grabbing his overnight bag, he got out and headed to the cottage.

Maybe he was just tired. The job up in Tampa had been dull and drawn out. Surveillance of a woman who was suing a big trucking company because a semi had clipped her Honda and left her "permanently disabled and in extreme mental stress." He had spent four days tailing her with a video camera, finally getting a shot of her banging her car floor mats against the fender of her car — after she had come home from the beauty salon. The film was played in court. The woman got two grand for medical bills. He got five grand for his pay. Good money for a P.I., he supposed. At least it was enough to keep him in grouper sandwiches at Timmy's Nook for the next few months.

The mailbox was stuffed. He dug out the fliers and envelopes and opened the door.

"Honey, I'm home," he said, throwing down his bag.

Issy came trotting out of the bedroom. The cat looked up at him, its tail swishing on the terrazzo.

"Okay, okay," he said with a sigh.

He headed to the kitchen, tossing the stack of mail on the counter. He shook a bag of Tender Vittles into the bowl on the floor. The other bowl was filled with clean water. At least his weasel landlord Pierre had been taking care of things like he promised. He had half expected to come home and see a cat carcass lying on the floor.

He pulled open the fridge. One Heineken and a carton of Chinese takeout probably left over from the Ice Age. He stood there for a moment, letting the cold air wash over his sweaty face, then grabbed the beer and closed the fridge.

There was one lamp on in the living room, but the small cottage seemed dark and stale from being closed up. He went to the TV and punched the remote, unleashing a rainbow of light and sitcom laughter into the shadows. Finally, after a moment, he muted the sound and tossed the remote aside.

He cranked open the jalousie windows, and the warm gulf breeze wafted in. He stood there, breathing in the salt and night-blooming jasmine, holding the cold beer bottle against his forehead.

He still wasn't used to it — even after three years of living in Florida. September would come and he would be waiting for that cool kiss in the air, yet the temperature stayed in the nineties. October would come and he would be expecting the first frost on the windows, but there was nothing but the cloud of humidity. And then came November, when the trees should have been turning brown and gaunt. But here . . . here in Florida, everything was green and lush and sultry.

He hated the holidays. Thanksgiving and Christmas. Back-to-back reasons to give in to that small but powerful part of him that wanted to slide into silence and solitude.

His eyes drifted to the answering machine on the counter. The red light was blinking. Ten messages. He rewound the tape.

The first one was a time-share come-on. Three hang-ups. A man wanting to hire him to spy on his "whore wife." Two more hang-ups. Then a familiar voice with its unmistakable Mississippi drawl.

"Oh! My . . . a machine! I didn't know you finally got one. Oh dear . . . how much time do I have? Louis, this is Margaret."

Louis took a drink of beer.

"I'm calling to invite you to Thanksgiving dinner. We're fixing to have a real feast this year — I'm making my sweet potato pie — and I know you don't have any family to go to —"

Louis could hear Sam Dodie yelling in the background, telling his wife what to say. She hung up, forgetting to leave a number. But Louis knew the Dodies' number by heart; he had spent many an evening at their table, eating Margaret's cooking, listening to Sam's war stories.

Now that his ex-boss had retired to Florida, Sam Dodie's need to talk about his years spent as a Mississippi sheriff seemed to grow. It was either listen to it or go fishing.

The next voice came on, the thin soft voice of a boy.

"Hi, Louis. It's me. I guess you're not home yet."

Louis leaned closer to the machine.

"I wish you could come over for Thanksgiving, but Ma says we gotta go see Grandma Cockran up in St. Augustine. Chewbaca is getting real big, but Ma says he can't sleep with me 'cause I got allergies." A long pause. "Okay, I gotta go. I love you. See ya!"

Louis smiled. Chewbaca was one of Issy's kittens, conceived last winter during Ben's kidnapping. Ben had needed a lot of time to recover from his experience, and Louis believed the kitten somehow helped him do that. He still worried about the boy, worried about him being twelve and not having a father in his life, worried about his being able to ever trust people again. That was why he tried to see Ben as often as he could. But work had been demanding lately and there didn't seem to be enough time.

The last message. Another familiar voice. Female, deep, deeply familiar.

"Hey there. It's me. Just wanted to let you know I pulled some strings and got Thanksgiving and Friday off. I've got two Swanson's turkey dinners and a good bottle of French Chablis on ice, so get your sweet ass over here as soon as you can. Call me as soon as you get in."

She hung up.

Louis just sat there, staring at the machine. He took a drink of the beer, then replayed her message just to hear her voice.

He hadn't seen Joe in weeks. She was a homicide detective for Miami PD. He had met her when she came over to help work the homicides connected with Ben's kidnapping. They had started an intense affair, and for Louis, it was just what he needed.

Louis finished off the beer. Two invitations to Thanksgiving dinner. Not bad. But now he had to choose. A great feast at Margaret Dodie's table. Or two days in bed with Joe. A slow smile came to his face. Well, maybe Margaret would save him some leftovers.

His eyes went to the pile of mail near his elbow. He began sifting through it. The

14

blue envelope with the familiar Michigan address made him stop.

His birthday — he had forgotten again. But Frances never did.

He slit open the envelope and pulled out the birthday card from his foster mother. He opened it and a crisp twenty-dollar bill fluttered to the counter.

November 18, 1988

Dearest Louis.
Well, here you are at 29! How the years have flown by! Though you are far, far away, always know that our thoughts and love are with you on this special day. We hope you can find some use for our little gift!
Love and kisses,
Frances and Phillip

It was written in Frances's frilly hand. The card came as regular as the sun every November 18, written by Frances, signed for them both, and always with a twenty tucked inside.

He picked up the twenty. It was only then that he noticed the piece of white paper that had fallen to the floor. He stooped to pick it up and unfolded it.

The note was in black ink, the handwriting heavy and unfamiliar.

Dear Louis,

Frances does not know I am writing this to you, and for now I would ask that you don't mention it to her. I suppose I should have called you about this, but every time I picked up the phone, I couldn't quite figure out what to say. Writing things down has always been easier for me. Although nothing about this is easy really.

I have a friend whose grave I have been tending for sixteen years. The cemetery is being relocated and since my friend has no family, I made arrangements to move the coffin. But I was told it is empty. As you can imagine, I am quite upset and do not know where to turn. No one will help me and I feel I owe this to my friend. There is no way I can fully explain all this in a letter, so I hope you will just trust me when I say I need help. I am sorry to have to burden you with this, but I am quite desperate.

Please don't tell Frances anything about this. If you were able to come home for Thanksgiving, she wouldn't suspect anything and I could explain it all to you then. But if you have other plans, I understand.

— Phillip

Louis stared at the letter, rereading the middle paragraph, then the final line. *If you have other plans . . .*

It was the first time Phillip had ever asked anything from him. Except the night when he was eleven, caught again going out through the bedroom window.

Where you going, Louis?

I don't know. Just away.

If you keep running off like this, they'll take you away from me. Do you want that?

I don't care.

But I do. Promise me you won't run away again.

All right.

And he hadn't.

Louis folded the letter and sat there for a moment, listening to the whisper of the surf. He picked up the phone and dialed Joe's number in Miami. He got the machine and left her a message asking her to call back. Then he called American Airlines and made a reservation to fly to Detroit in the morning.

17

Chapter 2

Phillip Lawrence turned the Impala into the driveway and cut the engine. Louis looked up at the yellow brick tri-level.

The first image that usually came to him when other people started talking about their childhoods was a house. Other things came, too — smells, emotions, mental snapshots of events. But those kinds of memories were fluid, changing for good or bad, depending on how, and when, a person chose to look back on them.

But a house was different. It was solid and permanent, and it allowed people to say *I existed here. My memories are real.*

His image of home had always been a wood frame shack in Mississippi. It was an ugly picture, but one he had held on to for a long time, convinced it symbolized some kind of truth about who he was or what he should be.

But all during the flight up to Michigan, it wasn't the shack he was remembering. It was this house. And now, here it was before him — unchanged, real.

18

Almost. The shutters were brown this year, and the silver maple in the front yard had grown taller, its stark, black branches stretching high against the gray sky. A short row of flat evergreens lined the cracked sidewalk, and the birdbath was still there out front.

Louis smiled.

"What's so funny?" Phillip asked.

Louis looked at Phillip. "Nothing. It's just nice to be home."

He pushed open the car door and climbed out. Phillip brought his suitcase to him, and they walked to the front porch, Louis automatically slowing in deference to Phillip's limp.

Christmas lights were strung around the eaves, and a wreath hung on the door. He recognized the wreath. Old newspapers stuffed into an oval of chicken wire, spray-painted red and green, and covered with gobs of shellac. He knew the back read: *Louis, Age 11.*

"It scares me what else Frances kept," Louis said, nodding toward the wreath.

Phillip unlocked the door and pushed it open. "Don't look in the attic then."

Louis paused in the front hall, the assault to his senses almost bringing a sting to his eyes. Pot roast and lavender air freshener. Three steps leading down to the living room and kitchen were just to his left. To the right, more steps leading up to the five bedrooms. The pale yellow walls of the hallway were covered with a montage of framed photographs.

Phillip asked for his coat and Louis shrugged out of it, his gaze moving slowly over all the photographs. Boys. Dozens of different faces, at all ages. Some in Little League uniforms, some Boy Scouts, some standing outside a camper-trailer, some around the big blue Dough-Boy pool that once dominated the backyard. Boys . . . all the foster kids who had passed through this home for more than twenty years.

"Leave your suitcase here, Louis," Phillip said. "Frances is anxious to see you."

Louis followed Phillip, the pot roast aroma growing stronger. She was standing at the stove, her hands clasped in front of her apron. She had put on a few more pounds, her face round and flushed from the heat of the oven. Her hairstyle was the same, a halo of light brown hair, a few curls sweat-plastered to her forehead.

"Louis," she said, coming to him. She crushed him to her soft chest. "Oh, it's so good to see you."

Another sensory flood. The feel of her cheek, soft as wilted rose petals, the smell of the Johnson's Baby Powder she always used and that he, as a boy, assumed was peculiar to all white women. A memory rushed up to him, of Frances's face coming close in the dark as she tucked him in bed and kissed him good night.

Louis finally pushed from her embrace.

"You look too thin," she said. "You're not eating."

He smiled. "I make do."

She gave a snort and turned to the counter, coming back with a tray. "Here," she said.

The tray held a container of Win Schuler's cheese and a plate of carefully fanned crackers and tiny pickles. There were two blue cloth napkins and a silver cheese spreader.

"How long until dinner?" Phillip asked, pulling two beers out of the fridge.

Frances wiped her forehead. "A while. Why don't you two go downstairs and have one of your visits? I'll call you when I'm ready."

Phillip nodded his head toward the basement door and Louis followed, carrying the tray. Louis slowed as he neared the bottom of the stairs. Knotty pine paneling and a bar. Blue-tiled linoleum he had helped Phillip install. Christmas lights twinkled in the mirror behind the bar. On the bar itself was an old radio, a blue rotary dial phone, a bowl of walnuts, and a miniature aluminum tree.

"Is that the same tree that was here when I was a kid?" Louis asked.

Phillip took a seat at the bar. "Yup. Probably twenty years old by now. Every year, she drags it out again."

Louis slid onto the stool next to him. "Please don't tell me those are the same walnuts."

Phillip smiled. "Could very well be. Want one?"

"I'll pass."

Phillip reached for a nut and the silver cracker. Louis knew Phillip was fifty-six, and except for the limp from the Korean War, he was lean and healthy. His face was still striking, and as Louis watched him now, he had a memory of one afternoon when he was twelve and was watching TV and happened upon the movie *The Day the Earth Stood Still.* He had looked at Michael Rennie and wondered what his foster father was doing playing a spaceman in some corny old black-and-white movie. It was a full year before he finally worked up the nerve to ask, and Phillip had just laughed and laughed. It was years later that Louis stopped thinking of Phillip Lawrence as some mysterious alien presence in his life.

Louis considered Phillip's face now. The network of lines had deepened and there was something else in his foster father's face he had never ever seen before — a deep, aching sadness.

Phillip felt his gaze and looked up. Louis looked away, picking up his beer and swinging his stool around on the pretense of looking around the basement.

"Nothing's changed. Place looks good," Louis said.

"Well, there's a lot of stuff that needs fixing, but one of the benefits of getting old is your eyes start going, so I don't notice it as much."

The trickle of memories continued. The basement was musty and outdated, but it was the best room in the house. This was where everything happened. Louis could almost see the heaps of crumpled holiday wrapping paper. See Phillip leading the Cub Scout meetings that he used to watch from under the steps, too shy, too scared, to join in. He could remember the indoor campouts in winter, a half dozen boys in

23

ragged sleeping bags, Phil sitting cross-legged whispering ghost stories.

"You seem different, Louis," Phillip said.

"Different how?"

"Different as in . . . calm. Maybe even happy."

"Things are good right now."

"Good. You've waited a long time."

Louis turned back to Phillip. He wanted to tell him that he seemed different, too. But instinct was telling him he had to leave it up to Phillip to bring up his friend and the empty grave.

The furnace kicked on, and hot air puffed down from the ceiling vents. From the kitchen above came the sound of clattering plates and Frances humming quietly. Louis reached for a cracker and spread some cheese on it. He heard Phillip take a deep breath and he figured he was about to tell him why he had asked him to come up.

But Phillip was quiet, cracking the walnuts.

Louis realized he would have to do the prodding. All those countless times when Phillip had been the one to urge him out of his shell. It felt odd to have the roles reversed.

"Phillip, why did you want me to come

24

here?" Louis asked. "What exactly is going on?"

Phillip glanced at him, then went back to the walnut, carefully picking the bits out of the shell.

"I don't know where to start," he said quietly.

"Try the beginning."

Phillip set the nutcracker down and turned to face Louis. "I've been visiting the grave of my friend for sixteen years. Last month, I went out there and there was a sign saying the place had been sold and that families could claim the remains for relocation."

"You said that in your letter," Louis said.

Phillip nodded. "When they found out I wasn't a relative, they wouldn't tell me anything. But there was this woman there, I guess she felt sorry for me or something. She told me that my friend's family . . ." Phillip paused. "They didn't want the remains."

Phillip brushed his hands together to get rid of the walnut shells. "I asked if I could do it and she said yes. So I signed a paper and made the arrangements for a new plot at Riverside back here in Plymouth. I even bought a new casket. But when they went to transfer the body, that's when they found out . . ."

Phillip stopped. His hands encircled the beer bottle, but he didn't move to take a drink.

"You said in your letter the coffin was empty," Louis prodded.

"No, it wasn't empty. It was filled with rocks. That's what they found when they opened it."

Phillip was sitting there, like if he let go of the bottle it would fall apart in his hands.

"So," Louis went on, "you think your friend could be alive?"

Phillip shook his head slowly. "No, no. I know that isn't possible."

"You said in your letter you didn't tell Frances. Why not?"

Phillip was very still, his voice low. "Because my friend is a woman I knew before Frances. I don't think Frances would understand."

Louis took a drink of his beer, his mind already forming questions, some too personal to ask. "Phil, I can't lie to Frances."

"I know, I know." Phillip looked at Louis. "I just want to find out what happened. Maybe there was just a mix-up at the cemetery, a bookkeeping error or something. Things like that happen, don't they?"

Louis nodded.

"I just want to see my friend reburied." Phillip's expression was beseeching. "Can you maybe just look into things? Can you help with that at least?"

"All right," Louis said.

There was a sudden noise above and they both looked up to see Frances standing at the top of the stairs, craning her head to look down.

"What are you two up to down here?" she asked.

"Just reminiscing a little, Fran," Phillip said.

"Well, dinner's ready and I want to hear everything that is going on in Louis's life. So get your butts up here now."

"We're coming up right now," Phillip said.

Frances went back to the kitchen. Louis could hear her footsteps above their heads, hear her humming again.

"I need to go to the cemetery," Louis said.

"We can go first thing in the morning." Phillip paused. "Thank you, Louis."

His voice had changed, like he was relieved the hardest part was over. But the sadness did not leave his eyes. Phillip slid off the stool and started up the stairs. He looked back and for an instant Louis had the feeling that Phillip Lawrence was a stranger all over to him again. This was a man with shadows in his soul.

Louis picked up his beer and followed Phillip upstairs.

Chapter 3

Louis hadn't been back to Plymouth in more than six years. After he graduated from University of Michigan in 1981, he had stayed in Ann Arbor to work on the police force there. He felt comfortable in the college town, comfortable in its rich stew of races, religions, and ways of thinking. Every time he had gone back to visit Phillip and Frances during the past few years, it had been while they were up North on vacation, sort of neutral territory. Never here, in Plymouth.

"So how's the old hometown look to you?"

Louis glanced over at Phillip, who was driving. "About the same," he answered.

Louis's eyes drifted back out the cold-fogged window. The Lawrences lived out on the edge of town, and Phillip had to drive through the small downtown to get to the freeway. Louis's eyes lingered on the square with its white band shell fully exposed by the bare trees. He could see the old columned bank and the marquee of the

Penn Theater: FIELD OF DREAMS. And there, on the corner, the old hotel.

"They've remodeled the Mayflower," Louis said absently.

"Yeah. But they kept that old wallpaper in the dining room."

Louis had a sudden memory of a sixth grade field trip. It was a slate-gray November day, just like today, and he remembered feeling alone and small as the bus let him and the other kids off in front of the Mayflower Hotel for their lunch.

He knew now that the Mayflower wasn't a fancy place. But it seemed like it then, with its dark green carpeting and shining wood desk and the sour-looking woman in a black uniform who handed them menus in the restaurant. The menu was huge in his hands and he didn't know anything. What to order. What to do with the heavy white cloth napkin. Where to go if he had to pee.

The teacher was standing up and talking about the Pilgrims, pointing to the wallpaper with its pictures of the *Nina, Pinta,* and *Santa Maria.* She was saying that they should all be thankful for the sacrifices of their forefathers who came here in ships to make their lives here possible. He had sat there listening to her, thinking, *well,*

30

they sure the heck weren't my *forefathers.*

"The town is changing," Phillip said.

Louis heard something in Phillip's voice and turned.

"All these young folks moving out here, looking for some lost idea of a perfect small town," Phillip said, his eyes steady on the road.

"Plymouth isn't perfect," Louis said carefully.

"They closed Cloverdale's, you know. Some chain came in on Main Street."

Phillip was shaking his head in disgust. But Louis was remembering soft Sunday evenings, walking to the old ice cream parlor, he and Phillip getting double-dip cones of lush black cherry ice cream and ignoring the stares of all the white faces.

Louis rubbed a sleeve over the fogged window. They were passing the high school now. The press of memories kept coming. Four years of being the only black kid in an all-white school. No one was mean, no one called him names. He was accepted, but almost like some weird mascot. Shared jokes in the john and always a seat in the cafeteria. But never an invitation to the parties at the white kids' homes.

Phillip was looking at the high school as they waited for the light to change.

31

"You still run?" he asked.

"Not as much as I should," Louis said. He was still back in high school, trying to bring a face into focus, the face of some asshole PE coach who told him he should go out for basketball. The man didn't care that Louis hated basketball, just kept pushing him until Louis started cutting PE. Finally, Phillip had a talk with the coach and then with Louis. Eventually, Louis went out for track just to please Phillip. But to his surprise, he liked cross-country. He liked the rush of the cool air on his face and the sound of his pulse in his ears. He liked the brain-cleansing feel of running. He liked the aloneness of it.

"Frances found your letter sweater the other day in a box in the basement," Phillip said. "She sent it to the cleaners so it would be ready when you came home."

"I don't want that old thing."

"Take it anyway," Phillip said. "Okay?"

The light turned green and they drove on in silence. Phillip reached down and jabbed the lighter, and with a gesture born of decades shook a cigarette from its pack and lit it with one hand, his eyes never leaving the road. He cracked his window and blew the stream out.

"What did you tell Frances about today?" Louis said.

"Just that you wanted to go for a drive."

"Phillip, I need to know something. How much exactly does she know about this? Does she even know you visited this cemetery?"

Phillip nodded. "She thinks it's an old army buddy."

"That's what you told her?"

Phillip nodded again. "I could never bring myself to tell her the truth."

Louis let that go. The landscape changed as U.S. 12 stretched into the Michigan countryside. Flat, and tufted with yellow grass, the air swirling with crumbling rust-colored leaves.

"Where are we going?" Louis asked.

"The Irish Hills."

Louis was trying to remember if Phillip had ever taken him to the Irish Hills. But he didn't need to think long. Phillip answered for him.

"I never brought you out there," he said. "I thought about it, but it would have meant taking Frances, too, and I just couldn't do that."

Louis formed the question, and then wasn't sure he wanted to ask it. But he knew he needed to. "The Irish Hills was your place with her?" he asked.

Phillip glanced at him, then turned his gaze back to the road. "Only for one weekend."

Phillip didn't say anything else and Louis held the rest of his questions. This wasn't some passing fling. It was something that had survived Phillip's thirty-one-year marriage to Frances. Longer than Louis had been alive.

A first love.

It wasn't something he knew much about. It sure as hell hadn't happened for him in high school. In the midseventies, many parts of the country were beginning to tolerate interracial relationships, but he never had the sense Plymouth was one of them. He had never gone to a dance or any other school function with a white girl on his arm. His first real girlfriend had been in college, but even she didn't come with those tender memories that should accompany a first love. Right now he couldn't even remember her last name.

He settled back in the seat, watching the empty land, feeling the cold swirl of air from Phillip's cracked window against the back of his neck.

There was no sign for the cemetery. Only a listing black iron gate stuck deep into the mud, as if it had been left open for quite some time. Two towering pines stood guard on each side of the entrance and the land beyond it was a flat expanse of brown grass bordered by thickets and trees. As they walked up to the gate, Louis could see a silent backhoe sitting at the far end next to a heap of black dirt. Near it was a gangly yellow hoist, used to lift the concrete vaults from the graves. Three muddy vaults sat off in the far corner of the cemetery.

Only the cawing of crows broke the still cold air. Louis looked up and spotted two of the birds staring down at them from the two sentry pines.

Phillip walked on ahead and Louis followed, scanning the ground. The grass wasn't very high, only five or six inches, but Louis didn't see any headstones or monuments. A yard or two into the cemetery, he spied a plot of freshly disturbed ground where he guessed someone had been dug up and the hole refilled. Then there was another, and a third, before Phillip finally stopped.

At his feet was an open grave, the

bottom puddled with dark water. Phillip knelt at the head of the grave and pushed aside the dead grass. Louis stepped closer.

A small stone square was pressed into the ground, no larger than six inches by eight inches. Louis squatted to look at the stone. It was well worn, but someone, probably Phillip, had scraped away the moss and mud, and the engraving was easy to read.

No name. Just a number — 1304.

"What kind of cemetery is this?" Louis asked, looking up at Phillip.

Phillip rose slowly, his eyes drifting back to the road they had driven in on, and beyond, to a cluster of taller trees. "There's a hospital over there. This is where they buried their unclaimed dead."

Louis looked off in the same direction as Phillip, but he saw nothing. "What kind of hospital?" he asked.

"A sanitarium."

"An insane asylum?"

"Yes."

"Your friend died there?"

"Yes. At least that's what I was told."

Louis looked back at the stone marker embedded in the grass. "And all these people got were numbers on their graves?"

"I suppose it started out as some kind of

privacy thing, maybe to keep the curiosity seekers from coming in and vandalizing the graves," Phillip said. "There were a couple of well-known criminals who were sent here back in the fifties and sixties."

Louis looked off at the far trees. Something was coming back to him. He stood up, facing Phillip. "This is Hidden Lake, isn't it?"

"Yes," Phillip said. "You know about it?"

Louis hesitated. He knew. He had heard about Hidden Lake many times, mostly in hushed conversations with other kids. Talk of crazy people screaming behind iron bars, stories of secret operations, torture, and brain removals. No one he knew had ever seen Hidden Lake, but every kid knew what it was like. Hidden Lake was hell, Halloween, and a chamber of horrors all rolled into one. It was where all the really crazy people were kept, where your mother would threaten to send you if you were bad. It was where all the insane killers were locked away.

A memory came to him suddenly. A serial killer from the late sixties, a man who prowled lovers' lanes, chopping off heads and eating the eyeballs of teenagers. The killer had been sent here, hadn't he? Or was that just another story whispered in tents at a summer camp, a story spawned of some boy's fevered imagination?

He knew now that none of it was true. He knew, too, that mental illness was something to be treated, not feared. Still, as he tried to imagine Phillip's friend in a place like Hidden Lake, he couldn't shake the images that were suddenly crawling out of the locked box of his own childhood nightmares.

He walked a few feet away and saw another stone marker almost hidden in the grass. "You mentioned that maybe some numbers got mixed up. Were you able to check that?"

Phillip shook his head. "No one will talk to me. The company in charge of transferring the bodies claims it's not their problem. And the hospital is being dismantled and there's only a few people left to clean things up. The records are either lost or just gone."

"What about the local police? Have you tried them?"

Phillip nodded. "They said if the hospital doesn't feel the need to report this, then it's not really their business. I get the feeling that all anyone wants to do is level the hospital and forget it ever existed."

Louis pulled a small camera from his

coat pocket and came back to the open grave. He took a picture of the stone marker, then moved to the nearby marker, brushed aside the grass, and took a photo of that one, too. He did the same with all four surrounding graves, hoping that having the numbers might help verify any errors.

He looked back to Phillip, who had knelt down by the open grave. He was pulling the dead weeds and grass away from the stone marker.

"What was her name?" Louis asked.

Phillip rose slowly and brushed the dirt from his hands. "Claudia. Claudia DeFoe," he said. He walked slowly away, his hands in his pockets.

There was a sign on the backhoe: SPERA & SONS EXCAVATIONS. Louis wrote it in his notepad. He looked over toward Phillip, who was standing at the cemetery entrance under the huge pine tree, lighting a cigarette. Phillip was wearing a gray overcoat, which seemed to accentuate his height and thinness, and his chopped gray hair was the same color as the sky. For a moment, he seemed to disappear before Louis's eyes.

Louis went over to him. "I think you need to show me this hospital," he said.

Chapter 4

They backtracked on U.S. 50 about a half mile. There were no signs for Hidden Lake, but Phillip easily spotted the small side road obscured by a tall stand of trees and slowed the car for the turn in.

Another iron gate, this one in better repair than the one back at the cemetery. There was a discreet sign on the gate that read HIDDEN LAKE. A uniformed man emerged from the red brick guardhouse as they pulled up. Phillip rolled down his window and the man leaned in to peer at them.

"What can I do for you?" he asked.

Phillip glanced at Louis, so Louis leaned across the seat.

"We wanted to see someone about claiming a deceased patient," he said.

"Sorry. We're closed for the weekend."

"We need to talk to someone in charge," Louis said. "If we come back Monday, who do I see?"

The guard shrugged. "Not sure. There's only a skeleton crew and I'm just here to keep folks out. But you can come back Monday and see for yourself."

Louis glanced at Phillip. He would have to come back alone Monday; he didn't want Phillip to have to lie again to Frances. Phillip started to put the car in gear.

"Wait a second," Louis said, leaning back over. "Can you tell me where . . ." He pulled the notebook from his jacket pocket. "Spera and Sons Excavations — do you know where it is?"

The guard had to think for a moment. "Go back up to U.S. 12 and head west. Just past the Mystery Hill, take your first left. Go a half mile and you'll see 'em."

"Thanks."

Phillip swung the car back onto the highway. He had been quiet since they left the cemetery. As they drove deeper into the hills, Louis stole a glance at him. Phillip was staring straight ahead out the windshield.

They passed through a town with a shimmering lake and dark clusters of pines and bare birches. A small wood sign welcomed travelers to Ardmore and underneath it read WHERE THE PAST IS PERFECT.

A few miles farther, Louis saw a sign for Mystery Hill. As he turned the corner, he saw Phillip twist his neck to look back at the faded yellow building.

"You want to stop?" Louis asked.

"No."

They saw the sign for Spera & Sons Excavations and Phillip pulled into the gravel parking lot. The compound was enclosed by a high chain-link fence, the top coiled in barbed wire. Behind the main building, Louis could see backhoes and other machinery in the muddy yard. There was a warehouse and beyond that a large white tent. If Louis was guessing right, this small company had won this hospital contract only because it was local and that the tent was probably a temporary holding area for remains not yet claimed or transferred to other graveyards.

Louis hesitated as he got out of the car, thinking Phillip should not go inside. But Phillip was already heading to the main building. Louis caught up with him and opened the door.

Inside, it looked like a construction company office — scuffed linoleum floors, harsh fluorescent lights, and scarred metal desks. The walls were covered in bulletin boards. The largest board, Louis noted, held a schematic of the cemetery. It was marked in a grid and shaded where graves had already been exhumed.

The office was empty, but a radio was playing softly, tuned to a country-and-western station. There was a door leading out into the warehouse.

"Hello! Anyone here?" Louis called out.

His eyes were drawn to a second bulletin board. It looked like an old architect's plan of a huge factory or development of some kind. He went over to get a better look.

The legend below the drawing identified it as HIDDEN LAKE FARMS ASYLUM AND HOSPITIAL. The drawing showed a sprawling compound of maybe a dozen buildings set down amid farm plots, pastures, and a small lake, all enclosed by a fence. Beyond the fence to the west, set away from the main compound in the surrounding woods, was a place designated only as CEMETERY. Without his glasses, Louis had to squint to read the date: 1895.

The flush of a toilet drew Louis's eyes back to a man emerging from a door. He was a big guy, with a wisp of black hair and glasses, the shoulders of his blue flannel shirt hanging loose on his round frame. He was carrying a yellowed paperback of Robert B. Parker's, *Looking for Rachel Wallace.*

"I'm John Spera. Can I help you?" the man asked.

Louis introduced them both, then told the man they were here to ask about one of the patients.

Spera set down the paperback and slapped open a thick ledger. "Name?"

Phillip answered, "Claudia DeFoe."

Spera's eyes came up quickly. "You're the guy who called."

"Yes," Phillip said.

"I told you on the phone, this isn't our problem, Mr. Lawrence. If the hospital wants to bury rocks, they can bury rocks. We just get paid to dig up the caskets."

Phillip's face twitched, and Louis stepped forward quickly. "Can we see her casket?"

Spera hesitated.

"What can it hurt?" Louis asked. "It's just rocks, right?"

"I don't —"

"You do have it, don't you?"

"Sure we do. We keep everything until someone claims it or we're told to send the remains somewhere else. Even rocks."

Now Louis was quiet, watching Phillip. His face was tight but his eyes had a flicker of something Louis read as distress.

"All right, but I got to warn you," Spera

44

said. "There's other remains out there. You sure you want to go?"

Louis looked to Phillip, who nodded. They followed Spera out the back door and across the gravel lot. Despite the cold, Louis detected a familiar scent in the air — the sour mixture of decomposition.

"Phil, you sure about this?" Louis said quietly as they walked.

"When I was in Korea we got caught in a bad night battle once, the kind of thing where nobody knows what's going on," Phillip said. "In the morning, I looked out and there were bodies hanging on the barbed wire and the sarge just said, 'You, you, and you, go clear the field.' So we did. I've seen dead bodies before, Louis."

They stopped and Spera threw back the flap of the tent. The smell engulfed them and Louis's hand flew to his nose. He glanced quickly at Phillip.

"Let's go," Phillip said quietly.

There were sixty or seventy tables set up in the tent. Each table held a pile of dirt and wood and one large clear plastic bag. The wood was what was left of the caskets, Louis guessed, the cheap boards now warped or waterlogged, some just in pieces. The bags held the bones and tatters of cloth. The few caskets that were still in one piece were stacked on plywood shelves at the back of the tent.

"How many graves are in the cemetery?" Louis asked.

"Over six thousand," Spera said.

They followed Spera as he wove his way through the tables. Louis couldn't help but look down as they passed. Each heap of bones had a tag attached, printed with two sets of numbers, Spera told them: the graveyard identifying number and a new number assigned by Spera. No names on any of them.

Spera finally stopped near the back of the tent next to a screened window. The outside flap was whipping against the canvas, and Louis was grateful for the fresh air.

On the table lay a pile of medium-size rocks, a scattering of dirt, and a few shards of boards dark with age and rot. The tag had the same number as Claudia's grave marker — 1304. Spera had given her the number 51.

Louis looked at Phillip. His skin was ashen as his eyes flicked over the pile of the rocks.

Louis cleared his throat to get Spera's attention. "The graves next to this one were untouched," he said. "Can you let us know when you get to them?"

Spera had to pull his eyes from Phillip. "I could do that."

Louis had asked mainly for Phillip's sake. He knew that the chances of Claudia's remains being in a neighboring grave by mistake were almost nil. Even if Claudia's remains were still in that cemetery somewhere, they could be in any one of those thousands of unnamed graves.

He touched Phillip's arm. Phillip turned away and started wandering the rows of tables, peering down into each heap.

"Mr. Spera," Louis said, "what can you tell me about the hospital?"

"Well, it's been here forever," Spera said. "It's just something we've all gotten used to over the years. When we were kids we used to hear these stories about —"

Louis shook his head and Spera stopped himself, watching Phillip.

"I do know," Spera said, "that out of all these graves, only twelve have been claimed by relatives. Seems most have been forgotten or folks just don't want to acknowledge them."

"What's going to happen to those that aren't claimed?" Louis asked.

"We send 'em over to county and they'll rebury them somewhere else," Spera said.

47

Louis turned back to Phillip. He had stopped at a plastic bag and was fingering the edge. Louis wondered if he had heard what Spera had said. But Phillip just walked away without looking up.

"Look, if you don't need me anymore," Spera said.

"Thanks, you've been a big help," Louis said.

Spera left. Louis stayed for a few moments, his eyes on the pile of rocks. Thousands of people buried in that cemetery but only twelve had been claimed. It was beyond sad, almost grotesque.

He looked up and didn't see Phillip. Then he spotted him over in a far corner of the tent. Louis started toward him and as he neared, he saw the white casket. It was sitting on a table by itself, apart from all the other decrepit wooden boxes. It was pearly white with gleaming silver handles. There was a tag attached to one of the handles on which someone had scribbled HOLD FOR P. LAWRENCE. Phillip was just standing there, staring at it.

"This was for her," Phillip said. "This is the one I picked out."

The cold air swirled in from the open tent entrance, the smell of decay eddying around them. Phillip reached out and put a hand on the coffin. He pulled in a deep breath that caught in his throat.

"Come on," Louis said, taking his arm. "Let's go home."

Chapter 5

Louis stripped off his jacket, taking a second to stand under the ceiling vent to warm up. When he reached back to take Phillip's coat to hang it on the peg next to his, Phillip was already heading to the kitchen.

Louis followed him. Still wearing his coat, Phillip veered off into the dark dining room. He opened a breakfront, pulling down a glass. He popped open a lower cabinet door and grabbed a bottle of Maker's Mark. Frances came in from the kitchen just as he was pouring the drink.

Her eyes went to the glass and then to Louis. "I was getting worried about you. How was the trip?" she asked.

Louis waited for Phillip to answer. When he didn't, Louis gave it a shot. "Fine. It was very cold." Louis nodded at the bottle still in Phillip's hand. "Phillip, pour me one. I could use some warming up, too."

Phillip took out another glass, poured a shot, and handed it to Louis. Louis didn't like bourbon, but he hid his grimace as he took a drink.

"So where did you go?" Frances asked, her eyes still on her husband.

Phillip took a slow drink.

"Did you go visit your friend?" Frances asked.

"Yes," Phillip said. "Louis and I were talking about him last night and I thought I'd take him out there."

Louis looked down into his glass.

"Maybe I should come with you sometime," Frances said.

"It's an old army buddy, Frances. You know I don't talk much about that."

"You've never even told me his name, Phillip."

Louis took a drink, wishing he was somewhere else. Jesus, this was awkward. Here they were, standing in a dark dining room, not able to look into each other's eyes, pretending everything was normal.

"Where is this cemetery?" Frances asked.

Phillip turned the glass slowly with his fingers. He wasn't going to answer.

"Irish Hills," Louis said.

"Really? I've been there," Frances said. "My parents took me out there once or twice. Is it still nice?"

No answer from Phillip again.

"We didn't see much of it," Louis said finally. "What we did see looked, you know, kind of run-down. An old amusement park, some old motels. All closed right now. Not much to see really."

Frances was watching Phillip. "I would have liked to go anyway," she said. "It's been so cold and I've been stuck in this house all week. I'd like a nice drive."

Phillip set the glass down carefully on the polished dining room table. "I better go get cleaned up," he said quietly.

Frances's eyes followed him out of the dining room. They heard the close of the bathroom door. Frances looked at Louis, and he saw something register in the bland prettiness of her round face, a slight tightness around her mouth. She picked up the empty glass, wiping the water ring with her sweater sleeve. She went back into the kitchen.

Louis stayed in the dark dining room. She knew. Wives always knew. Maybe Frances didn't know *what* was wrong, but she knew something was. And it occurred to him that Phillip was probably oblivious of all the vibrations his wife was putting out.

Thirty-one years . . . that was how long they had been married now. Moods and quirks had become second nature, as easy to read as a children's book. If Phillip had been behaving like this for several weeks, Frances would have to be blind not to know something was wrong.

Louis's mind tripped to Joe, and he let the image of her face come, welcoming it even, as something to dwell on instead of Phillip's secret. The chemistry born of their working a case together had deepened into something he had never expected. Was it love? He had no idea. Sometimes weeks could go by when he didn't see her, yet as soon as he did, it was as if she had always been there.

Almost ten months . . . that's how long he had been with Joe. And then, only on weekends, if they were lucky. But he always knew when something was bothering her. He could hear it in her voice. It would go just a hair huskier, and her speech just a beat slower. He never mentioned to her that he noticed. But he liked being able to tell.

Louis could hear Frances in the kitchen. He had to go in there. He just hoped she wouldn't ask something he couldn't answer.

The kitchen was bright after the gloom of the dining room. He went to the sink, poured out the bourbon, and rinsed the glass. He could feel Frances's eyes on him as he went to the refrigerator and got a Heineken.

"Do you have plans for tomorrow?" Frances asked.

Louis heard the slight edge in her voice. Suddenly he was getting tired of playing word games that skipped along the edges of the truth.

"Not really," he said, leaning against the counter.

Frances opened the oven and pulled out a pie. The kitchen was filled with the smell of pumpkin. "Will you be here for dinner?" she asked, without looking up.

Louis hesitated. He and Phillip had barely talked on the ride back from the Irish Hills. Phillip had pulled inward and had just sat there, head back, eyes closed. Louis had wanted to ask him questions, questions he needed answers to if he was going to figure out where to go next. But Phillip had deflected all his attempts to talk.

Frances set the pie down on the counter and turned toward Louis, clasping her arms across her chest, holding herself like she was cold.

"Louis, what's going on?" she asked.

"Pardon?"

54

"With Phillip. What's wrong?"

Louis struggled to keep his eyes on hers. "Nothing's wrong."

"Don't tell me that. Is Phillip sick?"

"What?"

"That's it, isn't it? Is it something awful that he can't tell me? Is that why he asked you to come home?"

Louis almost let out a breath of relief. "No, he's fine. Please don't worry about that."

"Then what is it?"

Louis gave her a shake of his head. "It's not my place, Frances."

She turned away, toward the sink, head bowed. Louis heard the sound of running water and when he looked up, Frances was rinsing bowls, her arms pumping. Louis left the kitchen, going out to the den. He paused to switch on a lamp and when he looked up he saw Phillip outside on the back patio.

Louis opened the sliding glass door and stepped out into the cold. Phillip was smoking a cigarette, dressed in a clean shirt and an old sweater, his hair wet from his shower.

"Frances thinks you're sick," Louis said.

"What?"

"She knows something is bothering you

and she told me she thinks you are sick and afraid to tell her."

"Good God," Phillip said softly.

Louis looked off into the bare trees of the backyard. He let out a long slow breath that spiraled up into the cold air. "Look, Phil, I appreciate what you're going through here, but please don't ask me to lie for you."

"I shouldn't have done that," Phillip said. "I apologize."

They were quiet. Phillip took a long drag on his cigarette, then bent down to snuff it out in the pail of sand that Frances always had kept on the patio as her one concession to his habit.

Phillip's eyes went to the sliding glass door. They could just see Frances's back in the kitchen from where they stood outside. Phillip reached into his pants pocket and pulled out another cigarette, and Louis knew it was just a ploy to buy them more time outside to talk.

"Tell me more about Claudia. How'd you meet her?" Louis asked, thinking that maybe if Phillip started with the good memories, it would be easier.

Phillip's Zippo gave his face a sharpness as he lit the cigarette. He stuffed the lighter back in his pocket and drew on the cigarette.

"It was the summer of fifty-one, at a beach party, one of those things with a bonfire and kids passing around a bottle," Phillip said. "I had a job at this country club over in Saugatuck to make enough to go back to Western. I had never seen her around town before that night on the beach. She was just there, sitting by herself, this little thing wrapped up in this big blue sweater. She had blond hair that smelled like lilacs. She was seventeen. Maybe that should have scared me off, but it didn't."

He paused to pick a bit of tobacco off his lip. "When she had to leave that night, I walked her home. Her family had one of those big stone fortress houses on Lake Michigan. We only had a week together. I went back to Western and she went home."

"That's the last time you saw her?" Louis asked.

"Oh no, no." Phillip let out a low, sad laugh. "Turned out we were neighbors of sorts. The DeFoes lived in Grosse Pointe Farms. My folks lived in the less desirable part of the Pointes, a place everybody called the Cabbage Patch. We grew up less than ten miles from each other and a galaxy apart."

Phillip had gone quiet again. Louis

could see the glowing tip of his cigarette as he took another drag. It was a moment before Phillip spoke again.

"We saw each other on weekends," he said. "She'd sneak out and her brother Rodney would drive her to the park by the lake and I'd pick her up on my motorcycle."

"What happened?" Louis asked.

Phillip let out a long breath. "Her mother found out and threatened to send Claudia away to school." He paused. "We decided to elope. It was nuts, crazy . . . she was so young. But I didn't care. I wanted her."

Louis was surprised, but he remained quiet.

"We made plans to leave late at night, after her mother was asleep. Rodney was going to bring her." Phillip took a hard breath. "I waited at the park, but she never showed up."

Louis waited, shivering in the cold. Phillip didn't seem to notice.

"The next day I went to her house," Phillip went on. "I stood out there, banging on that door, and finally this maid lets me in and tells me to wait." He paused. "I'll never forget standing in that goddamn library thinking Claudia was in that house somewhere that very minute and I couldn't get to her. So I starting yelling out her name. I was standing in that big foyer at the bottom of that staircase yelling her name and hearing it come back to me in that big empty house." He took a breath. "The butler or whatever the hell he was came back, then some security guy showed up and threw me out. He followed me down the road until I was past the guardhouse."

Phillip paused. Louis waited. The words were coming, but like slivers of glass painfully pulled through the prism of Phillip's memories.

"I kept calling," Phillip said. "But no one would talk to me. Then, a few months later, Rodney showed up at my door. He told me he was there for my own good, to help me get over her."

Another pause. It went on so long Louis feared Phillip had shut down. The ash from his cigarette fell to the patio.

"Then Rodney told me Claudia tried to kill herself," Phillip said. "That's why I couldn't see her. She had slit her wrists."

Phillip looked down at the cigarette butt in his fingers as if suddenly aware of it. He reached down and put it in the sand pail.

When he straightened, he went on, his voice steady.

"He said Claudia was sick, that she had always been mentally fragile. He told me — he begged me — to just let her go."

A light went on inside the house. From the corner of his eye, Louis could see Frances in the dining room, setting the table for dinner.

"What did you do?" Louis asked.

Phillip was silent.

"Phillip? What did you do?"

"I tried to forget her. And I did. I met Frances. And for a long time, I didn't think about Claudia. Then, a week before Frances and I were going to be married, I drove to Hidden Lake. I wasn't even sure she was still there. But she was. A nurse took pity on me and let me in to see her."

Louis glanced toward the dining room. Frances had disappeared. He hoped she wouldn't come out before Phillip finished.

"It was cold but sunny," Phillip said. "She was sitting on a sunporch. She was just sitting there, holding this blanket around herself, and she looked up at me. She looked up at me and she didn't see me."

Phillip turned and Louis could see his face clearly in the light spilling out from inside. Phillip's eyes glistened.

"I was scared," he whispered. "I was never so scared in my life."

"Phil —"

Phillip ran a hand over his face.

"I gave up," he said.

"What?"

"I gave up, Louis. I couldn't face it, any of it. Why she was there, what was happening to her, and that look on her face, like she had been erased. I couldn't face any of it." Phillip shook his head slowly and looked away. "I ran away. It wasn't my finest moment."

"But you went back," Louis said.

"Oh yeah, I went back in 1972," Phillip said. "It was my fortieth birthday. I went back to the hospital and they told me she had died there a year before."

"That's when you started tending her grave," Louis said.

"Not until the summer after," Phillip said.

"Phil, you were a very young man when all that happened."

"I ran," Phillip said. "Don't you see? I just left her in that goddamn place and ran." He turned quickly, taking a step away.

Louis looked at Phillip's back. He let out a long, slow breath. "Phil, you need to tell Frances."

"I know," Phillip said without turning.

Louis looked toward the patio doors. He could see Frances standing there, looking out at them. "We need to go in," he said.

Phillip was looking out over the yard. "What's next?" he asked.

"What?"

"The next step to finding her remains. What's next?"

Louis thought for a moment. "I can't go back to the hospital until Monday. Maybe I could try her family."

"We'll go tomorrow," Phillip said.

"No, I'll go alone. It's better that way. You're going to have to trust me on this."

Phillip gave him a nod and went inside. Louis sank into a lawn chair. The metal was cold on the back of his legs, and he felt a shiver move through his shoulders. But he didn't want to go inside.

It wasn't my finest moment.

He could see her face now. Her dark skin streaked with rain. Her eyes frightened.

I'm pregnant, Louis.

Louis stared out into the dark yard. He could barely make out the shape of an old rusted swing set.

I ran away. From Claudia, Frances, everything. It wasn't my finest moment.

Louis pushed up from the chair and went back inside.

Chapter 6

Nine miles. That's all it was. Louis had clocked it on the odometer as he drove north from the broken buildings of downtown Detroit to the manicured mansions of Grosse Pointe. Nine short miles from hell to heaven with a quick trip through the purgatory of Phillip's Cabbage Patch.

It was strange how little he really knew about his foster father. He had been thinking about it almost constantly since his talk with Phillip out on the patio. This was a man who had always seemed so grounded but at the same time so emotionally transparent. Yet now, Louis felt like he barely knew him.

Louis turned the Impala onto Jefferson, cutting down toward the Detroit River, as Phillip had directed him. He had never been to Grosse Pointe before — or the Pointes as some rich snot back at the University of Michigan had once told him it was called. The Pointes — a refuge of privilege and money rimming Lake St. Clair, the place where Detroit's auto magnates staked their claims and built their castles, where their sons and grandsons still held sway over their rust-belt kingdoms. The new money had long ago fled to the far suburbs. But in the Pointes, just nine miles from Detroit's decaying core, the old ways still lingered like the last moments of a fading dream.

His thoughts went back to Phillip. He knew that his family didn't have much money, that Phillip had worked hard to put himself through college but had never graduated. He guessed that meeting Claudia had interrupted that. Maybe that was why Phillip had been so insistent that Louis graduate from U of M, despite the fact that the Lawrences had made big sacrifices to keep him there.

Louis was on Lakeshore Drive now. He had expected the DeFoes to live in one of the mansions facing Lake St. Clair, but Phillip's directions were taking him away from the water to some place called Provencal Road. It turned out to be a winding private lane shaded by towering old trees. Louis slowed as he passed a sign with a picture of a person on horseback. He saw another discreet sign for the Country Club of Detroit but didn't see an entrance. There was a guard shack ahead, but when Louis saw no one inside, he continued on without stopping.

He had seen the homes of the rich before, the gleaming modern manses of the lawyers on Sanibel, the Spanish-style villas lining the Caloosachatchee River back in Fort Myers. But none of it compared to this.

Rambling old Cape Cods sprawling over acres of land. Hulking Tudors hiding behind towering walls of hedges. Aging art deco palaces peering out from behind iron gates. Then, suddenly, there it was, 41 Provencal Road.

It was an old red brick monstrosity with a steep-pitched slate roof and two double chimneys thrusting into the gray sky. Compared to the other homes, it had a gothic aura about it, the bare trees fronting windows of all shapes and sizes, from attic slits to a set of bay windows that stared out like dark eyes inspecting anyone who dared approach.

He pulled up in the half-circle drive and killed the engine. He was miles from the lake now, but a cold wind coming from the west made him pull up the collar of his jacket. At the massive carved wood door, he ignored the small plate that said SERVICE IN REAR and rang the bell.

There was an intercom near the bell and he waited, expecting to hear some servant's voice. Nothing. He rang again and waited. He was about to give up and leave when the door opened.

It was a man in a yellow sweater and gray slacks. He was tall and reed thin, in his midfifties, with straight thinning gray hair hanging over a dour face reddened by too much sun or too much time in the shower. Or maybe the bar, Louis thought, seeing the crystal tumbler in the man's hand.

"Yes?" the man asked. His unfocused eyes were a diluted pale brown, like the liquid in the tumbler. In the man's subtle raise of his chin, Louis could read the question: What is this black man doing at my door?

"I'm looking for Eloise DeFoe," Louis said.

The man leaned against the door frame, dangling the glass in his long fingers. "That would be my mother," he said. "If you're from Chavat's, you can just leave the flowers out here."

He started to shut the door, but Louis thrust out a hand. "My name is Louis Kincaid. I'm an investigator. I need to speak with Mrs. DeFoe, please."

The man's eyes took Louis in with one sweeping glance, lingered on his shoes, and came back to his face. "What are you investigating?"

"My business is with Mrs. DeFoe. Is she here?"

The man stared at Louis for a moment, then pushed the door open wider. "Oh, all right, come in, then."

He sauntered away, leaving Louis to close the door. Louis followed the tinkle of ice cubes through the cold foyer, down a dark paneled hallway, to a room on the left, set off by leaded-glass double doors. The room was lit only by two small table lamps and the soft glow of spotlights arching over the oil paintings, but Louis had a sense of dark paneling, heavy drapes, and plump chairs.

The man in the yellow sweater had faded into a shadowed corner. Louis heard the kiss of ice against glass as a refill was poured. The man came back toward Louis, the old wood floors groaning softly under his slippered feet.

"Wait here," he said. And he was gone, trailing scotch.

Louis stood in the center of the room. It smelled of furniture polish, must, and smoke from the dead fireplace. It made him remember that time when he was working on the force in Black Pool, Mississippi, and had gone to the funeral home to retrieve some evidence. The owner had made him wait, and Louis had sat there, listening to the weeping of a grandmother's mourners in the next room, listening and taking in the dusty perfume of the old woman's dissipating spirit.

He tried to imagine Phillip in this room. Tried to imagine him as a young man in love with a woman whose hair smelled like lilacs.

"My son said you wanted to see me?"

Louis turned. Eloise DeFoe was tall and brittle thin in a dark blue wool dress with a high collar. Her hair was white and cut in a severe chin-length bob with a slash of bangs. There was another slash of bright red at her lips. She had a silver-tipped ebony cane, but as she came into the room it appeared more an ornament than a necessity.

"Louis Kincaid," he said, coming forward with an outstretched hand.

She gave him her cold dry hand as she stared at him. She had the same pale brown eyes as her son, who had come up behind her and was leaning against the door frame.

"Rodney said you're an investigator," she said.

"Yes, I'm here about your daughter, Claudia."

She blinked. "My daughter is dead. She died in 1972."

Rodney came toward Louis. "I can't imagine what business you might have —"

"Just a moment, Rodney," the old woman said sharply, holding up a hand. She looked back at Louis. "What exactly do you want, Mr. . . ?"

"Kincaid. Something else has come up, ma'am," Louis said. "In the process of relocating the remains —"

"Relocating?" she interrupted. "What do you mean relocating?"

Louis hesitated, his confusion echoing Eloise DeFoe's. "Well, as part of Hidden Lake's closing down, they have to move the graves and your —"

Rodney pushed forward. "Mother, the hospital called about this a couple weeks ago. You haven't been well lately and I just didn't see any reason to bother you with something routine."

Louis stared at the guy. Routine?

"I wish you had told me, Rodney," Eloise DeFoe said.

"Everything is taken care of, Mother."

Louis watched them carefully. Eloise DeFoe was probably in her eighties, but she looked anything but feeble. There was a steeliness in her eyes that was disarming. She seemed mildly upset, but Louis couldn't tell if it was because he had brought up her dead daughter or because her son had left her out of the loop.

"Look, Mr. Kincaid, we can take care of this," Rodney said, taking his arm and leading him toward the door. "If there is something else I need to sign —"

Louis pulled away. "No, my business here isn't quite done. I came to tell you something else."

Eloise DeFoe was looking at him expectantly. Rodney had retreated behind the rim of his glass. Louis watched their faces carefully as he spoke.

"When we opened your daughter's casket, it was filled with rocks."

"Rocks?" Eloise DeFoe stared at him for a moment, then sank into a chair. "Good Lord," she murmured.

Louis looked at Rodney. He had gone pale.

A clock chimed out in the foyer three times before Eloise DeFoe spoke again. "Well, where are my daughter's remains then?"

70

There was nothing in the woman's face to read, not surprise, horror, or grief. Louis realized she was assuming he was working for the hospital and he decided to use this assumption to his advantage. "We haven't been able to locate them," he said.

Rodney set the glass down with a thud. "You're saying you've lost my sister?"

"We don't know," Louis said carefully. "We are looking into it and —"

"This is outrageous," Rodney said. "You can just go back to that hospital and tell your boss to expect a letter from my lawyer."

Louis glanced at the mother. She was just sitting there, stunned. He knew he was about to get thrown out and that he wasn't going to get any information about Claudia's past. He decided his best chance was to keep up the pretense of working for Hidden Lake.

"Now calm down, Mr. DeFoe," Louis said to Rodney. "You can help us out. Surely when your sister died, you were given some paperwork, a death certificate. Anything you have might help us."

"You lost all her records, too? I want you out of our house. Now."

Louis turned to the mother. "I'm sorry," he said.

"Please, just go," she said softly.

Rodney followed him to the door and waited stone-faced as Louis stepped outside.

"My mother isn't well," Rodney said. "Don't call her, don't come back here."

Louis started down the steps but then turned back. He couldn't let this go. "You don't care, do you?" Louis said. "You don't care at all where your sister's remains are. What kind of brother are you?"

Rodney slammed the door.

Chapter 7

Louis checked his watch. Just after nine. He had left Plymouth before his foster parents were awake, not wanting to give Phillip the chance to come along to Hidden Lake. There was a growing chill in the Lawrence house, and Louis didn't want to give Frances any more reason for suspicion.

There were only three cars in the parking lot when he pulled up to the hospital. He zipped up his jacket and got out, letting his gaze wander over the grounds.

From what he could see, the compound was huge, enclosed in a wrought-iron fence that had once been very elegant but was now topped with loops of razor wire. He could see maybe a half-dozen red brick buildings, some small and utilitarian looking, others large and elaborate with steep-sloped roofs and peaked dormer windows, spires, chimneys, and bell towers. He could see the top of three brick smokestacks attached to what he guessed was some kind of power plant. Beyond the smokestacks, more red brick buildings, and then a border of bare trees.

He remembered the schematic on the bulletin board back at John Spera's office. It had shown a lake on the property, but he couldn't see one. There was a narrow asphalt road that stretched from the parking lot and up the hill, disappearing into the pines. Maybe he would drive it when he was done inside. If it wasn't closed.

Louis jogged across the parking lot to the building signposted ADMINISTRATION. Like all the others, it was red brick but with an imposing stone portico of three columned arches. Carved in the portico was ANNO DOMINI 1895.

Louis found himself trying to imagine what the building might have looked like a hundred years ago, before the harsh Michigan winters had scarred the bricks and eaten away the stone steps, before the ivy, snaking over the stone arches and pillars, had gone brown and brittle.

A water-stained sign was taped to the front door that read CLOSING, DECEMBER 31, 1988. ALL VISITORS CLAIMING RECORDS OR LOVED ONES MUST REPORT TO THE MAIN NURSE'S STATION ON THE SECOND FLOOR.

Louis pulled open the door and stepped inside. The lobby had an austere beauty, like an old-fashioned bank, with marble

74

pillars and elegant fixtures. There were no lights, just a single shaft of pale light coming from a glass ceiling dome and settling in a pool on the terrazzo floor. Two corridors branched off into darkness and there was a wide marble staircase. Off in one corner was a glass showcase filled with curios and old medical instruments. A reception desk sat empty, its marble top caked with dust, a hand-printed sign propped on top: ALL INQUIRIES SECOND FLOOR.

The marble banister was cold under Louis's hand as he started up the staircase. The place felt so hollow he swore he could hear the echo of his own heart.

Then he heard something else. Footsteps from above, coming down. A man appeared at the landing between the first and second floor, drawing up short. He was tall and thin, about thirty, dressed in baggy hospital scrubs and an oversized gray sweatshirt. He peered at Louis, as if he were trying to focus, his fingers moving from his thin ragged beard to his red tufted hair.

"I'm going out," he said.

There was something in his look — and his voice — that told Louis this man was a patient, and he was surprised any patients still remained. Louis moved toward the wall to give him room to pass.

"My name's Charlie," the man said.

Louis gave him a nod. "Mine's Louis."

Charlie shifted and glanced slowly to the front door, as if he had to figure out exactly where it was. "I need to keep my head warm," Charlie said, holding out a woolly hat with red and green stripes.

"Good idea."

Charlie pulled the cap down over his head, leaving the tasseled chin ties hanging loose like braids.

"Do you like my hat?" Charlie asked.

"It's a helluva hat."

Charlie smiled and came down a few more steps. "Did you hear them?"

"Hear who?"

"I never hear them in the daytime, but I did today. Did you hear them?"

Louis tried to keep an even expression. "No," he said. "Excuse me. I need to go upstairs."

"I hear them."

"I'm sure you do," Louis said. "Excuse me."

Louis moved past Charlie and continued up the stairs. At the top, he looked back over the railing. Charlie had disappeared and the front door was easing shut behind him.

It was dim on the second floor, the only

light filtering through the barred windows. There was a big desk that looked like a nurse's station but it was deserted. Down the hall, Louis could make out a series of signs: RECORDS. PHARMACY. LOUNGE. SUPERINTENDENT. There were boxes stacked against the walls, along with three folded wheelchairs.

An odd sound made Louis turn. A woman was coming down the hall, her rubber-soled shoes squeaking softly on the linoleum. She was reading a file as she walked, and all he could see was the top of her head, a fuzzy circle of reddish brown curls. She was wearing a plain skirt and blouse covered with a baggy cardigan sweater that stretched almost to her knees.

When she saw Louis, she stopped. Her eyes were as blue as the Gulf of Mexico outside his cottage back home. They were the most vivid feature in an otherwise unremarkable pale face that set her age at somewhere close to fifty. He had to lean in to read her name tag: Alice Cooper.

She saw the question in his eyes. "I know, I know," she said. "But it was mine long before it was his."

Louis smiled, but it didn't seem to warm her.

"If you're here to claim a family member

you'll have to fill out the form," she said, ducking behind the counter of the nurse's station.

"No, I'm not. I just need some information. Are you the person I need to talk to?"

"I'm head of records here. Or at least I was." Her eyes narrowed. "Are you a reporter?"

"No."

"Then what kind of information do you want?"

"A friend of mine made arrangements to move one of the deceased patients from the cemetery to a place closer to his home."

She picked up a stack of files and started sifting through them quickly. The desk was heaped with them.

He went on. "But when they went to move her, the casket was full of rocks."

Her eyes came up to his face. "Are you a lawyer?"

"No, just a private investigator trying to help out a friend."

She blew out a long breath and ran a hand over her curls. "Yes, I remember now. Someone called us a few weeks ago about this. His name was . . . Lawrence, I think. Are you him?"

"No, but I'm working for him."

"What was the woman's name again?"

"DeFoe, Claudia DeFoe."

Alice shook her head slowly. "I felt bad for him, but I couldn't tell him anything because she was an E Building patient."

"What's E Building?" Louis asked.

She paused. "Are you sure you're not that reporter who's been calling here?"

"I'm a private eye out of Florida." Louis reached in his coat and flipped open his ID card. She gave it a careful look before he put it away.

"E Building housed the criminally insane and other patients who posed a danger to others," she said.

"This woman was here for depression," Louis said. "Why would she have been in E Building?"

Alice reached below the desk and pulled out a cardboard box. She didn't look up as she began to stack the files in it. "Sometimes the family doesn't know everything. People change after they come here."

"What about her records? Could I see them?" Louis asked.

She arched an eyebrow. "Medical records are confidential. As a private investigator you ought to know that."

"Look, I really am a P.I. and the only thing I am interested in is finding out what happened to this woman's remains."

Her expression changed slightly, the bright blue eyes not softening — Louis suspected she was too shrewd for that — but at least she wasn't looking through him as if he weren't there.

"I can't help you," she said, stuffing another folder into the already packed box. "I am in charge of seeing that the patient files are moved. But all the E Building patient files are locked up over there, and I've been told a special crew is coming to move them next week."

"To make sure they don't get in the wrong hands," Louis said.

"Exactly. Wrong hands, as in reporters'."

"What would reporters be after in this place?"

"Donald Lee Becker. Does that ring a bell?"

It took Louis a second to place the name. Donald Lee Becker had raped and murdered six young women at Michigan State in the sixties. He had claimed an insanity defense and had been institutionalized.

"Becker was here?" he asked.

She nodded. "In E Building. He died here. Last week, they found some bones on Becker's old farm, and now the reporters have starting coming around again."

"So what's going to happen to the E Building records?"

"Someone from the state's mental health association will go through them. Most will go to the county, some sealed and sent to the state."

Alice hoisted the full box with a grunt. Louis moved to help her, but she was already coming out from behind the counter. He watched as she went to the far wall and stacked it next to the others. He knew that once the state or county took possession of Claudia DeFoe's hospital records, he'd never get a look at them.

She came back with an empty box and started in on the next tower of folders.

"I met a man on the steps," he said.

Alice hesitated. "That would be Charlie Oberon."

"Is he a patient?"

"Kind of."

"I thought there were no patients left here."

Alice didn't answer for a moment. "There aren't. The last ones were moved months ago. We sent Charlie to a group home in Albion, but he ran away and came back here. We discovered his status has always been voluntary and he has no family." She looked up at Louis. "He's harmless."

81

"How long has he been here?"

"Since he was fifteen."

"What's going to happen to him?"

Alice stopped her sorting for a second, and when she resumed she didn't seem to be looking at the files. "I don't know," she said. "I've been letting him sleep in one of the old beds, but I don't know what's going to happen to him when we lock the doors."

A phone rang somewhere. Alice's eyes went down the empty hallway. Finally, the phone stopped, the ring echoing in the hallway.

Alice looked back at Louis. "Please don't tell anyone," she said.

"Tell anyone what?"

"That I let Charlie stay here."

When Louis didn't answer, she bent down and got another empty box. She began stuffing the box with the files she had just sorted. For several minutes, they were both quiet, Louis watching her as she finished filling the second box. Then she picked it up and started toward the stack of boxes at the far wall. Louis picked up the other box and followed her.

She looked up at him in surprise when he deposited it next to the others.

"Phillip Lawrence, the man I'm working

for, he's my foster father," Louis said. "He was in love with Claudia DeFoe. They were going to elope but Claudia's mother interfered. Claudia tried to kill herself and her mother sent her here."

Alice was quiet.

"She was only seventeen," Louis added.

The phone began to ring again. This time Alice didn't even look down the hall. She was looking hard at Louis, those keen blue eyes searching for a reason to trust him.

She walked back to the nurse's station. Reaching behind for a coat, she put it on. "I can't give you the records," she said. "But if you want to see E Building, I'll show it to you."

Chapter 8

Alice walked quickly, head bent against the wind, one hand holding the lapels of her wool coat closed.

"That was originally the tuberculosis sanitarium," she said, pointing to a building on their left. "After the TB epidemics subsided, it was transformed into a laundry and sewing department."

Louis glanced at it. Like all the buildings, it looked deserted, front door chained, windows dark.

"The smokestacks are the power plant. Everything was steam heated in the early days, and somewhere around the late twenties, it was reconstructed to provide heat, lights, and hot water to the whole institution."

Louis paused for a second, turning almost a full circle. "How big is this place?"

"A hundred and eighty acres," Alice said. "Over there was the bakery and kitchen, and beyond that, the firehouse and police station."

"A police station?" Louis asked.

"Not like you would imagine," she said. "More of a security force. They were trained to deal with the patients and, well, to be honest, the hospital didn't want outsiders coming in unless they had to."

They passed another brick building, three floors with dark, meshed windows. Alice saw him look up.

"That's the POG building. It was a dormitory for the homeless men who wandered in every winter. In the old days, Hidden Lake would take in the homeless and let them out every spring. They called them POGs."

"Pogs?"

"Poor Old Guys." Alice walked on, her shoes crunching on the frosted grass. Louis followed, his eyes still scanning the grounds as he tried to imagine living inside the iron fence with no contact with the outside world, your mind muddled with drugs or sadness or unseen demons. And he thought about the soothing curl of the waves on the gulf and the endless shimmer of blue that he looked out at every day, and suddenly he could not imagine being without it.

"That's E Building up ahead," Alice said.

It was four stories and like the others,

red brick with high chimneys, fronted by a plainer version of the administration building portico. All the windows on the second and third floors were barred, but the ground-floor ones were covered with heavy steel gratings. As they got closer, Louis could see that some of the ground-floor window gratings had been pried loose.

"Vandals," Alice said as they went up the steps. "This building has been closed for over two years."

She paused at the door and shifted her ring of keys to find the right one. It appeared to Louis that the original door might have been wooden but its replacement was heavy steel, with peeling paint that looked like some of the doors he had seen in prisons.

He glanced back. They were about a quarter mile from the main building and closer now to the heavy trees that abutted the back of the property. On the wind, he caught a hint of water and wondered if the lake was nearby.

"It's stuck," Alice said.

Louis used both hands to pull on the door and it opened slowly, the bottom scraping on the concrete. He followed Alice inside. She drew to a stop in the lobby.

"Oh my," she said softly. "I didn't know it was this bad."

The cold air was thick with mildew and dust and something else that smelled medicinal, but aged. The only light came from two front windows, a feeble spray of gray that washed over a small desk. The grimy terrazzo floor was littered with paper. There was a streak of black spray paint on the wall.

Louis's gaze drifted down the dark hallway. He could make out two elevators and farther down, double steel doors.

Alice turned to a stairwell on her left, tilting her head up. "The elevators don't work," she said. "We'll have to walk."

Again, he followed, listening to the echo of their steps, inhaling that thin scent of medicine in the air. Alice paused at the landing between the first and second floors. She just stood there, a slight frown on her face.

"What's the matter?" Louis asked.

She walked slowly to an exit door and peered out the small window. "Oh, nothing, really. Just something I remember," she said.

She was still looking out the window, so Louis came to her side and glanced out the small grated window. It overlooked an exterior staircase and a weed-choked parking lot.

"I was a nurse when I first came here in 1982, and I was assigned to this building for two months," Alice said. "I was new and this wasn't the kind of place where you asked a lot of questions. But I remember one day, the head nurse told me to take a patient to this landing and wait with her."

"What were you supposed to wait for?" Louis asked.

"I didn't know. But I did as I was told and for ten minutes we just sat here on these steps, not moving or talking."

"Then what happened?"

"This door opened," Alice said, pointing. "And a man came through it with two little girls, about four and six. They called the woman Mommy and rushed to hug her. The woman really didn't respond and barely raised her arms to hug them back, but the little girls didn't seem to notice."

Alice's eyes drifted up the stairs. "You see, children weren't allowed in here to visit. Their visit lasted fifteen minutes and then they were gone. I took the patient back to her bed and when I started to leave, she looked up at me and she thanked me for the children. I remember being surprised she even knew what had just happened, and I made sure I told the doctor the next day."

"What happened to her?"

Alice's eyes dipped to the third step. "The next day, the woman had forgotten all about her children and the family never came back. She died here a year later and was buried in the hospital cemetery." Alice took a heavy breath. "I often think about those little girls and that moment they had with their mother."

Alice looked directly at Louis. "But that's really all any of us have in the end, isn't it? Moments."

After a few seconds, Alice started up the stairs again, unlocking a door on the second floor. "This floor was where all the therapies were done," she said.

He saw the nurse's station first, a large desk enclosed in thick dirty glass with slots to pass medication through. There was garbage everywhere and the smell of urine hung in the air. Alice continued down the hall, stopping at a door. Louis looked in and saw a single claw-footed bathtub in the center of the room.

"Ice baths. They were used to shock the system," Alice said, walking away.

He followed her, catching up as she swung open another door. It looked like an examination room inside. There was one window, covered with steel mesh. A bed sat in the center, worn leather straps with large buckles dangling from each side, more leather at the foot.

"Electroshock therapy," Alice said.

Louis stared at the straps. "How did it work?" he asked.

"It was supposed to shock the brain back into functioning normally," she said. "They used it for everything, three and four times a week, even on things like depression. But it caused convulsions, sometimes so bad patients broke bones or their teeth."

"And afterward?"

"The patients were postictal . . . confused, disoriented."

Alice moved on, pushing open more doors, but Louis couldn't take his eyes off the table. Suddenly there was little he wanted to see. He was picturing Claudia DeFoe in this place and he couldn't help but wonder again how she ended up here with people like Donald Lee Becker. He was wondering, too, how in the hell he was going to tell all this to Phillip.

He fell into step behind Alice, stopping to look into the other small rooms. Some had padded walls, others old wood tables, a few just stacks of cardboard boxes. Most of the doors had been taken off their hinges and were stacked against the peeling walls or rusting radiators. The hallway walls were marked with graffiti — obscenities, crude drawings, and a symbol Louis recognized as a devil's pentagram.

"We've had a lot of trouble with break-ins," Alice said. "Kids think this is a cool place to party." She turned away with a disgusted snort, pulling up her coat collar against the wind whistling through a broken windowpane.

They passed a small pile of leather straps dumped in a corner and Alice saw him look down. She offered no explanation and he didn't ask.

"I'll show you the wards," she said.

Alice led him to another stairwell. Unlike the one on the first floor, this one was narrow, dark, and completely caged in heavy grating. Louis guessed it was because the stairs were used by the patients going down to therapy.

"The women were housed on the third floor," Alice said, heading toward another metal door. "The men were kept up on four."

The large room on the third floor was sectioned off by pillars, small barred windows every ten feet or so. In the dim light, Louis could count twenty metal beds, their white paint peeling, the bare springs cobwebbed and corroded. At each footboard sat a small metal locker. Off in one corner, there was a jumble of wood rocking chairs. The floors were littered with beer cans, garbage, and a couple of old striped mattresses.

"Seen enough?" Alice asked.

He said nothing, and Alice turned away from him. He knew the tour was over and he closed the door to the ward. The bang echoed through the hollow halls. Alice led him down a back stairwell and they emerged into a dark hallway. Louis was disoriented and headed toward what he thought was the exit. But it was just another plain metal door with PASSAGE 12 painted on it. There was no doorknob, no handle of any kind.

"This way, Mr. Kincaid," Alice called out.

Back in the lobby, Alice held the door for him, and he stepped back into the cold air.

He turned to look at her as she locked the building. "Thank you," he said.

"I hope you're able to help Mr. Lawrence."

"I need to know what happened to her

here," Louis said. "And where her remains might be now. I need to see her records."

Alice's face scrunched slightly as she stared into the gray sky.

"Please," Louis said. "He doesn't even know how she died."

"I'm sorry, Mr. Kincaid. I just can't."

He nodded, and they started back to the main building. It was just before noon now, but the day had not warmed up at all. The wind was stiff from the west, the leaves skipping furiously at their feet. Alice was pulling on gloves when Louis heard someone call out. He paused.

"Did you hear that?" Louis asked.

"Hear what?"

Louis took a step toward the trees behind E Building. The wind was coming through the branches, and he strained to hear, but there was nothing.

Alice came up to him. "People always think they hear voices out here," she said.

He looked to her. "It was real."

They waited a few seconds, listening, but when nothing else came, they both started down the path. But the cry came again. It sounded human, but wounded. Tearful. Scared.

"I heard that," Alice said.

Louis spun and started to the woods, but

93

he stopped suddenly. A man . . . his tall form slowly taking shape as he emerged from the deep shadows. He was struggling to walk. And he was carrying something long and limp.

Louis took another step.

A body . . . he was carrying a body. A woman.

As Charlie Oberon staggered closer into the light, everything came into focus. His bloody sweatshirt. A woman's lifeless, naked body, Charlie's long fingers pressed into her thighs. Arms, hanging limp, shreds of dark, wet leaves stuck to them. Her hair . . . long, blond, and thick with blood.

"She won't wake up," Charlie cried. "She won't wake up."

Louis broke into a run toward him.

Chapter 9

Louis reached for his gun, but he didn't have it. It was in the glove box of the Impala. He had no cuffs either. And he had no idea what he was looking at.

Charlie was motionless now, his face slick with sweat despite the cold, and his arms were trembling under the weight of the woman.

The woman was naked, her skin a pasty blue gray with splotches of red, small bits of leaves and twigs stuck to it. Caked blood streaked her blond hair.

"Set her down," Louis said.

Charlie's eyes filled with tears.

Louder and sharper. "Set her down. Now."

Charlie looked behind Louis at Alice, his eyes begging her for some sort of help. Louis motioned Alice forward, and as she stepped up next to him he could hear her quickened breaths.

"Talk to him, Miss Cooper," Louis said. "But don't get too close."

When she did not speak, he snuck a

95

glance. Her hand was at her lips, her powdered skin colorless.

"Talk to him."

"Charlie," Alice managed, "put Rebecca down."

"She won't wake up," Charlie said. "She's cold. She's cold."

"Put her down, Charlie," Alice said again.

Her voice was stronger now, her gaze steady on Charlie. And she took a step closer, then another. Louis started to reach for her, but she moved away from him.

"Charlie," she said, "put Rebecca down, please. Carefully."

Charlie dropped to one knee, easing the woman to the grass. She fell toward Louis, arms limp, head cocked to the side.

Bruises. On her face and shoulders. Raw, red marks around her wrists, ankles, and neck.

Louis forced his eyes away from the woman to Charlie. He had not moved, his head hanging low, arms at his sides. He was staring at her as if she were a broken toy he knew he could not fix.

"Charlie, back away from her," Louis said.

Charlie didn't seem to hear at first. Then he took a few steps backward, then a few more, finally collapsing on the ground about fifteen feet behind the body. He drew his legs in and crossed his arms over his belly, still staring vacantly.

Alice edged closer. Louis caught her arm. "Go call the police," he said.

Alice hesitated, her head jerking from Charlie to the dead woman and back to Louis. Her makeup was streaked with tear lines, and she looked scared.

"Go call the police," Louis repeated. "Now."

Alice ran across the grass. Louis eased toward Charlie. Charlie was still frozen, huddled into himself. Louis knelt near the body.

Her eyes were open, brown glassy pools. Her neck looked crushed, the skin reddish purple, deep finger marks clearly visible. He knew she was dead, but still he held a finger to her neck, then her wrist. But there was nothing. She was cold to the touch.

He looked at Charlie. "Did you kill her?"

"She won't wake up."

"Did you hurt her?"

Charlie looked up at Louis, his face drawn tight, his eyes pained. Louis had no idea what was wrong with Charlie mentally or how he comprehended the world, women, life or death, or anything else. And he didn't know how to talk to him.

"Charlie, where did she go to sleep?" Louis asked.

Charlie pointed back to the trees.

Louis rose. "Will you take me there?"

Charlie didn't move, his gaze drifting back to the body. Louis took his arm, urging him to his feet. When he stood, Louis tapped his shoulder to make sure he had Charlie's attention.

"Take me to where she fell asleep."

Charlie turned slowly. His sweatshirt was unzipped, half off his bony shoulders, but he didn't pull it up. He walked slowly into the brush, then the trees, careful to hold the branches back for Louis.

Louis kept glancing behind him, afraid he'd lose the way back to E Building, but he didn't want to stop. If there was a crime scene out here somewhere, he wanted to see it. And maybe preserve it.

The trees were thick now, the brush sharp and tangled, but Charlie moved unfazed through it. Finally, he stopped. It was a tiny clearing, filled with a thick blanket of leaves. Right in the center lay a white nurse's shoe, speckled with blood.

"Where are her clothes?" Louis asked.

Charlie didn't answer him as his eyes

drifted to the ground. At his feet were two small plastic flowers. Yellow daisies, the petals faded and cracked from the weather. Charlie bent to pick them up, but Louis grabbed his arm.

"Don't touch them," Louis said.

"They're mine," Charlie said. "I put them on her eyes. She needs them to wake up."

"Where did you get the flowers?"

"The cemetery," Charlie said.

Louis's eyes moved slowly over Charlie's shirt. The bloodstains were light smears, put there by cradling Rebecca's body against his chest. But Charlie had no blood on his green cotton pants. Or his face or his hands, except a few light smears. It was obvious the woman had been dead far longer than a few minutes, so if Charlie had killed her, when had he done it? Last night? Early this morning? And if he had killed her, why carry her out into the open?

Jesus. You're dealing with a crazy man, Kincaid. You have no idea what he did to her or why. You don't even know what's wrong with this man.

But he did know he needed to keep asking questions. And that he needed to keep it simple.

"Charlie, do you know what dead is?" Louis asked.

"Yes."

"Rebecca is dead," Louis said.

Charlie hung his head, drawing a hand across his face, smearing dirt on his cheek.

"You didn't mean to hurt her, did you?" Louis asked.

"I didn't . . . no. I didn't. But she cried . . . she cried all night. All night. I listened to her cry all night."

"Where was she when she was crying?" Louis asked. "Can you show me where she was?"

"I couldn't see her but I could hear her."

Damn it . . . this isn't making sense. Try again.

"Where were you when you heard her crying?" Louis asked.

"In the cemetery," Charlie said.

"You were in the cemetery last night?"

"I walk in the cemetery every night," Charlie said. "I talk to them."

"The dead people?"

Charlie rubbed his face again, looking off into the woods. For a few seconds, he was quiet, as if he was suddenly aware that talking to graves was something he shouldn't share. Louis wondered if there wasn't a small part of Charlie that understood he saw the world differently than most people did.

"The graves cry," he whispered. "I try to talk to them, but they never hear me."

"Do the graves talk, too?"

"No," Charlie said. "Just cry."

Louis started to ask another question, but he heard the distant wail of a siren. Charlie heard it, too, and his head shot up, his eyes scanning the trees.

"Police," he said. "The police are coming."

"Yes. Let's go back."

"No. No police. No police." Charlie's arms came out, fingers spread. "No policemen. Please. No."

"They won't hurt you."

"No police, please. Police hurt Mama."

Louis pulled on Charlie's sweatshirt to get him moving. Charlie tried to reach out to grab a branch, but Louis firmly eased him forward.

"Take me back, Charlie," Louis said. "Take me back to Rebecca now."

Charlie wiped his face again, the tears mixing with the mud and blood. "They'll take me away," he said.

"Take me back to Rebecca."

Charlie started moving, pulling nervously at the straps of his wool hat as he trudged through the brush. Every few steps, Louis would hear a soft sob or a low muttering about the policemen.

The siren suddenly cut off as Louis and Charlie broke the trees, coming back out into the compound behind E Building. There were two police cars parked on the grass. White with a streak of blue across the side. Alice was standing near one, her coat pulled tight around her.

Two cops were bent over Rebecca's body, and Louis directed Charlie toward them. He pressed back against Louis's hand, but Louis urged him forward, and as they cleared the trees, one of the cops looked up.

He wore a navy blue windbreaker with a thin gold stripe and a cap embroidered with Ardmore P.D. on the front.

"I'm Chief Dan Dalum," he said.

Dalum's face had the pink puff of a newborn baby, but a healthy gray-blond mustache and wire-rimmed glasses set his age close to forty. His voice was deep and melodious like that of a D.J. on a classical radio station.

"Louis Kincaid," Louis said.

"You're the visitor," Dalum said. He looked at Charlie. "So that makes him the patient then, the man who carried her out here?"

"Yes."

Dalum tapped his officer on the shoulder, then faced Charlie. "We're going to handcuff you, Charlie," Dalum said. "It's for your protection and ours. Do you understand?"

Louis could tell Charlie didn't understand, but Charlie let the officer handcuff him, his eyes searching for Alice. He saw her near the cruiser, and when the officer led him in that direction, he went easily.

Dalum looked back at the body in the grass, and then moved around her, positioning himself on the other side. His face was rigid, and Louis thought he saw him blanche slightly. Then his blue eyes came back up, settling on Louis.

"Why did you and Charlie go back there in the woods?" Dalum asked.

"I wanted to see if there was a crime scene," Louis said. "I was hoping he might talk to me."

Dalum's eyes stayed steady on Louis. "You talk like a cop."

"Ex-cop. I'm a private eye now," Louis said.

"Here in Michigan?"

"Raised in Plymouth, live in Florida now."

Dalum tipped up the brim of his ball cap. "And you're here at Hidden Lake why?"

"I'm just trying to locate a former patient for a client. Alice and I were coming out of that building," Louis said, pointing to E Building, "when we saw Charlie coming out of the trees, carrying her."

Dalum turned to look at Charlie, but he was almost invisible in the back of the cruiser. "Charlie say anything to you back there in the woods?" Dalum asked.

There was a defensive edge in Dalum's voice, and Louis understood why. No local cop wanted to be upstaged by an out-of-state P.I., especially on what was probably the town's first homicide in years.

"I'm not sure," Louis said. "It didn't make any sense to me, but maybe when you question him you'll hear something I didn't. Alice may be a big help, too. She knows him."

"Did you find a crime scene?" Dalum asked.

"No, it looks like she was killed somewhere else and just dumped there. No blood, no clothes, except for one shoe."

Dalum was quiet for a moment, his eyes drifting back down to Rebecca. Her skin had gone even bluer, and she looked more like a toppled marble statue than a human being.

"Let me get something from the car," Dalum said.

Louis nodded. Dalum walked back to his cruiser and leaned into an open window, picking up his radio from inside. Louis guessed he was calling the medical examiner or crime scene techs. When he was finished, Dalum walked to the trunk of the car and opened it. He returned with a green blanket that he laid over Rebecca. Then he looked at Louis.

"Show me this place you think she was dumped."

Louis led Dalum into the trees.

"I'm going to ask for your discretion on this, Mr. Kincaid," Dalum said.

"Of course."

"Most people around here are damn glad to see this place go away, and this kind of murder will just bring more looky-loos out here again."

"I understand," Louis said.

"For years, we've been swatting away reporters who wanted to write about people like Donald Lee Becker."

"Or the eyeball eater," Louis said.

"There was never an eyeball eater. It was just a myth," Dalum said, ducking under a branch.

"I know," Louis said.

"Yeah, but a lot of other people don't. They think he was real. Like the stories of

105

torture and brain removals that were supposedly going on inside."

Louis didn't want to anger Dalum, but he couldn't resist saying something. "In the early days, it *was* inhumane."

Dalum took a moment before answering. "Maybe. But they did the best they could with what they had. Many of these people had nowhere else to go. Even their own mothers didn't want them. As far as I'm concerned, this was a good place in many ways."

Louis let it go. He stopped and scanned the trees until he saw the break of the clearing. The single white shoe stood out against the brown ground. The yellow plastic flowers lay nearby.

"The flowers are Charlie's," Louis said, pointing. "He said Rebecca needed them to wake up."

Dalum stepped forward, looking at the flowers and the shoe. Then his gaze moved over the trees and he turned almost a full circle.

"Any thoughts on where she was killed?" Louis asked.

"Not a one. It's been about thirty degrees out here the last few nights. From the looks of her body, she was kept awhile."

"And it was probably done indoors," Louis said.

Dalum was still looking. "Yup. And as far as I know, all the buildings are empty except one."

"How many buildings are there?"

"Well," Dalum said, "I know they had a P Building, so if they all had letters, that would make . . ."

"Sixteen," Louis said.

Dalum exhaled a sigh.

Louis started to ask another question. He wanted to know how big the Ardmore Police Department was, if they had a homicide detective, and if they had the manpower for a search of this kind. But he knew it was none of his business. And a part of him didn't want to deal with another case. But he was seeing Rebecca, lying in the grass, her skin frosted blue. Seeing her and wondering what her last name was, and who was going to miss her tonight.

"I'll have to call in the state police," Dalum said.

Dalum didn't sound happy. Louis could guess why. Five years ago, Louis had his own experience with the Michigan State Police. It had ended his law enforcement career in Michigan.

"Maybe Charlie will just tell you where he killed her," Louis said.

Dalum's gaze swung quickly back to Louis. "You think Charlie Oberon killed that nurse?"

"I'm leaning that way," Louis said.

"Why?" Dalum asked. "Because he's a crazy man?"

Louis started to say no, but maybe Dalum was right. He had made a quick assumption, something no investigator should do. And he had made it because of what Charlie was. And, maybe even, where he was.

"Damn," Dalum said softly.

Louis glanced over at him. He was looking back toward the red brick buildings.

"I was really hoping they'd just let this place die peacefully," he said as if to himself.

He reached in his pocket and pulled out a white handkerchief. He tied it to a bare limb above the nurse's shoe. "I'll need you and Miss Cooper to come down to the station for a statement," Dalum said, starting back toward E Building.

"Of course," Louis said.

"Might take a couple hours."

"No problem."

Louis glanced at his watch. He knew Frances expected him back for dinner, but things at home had been so tense, he was dreading another evening with Phillip hidden behind a newspaper and Frances folding laundry.

But now there was something else, too. He had to explain to Phillip that the search for Claudia had come to a dead end, that they would probably never find her remains.

"So, your work finished here, Mr. Kincaid?" Dalum asked as they walked back to the cruiser.

"I think so," Louis said.

"Then you've really got no reason to come back here to Hidden Lake, do you?"

"No."

"Just as well," Dalum said.

Louis didn't answer. He stopped and looked back at the empty windows of E Building. As much as he wanted to help Phillip, he hoped he'd never have to come back to this place again.

Chapter 10

It was dark by the time Louis walked out of the Ardmore Police Station. Alice had asked for a ride back to the hospital, so he waited near the door, out of the wind, watching the street.

The shops were dark, CLOSED FOR THANKSGIVING signs on the doors. Christmas lights twinkled in the window of O'Malley's Hardware. A single car made its way slowly up the street, a faint sprinkle of rain shimmering in its headlights.

"Thanks for waiting."

Louis turned to look at Alice. He hadn't had much of a chance to talk to her once Chief Dalum had shown up and he wondered how she was doing. Her eyes were red-rimmed from crying, but there was something else in them, too — disbelief. The same disbelief he had seen in the eyes of so many other people whose quiet lives collided with catastrophe.

"You okay?" Louis asked.

Alice nodded, stuffing her hands in her pockets. "I just want to go home."

"You want me to drive you home?"

She shook her head. "No, just back to the hospital is fine. I need to get my car and lock up."

Louis led her to Phillip's Impala and helped her inside. She was quiet as he backed out of the space and flipped up the heater.

"Did you know her well?" Louis asked.

Alice sighed, folding her hands in her lap. "Pretty well, but we weren't close. Rebecca came to Hidden Lake before me."

Louis slowed for a stop sign, then drove on through, leaving the soft glimmer of Ardmore behind them as they headed out into the empty farmlands.

"Her last name was Gruber," Alice said.

Louis didn't reply, knowing nothing he could say would make this any better. But he did have some questions, ones he knew he shouldn't be asking because this wasn't his case. But he couldn't help it.

"Can you tell me more about Charlie Oberon?" Louis asked.

Alice didn't answer immediately, but her eyes were on him, looking for some level of trust. "I've known Charlie for six years," she started slowly. "And I've never known him to be violent."

"What's wrong with him?" Louis asked.

"We're not sure. He's been diagnosed as several things. Schizophrenia, mild retardation as a result of possible fetal alcohol syndrome or drug addiction. Maybe brain damage due to physical abuse as an infant. No one seems to be able nail it down since we have no history on him."

"Who brought him here?"

"The state. They found him wandering the streets of Jackson in the summer of seventy-four. He seemed to function on the level of about an eight-year-old. Things haven't changed all that much really."

She made a sniffling sound and Louis glanced over at her. But she wasn't crying, just reaching into her purse for a Kleenex so she could blow her nose.

They fell into a silence that was broken only when Alice had to give him some directions. Out here, in the emptiness of the hills and fields, with no streetlights to relieve the darkness, Louis wasn't quite sure where he was.

The blue and red bubble lights of a cruiser were visible well before they pulled up to the Hidden Lake entrance. Louis produced the pass Dalum had given him, and the two cops at the guardhouse waved him through. Beyond the administration building, he saw a flurry of lights — small jerking ones, like flashlights. The Ardmore Police Department didn't have any flood-lights, so Dalum was waiting for the state to bring some. The few cops here were protecting the scene and walking the grounds.

Louis swung the Impala in next to a cruiser, but didn't switch off the engine. He turned toward Alice. She was watching the flashlights, the Kleenex balled in her hand.

"It's going to be hard to go back in there," she said softly.

"Maybe you shouldn't," Louis said.

"I have to. I have to finish boxing the records."

"You shouldn't be alone."

"I won't be. The superintendent has arranged for extra security."

"Is there anyone else still working here?" Louis asked.

She shook her head. "It was just Rebecca and me. We were the last ones here. I was packing up the last of the records that were going to the state. She was helping the salvage company."

"There was a salvage crew here this week?" Louis asked.

"Yes, a foreman and his crew. All the buildings have been locked for months and

Rebecca had to take them around so they could do inventory."

"Who else was around?"

Alice had to think for a moment. "Three security guards, the old fellow at the guardhouse, and two others who were only here at night. One walked the grounds watching for vandals and the other was posted out in the cemetery to keep an eye on the exhumation company's equipment."

"Anyone else in and out?"

"Just a few people claiming remains in the last week." Now Alice had turned toward him. "Why are you asking?"

"No reason," Louis said.

Alice started to rummage through her purse, pulling out her gloves. "Well, thank you for the ride," she said.

"No problem."

Alice opened the door and started to slide out.

"Miss Cooper, wait," Louis said.

She looked back at him.

"Why do you think Charlie put flowers on Rebecca's eyes?"

She hesitated. "Chief Dalum asked me the same thing. You talk like a policeman."

Louis smiled. "I used to be one. It never really goes away."

"Do you think Charlie did it?" she asked.

"I don't know enough about him or Rebecca to answer that, Miss Cooper," Louis said.

She sat back in the seat, looking back out the windshield at the black hulk of the administration building. "Charlie loved Rebecca," she said. "She was the only one who really paid any attention to him, the only one who worked with him."

"Worked?" Louis asked. "How?"

"She figured out that he loved it when she read to him, and that he could remember things he had heard and recite them back. It didn't really matter what she read. Charlie just seemed to like to hear the words."

A small smile tipped her lips. "She used to read him Shakespeare." She saw the incredulous look on Louis's face and her smile grew. "Well, only *A Midsummer Night's Dream*. There's a character in it named Oberon. I guess he was the king of the fairies or something, and Rebecca told Charlie that's what he was."

When Louis said nothing, Alice went on. "She didn't mean it cruelly, and I'm sure Charlie didn't understand the play. He just knows his name is in it."

Alice's smile faded and in the faint lights of the dash, Louis could see her eyes, full of questions.

"He loved her," she said, more fiercely this time, as if she were trying to convince herself now.

"People sometimes kill the people they love," Louis said.

She looked away. "That's what the chief said."

The heater had fogged the windows, and Louis could barely make out the ghostly play of the flashlights out by E Building. Dalum had told him he didn't expect to find anything out there tonight. Tomorrow, in the daylight, Dalum and the state police would conduct a more thorough search.

A hundred and eighty acres. He wondered what else they'd find.

"Mr. Kincaid," Alice said.

"Yes?"

"Do you still want to see Claudia De-Foe's medical records?"

"Of course I do."

Alice was still for a moment, head down, her fingers working the Kleenex. "I'm going to make you an offer," she said. "I will show you the records, even let you copy them, if you'll do something for me."

He knew what was coming. And it surprised him that Alice would cross that line. But then he realized that she wasn't crossing it for him.

"You want me to prove Charlie didn't do this."

"Yes," Alice said. "Or at least prove beyond any doubt he did. So the town knows for sure. So I know for sure."

For an instant he wondered if she really wanted the truth. He had known other people, family members of accused murderers, who said they wanted to know the truth, but most didn't really. No one wanted to know that they were close — be it next door or by blood — to a killer. But he suspected Alice was different. She had seen the worst of things here. And in many ways, she had to be stronger than he was. Stronger than most cops he knew.

"You have a deal, Miss Cooper."

"Call me Alice," she said.

"When can I see the records?" Louis asked.

"We're closed now for Thanksgiving weekend," Alice said. "How about Monday morning? We don't have much time after that. The hospital will be closed by December thirty-first."

"Monday's fine. I'll be here early."

Alice pushed open the door against a

rush of cold air. She whispered a soft thank-you and she was gone.

Louis waited until she had climbed in her car and he saw the headlights go on before he even backed out. He followed Alice down the narrow drive and through the gate. She turned east, toward Ardmore. He sat for a moment, watching her taillights grow smaller.

His mind was already working on Charlie and Rebecca and the plastic flowers. And he was hearing Charlie's strange, childlike voice as they stood by the single white shoe in the woods.

I got them from the cemetery.

What were you doing in the cemetery, Charlie?

I walk there every night.

Louis turned west, easing down Highway 50, trying to find the tiny road that led to the cemetery. He knew why he was going, but the thought was so absurd he almost couldn't let it linger long in his mind: He wanted to see if he could hear the graves cry.

In the black cloak of darkness, he almost missed the road. But soon he saw the towering sentry pines that marked the entrance and he eased the car to a stop. He got out and went to the trunk, hoping

118

Phillip had a flashlight. He didn't, but it didn't matter. He didn't need light. Maybe it was better if he approached this in darkness.

A wisp of a moon scampered between the high icy clouds, giving him just enough light to see. He could make out the dark hulk of the backhoe in the far corner. He didn't see a security guard. Maybe he was out helping the cops, or more likely sleeping inside the backhoe. He was about to let it go when it occurred to him the guard could wake up, and in a panic, think Louis the killer and shoot him. So he walked to the backhoe, climbed up on the side, and peered inside. No one.

Maybe the guard had quit, afraid to sit in a cemetery with a killer running loose. Shit, maybe the damn *guard* was the killer.

Louis walked across the frozen dead grass, shaking his head. He would check it out with Dalum on Monday. But for the moment, he was glad the guard wasn't there. There was something about all this that required solitude.

Louis stopped in the center of the cemetery and looked around. For a moment, the wind died and a silence, as thick and heavy as the night, enveloped the cemetery. He closed his eyes, trying to focus.

On what?

On some part of himself that he had never used before? On something deep inside his brain that he wasn't even sure existed? On something that could allow him to see or hear or feel what Charlie Oberon did?

But there was nothing. Nothing but the steady pulse of his blood in his ears. Louis opened his eyes.

He walked away from the backhoe, his steps slow and quiet. He couldn't see the flat concrete markers, but sometimes he could feel them under his feet and he had the urge to step away from them, like walking on them was disrespectful. But he couldn't avoid them. The rows that had been so visible in the daylight now seemed distorted and he had no sense of the layout.

He stopped.

That silence again. No wind. Not even a sound of a car on the highway. Not the rustle of a branch.

He closed his eyes, drew in a breath, and held it.

What did you hear, Charlie?
The call of an owl in a tree?
The cry of a wounded animal?
The creak of a loose fence post?
The murmur of the pines?

The wind picked up suddenly, cold on the back of his neck, but he stood still, listening. And he guessed a minute went by. Then another. There was nothing. The silent nothing of the six thousand dead.

He pulled up the collar of his coat and walked back to the car.

Chapter 11

The snow started just before dawn. Louis had been lying awake in the guest room, the window cracked against the blast of heat coming up through the floor vent beneath the sofa bed. The sound of the snow kissing the eaves drew him to the window. It was beautiful, peaceful, the white specks swirling in the streetlights.

By six, he had gone down to the kitchen to make coffee, creeping past Phillip asleep on the sofa. Frances came down soon after, and by the time Louis finished the eggs she had made for him, Phillip had retreated to the shower. By noon, the snow had turned back to sleet, imprisoning the three of them in the house.

The smells were almost suffocating. Ginger, cloves, sage, roasting turkey, and those cloying cinnamon candles that Frances always lit on holidays. The living room was dark and too warm. Louis was having trouble keeping his eyes open.

"This is ridiculous."

Louis opened his eyes. "I'm sorry, did you say something, Phil?"

"They can't even get across the fifty-yard line."

Louis's eyes drifted to the television. The Lions were punting again. "What's the score?" he asked. He didn't really care, but if they talked about the game they didn't have to talk about anything else.

"Fourteen-zip, Vikes," Phillip said.

"Same old same old," Louis said.

"You got that right."

They fell into silence again. Louis watched the Vikings' running back plow through the Lions' line for another first down.

"We need a decent running back, someone like Anderson," Phillip said. "We need to get that Sanders kid out of Oklahoma State."

Louis gave a grunt to feign interest. His mind was miles away. He knew he had to tell Phillip about going to Hidden Lake yesterday, but he couldn't do it with Frances around. And the sleet had been so bad, Phillip hadn't even ventured out for a smoke.

The game had gone into halftime. Phillip was just sitting there, staring at the screen.

Frances appeared from the kitchen. She

looked at Louis. "Why are you sitting here in the dark?" She switched on the table lamp near his chair.

Phillip looked up at her, blinking. She held his eyes for a second, then looked away. "Would you two like anything? There's some cheese and —"

"I'd like a beer, please," Phillip said.

Frances paused just a beat. "It's a little early for a beer, don't you think?"

Louis jumped in. "I'd like one, too, Frances."

Her eyes were still on Phillip but then she gave a short nod and went back to the kitchen. Louis leaned in toward Phillip.

"Phillip, we have to talk."

He let out a long breath. "I know."

Frances came back out carrying a wicker tray. She set it down on the table between them. "The turkey is about ready," she said. "When will the game be over?"

Louis tried a smile. "It was over a long time ago, I think."

She was looking at him oddly, and for a second, Louis thought he saw her eyes tear. Then she reached out and touched his hair. "It's chilly in here," she said quickly. "I'll get you something to pull over yourself."

She was gone before he could tell her the

house was too warm. He listened to her footsteps going up the stairs, then reached to the tray. A bottle of Heineken for him, a can of Strohs for Phillip. With a plate of crackers, Win Schuler's cheese, and those god-awful little pickles.

Louis picked up one of the pickles. "Why does she keep giving these to us? We never eat them."

Phillips lips tipped up slightly. "I made the mistake of eating one once a long time ago and she's been bringing them out ever since."

Louis tossed the pickle back onto the plate. He leaned forward on his elbows. "Phil, I need to tell you what happened at the hospital yesterday."

"Did you find out where she is?"

"Not exactly. But I'm hoping I can find out more Monday."

"You're going back there?"

Louis nodded. "To look at her medical records."

Phillip picked up his beer and took a small drink. "So there's nothing else?"

Louis thought for a second of telling him about E Building and about Rebecca Gruber's murder. But Phillip needed something positive right now, even if it was only the hope of seeing Claudia's name on a piece of paper. At least that would be something real, something tangible, evidence that she had existed somewhere other than just in his memories.

He hadn't heard Frances come back down the stairs, but suddenly she was in the room. She stopped right in front of Phillip's chair. The light from the single lamp washed her face to an ashen stone color and gave a hard glitter to her eyes. She held two papers in her hand.

"Who's Claudia DeFoe?" she asked.

Phillip rose quickly. Louis did, too, his eyes jumping from Frances to Phillip. Phillip looked stricken, almost panicked.

Frances held the papers out. "You bought a casket for her. You bought a cemetery plot. And you're paying someone to bring her here to Plymouth from the Irish Hills?"

Phillip's shoulders drew tight. "You went through my wallet, Fran?"

Frances's eyes were moist, but Louis didn't think she'd cry. Not yet.

"Is this the army buddy you've been visiting for the last sixteen years, Phillip?"

Louis knew from the edge to her voice that Frances thought Claudia had been alive and that Phillip's visits had been romantic rendezvous, and his heart gave for her.

"I deserve an answer, Phillip," she said. "An honest one."

Phillip was staring at Frances. There was a stiffness to his jaw, but something had changed in his eyes. There was a faint fear there that came from the realization that he had let things go too far, kept his secrets too long.

"I'll leave you two alone," Louis said.

Frances looked at Louis. "Sure, go ahead and try to slink off like you've nothing to do with this. You should be ashamed of yourself."

Phillip finally reached out and touched her arm. Frances pulled away, her eyes filling with tears. Phillip motioned to a chair, tried to urge her down in it gently. Finally, she sat down, keeping hold of the papers, her eyes never leaving Phillip.

"I'll take care of this," he said, turning to Louis.

Louis started away, then glanced back at Frances. He wanted to apologize for the last few days, for keeping this from her, for not making Phillip tell her. But now wasn't the time.

Louis wandered into the kitchen. The turkey was still in the oven. A pan of dressing sat on the stove, and two pumpkin pies were on the countertop, near a glass of

127

eggnog and a plate of sliced cranberries. He looked up at the clock. Almost three.

He sat down at the table, spreading the newspaper, but he couldn't find anything he wanted to read. He could hear their voices, low and insistent, out in the living room.

He already felt different. Like something solid and unshakable had been snatched from under him. And he wondered if this was what kids felt like when they were first told their parents were getting a divorce. Growing up in foster homes, he had learned very early that nothing was forever. Especially good things. But then he had landed here in Plymouth, where things were not only good, they were unchanging, and no matter how long he waited for that bad something to happen, it never had. He had come to believe that forever was possible for some people.

The small kitchen was hot from the oven and finally, he went out the back door, standing under the overhang for a moment until the sleet drove him back in. The next half hour crept by like that, with him moving between the kitchen, the icy outside, and back again, taking bites of the stuffing as he passed.

He was remembering a night about a

month ago. Joe had driven over from Miami for a short weekend. They had stayed up until midnight, drinking and talking, and later, after making love, she had snuggled up against him and they had lain there, listening to the brush of the palm fronds in the rain.

I wish this weekend was going to last longer, Louis.

He had answered her before he thought about it. *I wish it would last forever.*

Maybe it was just a comment, an expected reply in an intimate moment. But still, he had said it, and maybe he had said it because at that moment he believed there could be a forever for him and Joe.

The kitchen had grown stifling, a hint of burnt meat now in the air. Still, no movement from the living room. Just muted voices. Louis switched off the oven, opened it, and took the turkey out. The skin was dry and cracked, most of the juices dried up.

He waited awhile longer, then sliced off some breast meat, and made himself a plate of turkey, cranberries, potatoes, and a biscuit. He sat at the small table, eating in silence.

Around five, he heard footsteps go up the stairs and the slam of a door. A few seconds later, Phillip came into the kitchen. He looked tired, his eyes red. He didn't speak, just went directly to the refrigerator and pulled out a beer. He left again.

A couple of seconds later, Louis heard the TV come on and saw the blue light filling the dark living room.

Louis didn't move from the table, but his eyes drifted to the yellow phone on the wall. Then he rose slowly and walked to it. He dialed Joe's number in Miami, and leaned against the counter, listening to it ring.

Twelve, thirteen, fourteen. *Pick up, Joe.*

And then her voice.

"It's me," he said.

"Which me?"

Her voice was playful and he felt the tightness in his chest lift just enough to make breathing easier.

"The me that needs to talk to you right now."

A silence, then, "Hang on a second." The clunk of the phone. He picked up a fork and the pumpkin pie and went to sit at the table, stretching the phone cord across the kitchen. By the time Joe came back on, he was digging into the pie.

"Where'd you go?" he asked.

"To turn off the oven," she said. "I'm making Thanksgiving dinner. Swanson's Hungry Man Turkey Special. Yum-yum."

He laughed.

"How's your turkey day going?" she asked.

"Not good," he said.

"Is that why you called?"

"I don't know. I think . . . I think I just needed to hear your voice, that's all."

"I was watching the Weather Channel. It's cold up there."

"Tell me about it."

A long pause. "What's wrong, Louis?"

A longer pause. "I miss you," he said.

"You'll be home soon."

Louis pushed the pie away and rose. He went to the counter, twisting the phone cord in his hands.

"Louis?"

"Yeah, I'm here. Joe, something's come up. I won't be home when I said. I might have to stay here awhile."

"How long?"

"I don't know. I'm helping my foster father out with a personal problem and things have gotten messed up. I can't leave them right now."

"What's the matter?"

Louis rubbed his forehead. "I can't go into it all right now."

Joe was quiet for a long time.

"You still there?" he asked finally.

"Yeah, I'm here."

Another silence.

"Joe —"

"Louis, I don't like this."

"Like what?"

"When you do this, when I know you need to talk but you won't."

Louis shut his eyes. He could tell her about it, tell her everything he had seen at Hidden Lake, because she was a cop and he knew she would understand. He could maybe tell her about Phillip and Frances and about how secrets kept too long could corrode a marriage. What he couldn't tell her was that he had secrets of his own, things in his past that needed to come out if there was ever going to be a chance for him and Joe.

"Louis?"

He had to tell her about getting Kyla pregnant and what he had said to her on that rainy night in his dorm room.

Go, then . . . get rid of it.

"Louis?"

"I have something to tell you, Joe."

She was silent, waiting.

"But I can't do it until I get home."

There was another long pause. It was so

132

quiet he could hear a purring sound and suddenly he could see her, sitting on that lumpy blue denim sofa cradling her big orange tabby cat.

"I'll be home as soon as I can," he said.

"I'll be here," she said.

Chapter 12

It was Sunday morning. Frances had left early to go to church. Phillip had slept late on the sofa again. Louis fixed himself a bowl of cereal and read every section of the Sunday *Free Press*. He was standing in the hallway looking at the gallery of pictures on the wall when Phillip finally came down from his shower.

"You get any sleep?" Louis asked.

"Not much," Phillip answered.

Louis's gaze went back to the photographs. "Is that me?" he asked.

Phillip pulled his glasses from his shirt pocket to peer at the photograph. It showed three boys sitting on a bench holding ice cream cones, a tan-skinned boy sandwiched between two bigger white kids. They wore T-shirts and jeans and the background looked like an amusement park.

"That's you in the middle," Phillip said.

"Was that Edgewater?" Louis asked.

"Yes."

134

"Who are the other two boys?"

"You don't remember them?" Phillip asked.

"No, sorry."

Phillip didn't seem to be in any mood to talk, but finally he pointed. "The one on the left is named Kevin. He's a doctor now. The other one is Jimmy. He's in Marquette Prison for murder."

Louis's eyes moved over the faces again. It bothered him that he couldn't remember the other boys, but he had been too miserable to care when he first got here. Phillip had been the one who had changed that, pulling him out of his isolation, holding his head above the pain until he could feel solid ground for himself.

"I need to get out for a while," Louis said. "Let's go for a drive."

Phillip slipped off his glasses. "Fran is —"

"She's at church," Louis said. "She said she wouldn't be home before three."

It was cold but sunny as Louis headed the Impala west on U.S. 12. Phillip was quiet, looking out at the cornfields. Louis was glad Phillip hadn't asked why they were going out to the Irish Hills. He wouldn't have been able to explain, because it was nothing more than a feeling. A feeling that Phillip was drowning and

135

needed something to grab on to right now.

And Frances . . .

She needed something, too. This morning, before she left for church, Louis had sat her down at the kitchen table and talked to her. He had apologized for his role in Phillip's deception, and she had accepted it. But there was a lingering hurt in her eyes. When he told her he wanted to take Phillip back out to the Irish Hills, he expected tears. But she just nodded.

"If going out there helps him, then do it," she said. "Help him finish this, Louis. Help him bury this so we can move on."

The monotony of the soy and corn fields was giving way to gently rolling pasture lands now. They were entering the Irish Hills. The road bent and dipped, dotted with small businesses. An antique store housed in an old brick tavern. A grocery with signs for bait fish and LaBatt's hanging in the dusty windows. A plain clapboard building called the Sand Lake Inn with a flicking neon leprechaun and a menu boasting deep-fried walleye dinner, $4.25.

They passed several tourist attractions — the Stagecoach Stop with its empty parking lot, the Mystery Hill with its shuttered ticket window. And the Prehistoric Forest with crumbling plaster dinosaurs and a weather-beaten woolly mammoth, its tusks propped up with cinder blocks.

Louis noticed that Phillip was taking it all in, his elbow propped on the window, his hand under his chin. The road curved and climbed and suddenly, two giant wood towers loomed ahead. At the crest of the hill, Louis slowed.

The towers looked like two stocky light-houses, with peeling white paint and huge fading letters that spelled out WELCOME TO THE IRISH HILLS.

"Let's stop for a second," Phillip said.

Louis pulled into the empty parking lot that faced a deserted miniature golf course. Phillip got out and started away from the car. Louis joined him.

"I could have sworn they were taller," Phillip said, his eyes moving up over the towers.

"Memories can be unreliable," Louis said.

Phillip glanced back at him and smiled slightly. "When did you become so philosophic?"

"It's not mine. It's from a friend."

Phillip looked back up at the towers. "There wasn't supposed to be two of them," he said, "but after the first guy built his, the fellow who owned the property next door got jealous and built one even higher. They kept adding on and adding on, waging their little war, and finally one day they just gave up. Those men are gone but the towers are still here." He paused. "They don't even look like they belong together, do they?"

Louis shrugged, deciding it was best to let Phillip wander.

"See that little bridge up there?" Phillip said, pointing. "One day somebody got the idea that the towers needed to be joined together forever. So they built a bridge between them."

Phillip pulled out his cigarettes and lit one. He drew in heavily, then let it out in one long, slow breath. For several minutes, they just stood there in the cold sun while Phillip smoked his cigarette. Finally, Phillip tossed the butt to the dirt.

"Let's go," he said. "I have something I want to show you."

They backtracked on U.S. 12 until Phillip steered him down a side road. It wound among small cottages, every once in a while offering up a glimpse of water beyond. Phillip pointed to a place called Jerry's Pub and told Louis to pull in.

Inside, a fire was burning and the guys at the bar — a gregarious mix of young longhairs in down vests and old guys in flannel — were watching the football game. Louis ordered beers and they took them outside to the leaf-strewn deck. Phillip stood at the railing looking out over the green-gray lake. He was quiet for a long time.

"This is Wampler's Lake. It hasn't changed that much since I was last here," Phillip said finally.

"When was that?" Louis asked.

"September 1951." Phillip set his beer bottle on the railing, his eyes scanning the far shoreline.

Louis could see something change in Phillip, a loosening in his shoulders, a softening in his eyes. Instinct was telling him this lake was where he had brought Claudia. And that bringing Phillip here now had been the right thing to do.

"It was Labor Day weekend," Phillip said. "Rodney brought her to the park near her house — her mother was away — and I picked her up on my motorcycle." A small smile tipped his lips. "She was afraid and clung to my back the whole way out. I drove faster so she'd hold on harder."

Phillip looked to the left, pointing. "There was a pavilion over there with an arcade. It had one of those machines

139

where you could put in a dime and make this claw thing pick up a prize. I won her this ugly fake silver ring."

Phillip was smiling now. "She wanted to go out on the lake on a powerboat ride, but it was fifty cents and I had just enough money left to pay for the motel room and a couple of burgers so I said no. I think she knew what I was up to."

Louis waited for him to go on. For a long time, the only sound was the gentle bump of a pontoon boat against the dock.

"We went upstairs to the dance hall," Phillip said. "It was the last night before they closed for the season and Fred Waring was playing. We danced and it was like I had caught on to the air and was holding it in my arms. It was so hot. She had a pink scarf and she used it to wipe my forehead."

Louis didn't move, didn't even want to take a breath.

"There were these little cabins over there," Phillip said. "She wouldn't go inside when I checked in. She was pretty nervous about everything. I took her back to the cabin and we made love. After, we laid there with the window wide open to catch any breeze, but there wasn't any. Just the music from the pavilion as they played the last song."

Slowly, softly, Phillip began to hum. Then hesitantly, the words came, in a whispered waltz.

"A boy and girl, they can kiss
good-bye,
and run down the hillside together.
But a man and woman, their hearts?
can cry
forever and ever
Though oceans may sever.
True be my true love. . . ."

Phillip fell silent, his eyes on the lake. And he said something so softly, Louis was sure he wasn't meant to hear it.

"I don't even have a picture of her."

Somewhere beyond the trees a church bell rang. It filled the silence. When it stopped, Phillip turned to him.

"Thank you, Louis," he said.

Louis wasn't sure what to say. Phillip didn't wait for a reply. He turned and left the deck.

Chapter 13

The drive back to Hidden Lake seemed longer this morning. Maybe it was the sadness of Phillip's journey back to the Irish Hills yesterday. Or maybe it was because, more than anything right now, Louis just wanted to go home.

But he couldn't leave things as they were. He had promised Phillip he would find out what he could. And he had promised Alice he would try to help Charlie. Right now, he didn't feel very confident he could do either.

The gates of Hidden Lake came into view. Near the guardhouse sat two Ardmore cruisers and a midnight-blue state police car. And a few feet down the road, parked almost in a ditch, was a rusty brown Civic. A man stood next to it, shivering in a tattered suede jacket and faded jeans.

Louis pulled up to the guardhouse. A cop walked to his open window and peered in.

"No visitors today, partner," the cop said.

Louis showed him the pass Dalum had

given him Friday, but the cop shook his head. "This is three days old," he said. "Let me make a phone call."

Louis shoved the car into Park and got out, leaning against the front fender. His eyes drifted to the man in the suede coat, who was now walking toward him.

He looked familiar. Thin and young, with spikes of orange-tipped blond hair. He wore blue wire-rimmed sunglasses, but Louis could see his face clearly and as the man grew closer, it started to come back to him.

I'll be damned.

It was Doug Delp, the reporter he had known up at Loon Lake a few years back. The guy was aggressive and obnoxious and Louis had almost decked him once or twice. But in the end, it had been Delp who probably kept Louis out of jail.

Delp's step slowed suddenly and he pulled off his sunglasses, staring at Louis. When recognition settled in, he came forward quickly, sticking out a wind-chapped hand.

"Louis Kincaid," Delp said. "What the fuck are you doing back here?"

Louis glanced down at Delp's hand and hesitated long enough for Delp to know he had to think about shaking it before he did.

143

Doug sniffed from the cold, jamming his hands back in his jacket pockets.

"I should ask you the same thing," Louis said.

"I'm here checking out Rebecca Gruber's murder," he said. "And looking for Donald Lee Becker."

"Becker's dead."

Delp grinned. "That's what people say about Elvis."

Louis didn't reply, glancing back at the Ardmore cop, who was still holding his radio waiting for Chief Dalum.

"I thought they ran you out of Michigan," Delp said.

"Well, I'm back."

"You still in Florida?"

"Yeah."

"Last I heard, you were a P.I. down there."

"You heard right."

Delp was looking at him through the blue lenses. Louis turned away from his scrutiny.

"Why you here at Hidden Lake?" Delp asked.

"None of your business."

"Does it have anything to do with Becker?"

Louis shot Delp a look. Delp smiled.

"Hey, it's juicy stuff, man. You heard, didn't you? They found some bones at Becker's old farm up near Mason. He admitted killing six women, and they found all six. So that poses the question, whose bones are these new ones?"

Louis stared at him.

Delp smiled. "This is going to make a helluva final chapter for my true crime book."

"You're writing a book on Becker?"

"Yeah, it's called . . ." Delp raised his hands, as if he were seeing the title on a marquee. "The Grim Reaper. The True Story of the Coed-Killing Farmer."

"Jeez, Delp," Louis said.

"Come here. Look."

Delp led Louis back to the Civic. Louis bent and peered in the driver's window. The car was a mess, filled with papers and boxes. Mounted on a makeshift holder near the glove box sat five police radios, their tops glittering as the tiny red lights zipped back and forth. On the passenger seat was a cardboard box labeled *D.L. Becker.*

"Looks like you got everything you need," Louis said. "Why you hanging out here?"

"I would kill for a look at Becker's hospital file," Delp said.

Louis shook his head. "Ain't going to happen."

"I would settle for some photographs of E Building and the name of Becker's doctor."

The Ardmore cop called to Louis, indicating he could go on through the gates.

Louis looked back at Delp. "I gotta go."

"So you aren't going to help me? After all I did for you?"

Louis ignored him, climbed back in the Impala, and drove through the gates. In his rearview mirror, he could see Delp huddled near his car.

Louis found Alice in her office, a small room not far down the hall from the nurse's station where he had first encountered her last week. When she looked up at him, her eyes were circled in shadows, and her red curls looked as tired as she did.

"How was your weekend?" Louis asked.

She took a second to answer. "I had family over," she said. "Of course they knew about Rebecca, but no one said anything. Saturday, Chief Dalum came to see me and I had to go over things again."

"I'm sorry," Louis said. "Is there anything I can do?"

Alice shook her head. "Nothing you're not already doing, Mr. Kincaid."

Alice didn't stand up, and he didn't want to seem pushy by asking her if they could walk to E Building right now. So he waited, his gaze moving to the window and the spiderweb of black branches against the cloudless sky.

"I have some information for you on Rebecca," Alice said. "Do you want to sit down?"

Louis slipped into a chair, then realized he didn't have his notebook with him. Alice was staring at him, and he hoped she hadn't noticed how unprepared he was. His mind had been on Claudia, not Rebecca. He saw a small steno pad on the edge of the desk and picked it up. Alice waited until he had flipped it open and plucked a pen from his pocket.

"Rebecca was at work Tuesday," Alice started. "I saw her on and off during the day up to about two. When I left before four, her car was still here in the lot."

"Okay."

"On Wednesday, her car was here when I arrived at nine, and I just assumed she had come in early," Alice said. "She had been working over in C Building with the salvage crews, so not seeing her was no surprise."

Louis looked up. "Do we know if she made it home Tuesday night?"

"She didn't," Alice said. "Chief Dalum told me he thinks she was abducted Tuesday afternoon and left in the woods at dawn Wednesday."

"So someone kept her for a day," Louis said.

Alice sighed as she nodded. "It seems that way."

"Did the chief tell you anything else?" Louis asked. "Like how she was killed or what had happened?"

"No," Alice said.

He would have to get that himself. He suspected Rebecca's death had been horrific, and that Dalum hadn't felt comfortable sharing that with Alice.

"Tell me about Rebecca's family," Louis said.

"She had a son, living with his father down South somewhere. No current boyfriends or angry exes."

"Have you talked to Charlie?" Louis asked.

"No," Alice said. "The chief won't let me. I'm sure he's scared to death in there. How long can they hold him without charging him, Mr. Kincaid?"

Louis gave a shrug. "Forty-eight hours usually, but in a small town, if no lawyer steps forward . . . well, the chief can end

148

up calling it all sorts of things. Even protective custody."

"That's wrong," she said.

"In this case, it's probably better for Charlie if he's in a cell. At least until we know."

Alice had no comment, but she reached into a desk drawer and withdrew a thin paperback book and held it out to Louis. "I thought you might like to read this."

A Midsummer Night's Dream. He took it, flipping through it. "You got this from Rebecca's office?"

"She didn't have an office," Alice said. "She had a locker, and the police took most everything. They didn't seem interested in this, so I asked if I could keep it."

"Have you read it?"

"Just enough to know why Charlie put flowers on Rebecca."

"Why?"

"In the story, the men place flowers on sleeping women's eyes," Alice said. "When the woman awakes, she falls in love with the first man she sees."

"And you think Charlie wanted Rebecca to fall in love with him?"

Alice rose suddenly, moving to the window, almost disappearing into the glare. Louis turned his chair so he could see her, but she spoke without turning back. "There was something about the way Charlie looked at Rebecca," she said. "I think . . ." She drew a breath and her voice grew huskier. "I think he might have tried to tell her he loved her and when she did not . . . could not . . . accept it, something happened to him."

Louis looked down at the paperback cover. A bare-breasted woman in a bride's veil was being groped by a half-man, half-donkey character. A full white moon shone above them. A small, naked crying child huddled on the bottom.

"So you think he was trying to put her to sleep so he could wake her up with the flowers?" Louis asked.

Alice faced him. "I don't know."

Louis knew he needed to talk to Charlie. If he could relate to him, using what was in the book, maybe Charlie would tell him what happened.

For a second, Louis had the thought that maybe that would be okay for Charlie. No way was Charlie competent to stand trial and he undoubtedly would be sent to a new hospital. In the end, his life wouldn't change at all.

He heard the jingle of keys and looked up. Alice was holding the ring out to him.

He slipped the book into his jacket pocket and took the keys.

"The big key opens the main door for E Building," she said. "The records room is at the end of the main hallway, on the first floor. The files are by admission date. Please make sure you lock everything before you leave."

"You're not coming with me?"

"I can't. The salvage men will be here in a few minutes and the superintendent is supposed to be coming by later." She nodded toward a copy machine. "I'd appreciate it if you could be gone by the time he gets here. Just bring her file back here and I will copy whatever you need."

"Thank you, Alice."

Louis left the administration building and walked quickly across the grass to E Building. He didn't see any cops, except the two at the front gate, but yellow crime scene tape was still draped across the trees, stretching deep into the woods. A salvage truck sat at a distance near another building.

Louis slipped the key in the lock and pulled open the heavy door. It scraped on the concrete and he debated leaving it open, but decided against it. He didn't need an open door attracting the cops or anyone else, so he struggled to close it, taking a second to relock it from the inside.

His breath clouded in the musty air as he moved down the hall, listening to the lonely tap of his footsteps on the terrazzo floor. A sudden wind at his face drew his eyes to a window. The grating was still in place, but the glass was broken, shards strewn on the sill and floor.

He moved on, past five or six closed doors, stopping at one with RECORDS stenciled on the pebbled glass window. He stuck the key in and went inside.

Boxes . . . so many he could not even tell how large the room was. There were walls of white cardboard stacked to the ceiling, leaving the lower three rows crushed to almost a third their size. He could not even read the dates on those.

He leaned against the doorjamb, drawing a long breath as he scanned the boxes. Maybe he'd get lucky. Maybe 1951 would be up high. He stood there almost a full minute, looking. There didn't seem to be any system to the dating on the boxes. He did not see 1951.

There was no space to work inside the room, so he started stacking the boxes in the hall. After one row, he was sweating, and he stopped to pull off his jacket.

A noise.

Just a tiny clink, like glass against metal.

He froze, listening.

The loose grating. At the broken window. Had to be it.

But he stayed still, laying his jacket down silently, waiting. When he heard nothing, he went back to work, reaching down to grab the box labeled 1933. It was wet and the soggy side ripped away, scattering folders and papers.

Damn it . . .

It took fifteen minutes to put the box back together, and he wasn't even sure he had the right records in the right folders as he jammed them inside. When he was done, he shoved the box away with his foot. Right behind it sat another, the date 1951 scrawled in thick black letters on the side.

He sat down on the floor, pulling the box to him, and opened it. It was fat with folders, but they looked to be in alphabetical order. He found Claudia DeFoe's, wiggled it free, and spread it open on his lap.

Man . . .

There were metal clips on each side to keep the documents in place, but the papers were loose, dog-eared and water-stained.

He pulled out his reading glasses. Charts. Log entries. Prescriptions. Treatments.

But he couldn't make much sense of it, couldn't even read the handwriting, except the scribbled letters THOR, which he guessed was Thorazine. He was going to have to ask Alice to help.

Putting his glasses away, Louis got to his feet. He set Claudia's file in the hall and started bringing the boxes back in. The room quickly filled back up, and for a moment, he wasn't sure they were all going to fit, but he crammed the last of them up against the ceiling and scanned the floor, making sure he hadn't lost any papers.

Clank.

He spun toward the rear of the building.

That noise wasn't the flap of loose metal grating. The broken window was near the front door. This noise came from the back. And it sounded like the slam of metal against metal.

The hall was brushed with sunlight, and he could see clearly that it went on about twenty feet before it split into a T at the end. There were four or five more doors, all closed.

Louis picked up his jacket and quietly slipped his Glock from the pocket, easing it from the holster. Then he waited, his

154

eyes locked on the end of the hall. Dust motes glittered in the shafts of light and he could feel the wind from the broken window against the back of his neck.

He moved forward slowly, shoving open each door, bracing himself for any flash of movement. But the rooms were empty, the windows closed. He continued on down the hall.

At the T, he stopped. To his left was an exit door, chained shut from the inside. To his right, more empty rooms. He moved on to the door he knew led to the upper floors, where the stairwell was grated all the way up. The door was unlocked, but the stairwell gate was chained at the first floor. He walked on.

One last room. A large one with double doors, propped open.

Louis moved inside.

The yellow walls were slashed with deep shadows that seemed to move as he did. Tables. Plastic chairs. A stainless steel sink and an old red and white Coca-Cola machine in the corner. Trash littered the floor. A Pabst Blue Ribbon bottle lay under the window. But the window was closed and barred on the outside.

And a smell . . .

Cigarettes. No, not cigarettes. Ashes.

He turned slowly, his eyes falling on a single cigarette lying on the stainless steel counter. It had been set on the edge and left burning, leaving a perfectly straight line of gray ash that stretched from the edge of the counter to the gold filter.

Louis bent and sniffed it. It was cold and stale. It could be months or even years old. And anyone could have left it, vandals, salvage men, or an employee sneaking a smoke while packing up the files.

Louis had started to turn back to the hall when he caught a whiff of something else.

Cigarette smoke. And it was fresh, hanging in the air like Phillip's did after he left the patio. Louis drew in a breath, trying to get a direction on the smell, but suddenly it was gone, leaving just that dusty medicinal odor in its place.

Louis eased back to the hall, his gun still level, his eyes lingering on the abandoned cigarette on the counter. He moved as quietly as he could, his ears still alert for anything. But there was nothing.

He walked back to the records room, and picked up his jacket and Claudia's file and locked the records room door. As he made his way to the main door, he glanced at the front stairwell, the one he and

Alice had gone up last Wednesday.

If someone had been in here a few minutes ago, chances were they were long gone, but still he felt the need to look. Maybe there was a stairwell he hadn't seen.

He pulled out Alice's keys and headed upstairs. On each floor, he did a cursory check of the rooms and closets. He went down the same steps he had come up and left E Building, again using both hands to push the door closed tight enough to lock it.

The cold air felt good in his lungs and he gulped in a deep breath, then another before starting across the grass. He had gone about fifty feet when he felt the urge to turn back.

The sun was hovering just above the roof, and Louis had to squint to bring the building into focus. The glare obliterated the grating and colored the windows black, and for a moment, they looked like something in an old fifties sci-fi movie, mysterious holes that led to another dimension.

Clutching Claudia's records, he hurried back to the administration building.

He was deep into copying the file when Alice came back into the office. She looked harried.

"You found it," she said.

"But I can't make much of it," Louis said. "I'm just copying everything until you can help me —"

"Oh dear, I can't," she interrupted. "Not now, at least. The superintendent is on his way."

"Alice," he said, "I just need a place to start. Please."

She hesitated, then picked up the file folder. She flipped through it quickly. Her eyebrow arched as she read something; then she looked up at Louis.

"What did you find?" he asked.

"Her attending doctor." She held out the paper. "It was Dr. Rose Seraphin." She waited, like she expected Louis to recognize the name, and when he didn't she went on. "She's a big name in psychiatric circles."

"So she's still alive then?" Louis asked, taking the paper and looking at the name.

Alice nodded. "I see her name in the journals. Last I heard she was affiliated with the medical school at University of Michigan. She would be . . . oh, in her seventies by now."

Louis slipped the paper in with his other copies. "Then that's where I go next. Thanks."

Alice's eyes went to the window. "Oh no,

158

there's the superintendent's car. You better finish up quickly. I'll go and keep him outside for a while."

Alice grabbed her coat and was gone. Louis went back to copying, keeping one eye on Alice, who was steering a fat man in a gray overcoat away from the front door. Louis was down to the last few papers when a picture caught his eye. It was old, a faded black-and-white photograph clipped to what looked like an admitting form.

Good God . . .

Louis quickly pulled his reading glasses out of his jacket, and when he put them on, Claudia DeFoe came to life before his eyes.

It was a head-and-shoulders shot, and she appeared to be wearing a hospital gown. Her hair was a white blond, hanging lank and uncombed over her white face. Her head was cocked to one side and there was a mark on her cheek that could have been a bruise or a smear of blood.

Her eyes . . .

God, her eyes.

Dark, wide, with a beseeching stare. Dark desperate eyes in that blank white face, like something trapped inside fighting to get out.

Louis took off his glasses. He could see

Alice and the superintendent coming back toward the door. He stuffed the original papers back in their folder and left it on Alice's desk. He gathered up his copies and slipped on his jacket, stashing the copies under his arm. He started for the door, but stopped.

He went back to the folder, pulled out the picture of Claudia, and slipped it in his pocket.

Chapter 14

Louis hurried across the quadrangle, weaving through the throngs of students. He hadn't been back to University of Michigan since his graduation eight years ago, and as he looked up at the cloisterlike stone buildings he had a fleeting thought that time seemed to stand still here. Nothing had changed.

As he was about to emerge onto South University, his eyes strayed upward. For a second, he was back in his dorm room.

And she was back, too . . . Kyla.

But there was no time right now. He had to get to Dr. Seraphin's office. It had taken only a phone call to the medical school to locate her. She was a professor emeritus affiliated with the department of psychiatry. He had discovered she was also on the board of the state psychiatric association.

It took him nearly an hour to find the right building in the sprawling maze of the medical school complex. A receptionist directed him to the fourth floor and he walked the hall, searching for the right door. There it was . . . and it was ajar.

He pushed it open quietly.

She was seated at a desk, her head bent over a thick book, her slender hand resting on the edge of the page. She wore one ring, something old and silver, silver as her short spiky hair.

"Dr. Seraphin?" Louis said.

Her eyes zipped to his face, and for a second he sensed she might have been expecting someone else.

"I'm sorry," she said, "I'm not taking any more applications."

Louis stepped into the office. "I'm not a student, Doctor. My name is Louis Kincaid. I'm a private investigator."

Dr. Seraphin rolled her chair back a few inches, crossed her legs, and studied him. She didn't look anywhere near seventy. She was a striking woman, dressed in a stylish quilted black suit jacket, black wool pants, and black boots with a spiked heel. The only color came from a red scarf around her taut neck.

"What are you investigating?" she asked.

"Missing remains from Hidden Lake Hospital."

She couldn't hide her surprise this time and she tried to cover it by turning away from Louis and closing the book. When she said nothing, he went on.

"My client is someone who wanted to relocate them, but the casket was filled with rocks."

She swung her chair back to face him. "Rocks? How can that be?"

"That's what I was hoping you'd tell me."

"I left Hidden Lake a long time ago," she said.

"I know that," Louis said. "She was a patient of yours by the name of Claudia DeFoe. I was told she died in 1972."

Dr. Seraphin's lips pressed together as her eyes dropped to the folder in Louis's hand. Her finger stroked the edge of the desk.

"Is that her medical record?" she asked.

"Yes."

"Where did you get it?"

"I can't tell you that."

Again, she was quiet for a moment. "What do you want from me?"

"Anything you can remember about Claudia DeFoe."

"I can't tell you much. That's all confidential."

"Can you at least tell me what she died of?"

"It's not in the file?"

"Not that I can find."

Again, Dr. Seraphin's eyes moved to the file in Louis's hand. Then she thrust out a hand. Louis wasn't sure he wanted to give the file to her, but if she was going to help at all, he had to trust her.

He gave her the file, and she opened it on her lap. She pursed her lips, then slipped a tiny rubber thimble on her forefinger and started flipping through the pages.

"Pneumonia," she said, looking up. The fluorescent light caught her face, paling it, and suddenly he could see a thousand fine wrinkles.

"Winter, seventy-one and seventy-two," she added. "I remember now. We had a flu epidemic. I recall we lost almost twenty people that month."

"Twenty people died from the flu?"

"Actually, most would have died of pneumonia and other forms of respiratory failure. The conditions in the wards weren't the best. They were damp and cold, and all the patients were confined to the indoors, which can take its toll on the elderly."

"Claudia DeFoe was only thirty-seven when she died."

Dr. Seraphin gave a small shrug. "Anyone with a compromised immune system can be susceptible."

"Okay," Louis said. "But why wasn't she in her grave?"

Dr. Seraphin ran her nails through her short hair, then closed the folder, keeping it on her lap. "I can only speculate," she said.

"Please."

"Patients did most of the menial labor at the hospital. It was part of their therapy," she said. "They would cook, clean, tend some of the elderly, do lawn work, or work in apple orchards, things like that. Some dug graves in the cemetery."

Dr. Seraphin fell quiet, and he gave her a second to travel back. When she started speaking again, her voice was gentler.

"Some of the higher-functioning patients, those we could trust with tools, had other jobs. They worked in the carpenter shop and built tables, and shelves and caskets."

Louis didn't know where she was going with this, but he stayed quiet.

"Of course, in the mortuary, we had orderlies to do the work," Dr. Seraphin went on. "Their job was to clean the bodies and prepare them for burial. And in the wintertime, it was also their job to keep the bodies organized, tagged, and cold enough to prevent decomposition."

"Excuse me?"

Dr. Seraphin looked at him, and it took her a second to understand his question. "The hospital had so little funding, so money was always a problem," she said. "Until the late seventies, we didn't even have any mechanical equipment and all the graves were dug by hand. We couldn't bury anyone in the wintertime so remains were stored in a cooler from around mid-December until April."

Louis turned away from Dr. Seraphin, a sourness in his throat that he knew showed on his face. Dr. Seraphin was quiet for a moment, and he could hear papers rustling and the squeak of her chair as she rocked. Then her voice.

"That December, with the flu outbreak, anything over five or six bodies would have been more than we could store."

"So what happened to them?" Louis asked.

"I am sure we cremated as many as possible," she said. "We had the permission of the families, of course. It was routine admission procedure that families signed a form about disposition of remains should their loved one pass away while institu-

tionalized. Some chose burial, some cremation." Dr. Seraphin hesitated. "Given the
state of our workforce and our storage
problem that winter, it is possible a few remains were cremated by accident."

Louis pointed to the file still in the
doctor's lap. "What does it say about
Claudia DeFoe?"

Dr. Seraphin knew right where to look.
"It says burial."

When Louis said nothing, Dr. Seraphin
went on. "My guess would be that
someone made a mistake and cremated her
along with the rest of the flu victims. Not
wanting to lose his job, he probably put
rocks in a casket before turning it over to
the grave diggers to bury."

Louis drew in a tight breath.

"The grave diggers would not have
known the difference," Dr. Seraphin said
softly. "They were barely functional."

Louis rubbed a hand over his face. He
had known from the moment he walked
into E Building that whatever he found out
about Claudia was going to be tragic. He
hadn't even told Phillip about E Building
yet. How in the hell was he ever going to
tell him this?

There was one shred of hope here.

"Doctor," Louis said, "I didn't see a mausoleum in the cemetery. Where did they keep the cremated remains?"

"The place you're thinking of is not called a mausoleum," she said. "It's called a columbarium. We kept the cremated remains in a vault in the mortuary."

Dr. Seraphin was quiet, her eyes steady on face. He had the feeling she was evaluating him, trying to read something into his questions or the expression on his face.

"You think we were monsters," Dr. Seraphin said.

Louis wanted to say, *no, I don't think that. I know you did the best you could.* But there was a part of him that did think what had happened to Claudia and the others was inhuman.

Dr. Seraphin rose suddenly and picked up her coat. As she slipped it over her slender shoulders, she looked back at him.

"In some ways, it *was* barbaric, just as much of medicine was," Dr. Seraphin said. "But we did the best we could with what little money we had. We learned and we found better ways of helping people."

When Louis still said nothing, Dr. Seraphin picked up her briefcase and motioned to the door. "I'm sorry but I have an appointment. Will you walk out with me?"

She picked up Claudia's file and they started down the hall toward the stairs. Dr. Seraphin spoke as they walked.

"People always focus on the horror stories," she said. "But we had many other benign therapies you don't hear about — relaxation techniques, audio and visual stimulation. We used to try to treat depression by having the patients watch love stories, and episodes of shows like *I Love Lucy*."

She paused and turned to him. "People *did* get better at Hidden Lake. Many, many people went home better than they came in."

They reached the bottom of the stairs and Louis held the door for her. She stopped to slip a pair of sunglasses from her pocket. They were large and black, covering her eyes completely.

"How long were you at Hidden Lake, Doctor?" Louis asked.

"Nearly twenty years," she said, as she started walking again. "I rose up through the ranks and I was instrumental in correcting many deficiencies. But there was only so much I could do as assistant deputy superintendent. As third in command, I had no real power to move the board toward more progressive treatments. And as a private institution, we were always strapped for funds."

Again, Louis was quiet. They were walking toward a shiny black Volvo. There was a man standing next to it. Beefy and tall, and wearing a dark suit and hat.

Dr. Seraphin suddenly stopped, about ten feet from the Volvo. Louis could see the driver watching them intently.

"May I ask your background, Mr. Kincaid?" Dr. Seraphin asked.

"Nearly three years a private investigator and before that, a cop. Why?"

"You have that look of someone who is dealing with mental illness for the first time."

"And what kind of look is that, Doctor?" he asked.

"Appalled, somewhat fearful." She smiled when she saw his disbelief. "Please, it's perfectly normal to feel that way," she said gently. "I've worked with the mentally ill all my professional life and I learned a long time ago the line between what is real and what is not is very thin. Sometimes it is even invisible."

Dr. Seraphin held out the file. "We all fear what we can't see."

Louis took the file. Dr. Seraphin extended a hand to Louis. "Good-bye, Mr. Kincaid," she said.

Louis shook her hand. Her palm was

soft, creamy, but ice cold. He watched her walk to her car and slip inside. The Volvo pulled away, and he stood there for a moment, clutching Claudia's file to his chest.

Chapter 15

"I need to see the mortuary."

Alice stared at Louis for a long time through the open driver's-side window of her car. Without a word, she reached back to get her tote bag, got out of her car, and shut the door. When she turned back to face him, there was such a look of distress on her face that Louis regretted just blurting things out before she even had a chance to get into the building.

He could almost read her thoughts. That he wasn't holding up his end of the bargain to help Charlie. That he was some ghoulish voyeur no better than that damn reporter Delp. That she had been wrong about him and shouldn't have trusted him.

"Alice," he said quietly, "I wouldn't ask if it weren't important. I know you think I'm —"

She held up a hand. "It's all right." She gave him a wary smile. "Is it okay if I go to my office first?"

Louis followed her up the stone steps and waited, stamping his feet against the cold as she unlocked the door. Inside was almost as cold as outside.

"Oh no, they must have shut down the boiler," Alice said. "We're going to be without heat from now on, I'm afraid."

"When do you have to be out of here?" Louis asked.

"December thirty-first."

"Then what?"

"The demolition people come in. They're going to start on the western side of the compound and work eastward toward the buildings over by the lake."

"So there really is a lake?"

She looked at him oddly. "Of course. It's over by the east edge of the property out by the cemetery. It is quite lovely, really." She heaved a sigh. "I heard they are going to build condos around it."

Alice plopped her tote down and pulled out a huge thermos. "Coffee?"

"Alice, I think I love you."

She smiled and poured out the steaming black brew. Louis was about to ask for sugar when she dug in her desk drawer and tossed out a handful of packets and little restaurant cream cups. "I steal them from McDonald's," she said.

For a minute or two, they just stood sipping their coffees as the cold air swirled around them. Then Alice set her cup down and capped the thermos.

"Let's go get this over with," she said, pulling out her key ring.

The morning sun was a pale yellow smudge behind the gray scrim of clouds. Alice took him out a back door and they hurried down a cracked concrete walkway heading in the direction of E Building. They passed a small wood building with a COMMISSARY sign above the entrance, and then the power plant. Louis thought again about what Alice had told him that first day, that Hidden Lake had been a city unto itself, with a bakery and laundry, a post office and dairy, even its own farm-lands where inmates picked apples and pressed cider for sale to the outside world. It was a place where a person could live, work, die, and be forgotten without ever stepping outside the iron gates.

"That's the hospital," Alice said, pointing to a mammoth spired building ahead. "It's one of the oldest buildings here and was even open to the public during the Depression. They charged a dollar eighteen a night for a bed. The mortuary is in the basement."

The salvage crew had already stripped most of the furnishings, fixtures, and doors, and now the empty halls with their gaping door frames had the desolate look of a place waiting to die.

Louis followed Alice down a long metal staircase and along a plain tiled corridor with many doors and overhead steam pipes. At a door with MORTUARY stenciled on the glass, she slipped in the key and stepped aside to let Louis in.

He bypassed the outer office and headed straight into the working area. Although everything had been stripped, he could guess that this was where the bodies were washed and prepared for burial; there were still pipes in the walls, rusting drains, and holes in the peeling linoleum where tables had once been bolted. The walls were stripped of all shelving and anything that could be sold. A very old and very yellowed hand-lettered sign still hung on one wall: PRIMUM NON NOCERE.

Louis had seen the sign in hospitals before. "First do no harm," he translated out loud. "Strange thing to put in a morgue."

"Even the dead deserve respect," Alice said quietly.

Louis looked back at her. She was standing at the door, shoulders hunched up in her coat. "If you don't mind, I think I'll wait out in the hall," she said.

Louis heard Alice's retreating footsteps and the banging echo of a door. It wasn't until that moment that he realized what he was going to do. He had the hope that whoever cremated Claudia by mistake had at least been decent enough to provide her an urn. And if he could find it, he was going to just take it.

He went back to the hallway and looked around. All the signs had been taken down, so he went along, opening doors. Broom closets. Offices. Supply rooms. Another one of those heavy steel doors, this one with PASSAGE 7 painted on it but again, with no doorknob or handle.

He moved into a large white-tiled room that he guessed had been used for embalming. There was a small door leading off it. He tried it, and it opened with a wheeze of cold musty air.

Five wooden steps leading into a dim room. He went down two steps and peered into the gloom. Rough stone walls and some wood shelves. Another storage room. He was about to go back up when a glint caught his eye. He reached up and pushed the door open wider for more light. The wood shelves were filled with tin cans. He went down the last three steps.

The shelves completely lined the small stone room, running from the concrete floor to the low ceiling. Each shelf was filled with the tins, each about the size of a paint can. But as Louis came closer he could see they weren't tins but were made of copper, the once-shiny metal now dull and green with corrosion.

Labels . . .

Maybe half the cans had labels, but they were frayed, peeling, or water-spotted. Louis groped for his reading glasses and picked up one of the few cans that had a piece of a legible label.

Large black letters: HIDDEN LAKE HOSPITAL.

And below that in faded typing: 4/12/34 ANDREW. The rest of the label and the rest of the name was gone.

Louis felt a grab to his gut and he threw out a hand to grip the shelf.

These were . . . people.

His eyes came up from the can in his hand, and moved over the shelves. Rows and rows of them. His chest drew tight, and the air was suddenly thick with the smell of dirt and decay.

He swallowed back a rush of nausea, but still he could not draw a full breath. He spun away from the shelf and was halfway to the door before he realized he still held a can in his hand.

He stopped and looked down at it, then gently placed it back on the shelf. He turned and left the room, his footsteps growing faster as he made his way back up the steps to the entrance.

Alice was standing outside on the grass. "What's the matter?" she asked.

He pulled in some cold air, trying to find the words. His head was still thick with the smells of the room, and his thoughts were jumbled.

"Louis," Alice said, "talk to me. You look sick."

He told her what he had seen and when she said nothing, he explained what Dr. Seraphin had said about the possible mix-up in bodies and how he had hoped Claudia would be among the cremated remains.

"I need to go back down there," he said. "I need to make sure she's not down there."

Alice grabbed his arm. "No, Louis. Let it be."

"Alice, I have to —"

"No, not now. You don't have to do anything right now. You're going to come back to my office with me and I am going to call

178

John Spera. He will come and get them."

Louis looked back at the hospital. "If she's down there, Alice, I have to do something —"

"Let Mr. Spera do his job. Then you can go to him and see if she is there."

Louis felt Alice's firm but gentle tug on his arm. He reached up to wipe his brow. His hand was shaking.

"Come on," Alice said softly.

He walked with her back across the frozen grass.

Chapter 16

Alice hung up the phone and leaned back in her chair. "Mr. Spera wasn't there, but his son said he would make sure his father knew about the cremated remains as soon as possible."

Louis was slumped in a chair across from her desk and nodded woodenly. "How can something like that even happen?" he asked, almost to himself.

"I don't know," Alice said.

They were quiet for a long time. A banging sound drew Louis's gaze to the window. Some men were loading doors onto one of the salvage trucks. He shivered, wrapping his arms around himself. When he looked back at Alice, she was watching him closely.

Suddenly, she opened a drawer and pulled out a thick manila folder, setting it on the desk between them. Louis recognized it as Claudia DeFoe's original medical file.

"I took a look through this yesterday," Alice said. "Did you get a chance to go through it yet?"

"Just a quick glance. It doesn't make a lot of sense to me."

"Well, maybe I can help."

Louis sat up straight, scooting the chair closer. Alice flipped the folder open and studied the various forms for a long time before looking up at Louis.

"Most of this looks pretty normal to me," she said, sifting slowly through the papers. "It's just the usual progress reports from her doctors, logs of the therapies she underwent, routine nurses' notes." Alice went back to reading, then looked back up at Louis. "Maybe if you could tell me what it is you're hoping to find . . ."

Louis shook his head. "I don't know. I guess I just want to *know* her."

Alice's expression had just a hint of pity in it. "Some of what you find in here might be a little hard to take, Louis."

"That's all right," he said. He jammed his hands in his coat pockets, waiting while Alice read some more papers.

"Maybe we could start with the intake form," Alice said, pulling out a paper. "Claudia was admitted to Hidden Lake in October 1951 by her mother, Eloise DeFoe." Alice hesitated. "She had multiple self-inflicted lacerations on both wrists. The doctor noted that her mood was alternately hysterical and disoriented."

Louis thought of the photograph of Claudia he had taken from the file, how the masklike quality of her face contrasted with the wild look in her eyes.

"She was admitted to B Building," Alice went on. "That's the ward for the general women's population." She picked up a different form and studied it.

"What's that?" Louis asked.

"Drug log. I'm just trying to see what they gave her. Here it is. She was on Thorazine, twenty milligrams per day." She looked up at Louis. "I'd say that would be a routine protocol for a suicidal girl and a fairly low dosage. It would make her . . . compliant but not out of it."

Louis nodded.

Alice went back to reading. "She was kept on suicide watch, but I can't find any notes of other attempts. In fact . . ." Alice picked up the drug log again. "She was totally off the Thorazine by late November."

"So she was getting better," Louis said.

"Looks like it." Alice sniffled. "My, it's cold in here. Why don't you pour us some more coffee?"

Louis got the thermos and poured two fresh cups while Alice continued her reading.

"Claudia was admitted to the general infirmary in late December, but it doesn't say why," Alice said. She looked back at the drug log. "Apparently, she was treated for a nervous stomach, because it says here she was given something for stomach distress."

"So why did she end up in E Building?" Louis asked.

"Good question," Alice murmured, her head bent over the records. She had five different forms spread out on the desk now, trying to piece together Claudia's history. It was quiet. Louis could hear the salvage guys talking and laughing out in the yard.

"All right," Alice said quietly. "She was moved to E in September of 1952. It looks like she had some kind of breakdown."

"Is that normal?" Louis asked.

Alice looked up, a sad smile tipping her lips. "Normal? That's not a word we use a lot here. Let's just say it happens. People can be fine one day and you think they are getting better. Then something snaps inside them and they fall back down into these . . . holes. A few, with the right help, climb back out. But some just can't. Some are just . . . I don't know, too fragile."

Louis was remembering the story Alice had told him about the mother visited by her two children who had a moment of clarity, then slipped away forever. He wondered if Alice was thinking about it, too, because there was a far-off look in her eyes as she sipped her coffee.

"Can you tell much about what happened to Claudia after she went to E?" Louis asked.

Alice went back to the forms. "She was back on the Thorazine at a much higher dosage." Alice shook her head slowly, pulling one of the forms closer. "Things went downhill from there. Ice-bath treatments several times a week. Apparently that didn't work so they tried electroshock therapy."

Alice let out a long sigh. "It looks like she broke her arm during one of the treatments."

Louis shut his eyes against the image of that heap of leather straps he had seen in E Building. When he opened his eyes, Alice was looking at him.

"Go on," he said quietly.

"By the summer of 1953, they were using insulin shock therapy on her," Alice said.

"What in God's name is that?"

Alice hesitated. "The patient would be strapped down and injected with enough insulin to bottom out the blood sugar. The patient would go into severe convulsions or seizures. It was looked at as safer than electroshock. They didn't realize until years later that they were killing the patient's brain, leaving holes."

"Jesus."

"Patients were often left worse off than when they came in. The long-term effects could be anything from mild delusions to incoherent babble."

Louis rose slowly and went to the window. The salvage workers had driven off with their plunder.

"This is odd."

Louis looked back at Alice. He almost didn't want to hear anything else.

"It looks like Claudia tried to escape once," Alice said.

"Escape?" he asked. "How?"

"It was late summer, 1952, about ten months after she arrived, before she was sent to E Building."

Louis moved back to the desk. "What'd she do?"

"Claudia and another young patient by the name of Millie Reuben snuck out of the ward after dinner and climbed over the fence behind B Building."

"The fence with the razor wire?"

"It would not have had razor wire then. It would have been fairly easy for a young girl to get over."

"How far did they get?"

"A half mile or so," Alice said. "They were found in the middle of an apple orchard by a local farmer who recognized the hospital dresses and called the police. They were returned in less than an hour. The nurses wrote that Claudia was hysterical and incoherent and that restraints were necessary."

Alice fell quiet, reading down the page. Louis edged closer, but the handwriting was small, and he couldn't read it upside down.

"That night," Alice went on, "she was transferred to E Building and received her first ice bath. I guess that is your answer as to why she ended up in E Building."

"Did she ever try to escape again?"

Alice's head came up. The tip of her nose was red from the cold. "She would not have had the chance once she went to E Building."

Louis sank back into his chair, resting his elbows on his knees. He could see them, two young women, running through an apple orchard, desperate enough to want to be free yet incapable of finding their way. And for an instant, his image of Claudia changed to something prettier and brighter, as if her run through the orchard was the last real moment she would have before they took it all away.

"Alice," he said, "is there any way you can get to Millie Reuben's file?"

Alice's eyes narrowed. "I don't think I should."

"Please."

"I'm sorry. It was different with your friend. But there's still confidentiality to consider."

He didn't press it. Alice's gaze turned to the window. The pane had a thin layer of frost on it, blurring the trees outside. He wanted to leave, but he knew Alice expected some information from him on Charlie. But he had nothing to tell her. He hadn't yet made it to the Ardmore Police Station to even speak with him.

The phone rang and Alice glanced at it, then lifted the receiver slowly. Louis could hear a man's voice on the other end. Strong, but slow. Alice listened for a minute; then her face started to change as her eyes came to Louis.

"Yes, Chief," she said. "Yes, I understand."

She hung up.

"What's wrong?" Louis asked.

"That was Chief Dalum," she said. "They've found some bones."

Chapter 17

The bones had been buried in a shallow grave on the north end of the cemetery. John Spera and his crew had been working nearby, exhuming grave number 978, when a brownish-colored human skull tumbled from the claw of the backhoe. Spera had promptly stopped and called Chief Dalum.

Two of Dalum's men borrowed spades from Spera and carefully dug a wide hole around the area where the skull had been found. It didn't take long for them to uncover a rib cage and right arm bone. Dalum immediately called the county for the crime scene investigators. No one was sure if this was a crime scene, but Dalum wasn't going to take any chances.

Dalum had seemed surprised when Louis showed up at the cemetery entrance, but he waved to his officer to let him in. When Louis explained he had been visiting Alice, Dalum just nodded and brought him over to the grave. Now the three of them stood — Dalum, Louis, and Spera — watching as one of the technicians carefully brushed away the last of the dirt that had concealed the skeleton.

Spera suddenly turned away, going over to stand next to his backhoe operator. Louis watched him. The wind was in Spera's face, tearing his eyes and whipping his thin dark hair into a frenzy. The man had been digging up graves for weeks now, and Louis knew there was a certain stoicism that went with that. But now Spera had the same look Alice had last week when Charlie walked from the woods carrying Rebecca Gruber — the look that came from being touched by something close to evil.

Spera had a rolled paper in his hand, and Louis guessed it was the layout of the cemetery. He walked over to Spera and asked if he could see it. Spera unrolled it and as he tried to smooth it against the side of the backhoe, it snapped furiously in the wind.

"We're right here," Spera said, pointing a callused finger at the grid. "Number 978 is the farthest grave at the back of the cemetery. The graves end right there. That skull shouldn't have been where it was."

There was a slight defensiveness in Spera's voice, like he felt this was his fault somehow.

Louis looked north beyond the cemetery boundaries. No fence, just heavy brush, then nothing but tall trees so thick they formed a twisted wall of branches as far as Louis could see.

"What's beyond those trees?" Louis asked.

"Farmland," Spera said. "Apple orchards mostly."

Louis looked back at the map, then at the spot where the bones lay. There was less than a yard between grave number 978 and the bones, but probably a good fifty feet of nothing to the north trees.

"Do you have any idea why this area from here to the back was not used for burial?" Louis asked.

"Nope," Spera said. "I just go by the map."

Spera rolled up the paper and walked back to his worker. Louis turned and headed to the north trees, scanning the ground as he walked. He didn't see any stone markers embedded in the ground. There were no graves here. Just grass.

He stopped when he got to the high brush. It was too thick to venture in, and he strained to peer into it. It was wild and tangled, unlike the woods behind E Building, which were maintained by the hospital with plenty of paths and clearings.

"Kincaid, come on over here. I need you to see this."

He headed back to Dalum. He was standing legs wide, arms folded across his jacket as he stared down at the bones, now fully exposed.

Louis guessed the skeleton was still positioned as it had been when it had been dumped and buried. On its side, legs drawn up, both arms folded to one side.

The technicians rose, nodding to Dalum, who in turn nodded to Louis. They both knelt down for a closer look.

"I'd guess it's a child," Louis said. "Or a teenager since the bones are small. I'd estimate the height at no taller than about five three."

"I take it you agree with me that no way is this a patient they just didn't happen to have a casket for," Dalum said.

Louis nodded. "It's not deep enough and there's no clothing."

"You have a guess on how long she's been here?"

Louis looked at him. "She?"

Dalum shrugged.

"No idea, Chief." Louis fell quiet, staring at the bones. A thought was pushing its way to the front of his brain, but it was so far-fetched he couldn't believe it had even occurred to him. Could this be Claudia? His eyes swept over the cemetery. They were a good thirty yards from where her marker was. And it was pretty damn unlikely she would have been dumped like this and so hastily buried. But the bones did look old.

The sun crawled out from behind a cloud. Louis was about to stand up when something caught his eye in the dirt. It was a tiny flash that came to life for just an instant in the sun and was gone.

"Chief," he said, pointing.

"What is it?" Dalum asked, squinting.

Louis carefully wedged a finger in the dirt and popped the object out of the ground. It was dirt-encrusted and he still couldn't tell exactly what it was. He picked up a stick and used it to flick away more dirt. It was a ring.

"I'll be damned," Dalum said.

Louis glanced back at the crime tech, who was putting away his tools. He used the stick to scrape away some of the dirt, enough so they could see an emblem and a stone. It looked like a class ring.

"Better leave it," Dalum said.

Louis nodded and dropped the stick, as Dalum called over the tech guy. Louis rose, brushing the dirt from his hands.

The tech guy was working on the ring now, and Louis knew it would eventually make its way into a nice clean evidence bag. Soon enough they would have a school and a date and a lead on an ID. One thing was sure right now, however. Whoever this was, it wasn't a Hidden Lake patient, because Alice had told him patients weren't allowed to wear jewelry.

Louis felt a strange surge of disappointment that it couldn't be Claudia. At least he would have had something to take back to Phillip, something less horrible than one of those pathetic forgotten cans.

"Kincaid?"

He turned back to Dalum.

"Can I ask you something?"

"Sure."

"Why are you hanging around here? What exactly is it that you're investigating here?"

Louis hesitated. It didn't seem right, telling a stranger the intimacies of Phillip's past. But if there was even the slimmest possibility this was Claudia's remains, then Dalum had a right to know. Louis told the story, told Dalum about Phillip and Claudia, about the rocks in the casket, about Dr. Seraphin and the copper cans in the bowels of the hospital. Before he knew it, he had also told him about Eloise DeFoe committing her only daughter, and about Rodney DeFoe not even wanting to bring his sister's remains home. When Louis was finished, Dalum was staring at him.

"You think your case has anything to do with these bones? Or Rebecca Gruber?"

"No," Louis said.

"Why not?"

"Patients weren't allowed to wear jewelry. And Claudia DeFoe died in 1972. That puts sixteen years between her and Rebecca Gruber. Too much time."

Dalum put his hands on his hips and scanned the cemetery. "Two women dead," he said almost to himself. "Both left in the same place. This can't be a coincidence."

"Chief, I have something to tell you," Louis said. "It may not have anything to do with this, but I don't think we can discount anything right now."

Dalum looked at Louis.

"I was in E Building yesterday," Louis said. "I heard a noise. I didn't see anyone."

"But?" Dalum said, sensing Louis had more to say.

Louis shook his head slowly. "I don't know."

Dalum took a long breath, his hands

slipping into his jacket pockets. Louis knew Dalum was probably taking this personally, like it was an invasion in his small hometown. He knew, too, that it was going to be hard for Dalum to hand things off to the state or county boys. But any small-town cop who was worth a damn knew there was no choice.

A whirring noise made Louis turn.

Shit. It was Doug Delp.

Dalum spun around. "What the hell? How'd you get in here?"

Delp let the camera fall so it hung over his suede jacket. He held up his hands. "Hey, Chief. I'm just doing my job."

"Get out of here! Pete! Escort this asshole back behind the line."

A hulking officer appeared and clamped a mitt on Delp's shoulder. Delp looked to Louis for help, but Louis offered nothing.

"I know you found bones," Delp hollered as the officer gave him a shove. "I know you've got the whole damn county on their way down here."

The officer grabbed Delp's jacket again.

"Damn it, wait a minute!" Delp said. "I have information. I can help you."

"Get him out of here now, Pete," Dalum said.

"Becker did it!" Delp yelled. "Donald

Lee Becker, that's your guy."

Louis and Dalum stared at Delp.

"Becker's dead, you moron," the chief said. "Now get out of here before I run you in."

Louis watched the officer drag Delp off toward the cemetery entrance. Just outside the two towering pines, the officer gave Delp a shove and the reporter stumbled toward his Civic. But he didn't get in. He just stood there, looking back at them. The officer came back, shaking his head and circling a finger near his temple as he walked past Louis.

Dalum turned his gaze from Delp. "Is that the guy who's been bothering Alice and everyone?"

"Yup," Louis said.

"Never seen him before. What paper is he with?"

"He's not. He's here to get material for a book about Becker."

Dalum shook his head. The crime scene tech was waving him over, so Dalum left Louis standing alone at the edge of the shallow grave. Louis stared down at the bones. When he looked up, his eyes went back to the cemetery entrance. Delp was still there.

Louis walked through the brown grass

and out through the pine trees. Delp watched him coming, leaning against his car smoking a cigarette.

"I saw that," Delp said. "I saw what that cop did. You think I'm nuts. But I'm not. Donald Lee Becker is alive."

Louis pointed back to the cemetery. "Becker is in there, Delp, has been for eight years."

Delp stuck the cigarette in his mouth and used both hands to rummage through his pockets. He pulled out a creased photograph and held it up. "See this? This is Donald Lee Becker. It was taken at his farm up near Mason."

"So?"

"It was taken three years ago," Delp said.

Louis took the picture from Delp. It was a blurry black-and-white shot of a guy standing in a cornfield. "You can't tell who this is," Louis said.

"Eyewitnesses," Delp said. "They've seen him."

"Yeah, sharing a Slurpee at the 7-Eleven with Elvis."

Delp snatched the photo from Louis's hand and stuffed it back in his coat pocket. He tossed his cigarette to the dirt, un-looped the Nikon from around his neck, and aimed it toward the cemetery.

Instinctively, Louis held a hand up in front of the lens.

"Hey, man," Delp said.

"Knock it off."

"I got a right —"

Louis grabbed the camera. He knew he had no authority here, but the guy was a ghoul, lurking around taking pictures of bones before Dalum had even had a chance to figure out who it was.

Louis turned the camera over, looking for the latch to release the film-loading mechanism. Delp realized what he was doing.

"Hey, don't do that, man," Delp said, groping for the camera. "Don't expose the film. All my shots of the asylum are on this roll."

"The asylum?" Louis asked, holding the camera at arm's length.

Delp put on a defensive face. "Yeah. What's wrong with that?"

Louis looked hard at Delp, remembering the noise he had heard and the cigarette smoke he had smelled the day he was in E Building getting Claudia's medical records. "Have you been inside E Building?"

"E Building?" Delp asked.

"Yeah," Louis said. "The building Becker was in."

Delp ran a hand across his nose. "No."

"Why don't I believe you?" Louis asked.

Delp was quiet. Louis looked down at the camera. He hit the Rewind button and the Nikon gave out a loud whirring sound.

"What you doing?" Delp said, grabbing for it.

Louis jerked the camera away. When it was finished rewinding, he popped open the back and took out the film, putting it in his pocket.

"You can't have that!" Delp said.

"I'll get the other pictures back to you."

"Yeah, thanks a lot."

Louis handed him the empty camera. "You're lucky the chief didn't throw you in jail for obstruction," he said.

"Let him. It would make a good chapter in the book." Delp leaned against the car again. He pulled out his pack of Kools, hesitated, and held it out to Louis.

Louis shook his head. Delp lit one for himself and looked back at the cemetery.

"So how old you think those bones are?" he asked.

"No way to tell."

"But it's a female, right?"

"No way to tell."

"You're jerking my chain, Kincaid."

Louis was silent.

"Well, they looked old to me," Delp said. "You know, Becker was in this place from the early sixties until 1980, don't you?"

"I don't care."

"Becker died here. Under mysterious circumstances, they say."

Louis didn't look at him. He heard a door open and looked over to see Delp putting his Nikon back in a bag on the front seat. Louis's eyes went to the box on the backseat. It was stuffed with folders, *D.L. Becker* scrawled in black marker on the side. He looked away as Delp emerged.

Delp leaned against the car again, his gaze going back to the cemetery. "They don't have any names. Did you know that?"

Louis nodded slowly.

"Weird, huh? Wonder why they did that. Why did they only give them numbers?" he said.

Louis was quiet.

"The hospital people won't tell me which grave is his," Delp said. "You don't happen to know, do you?"

"Nope."

"Well, I guess it doesn't matter because Becker ain't in it." Delp took a drag on his cigarette. "But it would be kind of cool to find out who is."

Louis was silent.

"Don't you think it's kind of strange?" Delp said.

"What?"

"That the hospital won't tell me where he's buried."

Louis turned to face him. "It's none of your fucking business, Delp."

Delp gave a short laugh. "You just don't want to admit that I'm onto something here with Becker. He's alive, man. He's alive and out there killing girls again."

"You're nuts." Louis started away.

"*I'm* nuts? You came over here. You listened to me, man." Delp's laugh followed Louis as he went back into the cemetery.

Chapter 18

It didn't look much like a police station. Louis had been here last week, to give his statement on Rebecca and Charlie, but he hadn't really taken a good look at it.

The walls of the Ardmore station were a golden brown, the desks mahogany, the floor carpeted in a thick but well-worn forest green. A fire blazed in a fieldstone hearth near the back of the main office.

The fire was warm on Louis's back, but it was making him sleepy. The day had been a long one that had started ten hours ago in Ann Arbor with Dr. Seraphin, followed by his trip down into the mortuary, and talking with Alice about Claudia's records. Then the new bones. And just when he thought he was on his way home, Dalum had made a suggestion.

Why don't you come back to the station with me, Kincaid?

He hadn't said why, but Louis knew. Dalum wanted to talk about the bones, Rebecca, and probably Charlie. And just as Louis was about to decline, he remembered that look on Alice's face a few hours earlier. *When are you going to help Charlie?*

So he had agreed.

Dalum had gone into his office with a grim-looking man in a navy peacoat and a gold badge on the pocket. Louis guessed he was an investigator with the state. Out here in the lobby, a few Ardmore officers worked the desks.

Alice had been here earlier, but when she could offer no thoughts on the bones, Dalum sent her home. She had left with the look of a woman whose whole life was starting to crack. And Louis found himself wondering if she had a husband or a friend she could talk to.

Dalum's door opened and Louis looked up. The state investigator pulled on his coat and left the station, and Dalum waved Louis in. Louis went into the office, closing the door.

Dalum was behind his desk. Behind him was a window fogged with condensation. And on Louis's left, a wall of shelves with a rainbow of book spines. Michigan law books. Lenawee County plat maps. Lenawee County history. Law enforcement handbooks. *Cultivating Beautiful Roses. Investigating Unexplained & Strange Phe-*

nomena. Psychics: Law Enforcement's New Tool? The Deep by Mickey Spillane. *Study Guide for the Florida Law Enforcement Officer's Certification Examination.*

Louis turned quickly. "You thinking of relocating?"

"I was. But then I met my wife, Dee," he said, turning a photo on the desk to face Louis. The woman in the picture was a brunette, maybe forty, with eyes that were not afraid to still seduce the camera.

"That was twenty years ago," Dalum added, nodding to the books. "I kept the Florida study guide just in case she ever left me."

Louis smiled. Dalum set out two small glasses, then picked up a ceramic decanter. It was a figurine of a drunk cop leaning against a lamppost, gun in one hand, whiskey bottle in the other. When Dalum uncapped it, a song tinkled out. "Show Me the Way to Go Home."

Dalum poured two glasses and held one out to Louis. Louis took it down in one gulp. The burn felt good.

"So," Dalum said, reaching for a manila folder, "you interested in what we know about Rebecca Gruber?"

Louis only nodded, his throat still on fire. He didn't want to tell Dalum that

Alice had already given him some details.

"Based on what Alice said, and the last time the salvage men saw Rebecca, we're guessing she disappeared Tuesday afternoon," Dalum said. "Her abductor kept her about fifteen, sixteen hours, then dumped her in the woods behind E Building, where Charlie says he found her Wednesday morning."

"You find anything close to a murder scene?" Louis asked.

"We searched every building," Dalum said. "We didn't find a thing."

Louis had another question, but he was afraid if he asked it, Dalum might think he was questioning his competence. But he wanted to know exactly where things stood.

"Have you talked to all the salvage guys? And the security guards?"

Dalum nodded. "We've cleared all but one, the graveyard security guy. I've known him for a few years, and he seems clean, but it's hard when your alibi is working alone in a place where a murder is committed. I don't believe he's involved."

Dalum was fingering the folder in his hand and he didn't seem anxious to open it.

"You have any other locals in mind you think might be involved?" Louis asked.

Dalum shook his head.

Louis motioned toward the folder. "Is that Rebecca Gruber's autopsy?"

Dalum sighed and opened it. "She was raped, but they didn't find any semen or fluids. The M.E. says the perp used an object, something long and sharp, with a jagged point. It ripped up her insides pretty bad."

Dalum's voice had grown tight and he paused, head down. The light bathed his thick curly hair a white gold. For a few seconds, the room was very still. Then he went on.

"She was beaten and the red marks on her neck and wrists were likely restraints. She was manually strangled. He crushed some of her vertebrae."

Dalum's eyes flicked down to the empty shot glasses. But he kept reading. "And she was burned with a cigarette." He slipped a photo from the folder and held it out.

It was a glossy, color photo of Rebecca Gruber's inner thigh. In the soft depression of pale skin up near her pubic hair were three small red scabs, aligned in a row. Louis looked up. Dalum was holding a second photo of Rebecca's other leg. It had the same three burns.

Dalum slid the photos inside the folder

and set it down, dropping slowly to his chair. Louis reached for the decanter, poured two more shots, and sat down in a chair across from Dalum. They drank in silence, the rattle of the wind on the window the only sound.

The photo was vivid in Louis's mind. Burning was the kind of thing a killer would do while the victim was alive. So he could watch her, smell her skin burn, and hear her scream.

Did you hear them?

Louis stiffened.

I heard her crying.

Where did you hear her, Charlie?

In the cemetery.

Louis stood up. "Chief, can I see Charlie?"

"Now?"

"Yes," Louis said.

"I don't know how much he'll tell you," Dalum said. "He won't talk to us at all. Just keeps asking about Alice and Rebecca and saying he wants to go home."

"I have something that might help," Louis said.

Dalum eyed Louis for a second, then stood up. "All right, then. I'll take you to him."

Charlie stood up quickly when he saw

Chief Dalum and Louis standing at the bars to his cell. He wore an oversized gray cotton jumpsuit, the letters A.P.D. stenciled over the chest. His hair was tangled, and his face was slashed with shadows. In the dim light of the cell, he looked like a frightened animal.

Charlie didn't move until Dalum unlocked the cell. Then he shuffled backward deeper into the shadows. Louis went in the cell and Dalum closed the door. He hesitated a minute in the corridor, then walked away.

"Hello, Charlie," Louis said. "Do you remember me?"

Charlie nodded, his body now pressed against the wall.

Louis held out the book Alice had given him, *A Midsummer Night's Dream*, making sure Charlie saw the cover. Louis had read enough of the book to know that special flowers were placed on the sleeping eyes of men and women. The juice from the flowers would leak into the eyes and when the person awoke, he or she would fall in love with the first face seen. Oberon was some kind of king who was trying to get his queen Titania to give him her baby so he could use the child as his page. But Titania had been a victim of the flowers and was in love with a man who wore the head of a donkey.

Charlie was staring at the book. "That's Rebecca's," he whispered.

Louis nodded. "I know. Will you talk to me about it?"

Charlie didn't move. Louis held out a hand, hoping to draw him back to the bunk, but Charlie stayed against the wall.

"Can you tell me what this book is about, Charlie?"

Charlie's pale eyes clouded with confusion.

"Can you tell me about the flowers you put on Rebecca's eyes?"

"Where are the flowers?" Charlie asked.

"The chief has them," Louis said. "They're safe."

Charlie's hand came out slowly, palm up. "Can I have that?"

Louis hesitated, then gave him the book. Charlie stayed against the wall and opened it.

" 'You spotted snakes with double tongue, thorny hedge-hogs, be not seen,' " Charlie said. " 'Newts, and blind-worms, do not wrong. Come not near our fairy queen.' "

Charlie looked up at Louis, then back at the book. " 'To bring in — God shield us!

— a lion among ladies, is a most dreadful thing, for there is not a more fearful wildfowl than your lion living!' "

"Charlie . . ."

Charlie looked up at Louis, his eyes wide. " 'I have a reasonable good ear in music!' " he said. " 'Let us have the tongs and the bones!' "

It took Louis a second to realize Charlie wasn't reading from the book but merely repeating words and phrases he remembered. It wasn't making any sense and Louis let him go on until he started to turn a page; then he interrupted him.

"Charlie, I need to ask you a question."

Charlie looked up. " 'I am slow of study . . . I'll speak in a monstrous little voice.' "

Louis wasn't sure how to go about this, then decided straightforward was the best. "Did you love Rebecca?" he asked.

Charlie's eyes went back to the book in his hands. " 'This passion, and the death of a dear friend, would go near to make a man look sad —' "

"Charlie, stop reading for a minute."

The pale eyes came up to focus on Louis. "Let's put the book away for now, okay?"

Charlie nodded and closed the book.

"Charlie," Louis said quietly, "did you love Rebecca?"

211

"Yes," Charlie whispered.

"Did you ever tell her you loved her?"

Charlie held the book to his chest and his eyes squeezed closed. Louis suspected Charlie was about to tell him that yes, he had professed his love to Rebecca, but that Rebecca had rebuffed him.

"I was a changeling child," Charlie said.

"A what?"

"I was Rebecca's changeling child. She said I was left for her a long time ago because I was sick."

Louis stifled a sigh. "Left at the hospital?"

"Yes," Charlie said. "I was left because I was sick."

"Who left you there?"

"The fairies."

Louis moved to the bunk, sitting down.

Charlie took a step toward him. "You don't believe me."

Louis looked at him quickly. He was surprised Charlie had picked up on his frustration. He hadn't thought him capable of that kind of perception.

"Tell me again how you heard Rebecca crying," Louis said.

"That night she cried and the graves cried back to her."

"Have the graves cried before?"

"Sometimes."

"When did they cry before?"

Charlie came closer, the book still against his chest, but the frightened look in his eyes was gone. "A midsummer's night before."

"How long is that?"

"A long time. It was warm."

"Last summer?"

Charlie's face blanked and Louis knew he had no conception of how long ago he heard anything. "Were you a child or a man when they cried before?"

"I am a changeling child."

"I know that," Louis said. "But when did the graves cry before?"

Charlie stared at him for a minute, then slowly came closer. To Louis's surprise, he sat next to Louis on the bunk, their shoulders touching. Louis wasn't sure where else to go with this. He could ask him about the bones, but he didn't know how to approach it in a way Charlie would understand.

"Charlie," Louis began, "did you ever see anyone else sleeping like Rebecca was sleeping?"

Charlie's eyes widened, and Louis thought he even blushed.

"With no clothes on?" he asked.

"Yes," Louis said.

His answer was whispered. "No."

"Did you ever try to put flowers on anyone's eyes before Rebecca?"

"No."

Louis knew he needed to ask something else. "Charlie, do you know what sex is?"

Charlie's gaze swung to the concrete floor and his breathing quickened. Louis didn't make him answer. It was pretty clear he knew what it was, in some form or another.

"Did you and Rebecca have sex?"

Charlie said something, but Louis didn't hear it. He leaned closer. "Have you?"

" 'I must go seek some dew drops here and hang a pearl in every cowslip's ear,' " Charlie whispered.

Louis touched his arm. "Charlie . . ."

" 'So we grew together, like to a double cherry, seeming parted, but yet a union in partition . . . two lovely berries molded on one stem —' "

"Charlie, answer my question, please. Did you have sex with Rebecca?"

When Charlie's eyes came up, they were filled with tears. "No. That would be bad."

Louis let it go, trying to figure out what else to ask, but nothing was coming. Maybe he would talk to Dalum about letting Alice question him. Maybe Charlie's ramblings would make more sense to her. Or maybe they needed a psychiatrist.

Louis started to get up, but Charlie's hand came down on his forearm. Louis almost pulled away, but he didn't.

Charlie was staring at him, his eyes moist with a need that seemed to swell up from somewhere deep inside. In the drifting darkness of the cell, Charlie looked as sad and empty as Louis had ever seen any human being look. And in that sadness there was a speck of normalcy that told him Charlie understood he was not the same as everyone else and never would be.

Suddenly, Louis could not imagine this man putting his hands around anyone's neck and crushing it.

"Will you read to me?" Charlie asked.

"Read?"

Charlie held out the book.

Louis hesitated, then took the paperback, opening it to the middle.

" 'I may never believe these antic fables, nor these fairy toys,' " Louis read out loud. " 'Lovers and madmen have such seething brains, such shaping fantasies that apprehend more than cool reason ever comprehends —' "

Charlie interrupted. " 'The lunatic, the lover, the poet, are of imagination all compact. One sees more devils than vast hell can hold.' "

Dalum was pouring another shot when Louis walked back into his office. He held the bottle up to ask if Louis wanted one, but Louis shook his head. He was tired. All he wanted to do was go home and sleep.

"Well?" Dalum asked.

"Nothing," Louis said. "I can't relate to him, Chief."

"Sounded like you were doing a pretty fair job of it."

Dalum swallowed his whiskey and set the glass down. Then he motioned to the chair for Louis to sit, but again Louis shook his head.

"I have to get going. I have a long drive."

"I'll walk out with you," Dalum said, grabbing his parka.

They left the station, Dalum staying in step as they made their way down the block toward the Impala. Louis knew the chief's car was parked back behind the station and that Dalum was taking this walk for some other reason. But he stayed silent, waiting for Dalum to say whatever it was he needed to say.

When they stopped at the Impala, Louis faced him. Dalum looked tired, his face showing the same tiny cracks that Alice's had earlier today.

"I have a favor to ask you," Dalum said.

Louis waited, shoving his hands in his jacket pockets and stiffening his body against the wind.

"I don't know you very well," Dalum said. "I haven't even run a check on you. But I have to confess, I am damn impressed. I've never seen a cop, or ex-cop, sit in a jail cell and read Shakespeare to a murder suspect."

Louis looked down, a little embarrassed. "Just trying to get him to trust me."

Dalum shook his head. "It was more than that. This is a special kind of case we have here. And I think you know that. I think the bones we found today are from a second murder victim, and I'm already wondering if there are more buried out there."

"I was wondering the same thing."

"Do you want to be a part of finding out?"

Louis looked down, the air cold on the back of his neck. He'd seen his share of dead bodies and handled numerous homicides, but no matter how many he worked, he was drawn to the next with the same fervor as his first. But there was something

217

about this place that told him this was one he needed to walk away from.

"Look," Dalum said, "I love this town, and that hospital has been a part of Ardmore for a long time. I just want to do what I can to help it die peacefully, and there's a good chance that won't happen with that detective from the state getting his hands in it." He paused. "I could really use your help on this."

"All right," Louis said. "I'll do what I can."

"Good. I'd like to make it official, though," Dalum said. "I'd like to deputize you."

"Deputize me?"

"Yes," Dalum said. "The town of Ardmore has given me the authority to deputize any number of people I need in the event of a natural disaster or any other time I feel there is a danger to the community." Dalum gave a small smile. "And I think we have a danger to the community out there. Am I right again?"

"Yes, you are."

"Okay then," Dalum said. "I'll get you an ID card and a badge ready. You'll get more answers and more respect flashing some tin."

Louis extended Dalum a hand. "Okay. We have a deal."

"I should have the ring back by noon to-morrow," Dalum said. "And we'll go from there. How's that, Mr. Kincaid?"

"Sounds good. But call me Louis, please."

Dalum gave a short nod and Louis turned away and climbed in the Impala. As he started it, he watched Dalum walk back toward the police station. His hands were back in his pockets, his head ducked against the wind.

Louis turned on the heater and held a hand in front of the vent, waiting for it to get warm. His gaze moved to the quiet storefronts, and the glitter of Christmas lights that had appeared since last week, but his thoughts went back to what Dalum said about getting more respect flashing some tin.

He hadn't had a badge in his pocket since . . . when? Winter, 1984, in a small Michigan town similar to this. Right after that, he had left for Florida and had never thought he'd be back here working a homicide.

Louis felt a stab of guilt. He wasn't any closer to finding Claudia's remains and now his time and energy would be spent on helping Dalum track down a murderer. But he couldn't ignore that kick of adrenaline that was coursing through his veins like some weird cop narcotic. He pushed the car in gear and pulled away from the police station, heading out into the darkness of Highway 50.

Chapter 19

The voices woke him. They were loud and sharp, and coming from downstairs somewhere. Louis sat up in his bed, shaking off the sleep, trying to make sense of what he was hearing.

Phillip was shouting, and it was a sound so foreign Louis couldn't immediately comprehend it. He didn't think he had ever heard Phillip raise his voice. But what was even more surprising was that the person he was arguing with wasn't female — it wasn't Frances. It was another man.

Louis threw back the blanket. He was wearing only pajama bottoms and he grabbed a T-shirt, yanking it on as he hurried down the stairs. He came to a quick stop as he neared the landing at the front door.

Rodney DeFoe was a few steps inside the house, his face shoved into Phillip's. He stopped in midsentence when he saw Louis.

"Ah," he said. "The so-called investigator."

"He's my foster son," Phillip said.

"He's a liar, too," Rodney said. "He said he worked for the hospital."

"So what?" Phillip said. "You wouldn't have even let him in the front door if he told you the truth."

Rodney stared at Phillip, then gave him a disgusted shake of his head. "Why are you doing this, Lawrence?" he asked. "What are you looking for? She's dead. She's been dead for more than fifteen years."

"I owe her this much."

Rodney gave Phillip that same arrogant look he had thrown at Louis when he answered the door in Grosse Pointe. "You owe her? Yes, you do. But you can't give anything to a dead woman. It's too late."

Phillip's face deepened in color and Louis slowly came down the remaining three steps. He was tempted to throw Rodney out of the house, but he wasn't sure Phillip didn't need this confrontation. Maybe it was long past due.

"At least I'm trying," Phillip said. "What about you? What did you ever do for her? She trusted you. I trusted you and you failed both of us."

Rodney's shoulders drew back, his gaze flicking between Louis and Phillip.

"Tell me what happened that night we

were supposed to elope," Phillip said. "Tell me why she didn't come."

"Let it go."

"Tell me!"

"I already told you, back when you were calling all the time," Rodney said. "I told you Mother found out and she and Claudia argued. A few hours later Claudia slashed her wrists."

Phillip didn't say a word. Louis was watching him closely, afraid he would throw a punch or lose control completely. But he was very still, his hands stiff at his sides.

"And you did nothing to save her," Phillip said. "You were there inside that house. You could have helped her."

"There was nothing I could do," Rodney said. "The damage was already done. She was never the same after that. No one could help her after that. And now it's too late for either of us, isn't it?"

Phillip shook his head. "It's not too late to bring her some sort of peace. That's all I'm trying to do."

"You're trying to bring yourself some peace. And you won't be able to do it."

"Let me try," Phillip said.

"No," Rodney said. "She's not your problem. Mother and I have decided to take care of it."

Phillip took a small step toward Rodney. "You bastard. You let her die in that place. You didn't even claim her body. Why are you doing this now?"

Rodney stared at Phillip for a moment before speaking, as if he knew his words would prompt a reaction and he needed to prepare himself for it.

"Because Mother would rather she stay lost than be buried out here and have her grave tended by you."

Phillip's fist came up and before Louis could stop him, he slugged Rodney. Rodney tumbled backward into the storm door, crashing it open. Phillip moved to go after him, but Louis grabbed his shoulders.

Phillip jerked away from him, and leaned against the wall, trying to catch his breath. Louis kept his hand on his shoulder for a moment to make sure he was going stay there, then looked at Rodney. He had tumbled down the front steps and was crawling to his feet, his fingers wiping a smear of blood off his lip.

Louis stepped to the porch. "Leave."

Rodney touched his lip again, looking at Phillip inside the doorway. "He's pathetic," Rodney said.

"Leave, now."

"You need to tell him if he keeps this up

I'll have some kind of restraining order filed against him."

Rodney held Louis's gaze for a long time. There was a stony coldness in Rodney's eyes that matched the icy morning air, and Louis had a weird thought about how different the look was from Charlie Oberon's soft sadness. And he had to wonder just who was the crazy one anymore.

"I'm going to keep looking for her," Louis said.

"Legally, her remains belong to her mother," Rodney said. "So even if you find her he will only lose her again. Do you really want to put him through that?"

Louis didn't reply. Rodney turned and walked back to his car. Louis waited until he had driven away, then went back inside the house.

There was no one on the landing. Louis moved down the steps to the living room, stopping at the doorway.

Aw, man.

Frances was hunched in the chair near the television, her yellow robe pulled tight around her. Her head was down, Kleenex clutched in her trembling hand.

Phillip was standing at the window, arms folded, head bowed. And spread across the sofa and ottoman was a slew of papers and an empty manila folder. Resting on top was the admitting photo of Claudia.

Louis drew a hard breath and walked to the sofa. He started picking up the copies of Claudia's patient file and stuffing them back into the folder. He had left the file up in the guest room, and Phillip had taken it. Louis tried not to let his anger show, but he could feel the slow burn starting across his shoulders.

"I wasn't finished with them," Phillip said.

Louis didn't even look up. "I was going to show them to you when I understood them better."

Phillip came to him. "Louis —"

"We'll do this later, Phil."

Damn it. He couldn't get the papers back in the folder neatly and he finally just gathered them all up in both arms and started back upstairs.

Phillip followed him. "I read what they did to her. I saw how she looked."

"Phil, stop."

Phillip caught his arm. "You haven't talked to me in days. I don't know where you've been or who you've spoken to."

Louis leaned against the wall, Claudia's folder against his chest. Phillip's eyes begged for something.

"There's a chance she was cremated," Louis said quietly. "I'll be able to look at some things in a few days, and we might know something."

Phillip nodded, trying to accept this new possibility. He slumped against the wall. "Where are you going today?" he asked quietly.

"Back to Ardmore," Louis said.

"May I come this time?"

"No. I think you should stay here."

Phillip looked back down the empty stairwell. "You're right. I need to stay with Fran." He ran a hand over his face. "I'm afraid I've messed this up so badly it's too late to make things right with her."

"I don't think so," Louis said.

Phillip hesitated, then gave a wooden nod. He started back down the stairs. Louis continued on up. He closed the bedroom door with his foot and dumped Claudia's records on his tangled bedding. He sat down next to it.

He just wanted this over. He needed it to be over and he knew Phillip and Frances did, too. And for an instant, Louis considered letting Phillip believe Claudia had been cremated no matter what he eventually found at John Spera's.

But he knew it would be no different

than what Eloise and Rodney DeFoe had done, sticking Claudia away somewhere and pretending she didn't exist.

Louis looked over at her medical records and slowly started putting them inside the folder, making sure they were straight, and hooking each paper over the metal tabs that held them in place. When he got to her picture, he kept it in his fingers for a moment.

He stared at it, trying to see some glimmer of light, a hint of the beauty that Phillip had seen more than thirty years ago, but there was nothing. He set it aside and finished putting the folder back together. Then he carried it to the dresser, slipping it in the drawer, under his shirts.

It was time to let her rest for a few days.

Chapter 20

Dalum called later that day to tell him that the ring they had found in the grave was from a high school in a town called Napoleon up near Jackson.

"No name on it but the year is 1987 and there's an engraving inside that might be the initials SS," Dalum told him.

Louis was thankful for an excuse to get out of the house. "I'll go up to the school today," he said.

"That's what I was hoping," Dalum said. "Swing by and pick up the ring first. You might need it."

The town of Napoleon wasn't hard to find. It was a crossroads farming village less than twenty miles north of Hidden Lake, straight up Highway 50. Louis just hoped finding the owner of the class ring would be as easy.

The sprawling fifties-style high school was surrounded by corn and soy fields, with the thrusting tower of a grain elevator off on the flat horizon. The parking lot was filled. Louis swung into an empty spot and noted a sign in front of a blue Ford: RE-SERVED FOR PRINCIPAL WIGGINTON.

Inside, the halls were noisy and crowded with kids, and Louis glanced at his watch. Noon. He found the administration office and went in.

"I'd like to speak with the principal, please," he told the woman behind the desk.

She squinted up at him over black half lenses. "Are you Mr. Jeffries?"

"Excuse me?"

"Bobby Jeffries's dad. Are you him?" She pointed a pencil toward an inner room where a young black boy sat slumped in a chair.

"No, I'm here on official business." Louis pulled out the ID card Dalum had given him.

The secretary's eyes widened when she saw the official seal. "Goodness. Well, I'm afraid Miss Wigginton isn't here right now."

Louis put away the card. "When will she be back?"

"Oh, she's got lunch watch today." The woman leaned over and pointed her pencil down a hall. "Follow this almost to the end, turn right at the pirate. She's in the cafeteria."

Louis thanked the woman and started down the hall. He passed signs for the upcoming homecoming game. The float contest theme this year was kitchen appliances and signs shouted TOAST 'EM PIRATES! NUKE GRASS LAKE!

Louis followed the noise until it built to a crescendo of laughter and clattering cutlery. He turned right at the giant papier-mâché pirate.

The lunchroom was crowded and Louis stood at the entrance scanning the room, but except for a few food handlers in hair nets, didn't see any adults. Then he spotted her, a blond woman in a red blouse sitting at one of the tables. He went over to her.

The girls she was sitting with looked up at him quizzically. "Miss Wiggs," one whispered, nodding up.

The principal turned, looking up at Louis. She was in her fifties, an attractive woman with streaked blond hair and a guileless expression.

"Yes?"

"Excuse me, ma'am —"

This sent the girls into a spasm of giggles and the principal shushed them.

"I need to talk to you in private," Louis said. "It's about one of your students."

The girls giggled again, and the woman abandoned her plate of turkey and mashed potatoes and steered Louis toward the entrance. Louis pulled out the Ardmore police ID, and the principal looked at it in surprise.

"What is this about, Officer?" she asked.

"I'm trying to trace one of your students who disappeared."

The principal let out a sigh.

"Is this about Sharon?" she asked.

"I don't know, ma'am," Louis said. "I don't have a name yet. Just this." He pulled a plastic evidence bag out of his pocket and held it out.

She took it, turning it over in her fingers, feeling the ring through the plastic. "Where did you find this?" she asked.

"Can we go somewhere quiet and talk?"

She nodded and started back down the hall. Back in her office, she shut the door and indicated a chair to Louis. She was still holding the evidence bag as she sat down across her desk from him.

"Who is Sharon?" Louis asked.

"Sharon Stottlemyer, one of our students here. She disappeared last year."

"Disappeared?"

The principal nodded. "No one really knows what happened. One day she was here and the next . . . she wasn't."

"Could you be more specific?"

Miss Wigginton was looking at Louis with great curiosity. "The police already talked to me a year ago. They talked to everybody around here. Why are you here? And why a policeman from Ardmore?"

Louis nodded toward the bag. "We found the ring in a grave near Ardmore. We think whoever owned that ring was murdered."

She set the evidence bag on the desk and shut her eyes. Louis waited for her to recover her composure. When she opened her eyes, they were teary.

"I knew she didn't run away," she said softly.

"Pardon?"

"Sharon. The police thought that's what happened to Sharon. That's what they told her parents, that she ran off. But I knew that wasn't it."

"So you knew her?" Louis asked.

Miss Wigginton nodded slowly. "We only have three hundred kids here. I know them all. Some better than others, but I know them all."

"Did you know Sharon Stottlemyer well?" Louis asked.

"She was a quiet girl," the principal said.

"Not one of the popular kids. She was on the fringes like some are." She paused, thinking. "Eccentric, moody, always wore black and came in one morning with her hair cut off and dyed black. I remember at graduation, when she came up onstage to get her diploma, she shook my hand and gave me this little smile and said, 'I'm outta here, Miss Wiggs.' "

"What about friends?" Louis asked.

Miss Wigginton was staring at the ring on the desk and she looked up at Louis. "Sharon had one very good friend, if I remember."

She rose suddenly and went to a shelf, pulling down a dark green book. It was a yearbook, Louis saw, as she brought it to the desk. She flipped to the back and then turned the book around. "This is Sharon," she said, pointing.

Sharon Stottlemyer wasn't pretty in any conventional sense. Her hair was cropped like she had cut it off herself and dyed a flat black. Her eyes, rimmed with heavy black liner, held a sadness that the photographer, in his desperation to extricate a happy senior portrait, had been unable to disguise.

Miss Wigginton turned the page. "This is Allison Deitz, her best friend."

Louis noticed that Allison Deitz had been a junior last year. "Is Allison still here?" he asked.

"Yes. She's a senior now."

"I'd like to talk to her," Louis said.

Miss Wigginton hesitated. "I'd like to know more first," she said. "How do you know Sharon was . . . was . . ."

"We found the ring in a shallow grave on the grounds of a hospital down near Ardmore," Louis began.

"Hospital? You mean Hidden Lake?"

Louis nodded.

"What was Sharon doing at Hidden Lake?"

"That's what I need to find out. Can I talk to Allison, please?"

The principal didn't hesitate. She punched an intercom button and told her secretary to summon Allison Deitz to the office. An uncomfortable silence filled the small office as they waited. Louis could see the questions in the principal's eyes. After a few more minutes of silence, the secretary opened the door and ushered in a plump girl. She looked up at Louis curiously from between two curtains of dyed black hair.

"Have a seat, Allison," Miss Wigginton said, indicating a chair near Louis.

235

Allison slid into the chair, clutching her loose-leaf binder to her chest. Her nails were purple and she wore a ring on every finger, one of them a huge skull.

"Allison, this is Mr. Kincaid," the principal said gently. "He's a policeman and he needs to ask you some questions about Sharon."

The girl's heavily lined blue eyes came up quickly to Louis. She seemed to shrink in the chair. The principal nodded to Louis. He slid his chair closer.

"Hello, Allison," he said.

She murmured a hello back.

"Miss Wigginton tells me that you were Sharon's best friend," he said. "Is that true?"

She nodded.

"I know this might be hard for you to talk about, but I'm trying to find out what happened to her, and you can help me with that."

"Sharon's dead, isn't she?" the girl said.

Louis glanced at the principal, then looked back at Allison. "Why do you say that?" he asked.

"Because I know she didn't run away like everyone says," Allison said. "She would never do something like that and

236

not tell me. She just wouldn't. We told each other everything."

"Allison," Louis said gently, "do you know what Hidden Lake is?"

Allison shifted in her chair, clutching her binder tighter.

"It's a hospital," she said softly.

"Do you know why your friend might have gone down there?"

Allison was quiet, her eyes downcast.

"Did you or she know anyone who lived around there?"

Silence.

"Maybe she went to visit someone in the hospital?" Louis prodded.

A bell rang out in the hall and the muffled noise of the kids changing classes filtered in to them. Allison sat there, motionless, her eyes on the floor. Louis focused on her hands clutching the binder. Her knuckles were turning white.

"Allison, you have to help me," he said. "Please."

When the girl looked up at him, her eyes were filled with tears. "I told her not to go there," she said. "I told her there were crazy people at that place."

"Why did Sharon go to Hidden Lake, Allison?" Louis asked.

The girl shook her head slowly, shutting

her eyes tight as the tears fell, leaving black streaks on her cheeks.

"Allison . . ."

"She made me promise not to tell anyone," Allison said. "I'm sorry . . . I'm sorry. I know I should have told, but I promised Sharon I wouldn't."

"Did Sharon go there to see a doctor?" Louis asked.

Allison's face was hidden behind her hair. She ran a shaking hand over her face, sniffling.

"Allison, did Sharon go to Hidden Lake to see a doctor?"

An almost imperceptible nod of the head. Louis glanced over at the principal, who looked stricken. She pushed a box of Kleenex toward Louis. He plucked out some tissues and held them under Allison's bowed head.

Allison took them and wiped her face. She was crying outright now, small hiccups of sobs. Louis touched the girl's hand.

"Thank you, Allison," he said.

Louis looked at the principal. She rose slowly and nodded toward the door. Louis followed her out and closed the door behind him. Miss Wigginton folded her arms across her chest as she looked back through the glass door at Allison Deitz.

"Why?" she said softly.

"Why what?" Louis asked.

She looked back at Louis. "Why would Sharon go all the way down there to see a doctor?"

Louis knew the answer. He suspected the principal did, too.

Hidden Lake was a thirty-minute drive down Highway 50, close enough to be convenient but far enough away to be private. If Sharon Stottlemyer had been troubled and gone there for help, it had to be because she didn't want anyone to know. She had probably been eighteen, old enough to sign herself in. At least now he could check Hidden Lake's admissions records. But there were still many other questions without answers.

"I need to speak to Sharon's family," Louis said. "Do you have an address?"

Miss Wigginton nodded and went to talk to a secretary. She returned with a piece of paper and gave it to Louis. He picked up the yearbook.

"It would help if I could take this," he said.

"Of course." The principal was looking back through the glass at Allison Deitz, huddled in the chair.

"They keep it all inside," she said.

239

"Some of them you can see it and maybe help. But others . . ." She shook her head slowly. "Some just fall."

She looked back at Louis. "I'd better get back in there. Please call me if I can be of any more help."

The Stottlemyers lived in a white frame house on East Street just a few blocks from the high school. It was a pretty house, two stories with a big wraparound porch and several bird feeders hanging in the bare trees of the front yard. As he went up the walk, Louis could see lights on inside and a curl of smoke coming from the chimney. His knock was answered by a round-faced woman with brown hair and dark eyes, and Louis had the thought that it was exactly what Sharon Stottlemyer would have looked like if she had lived to be forty-something.

"Mrs. Stottlemyer?" he asked.

"Yes," she said warily.

When he produced the police ID, her face crumbled inward and the word came out in one long exhalation. "Sharon," she said.

"May I come in, ma'am?" Louis asked.

She nodded and held out the storm door. It was a small living room, lamps lit against the afternoon gloom, a big black dog lying in front of a low-burning fire. Mrs. Stottlemyer motioned for Louis to take the sofa and she went to a worn wing chair, setting aside a pile of blue yarn and knitting needles.

"Have you found my daughter?" she asked. Her voice was soft but firm, and Louis had the feeling she already knew that her daughter was dead.

"We think so," Louis said. "We'll need dental records to be sure."

The woman's eyes were fixed on Louis. "Then Sharon is dead."

"We found a body in a shallow grave," Louis said. "There was no identification, just this ring." He held it out the evidence bag and Mrs. Stottlemyer took it. She picked up the glasses on the cord around her neck and put them on to look at the ring. After a few seconds, her hand closed around the plastic bag.

"Where did you find her?" she asked.

"On the grounds of Hidden Lake Hospital."

Mrs. Stottlemyer closed her eyes. "Oh my God."

Louis gave her a minute, sensing she was remembering something, or making some connection between her daughter and the hospital. One that was painful.

"She . . . she said something a few weeks before she disappeared," Mrs. Stottlemyer said. "I didn't think anything of it at the time, but now . . ."

"What was it, Mrs. Stottlemyer?"

Her eyes came to Louis. "She asked me if I ever got sad."

"Sad?"

She nodded. "I told her that everyone gets sad sometimes. But that being sad was nothing more than a mood and that . . ." Mrs. Stottlemyer drew a thick breath. "And that all she needed to do was think positive thoughts and stay busy."

Louis looked down. Mrs. Stottlemyer's soft sobs started to fill the small living room. "Mrs. Stottlemyer," he said, "do you have someone you can call to stay with you?"

"My husband will be home soon," she said. "And I have a friend next door."

Louis stood up. Mrs. Stottlemyer looked at him and her hand came up, holding the evidence bag. "Can I have her ring back?"

"Not yet," he said. "But we'll return it to you when we can."

She handed the bag over. "I'm so sorry," he said.

She didn't reply, just accompanied him to the door and closed it softly behind him.

Louis headed down the narrow walk to his car. As he opened the car door, he glanced over his shoulder at a group of small children playing in front of a bright blue house a few doors away.

Two of the kids were chasing each other, another was up in a tree, a fourth was wrestling with a shaggy brown dog, and a fifth was blowing bubbles that disappeared quickly into the icy air.

Chapter 21

The drive back from Napoleon gave him plenty of time to think. But everything was scattered, his thoughts ricocheting between Sharon Stottlemyer, Rebecca Gruber, and Charlie Oberon. Every instinct was telling him Charlie had nothing to do with either woman's death. Yet there was this small part of him — a part he didn't want to acknowledge — that wanted to believe that someone like Charlie could kill.

What had Dr. Seraphin said? *The line between what is real and what is not is very thin. Sometimes it is even invisible.*

He was thinking of Phillip now. Thinking that Phillip's hold on reality wasn't very good right now. He had attacked Rodney DeFoe. Not that the bastard didn't deserve it. But still, Phillip was showing every sign that he was coming apart. And Frances . . . he didn't even want to think about what all this was doing to her.

It started to rain. He switched on the wipers and then upped the heater a notch. Right now, all he wanted to do was go

244

home and knock down enough Heinekens to numb out for a couple of hours.

Through the blur of the wipers, a sign caught his eyes. He had passed Spera's place.

There was no excuse for not going back and finding out if Spera had any information about Claudia being cremated. He swung into a driveway and turned around.

Spera was standing by a truck backed up to the tent. The truck was an old U-Haul painted over white with red lettering, SPERA & SONS EXCAVATIONS, on the side. Spera was wearing a yellow rain slicker and stopped to wait as Louis ran from the car through the pelting rain. Spera motioned him back inside the tent.

"Lousy weather," Spera muttered.

Louis nodded, wiping his face. He noticed the open back of the truck. Stacked inside were the cans from the Hidden Lake mortuary.

"Is this all of them?" Louis asked.

"Yup. The ones we found names on are over there," Spera said, pointing back in the tent.

Louis turned and saw the table where about a hundred of the corroded copper cans were carefully lined up. He went over to the table, his eyes scanning the labels.

"She's not there," Spera said, coming up behind him.

Louis's eyes went back out to the truck.

"The ones still on the truck have no labels at all," Spera said.

Louis looked back at the cans. He leaned closer. There were numbers stamped on the tops. He hadn't seen them the first time in the darkness of the mortuary storeroom. He turned to Spera. "What about these numbers?" he asked.

Spera shrugged. "I was hoping it was a numbering system of some kind, but I can't find anything that matches anything in all the records the hospital folks gave me."

"You're sure?" Louis asked. "Maybe they're —"

"Look, Mr. Kincaid," Spera interrupted. "I know you want to find your loved one, but I got a job to finish here, and things are just one big mess right now."

There was more than a hint of exasperation in Spera's voice. "I got a bunch of strange bones with *no* casket," he went on, "and a bunch of rusty cans with no *names*. I got the cops telling me I can't do any more digging in the cemetery because now it might be a crime scene. I got a developer calling me every day wanting to know when I'm going to be finished. I got reporters nosing around."

He stopped just long enough to pull in a breath. "And now I got this DeFoe guy coming around."

"Rodney DeFoe came here?" Louis asked.

"Yeah, Rodney, that was his name." Spera shook his head. "He came by two days ago wanting to know where your friend Mr. Lawrence lived."

"You told him?"

"Not me. I wasn't here. But he told my son he was an old family friend of Mr. Lawrence and wanted to get in touch, so Andy looked up the address."

Louis suppressed a sigh. Well, that explained how Rodney got to Phillip.

Spera was shaking his head. "Kind of funny, don't you think. First the guy wants nothing to do with his sister's remains and now he tells Andy that if we find her he's the only one we should call."

Louis thought about what Rodney had told Phillip yesterday: *She's not your problem. Mother and I have decided to take care of it.*

Louis's eyes swept over the tent, to the lines of cans, back to the muddy caskets stacked like cordwood. The white coffin that Phillip had bought for Claudia was still sitting alone on a table in the corner covered with plastic. The rain was whipping the flaps of the tent, bringing the swirling smell of dead earth to his nostrils.

She's not your problem. Then why in hell did he feel like she was?

"Hey, you okay?"

Louis looked at Spera. "Yeah. I just don't know where to go next with any of this."

Spera pursed his lips. "Hold on." He ducked out into the rain and pulled down the back of the truck and locked it. "Come on inside and let me get you some coffee," he said.

Louis followed him through the rain and into the office. Spera shook out of the slicker and went into the bathroom, tossing a towel at Louis when he came back out. "Have a seat while I make a fresh pot."

Louis rubbed his face dry with the towel and wandered over to the bulletin board where the plans and diagrams of Hidden Lake were displayed. There was a new one posted, a copy of the grave plot map that Spera had shown him out in the cemetery yesterday.

About an eighth of the cemetery plots were shaded black, the rest left blank. The black ones were all toward the back of the cemetery where the bones had been found, except for a handful scattered throughout.

"Are these black ones the graves you've already dug up?" Louis asked, turning to Spera.

"Yeah," Spera said, coming out of the bathroom with a pot of water. "We started at the back so access would be easier as we went along. Except for the ones we dug up first because families asked for the remains."

"Where is Donald Lee Becker buried?" Louis asked.

Spera turned, a bag of coffee grounds in his hand. "Why are you asking about him?"

"I don't know," Louis said quietly, still looking at the map.

Spera set the coffee brewing and came over to Louis. He pointed a grimy finger at a plot in the far bottom corner. "This is him. I'm not going to get to him for weeks yet at this rate."

"You sure that's him?"

"Sure I'm sure. I looked him up not more than an hour ago."

"Why?"

"Some reporter was here asking me about him."

"Was his name Delp?"

Spera went back to the coffee machine. "Yeah, you know him?"

"Unfortunately." Louis was still looking

at the black plots. "You didn't tell him, did you?"

"Hell no. How do you take your coffee?"

"Black, lots of sugar."

Louis came over to the desk where Spera had set out a Garfield ceramic mug and a pile of Sweet n' Low. Louis took a seat and stirred in the sweeteners.

"That Delp guy was asking me about you, too," Spera said, sitting down behind the desk.

"He wanted to know what you were doing here."

"What did you tell him?"

"That it wasn't any of my business. I'm just the lowly grave digger. I'm just here for comic relief in this little drama."

Louis smiled.

Spera was toying with his coffee mug. "What are you really doing here, Mr. Kincaid?"

"I'm just trying to find Claudia DeFoe," Louis said.

"Was that her bones we came across?"

Louis shook his head slowly.

"That reporter thinks Becker is alive," Spera said. "He thinks Becker killed the nurse they found last week."

Louis picked up the mug and took a drink of coffee.

"I remember when Becker was here," Spera said. "Everyone around here was talking about it, scared he'd escape. And rumor was he didn't really die, that he really did escape and the hospital just said he died to calm the local folks down."

Louis looked up at Spera. "Don't tell me you believe he's still alive."

Spera leaned back in his chair, shaking his head. "If you'd asked me that a week ago, I'd say you were crazy. But with all that's going on, I'm almost ready to believe anything is possible in that place."

Louis's eyes went back to the wall map of the cemetery plots. Spera was quiet for a moment, then he disappeared into the back room and returned with two tubes of rolled paper and a set of stapled papers.

"What's that?" Louis asked.

"A copy of the cemetery layout, a map of the hospital, and the log sheet of names of who's in what plot."

Louis was confused.

Spera gave a sad shake of his head. "This whole job is starting to get to me," he said. "All I want is for it to be over with. It's my job to put these poor souls to rest, but things have gotten so messed up, I can't even do that."

Louis's gaze dropped to the papers

Spera was holding out. "I don't know how I can help you."

"I don't know either," Spera said. "I got a feeling no one is going to be at rest until your lady Claudia is. So take a look at these. Maybe it will help, maybe it won't."

The rain had turned to sleet by the time Louis pulled out of Spera's place, and as he turned east, he found himself stuck behind a slow-moving semi. He was only doing about thirty when he rounded the last curve out of the Irish Hills and saw the rusted Civic in the parking lot of the Sand Lake Inn.

He pulled into the muddy lot, facing the large front window. Through the swipe of the wipers, he spotted Delp's red-tipped spike hair. He went inside.

Delp was sitting at the counter and looked over when he heard the door.

"Well, well, look what the wind blew in," he said, then swung back on his stool to take a drink of his beer.

Louis went to the counter and stood directly over the reporter.

"Hey, you're dripping on me, dude."

"I'm going to do more than that if you don't knock it off," Louis said.

Delp leaned back, holding up his hands.

"Whoa. What'd I do now?"

"You were bugging Spera, and I'm getting tired of you bugging people," Louis said. "And if you got a question about me, you ask me."

Delp just stared at him for a moment, then nodded toward the empty stool next to him. "Fair enough. Sit down. What you drink? I'm buying."

Louis hesitated, glancing around. The place was one big room backed by an old-fashioned soda fountain counter and a scattering of tables covered with red-checked tablecloths. Back when U.S. 12 had been the major highway from Detroit to Chicago, the place had probably been humming with hungry travelers. It reminded Louis of roadside diners he had seen in the South, places where the cars didn't stop anymore but the slow ebb and flow of life kept going.

Louis slid onto the stool just as the waitress set a plate down in front of Delp.

"What's that?" Louis asked.

"Liver and onions."

Louis grimaced even as his rumbling stomach was telling him that it didn't smell half bad. When the waitress returned, he ordered a hot roast beef sandwich and a beer.

Delp was wolfing down his food but finally came up for air. "All right then," he said, "if I ask you a straight question, you going to give me a straight answer?"

"Depends," Louis said.

Delp wiped his face with a paper napkin. "So what are you doing here?"

Louis took a swig of beer to buy time before he answered. It was probably just a matter of time before Delp found out he was helping Dalum. And there was a good chance Delp would also find out about Claudia, and the last thing he needed was Delp showing up on the Lawrences' doorstep.

The waitress brought his food. Louis took two big forkfuls of the gravy-covered sandwich before he spoke. "Look, if I tell you why I'm here, I want your word you won't write about it."

Delp shook his head. "You know I can't promise that."

"It's got to do with my foster father, something personal."

"You've got a foster father?"

Louis ignored him. "I swear, Delp, if you so much as make one phone call to his house, I'll break your goddamn neck."

"Little drastic, don't you think?"

"Not at all."

"Okay, okay. You got my word."

Louis told Delp about his search for Claudia's remains, giving only enough details to be convincing. When he was finished, Delp was shaking his head.

"What's the matter?" Louis asked.

"I don't know if I can keep that promise, man. That is a helluva story."

"Look, you weasel —"

"If your missing woman was murdered by my man Becker, then she's part of my story."

Louis just stared at him.

"Come on," Delp said. "Don't tell me that didn't already cross your mind."

Louis looked away, down at his roast beef sandwich. He picked up a fork and took a bite, mainly because he didn't want to look at Delp.

"All right, when was your missing woman in Hidden Lake?" Delp asked.

"She was committed in 1951 and died there in 1972," Louis said.

"Becker was there from 1963 to 1980."

Louis was quiet, pushing the mashed potatoes around with his fork. He wasn't about to tell Delp that Claudia had been confined to E Building, just one floor below Becker.

"And if Becker killed a patient, don't

you think the hospital just might want to keep that little fact quiet?" Delp went on. "Don't you think they might even accidently *misplace* said patient's body just in case someone ever asked?"

Louis pushed his plate away. In the mirror behind the counter, he could see his and Delp's reflections.

"Quid pro quo, Kincaid," Delp said.

Louis didn't say anything.

"Tit for tat. You show me yours, I'll show you mine."

Louis faced him. "What do you want from me, Delp?"

"Anything I can get on Becker."

"What do I get in return?"

"My help. And my word that I won't write about your missing woman. *If* she turns out to have no connection to Becker."

Louis stared at the reporter for a moment. "Okay," he said.

"Great. So how about you start by getting me a copy of that dead nurse's autopsy report?"

"Why?"

"Just to see if the M.O. fits."

"How about if you tell me about Becker and I'll tell you if it fits?"

Delp shrugged. "Becker killed six

women, all the same way. Strangled them, crushed their necks, and left them naked outdoors."

"So do most serial murderers." Louis hesitated. He had to ask, there was no other way. "Did he mark his victims in any way?"

Delp looked at him with new interest. "Mark? The Gruber woman was marked? How?"

"Cigarette burns on the inner thigh."

Delp shook his head. "I'll go back and check through my files, but I know that all Becker's victims were found in an advanced state of decomposition. Probably no way to tell."

Louis was quiet, sorry he had shared that detail with Delp. He still didn't trust him, and he knew Dalum intended to keep that fact secret from the public.

"I do know," Delp said, leaning close, "that Becker was a smoker. Had a carton of Camels in his car when they arrested him."

Louis could see Delp's Civic outside the window, and he remembered it was filled with boxes and files. To know what they found in Becker's car, Delp had to have gotten a copy of the evidence log or the arrest reports.

"What else do you have on Becker?" Louis asked.

"Everything from police interviews to crime scene photos to copies of one of the dead girl's diaries."

Louis shook his head. "Where'd you get it all?"

Delp grinned. "Bought some. Stole some. Some was public record. Met a few greedy cops along the way. But there's one thing I don't have that you can get me. I need Becker's death certificate."

"Get it yourself. It's public record," Louis said.

Delp made an obnoxious sound like a game show buzzer. "Wrongo, LaBatts breath. It's sealed. Now why do you suppose the state did that?"

"To keep it away from ghouls like you."

Delp held up his empty beer bottle for the waitress to see. "I think it's because Becker escaped from that hellhole and the hospital had to cover it up, just like they covered up your friend's death."

The waitress set down a fresh bottle in front of Delp. "Becker's out there, man," he said.

"Becker's out there in that cemetery," Louis said.

"Sure. Just like your missing woman was."

Louis shook his head. "You're believing your own hype, Delp."

"Okay, then, let's find someone who can tell us," Delp said. "Someone besides a doctor or nurse who are afraid they'll be sued. Like a former patient who knew Becker or Claudia."

Louis looked down at his bottle. Delp was right. The hospital staff wasn't going to tell any secrets. And if he was going to take this crazy Becker theory to Dalum, he needed something solid, needed to know more about what it really had been like inside Hidden Lake.

And there was someone who could tell him. The woman who had tried to run off with Claudia in 1952. What was her name? Millie something. Millie Reuben.

Alice had refused to give him her files, but he knew Dalum could find out where Millie Reuben was. If she was still alive.

"What are you thinking, Kincaid?" Delp asked.

Louis stood up and tossed some money on the counter. "Nothing."

"You have an inside contact, don't you," Delp said. "You have a former patient you're going to see, right?"

"Doesn't matter, Delp," Louis said, slipping on his jacket. "You're not going with me anyway."

"Quid pro quo, Kincaid."

Louis shook his head. "Not this time."

Louis left the restaurant, pausing under the overhang to zip his jacket. Louis heard the slam of the storm door and smelled cigarette smoke, knowing Delp had followed him out. Louis put up his collar and stepped out into the sleet. As he was unlocking the car, Delp grabbed his arm.

"Kincaid, if you guys dig up Becker, I want in."

"No promises."

"Then how's this for a headline?" Delp said. "A Foster Son's Lonely Search for the Missing Bones of a Poor Little Rich Girl."

"I ought to deck you," Louis said.

"Aw, come on," Delp said. "If Becker's grave is empty, it'll be national news. Just let me break the story."

Delp was shivering, the damp Kool dangling from his lips.

"All right," Louis said, slipping in the car. "I'll do what I can."

"I'll give you an acknowledgment in the book."

260

Louis jerked the car door closed and started the engine. Delp tossed the cigarette to the dirt, gave Louis a small wave, and hurried back inside the restaurant.

Chapter 22

Louis took a drink from the can of Dr Pepper, careful not to take his eyes off the twisting road. The last sign he had seen said DEXTER 6 MILES. He passed under an old stone railroad bridge, and started seeing a scattering of Victorian houses set back among the trees. He passed a sign for the Dexter Cider Mill; then the town came into view and he slowed.

The row of storefronts were painted in rusty reds and shades of gray. There was a small Victorian clock tower set on an island in the middle of the street. Beneath it, huddled on a green bench, were two old men in checkered flannel jackets and leather caps with earflaps.

Farther along, he passed a weathered wooden gazebo. Inside the gazebo were two teenagers who, in between kisses, were watching workers string a banner from the streetlights that read A VICTORIAN CHRISTMAS.

He took a right at Apple Orchard Lane, and less than a block later, he saw the house that Millie Reuben had described to him on the phone, a pale pink Victorian with a wraparound porch. He pulled in behind a blue sedan, picked up the thin manila folder off the seat, and walked to the door. He knocked.

When he had called, he had told Millie Reuben that he wanted to talk about Hidden Lake, and after a long silence, she had agreed, without even asking him why.

There was a white lace curtain over the door's glass inset. It moved suddenly, a pair of eyes appearing. Then the door opened.

He knew Millie Reuben was in her midfifties and he had been expecting a hollow-eyed, broken woman. But Millie Reuben had loose, brown curls and was wearing a leopard-trimmed, velour pantsuit. Her face was lightly lined with a brush of rose at her cheeks, but she wore no mascara or eye shadow. She didn't need to. Her deep-set, thickly lashed eyes were flecked with yellow and green, and he knew instantly they had once been her most beautiful feature.

"Millie Reuben?" he asked.

"You must be Officer Kincaid."

"Yes. May I come in?"

Millie stepped back and let him inside,

then led him to a living room filled with sunshine from a large bay window. The place was pine-scented with an undernote of something sweet he thought he knew but couldn't quite imagine in this old house.

Millie motioned for him to sit and he propped himself on the corner of a hard-tufted couch. Millie started to sit down, but her eye caught a shadow behind her and she turned.

"Go stir the stew, Ruthie. He's not here to see you."

The shadow disappeared and Millie reached to an end table and opened a silver box, taking out a cigarette. "My sister," she said as she lit the cigarette with a red Bic from her pocket.

She grabbed an ashtray and came to sit across from Louis. "I'm sorry," she said, waving her cigarette. "Does this bother you?"

"No."

"Good," she said. "Not that it would make any difference to me. Ever since I got out of that place, I've made it a point to do exactly what I want to do when I want to do it."

"I understand."

"So," she said. "Why do you want to

know about that place? Is someone suing them?"

"No," Louis said.

"You writing a book?"

"No."

"Then what?"

"Miss Reuben," Louis said, "I realize this might be hard for you —"

Millie shook her head quickly. "I used to talk about this stuff every week with my shrink. I saw the same one for years and trust me, he got memories out of me about that place I didn't know I had. I'm fine with all of it now."

She reached over and opened a drawer on the end table. It was full of brown prescription vials.

"Really, I am," she added.

Louis wasn't so sure. Maybe it would be best if he started with something other than Donald Lee Becker.

"Do you remember Claudia DeFoe?" he asked.

Millie closed the drawer and sat back, blowing out smoke. "Nice little rich girl," she said. "Not that having all that money ever helped her any. Money didn't do you a damn bit of good in that place."

"When did you meet her?"

Millie had to think for a minute. "Right

after I went in," she said. "Let's see, my father committed me in the summer of 1952. She'd been there awhile by then."

"May I ask why you were committed?"

Millie's eyes swept back to Louis quickly and he was sure she was going to tell him it was none of his business. "I was a heroin addict," she said. "My boyfriend got me hooked, and when my father found out, he had me arrested. I stabbed a police officer with a kitchen knife and then stabbed myself."

Louis looked down at the folder in his hand.

"I was high," she said, stiffening. "I never would have hurt myself or that cop without that crap in me."

When Louis said nothing, Millie went on. "They detoxed me and a month or so later I was bunking next to Claudia in that place. She was the saddest person I ever met, I think."

"Sad, how? Suicidal?"

"Oh no, not like that. I never heard her talk about hurting herself."

"She slashed her wrists. That's what put her there."

"I know. But she told me she didn't even remember doing that," Millie said. "Like I didn't remember much about stabbing the

266

cop or myself, either. Besides, that one thing didn't make her a lunatic."

Louis opened the folder and reached for the photograph of Becker, but Millie was talking again.

"She used to cry all night," she said. "I never heard someone cry so much."

His next question popped into his head and he almost thought about not asking it. "Did she talk of anyone?" Louis asked.

Millie's lips turned up in a sad smile. "She was a romantic, that one was. She talked of a boy named Phillip. And how they were going to get married, and how she and him and their children would live in this beautiful house on Lake Michigan."

Louis lowered his eyes, but they fell on the mug shot of Becker. He closed the folder again. "Did she ever seem to get better?" he asked.

"Better?" Millie asked. "In that place they didn't want anyone to get better. They only wanted you to comply. And if you didn't you went to E Building."

"That's where she went after you and she tried to escape, right?"

Millie seemed surprised he knew, and she took a second to stab out her cigarette in the ashtray and then gave him a long look. "If you know that, then you know what they did to her in that place. They say she died of the flu, but it wasn't that. It was that place. It killed you in ways you didn't even know you could die."

Louis didn't want to go back into this, but Millie kept talking and he had the sense that outside of her therapist, she didn't have anyone to talk to about this. Or at least anyone who wanted to hear it.

"Do you know about the therapy they gave her?" Millie asked.

"I know about the shock and insulin treatments."

"And about the isolation periods?"

"No," Louis said. "I haven't read the whole file yet."

"She would disappear for months at a time, and when I'd ask, they'd tell me she was on punishment and in isolation and if I wasn't good, that's where I'd end up, too."

He knew what effect long periods of isolation had on convicts in maximum-security prisons. He could not imagine the effect on a young woman already under the influence of drugs and suffering from depression.

His eye caught a shadow lurking just inside the kitchen, and Millie saw him glance toward it.

"Excuse me," she said. She walked quickly to the kitchen door and in harsh whispers again told her sister to go find something to do. When Millie returned, she carried an amber-colored drink with ice.

"I was isolated once," she said, setting the glass aside and lighting another cigarette.

Louis opened the folder and slipped out the photograph of Becker, hoping to get Millie back on track. But she kept talking.

"They locked me in that isolation room downstairs and I remember it was cold and wet." She nodded briskly. "It was February 1964. I remember because those Beatle guys were supposed to be on television that night and I had been good 'cause I wanted to watch them —"

"Miss Reuben," Louis interrupted.

"But they took me anyway," she said, her voice changing to something deeper and more distant. "They came and got me in the afternoon and they took me down there and they strapped me down and they just left me there."

Louis held up a hand, hoping she would see he wanted to talk about something else, but her eyes weren't on him. She was staring beyond him and she was remembering. He wasn't sure what to do. He had no idea whether she could make that mental journey back to E Building, and he didn't want to be here with her alone if she couldn't.

"That's the first night I was raped."

Louis watched her carefully, not quite sure he had heard her right. Millie hadn't moved and her cigarette ash was growing long between her fingers.

"Who raped you?" Louis said.

Millie was still.

"Miss Reuben?"

Suddenly, her eyes focused on him, and she flicked her ash twice toward the table, missing the ashtray. "I don't know," she said. "It was dark and I was full of pills. I felt him and I saw him, but I didn't see him, do you know what I mean?"

"Do you know anything else about him?"

"I know he was a patient," Millie said. "He wore the blue tunic the men wore and he had a plastic ID bracelet on his wrist."

"How would a patient get into a locked room?"

Millie shrugged. "Probably let in by some orderly who wanted to watch."

Louis drew a breath and looked back at the papers he had in the folder. Under

Becker's photograph was a newspaper account of his arrest and incarceration at Hidden Lake. Louis knew the date, but he doubled-checked now. Becker had been sent to Hidden Lake in 1963.

He glanced up at Millie. She was quiet, the cigarette at her lips, her eyes steady on the window. Then he held out the photo of Becker, bracing himself for her reaction — anything from a gasp to hysteria.

"Is there any chance this is the man who raped you?" he asked.

Millie stared at it. "That's that weirdo Becker. But I don't know if he was the man who raped me."

"Did you know Becker?"

"I saw him around," Millie said. "The men and women were always kept separate inside E Building. We didn't even eat together, but occasionally, if we were good, every few weeks, they'd let us out and we could walk the grounds. Sometimes, you could visit with the men then."

"Wasn't Becker under guard?" Louis asked.

Millie shook her head. "The inmates ran the prison, if you know what I mean. I saw him alone sometimes."

Louis put the photo away.

"The night of the Beatles," Millie said,

271

"that wasn't the only time I was raped."

Louis looked back at her. She had the expression of someone who was remembering a disturbing but foggy dream rather than a nightmare, and he was suddenly thankful that she had been too drugged to remember the specifics.

"How many times?" Louis asked. "Do you know?"

"A dozen or so, all during that same time."

Louis stared at the floor. He was trying to imagine how Becker might have gained access to the women when something else edged into his brain. The autopsy photo of Rebecca Gruber's thighs.

"Miss Reuben," he said softly, head still down, "may I ask you a very personal question?"

"Sure."

"Did your rapist burn you?"

When Millie didn't answer him, he looked up at her. The beautiful speckled eyes misted as she blew a long, thin stream of smoke from her lips.

"They told me later I did that to myself with cigarettes," she said. "But I knew I didn't."

"Where did he burn you?"

Her hand moved slowly to her leg, and

she touched her inner thigh with the tip of her finger. "There. On both sides."

"Three burns?"

"Three with each rape. My legs are full of marks."

Louis rubbed his forehead, listening to the rattle of pans in the kitchen. The sweet smell in the house seemed stronger now, a mixture of air freshener, incense, and that other smell he now was sure was pot.

"I heard about that girl who was murdered down there," Millie said. "The newspaper said she was a nurse."

"Yes."

"Was she burned, too?"

"Yes."

"And you think Donald Lee Becker did it?"

"Becker died in 1980."

"Inside that place?"

It was then he realized she had never said Hidden Lake. She had called it only "that place." He nodded in response to her question.

Millie shook her head. "You seen his body, Mr. Kincaid?"

"No."

"Then don't be so sure he's dead," she said.

Millie had that same crazy look Delp

had when he talked of Becker being alive. By 1980, she had already been out of Hidden Lake for six or seven years. She couldn't know anything about Becker, how he died or where he was even buried.

He stood up. "Thank you for your time," he said. "And your honesty."

"What the hell, it's therapy, right?" she said with a shrug. She walked him to the foyer and opened the door. As he started out, she touched his arm.

"Why were you asking about Claudia?"

"I'm working for someone who knew her a long time ago," he said. "I'm working for Phillip."

Millie looked surprised. "So there really was a Phillip," she said. "I thought the girl was just crazy with all that talk."

"She wasn't crazy," Louis said.

Millie smiled. "None of us in that place were. Don't you know that?"

Chapter 23

Louis parked the car in front of the Ardmore Police Station, and turned off the engine. But he didn't move from the driver's seat.

He had called Alice from a pay phone as soon as he left Millie Reuben's house and asked her to pull Donald Lee Becker's medical records. Alice had refused, claiming confidentiality. Louis then told her he had found Millie Reuben and that she had the same burns Rebecca Gruber had.

"I still can't give you those records, Louis," Alice had said. "I just can't. Please don't ask again."

"Then just pull his death certificate, Alice. Please."

"You can get that from the public records."

"No, I can't. The state sealed it."

With that, she had reluctantly agreed to get the death certificate, and they arranged to meet at the police station around three. It was ten after, but he didn't see her car yet.

It was going to be hard, approaching Chief Dalum with all of this. There was now a definite link between Rebecca Gruber and Millie Reuben, and Dalum might even be willing to concede that Sharon Stottlemyer could be connected, despite the fact they would never prove she was burned or raped. From there, it wasn't a big stretch to see that a former patient was the likely perpetrator. But Louis knew Dalum wouldn't buy Becker — a dead man — as a viable suspect.

Louis wasn't sure he did, either. Except for the one fact that in a case where nothing else made sense, Becker did. If Claudia's body had gone missing, why couldn't Becker's?

Louis pushed open the car door and went inside the station. An officer near the front desk gave him a nod. "Chief's down the way, getting a sandwich," he said.

Louis hung his jacket on a hall tree and started for the coffeepot in the corner. He poured himself a cup and glanced at the clock. It was 3:20. Alice was probably having a hard time finding Becker's folder in the crowded records room in E Building. He had made her promise to take a security guy with her. He hoped she had. Maybe he should have gone himself.

"Charlie's been asking for you," the officer said.

Louis glanced at the closed door to the cell block. "Mind if I go back?"

The officer shrugged and grabbed a set of keys from a drawer and took him back. Charlie was seated on the lower bunk, *A Midsummer Night's Dream* open on his lap. He looked up when he heard footsteps and broke into a grin when he saw Louis.

"Hello, Mr. Kincaid."

"Hello, Charlie."

The officer opened the cell door and let Louis inside, then walked away without locking the door. On the top bunk, Louis saw a McDonald's bag, and next to that, an unopened package of Hostess cupcakes. He guessed the cops were starting to consider Charlie more of a guest than a possible killer.

"Can we talk, Charlie?"

Charlie closed the book and stood up, setting it on the top bunk, beneath the McDonald's bag. Then he faced Louis.

"Miss Alice is coming," Charlie said.

"Yes, I know," Louis said. "But can I ask you about something else?"

"Yes, sir."

"Do you know the name Donald Lee Becker?"

Charlie's face tightened and his eyes started to flick around the cell, finally dropping to the floor where they stayed. "I heard about him."

"Did you ever see him up close? Ever talk to him?"

Charlie shook his head. "We were scared of him."

"Who was?"

"All of us."

Louis leaned against the bars. "I don't blame you. Did you ever hear stories about him?"

"Stories?"

"Yes," Louis asked. "Stories, like you read in books. Heard about things he was doing. Stuff like that?"

"Donald Becker lives in E."

"Yes, he did. Were you ever in E Building?"

Charlie sat down slowly, silent. Again, his head was down and he seemed to be drawing back into himself. Louis moved to sit next to him.

"Were you ever in E Building?" Louis asked again.

"I'm sorry."

"Don't be sorry," Louis said.

"I wasn't supposed to be there."

"You and a lot of other people, Charlie. It's okay."

Charlie rubbed his hands together, then stood up and walked a circle around the cell, his hands moving to his hair. He raked it, then seemed at a loss as to what to do with his hands and raked his hair again.

"I'll be in trouble if Miss Alice knows. Please don't tell her."

"I'm sure she already knows, Charlie."

Charlie stopped walking. "No," he said. "She told me not to go in there. And I promised. I promised."

Louis lifted a hand to calm him down. "Were you in E Building recently?"

"I promised. I promised."

"Charlie, listen to me. When were you in E Building? Like just before you found Rebecca? After there were no more patients there?"

"I went in the window."

Louis thought about the noise he had heard that day he was getting Claudia's file, but Charlie was already in jail by then. But maybe Charlie had seen something or someone before that.

"Charlie, what do you do when you go inside E Building?" Louis asked.

"I talk to the people there," Charlie said.

"What people?"

"The people in the walls," Charlie said.

Louis stifled a sigh. "Do they talk back?" he asked.

Charlie was staring at him, like he had the other night, when he sensed Louis wasn't believing him. Louis leaned forward on his knees.

"Do they talk back?" Louis repeated.

"No. Just noises."

"What kind of noises?"

Charlie looked around the cell, then walked to the corner and tapped a water pipe with his knuckles.

Louis kept his expression even. "Have you ever seen the people?"

"No one sees them."

"How do you know it's people?"

"I smell them."

Louis stared at Charlie, something starting to gnaw at his brain, and again it sounded crazy, but he had to ask.

"What do they smell like, Charlie?"

Charlie shifted his weight and looked around, as if he was trying to figure out how to answer Louis.

"Like cigarettes?" Louis asked.

Charlie pulled his lips into a thin line and gave Louis a quick nod. "No smoking in E. No smoking allowed."

Louis heard the clang of a door and a few seconds later, Alice appeared at the bars. She carried a thick folder, held closed by a rubber band, and a basket covered with a white napkin. He could smell hot food — chicken maybe — and he knew she had brought Charlie dinner.

Louis pushed open the door and Alice came in. Charlie was smiling, his eyes on the basket.

"You brought the apple babies," Charlie said.

"I brought chicken, Charlie," Alice said.

Alice set the basket on the lower bunk and looked at Louis as she dug into the folder and withdrew a single, folded paper. She held it out.

"Becker's death certificate," she said.

Louis took it and opened it. It had Becker's name on it, and was dated March 22, 1980. Cause of death was emphysema.

"Charlie," Alice said suddenly, "what are you doing?"

Charlie was bent over the food basket, and he had strewn the chicken, silverware, and napkins across the bunk.

"Charlie," Alice said sharply.

"Where are the apple babies?" he said, looking at Alice.

"What are you talking about, Charlie?" Louis asked.

"The apple babies!"

281

"Charlie, calm down," Alice said.

"The changeling child needs the apple babies to go home," Charlie said. He was staring at the empty basket, tears welling in his eyes. Alice moved to him, placing a hand on his shoulder.

"You *are* going home," she said softly. "Pretty soon. I promise you."

Charlie crossed his arms over his chest and walked to the corner, leaning his head against the wall. Louis could hear him mumbling something about the apple babies.

"I need to talk with Chief Dalum," Louis said.

Alice nodded, and Louis thought she'd stay with Charlie, but she walked with Louis halfway down the corridor.

"I could lose my license for giving you Becker's death certificate," Alice said. "Please be discreet."

"I will," Louis said. He glanced at the fat folder still in her hand. "Is that his complete hospital file?"

She nodded, clutching it to her chest.

"Why did you bring all his records?"

Alice sighed. "If you do go ahead and exhume Becker and his casket is empty, then it's not going to be hard for Chief Dalum to get a subpoena for these," she said. "I thought I'd save myself a trip back to E Building."

"Strange vibrations inside that building," Louis said.

"It's just the old pipes and things like loose gratings and falling glass."

Louis didn't argue with her. He knew she felt the same weird presence inside E Building that he and Charlie had. She just wasn't ready to admit it.

Dalum was staring at him, but Louis couldn't read his look. He had just spent the last ten minutes telling Dalum about Millie Reuben and her stories of rape and burns, and how that all connected to Rebecca Gruber. And maybe to Sharon Stottlemyer.

"And this Millie Reuben said a patient raped her? Back in 1964? Hell, Louis, the man would have to be, what, sixty something now?"

"Not necessarily," Louis said. "Not if he went in when he was in his early twenties. He'd still be in his forties."

Dalum gave a deep sigh and dropped down into his chair. "So we're looking at a patient who raped and burned Millie Reuben and was maybe caught or not caught because of that, but then was released at some point and now, more than twenty years later, is back here killing women and leaving their bodies on the grounds."

Louis nodded.

Dalum came back to his desk. "So we're looking at a patient probably released within the last few years."

"Or one who escaped."

Dalum's brow went up. "Becker? You've been talking to that reporter."

"I know it sounds crazy."

Dalum gave a long stare, then shrugged. "I'm not so sure I know what crazy is anymore, Louis. I'll hear you out."

"Okay," Louis began. "Becker's M.O. was to strangle his victims by crushing their necks. Just like Sharon Stottlemyer and Rebecca Gruber. He also left his victims naked in shallow graves."

"Did he burn them?"

"We don't know. The bodies were too decomposed."

"Maybe he told something to his doctor," Dalum said. "Have you seen his medical records?"

"Alice has them," Louis said. "But we can't look at them without a subpoena. And no judge is going to give us one with a dead guy as a suspect."

"Anything else you know about this guy?" Dalum asked.

"Delp claims Becker's been seen back around his hometown, but that's probably just rumor. But we do know he was a smoker." Louis set Becker's death certificate on the desk. "This is his death certificate. He supposedly died of emphysema."

Dalum was looking at the death certificate.

"There's something else, too," Louis said. "Do you remember what I told you last week, when I was in E Building getting Claudia's medical records, that I heard a noise?"

"Yeah."

"There was something I didn't tell you. I thought it was my imagination until a few minutes ago when I talked to Charlie."

"Go on."

"I smelled cigarette smoke. Charlie told me he smells people in that building, too. Becker was housed in E Building."

"You're thinking he's living out there somewhere?"

"Yes."

"We looked everywhere, Louis. We checked every building. Every closet, every rat hole. You saw the garbage out there and we have no way of telling what was left by

285

salvage crews or vandals — or if someone was living in there."

Dalum rose slowly and walked to the frosted window. The office was quiet. Louis spotted the drunken cop decanter on Dalem's desk and thought about grabbing a shot. But the roads were still slick and he had that long drive back to Plymouth. It was already getting dark. Maybe he would grab a motel room here somewhere.

Dalum turned. "Well, we don't need a court order and we already have a backhoe sitting out there doing nothing," he said. "I guess no one's going to care if we dig up Becker a few weeks earlier than we planned."

"Tomorrow?" Louis asked.

Dalum gave a short nod. "Best to do it quickly. We'll start at dawn."

Louis stood up. "Dawn?"

"I think a little secrecy is warranted until we know for sure," Dalum said. "If Becker *is* in that grave, I'd just as soon the state investigators didn't get wind of what we were thinking here today."

"I understand."

"You got some dental records or something we can use for a comparison?" Dalum asked.

"I know someone who probably does."

Dalum shook his head slowly. "One thing we didn't mention. If Rebecca's killer is the same guy who raped Millie Reuben in 1964, that clears Charlie."

"Yes, it does," Louis said.

"I guess I'm going to have to release him, but I'm a little reluctant until I know for sure all these rapes were by the same guy."

"I know."

"Plus, I don't where he'd go. The hospital will be closed soon," Dalum said, pulling on his jacket. "I guess we can let him stay here a few more days."

"Good idea."

Dalum gave another nod and took a long breath, his eyes swinging up to the clock on the wall. "I'm heading home early," he said. "Why don't you come along and Dee will fix us some dinner? You look like hell."

"Sounds great."

"You want to stay the night at my place?" Dalum asked. "We've got a fold-out sofa you can use."

"That would be nice," Louis said. "Save me a long drive in the morning."

Louis followed Dalum to the outer office and was almost to the door when he remembered Alice was still in the cell block.

He asked Dalum to wait a second and walked back.

Charlie and Alice were seated on the lower bunk, eating the chicken. A uniformed officer stood at the end of the corridor, wiping his mouth with a napkin.

Louis motioned Alice to the bars. When she neared, he spoke softly so Charlie could not hear them.

"There's a good chance we're real close to clearing Charlie," Louis said.

Alice's face brightened and he realized it was the first time in days he had seen her smile. "Thank you," she said.

"You might start thinking about what we can do with him when we do clear him and the hospital shuts down completely."

"I have thought about it," she said. "I'm going to ask him if he wants to come stay with me."

Louis couldn't help but stare and he knew she saw the concern. "You look surprised, Louis," she said.

"I am."

"Charlie's not dangerous," she said. "And I've lived alone for almost ten years. I think we'd be good company for each other."

"Well," Louis managed, "if that's what you think best."

Alice still had that small smile on her lips. "I've spent my whole life working with people like Charlie. They don't scare me. In fact, I've found I can learn a lot from people who see the world through a different prism."

Louis glanced at Charlie. He had felt something similar the other night, when he was reading to Charlie, and he had seen the same guileless smile on Charlie's face when he had walked in a few minutes ago. But the image of Charlie carrying Rebecca from the woods was there, too.

He started to ask her not to take Charlie home until they knew for sure, but she had turned away from him and was sitting down next to Charlie on the bunk.

Alice was trying to explain to him that one day soon there would be no hospital and he needed to understand some things. Charlie was still talking about the apple babies and how he wanted to go home.

Louis walked back to the office, their voices a soft echo in the concrete corridor.

Chapter 24

The air was raw, the sky a solid wash of white, and the grass crisp with a light sprinkle of snow that had begun falling just before dawn.

Louis looked at his watch. Seven-fifteen.

They had been here about twenty minutes, arriving just as the darkness was fading to a ghostly white dawn. During that time, Louis had walked the cemetery as he had the first night he left Charlie, the night he went in search of the crying graves. Like that night, he had heard nothing.

But standing in the darkness had given him time to think and imagine. He knew it was his mind playing with him, but he found himself wondering what the killer was doing right now. Had he spent the night inside one of the empty buildings? Was he out there in the trees watching them now? Had he already picked out his next victim?

Last night, Louis and Dalum had discussed putting an officer out here full time until the place closed down completely and Alice and all other workers were gone. Dalum had told him he had already asked the state police, but that they didn't deem it necessary at this point. After all, they said, there was a security team at the hospital. And they themselves had the case under control. They were researching other women who had been reported missed over the last year. And they even had a few suspects, they told Dalum.

Louis guessed not one of them was named Becker.

He heard the grind of a backhoe and he turned to see it rumbling toward him. Spera was propped high on the driver's seat, wrapped in a red flannel jacket, a wool cap pulled down over his head.

Spera drove the machine up close, then cut the engine. He hopped down off the seat and walked to Louis and Dalum, his gaze lifting to the flakes drifting from the sky.

"We better get this over with," Spera said.

Louis pulled out his copy of the grave log Spera had given him. Spera did the same.

"I want to make sure there's no mistake here," Spera said. "I got him listed in number 6888."

"Same here," Louis said.

The three of them walked a few feet toward the back corner of the cemetery. Louis and Dalum had already cleared the dirt and weeds away from Becker's marker, but it was powdered now with fresh snow and Dalum bent to brush it away. The numbers chiseled in the stone were clear: 6888.

"Okay then," Spera said.

Louis and Dalum walked away, giving Spera room to work. The backhoe roared to life again and the digging started. Louis led Dalum farther away from the noise and as they walked, he noticed he wasn't far from Claudia's grave. And he tried to remember what number she was.

"Your buddy's here," Dalum said.

Louis looked up to see Delp coming toward them. He walked like he was drowsy, and his hair was flat on one side like he'd slept on it and hadn't combed it yet. Louis stepped forward to meet him.

"Did you bring them?" Louis asked.

Delp put a hand inside his jacket and withdrew two items. One was a small manila envelope that Louis suspected held Becker's dental records. The other was a single piece of white paper.

"What's the paper?" Louis asked.

"You're going to want to kiss me for this," Delp said.

"I doubt it. What is it?"

"Becker's booking sheet from Mason."

"And how does that do us any good?"

Delp snapped the paper open. "It lists the distinguishing scars and tattoos, as you know."

"So?"

"Becker has an eleven-inch scar on his right forearm. Just below the elbow from a broken arm he got as a teenager. It was a clean break of the ulna, and my guess is it's still going to be visible on the bones today."

"Can I see that?" Dalum asked.

Delp handed Dalum the paper, giving the X-ray envelope to Louis, then started to step around him. Louis grabbed his sleeve.

"Give me your camera," Louis said, putting out his hand.

"C'mon, Kincaid. Quid pro quo. I gave you his dental records and I even threw in his booking sheet and I can't even take a look?"

"Look all you want, but give me your camera," Louis said. "And you know the deal. If he's in there, none of this ever gets written. This morning never happened."

Delp blew out breath laced with stale beer and slapped his camera into Louis's hand. Then he wandered over to watch Spera.

Louis pulled the small X-ray out of the envelope and held it up to the weak light. Becker had a full set of small, square teeth. On the lower right, there was a filling and on the upper right, there was a gap between the last two teeth.

The X-ray had a sticker on the corner, with Becker's name and a date. June 1962 — before Becker was arrested. He hoped this was good enough.

"This guy looks like he's wound a little tight," Dalum said, handing Louis the booking paper.

The picture of Becker was black and white, shading the jail smock gray and Becker's razor-cut hair almost black, but Louis saw that both his hair and eyes were listed as brown.

Becker was twenty-two in the photo, and at first glance looked like a college student, with wireless glasses and a studious expression. But there was something about the way his thick brows formed a single line over his eyes, and the half smirk of his bowed lips that hinted at something darker.

Louis folded the paper and stuffed it in his pocket, then turned up the collar of his jacket. Dalum had given him some gloves this morning, along with a clean sweatshirt emblazoned with I VISITED HELL MICHIGAN, but he was still cold.

Suddenly, it was quiet.

Louis and Dalum walked back to the open grave. There was still a layer of dirt in it and Louis could not see the concrete vault.

"Normally, I got a crew who does this," Spera said, coming up behind them and carrying two small shovels and black rubber gloves. "But you wanted to keep this secret, so I need a little help."

Spera held out the shovels and gloves. "You guys go ahead and shovel off the rest of the dirt, down to the vault lid. I'll go get the hoist."

Louis took the shovels and Spera walked away. Louis looked at Dalum, then at Delp, who was standing on the other side of the grave.

"I don't do manual labor," Delp said.

Louis and Dalum eased themselves into the grave. "Wait," Dalum said, reaching into his pocket. He opened a small jar of Vicks VapoRub and spread some under his nostrils. He handed it to Louis, who did the same.

They started digging. The stench was awful, and was getting worse with every heap of dirt they tossed out. After a few minutes, Louis paused, his hand over his nose. He looked up at Delp.

"You might want to back off, Delp," Louis called.

Delp grinned and whipped a small white painter's mask from his jacket pocket.

"You're going to need more than that," Louis said.

Delp said something, but it was muffled behind the mask. From behind him, Louis heard the hum of another machine and saw Spera bringing the hoist into place.

"I hit concrete," Dalum said.

Louis helped him finish up; then Spera and his son Andy climbed down again and lowered the chains into the grave. Louis and Dalum hooked them to the iron eye-holes on the sides of the concrete vault and climbed out, pulling off the gloves and walking as far away from the grave as they could. After drawing a full breath, Louis turned and watched as Spera operated the hoist, lifting the vault from the hole.

The vault dripped muddy water as it rose into the air. And suddenly the smell was everywhere. Louis pulled his sweat-shirt up over his nose. It wasn't until Spera had the vault back on the ground and Andy was headed toward it with a crowbar that Louis forced himself to move forward.

It took three good jerks of the crowbar, but the vault finally slid open, the heavy lid dropping to the grass. Louis's hand came to his nose again.

Aw, Jesus . . .

Grave juice . . . that's what cops called it. The wood casket was floating in a fetid brew of rancid, muddy water, dark with decomposed flesh.

Louis heard a groan, and his eyes moved immediately to Delp. Delp had ripped off his mask and was hunched over, already in his second or third spasm of vomiting.

"You want one of these, Louis?" Spera asked, holding out a gas mask.

"Yeah," Louis said.

Spera gave one to Dalum, too, and then went about helping Andy slip straps under the casket. When he was finished, Louis and Andy took one side and Dalum took the other, and they lifted the casket from the vault. The wood was soft and warped, and the whole casket started to bow as they tried to get it up over the sides of the vault.

"Steady!" Spera called.

The casket gave a groan, and before

Louis could do anything, the wood panel on the side split away, and the front end started to dip.

"Hold it! Hold it!" Spera yelled.

But it was too late. Just as they got the casket over the side, part of the bottom gave out, washing their feet and ankles with thick black water.

"Damn it," Louis hissed.

Then the rest went, the wood ripping like wet newspaper, and the body fell to the ground with a thud.

For a second, they were still; then Spera moved aside the straps and they stared at the body.

It lay faceup, the arms extended by the fall. The clothes were intact, a plain shirt and dark trousers, both wet and muddy. The hands were black with decay and tapered into grotesque gobs of bumpy, dark mush. The hair was combed straight back, wet and speckled with mud.

But it was the face Louis couldn't stop looking at.

The skin was waxy, flesh-colored, and except for a rotted black hole on the left side of the mouth and another one down the neck, the corpse looked almost normal. There were a pair of rusty, wire-rimmed glasses lying by the head.

It was Becker, Louis knew. Older, fatter, and eaten with grave rot, but it was him.

Louis looked up, meeting Dalum's eyes behind the glass of the mask. Dalum knew, too. Louis felt a hard rush of disappointment and he lifted his gaze up. Spera was coming back from his flatbed truck with a body bag.

Louis moved forward to help slip Becker's body into the bag. Parts of Becker's hands and feet came off and by the time the bag was loaded on the truck, Louis's stomach was turning.

"If you guys will stay and keep an eye on all this," Spera shouted through the mask, "I'll go get a few of my guys and come back and clean it all up."

Louis nodded. Dalum nudged him and motioned with his head toward the pine trees near the gate. Ahead of them Louis saw Delp. He was standing upright, shivering, his hands covering his face.

As Louis and Dalum passed, Delp stumbled after them. No one stopped until they got to Dalum's car. Louis jerked off the mask and his gloves, tossing them to the ground. The air wasn't great, even under the pines, but it was breathable. He glanced at Delp.

"You okay?"

Delp's skin was wet and gray, and he was staring off toward Becker's grave.

"It was him, wasn't it?" Delp whispered.

"Looked like it."

"How come he still had a face?"

"It's called adipocere," Louis said. "It's a chemical process that happens as the body fat is altered somehow, and the body doesn't decompose."

"I've heard it called grave wax," Dalum said.

The smell was still strong and Louis looked down at his sneakers. Shit. They had the grave water on them. So did the cuffs of his jeans.

"So," Delp said, his voice stronger now, "where do we go from here?"

Louis looked to his right, toward the trees and the hospital beyond them. He knew where they needed to go. They needed to go back to where the murderer had felt at home, the place he still haunted. E Building. That's where they would find him, among the hundreds of records stacked in that musty little room.

Louis wiped a hand over his cold, sweating brow.

But there were so many records and the attacks spanned more than two decades. And there was no way a judge was going to give them a warrant to randomly search confidential files for a nameless and faceless killer.

They had to narrow this down. They had to know what kind of man they were looking for. And that could only come from someone who worked in E Building for a long time. Someone who knew these guys better than they knew themselves.

He looked at Dalum. "Chief, can we get a list of people admitted during a certain time period?"

Dalum shrugged. "You mean just admission dates and names?"

"Yeah."

"I suppose we could. Nothing confidential about that," he said. "That's going to be a helluva list, Louis."

"I know. But we need it to narrow down the suspect pool."

"But all we'll have is names," Dalum said. "We won't know anything about these people. It'll take weeks, maybe years, of legwork to even start eliminating people."

Louis was staring at the point in the milky sky where a single red brick chimney could be glimpsed above the trees.

"I know someone who can do it faster," he said.

Chapter 25

Louis was slumped in a hard metal chair when Dr. Seraphin came out of the elevator. She stopped, her keys in her gloved hand, and looked at him in surprise.

"Well, hello, Mr. . . ." she began.

"Kincaid," Louis said, standing and stretching. He had been waiting outside her office for the last hour.

A smile creased her wind-ruddy cheeks. "Louis, right?"

"Right. I need to talk to you, Doctor," he said.

"Well, I have someone coming in soon," she said, shifting the strap of her black alligator briefcase up her shoulder.

"It's important," Louis said. "We might have another murder victim at Hidden Lake."

Dr. Seraphin's smile faded. "Good Lord."

"We found some bones buried in a shallow grave and we were able to trace them to a young woman who came to the hospital last year for outpatient help."

Two students passed them in the narrow

hallway, giving Seraphin and Louis a strange look.

"I think you'd better come in," Dr. Seraphin said, unlocking the office door.

Louis waited as she took off her gray cape and gloves, and slid her briefcase under the desk. When she motioned for him to take a chair, he sat down across from her desk.

"So why are you here to see me?" she asked.

Louis recounted everything he knew so far, including his talk with Millie Reuben and the fact that Rebecca Gruber had been burned. He told her also about exhuming Donald Lee Becker's body. The doctor's face remained impassive throughout, and Louis had the sense that she was taking this all in not as any woman might but as a psychiatrist would — with a calm, clinical interest.

"We think whoever killed them is a former patient," Louis concluded. "Someone probably released in recent years."

"Why recent?" Dr. Seraphin asked.

"If this patient had been out for a long time, we would have other victims," Louis said.

"Maybe there are more and you just haven't found them," she said.

303

Louis nodded. "That's possible."

Dr. Seraphin leaned her elbows on the desk and clasped her hands in front of her face. "So what exactly do you want from me?" she asked.

"Help in finding possible suspects."

The doctor's eyebrows shot up.

"There's not a judge in the world who will grant me access to medical files," Louis said. "And I don't even know what I am looking for. He may not ever have been convicted of anything, so I can't just look at criminal records."

Dr. Seraphin shook her head. "I'd like to help you, Mr. Kincaid, but as I told you, I left Hidden Lake a long time ago. If the person you are looking for was in fact released recently, I wouldn't know him."

Louis stifled a sigh. She was right of course.

"And while I am certainly not one to question the police's logic, I think you could be wrong about this being a recently released patient," Dr. Seraphin added.

Louis sat up straighter in his chair. "Why?"

"Well, most patients were released back in the seventies," Dr. Seraphin said.

"The seventies?"

"It was part of a mass movement to

deinstitutionalize the mentally ill. The thinking was that the best approach was to integrate them into society rather than keep them locked up." She shook her head slowly. "I'm not so sure now it *was* in fact the right thing to do. But then, the entire history of mental health is really nothing but trial and error when it comes down to it. There is a lot of — what is the sports cliché? — Sunday morning quarterbacking."

"Monday morning," Louis said with a smile.

She smiled back. "We've tried hard. But the public generally still thinks of mental health professionals as quacks or monsters."

"So why were all these patients released?" Louis asked.

"Well, I'd have to put it in perspective for you."

Louis wasn't sure if she was patronizing him or not. But he knew if he was going to get anything helpful from this woman, he had to appeal to her ego.

"Your opinion could help me, Doctor," he said.

She leaned back in her leather chair. "I'd say you'd have to go back to the Civil War to get a clear idea of what has happened in mental health. After the war, many sol-

305

diers suffered from what we now call post-traumatic stress syndrome. But then, they just warehoused them in asylums so no one had to deal with them. The places were so overcrowded, doctors got desperate and went back to using restraints, shock therapy — and mass doses of opium."

Louis shook his head slowly.

"By the turn of the century, asylums were opening up all across the country, most of them modeled after the Victorian design of a man named Thomas Kirkbride," Dr. Seraphin went on. "He had the idea of putting the least disturbed patients closer to the center building to encourage interaction with the staff. But if the patients' conditions worsened they were relocated farther away."

"Like in E Building," Louis said.

She leveled her sharp gaze at him. "You've seen E Building?"

"I've been on the grounds."

"Well," she went on, "then you know that Hidden Lake was like a small city. All the asylums like it were. They were very efficient communities with their own farms, dairies, greenhouses, transportation systems — and graveyards, of course. And most of the patients worked to support the 'family,' so to speak."

She paused, then opened a desk drawer. After a moment of rummaging through some files, she pulled out a small card and a yellowed newspaper clipping. "I kept these when I left Hidden Lake."

She handed them to Louis. The postcard was an old color-tinted photograph of the Hidden Lake grounds with people sitting on the grass around a lake with weeping willows in the foreground and the Victorian spires of the asylum in the background. The lettering said GREETINGS FROM HIDDEN LAKE. The newspaper clipping was from the *Detroit Journal* dated 1906. It was a cartoon showing a group of hobos gathered around a piano in a parlor singing. The caption said WELCOME TO HOTEL HIDDEN LAKE.

"I don't get it," Louis said, looking at Dr. Seraphin.

"Respectability," she said with a small smile. "The postcards were sort of an early PR campaign, sent out so family and friends of the patients felt better about committing their loved ones."

She nodded to the clipping. "Respectability brought lots of new customers. Adult children who couldn't cope with their aging parents would just commit them, thinking Mom or Dad would be just fine." She let out a sigh. "And in the winter, the asylums would fill to bursting with the homeless who had nowhere else to go."

Louis remembered Alice's explanation of the POGs, the "poor old guys."

"Many of the people in these places weren't mentally ill at all," Dr. Seraphin said. "But there were no real criteria for accepting or rejecting patients, so asylums became dumping grounds to just hide away anyone society didn't want to deal with."

Louis stared at the cartoon for a moment, then put it down. "Depressing," he said.

"The severe overcrowding led to a sharp decline in care," Dr. Seraphin went on, "which led to a return to old practices like restraints, ice baths, and shock therapy. But then, in the 1930s, mental health got the answer to its problems — transorbital lobotomy."

"That's what they gave to Jack Nicholson in that movie," Louis said.

Dr. Seraphin gave a nod and a grimace.

"How did it work?" Louis asked.

Dr. Seraphin let out a long breath. "First they would sedate the patient, then insert a device through the eyelid into the frontal lobe. They would then tap the device with a hammer and after the appropriate depth was achieved, manipulate the device back and forth in a swiping motion within the patient's head." She paused. "It was very quick, very efficient, and very popular."

She saw the horrified look on Louis's face and went on.

"The lobotomy was mental health's darkest hour, and I only tell you this so you can understand how far we have come," she said.

Louis leveled his eyes at her. "I'm here to learn from you, Doctor, not condemn you."

She was silent for a moment. Then she carefully gathered up the old postcard and the newspaper clipping and slipped them back in her desk drawer.

"So how did things get from lobotomies to mass patient releases?" Louis asked.

Dr. Seraphin looked up. "To oversimplify things, Thorazine."

"That's a drug," Louis said.

She nodded. "Thorazine and other drugs made it possible to cut down on the time patients needed to spend in hospitals. Plus, opinion shifted. It was thought that with proper medication, patients could function on their own in society."

She toyed with the edge of a folder on her desk. "The intention was good. The idea was to protect the rights of mental patients."

Louis was getting impatient. "So how does this explain how a serial rapist and murderer could have been let loose?"

Her eyes shot up to his. "I am sure that did not happen at Hidden Lake."

Louis shook his head slowly. "With all due respect, Dr. Seraphin, what you have been describing makes me believe just about anything is possible."

She stared at him for a moment, then folded her hands and placed them on the desk. "In 1960, there were half a million people in mental institutions in this country," she said. "Things changed fast — legislation, insurance, public opinion, psychiatry. Places like Hidden Lake were expected to do everything — train staff, treat and diagnose outpatients, do research. Before, Hidden Lake had been like a caretaker, but it got so we were being asked to do everything with no funding or support. It was like a Model T trying to compete in the Indy 500."

She paused. "I knew it was going to end," she said softly. "I had worked at Hidden Lake for more than twenty years, but I knew the world was closing in on us and it was just a matter of time."

Louis waited. The doctor was staring at her folded hands. Finally she looked up. "The end for places like Hidden Lake came, for all practical purposes, in 1972."

"Why then?" Louis prodded.

"A federal court ruled that patients couldn't work unless they were paid."

She gave a small laugh. "Sounds so benign, doesn't it? But that was the proverbial straw that broke the camel's back. We had always relied on the patients to run Hidden Lake — the gardens, the dairy, the kitchens, the apple orchards. We made quite a tidy profit selling apples and cider and such."

She looked up at Louis. "But it wasn't just the money. The work was good for the patients. It gave them a sense of purpose, of being part of something real and productive."

She shook her head. "After that, there was more pressure to move patients. We were even given monetary rewards for decreasing the number of our inpatients. We released three-fourths of our population in the early seventies."

"Where did they go?" Louis asked.

"Halfway houses, nursing homes, some

back to their families." She shook her head slowly. "Many just ended up on the street. It was very traumatic for patients."

Louis thought of the homeless men and women he had seen crouched in the storefronts of downtown Fort Myers or hunched on beachfront benches. He thought of Charlie, finding his way to the gates of Hidden Lake with nowhere else to go.

And he thought of some faceless, senseless, murderous man who had somehow been let loose from Hidden Lake decades ago and now had come back to haunt its ruins.

"Dr. Seraphin," Louis said, "why would he come back?"

She stared at him. "Excuse me?"

"Whoever killed these women at Hidden Lake. Why now? Why would he come back and commit his crimes there?"

She leveled her piercing eyes at him. "Because it's his home."

There was a soft tap on the glass of the door. Dr. Seraphin's eyes went to the door and then to her wristwatch. "I'm so sorry," she said, "but I have an appointment."

Louis rose, picking up his jacket. The doctor got up and went to the door, opening it. A young woman, clutching some books, was waiting.

"Go on in, Mona, I'll only be a moment," Dr. Seraphin said. She led Louis out into the hall and closed the door behind her.

"I need your help," Louis said.

"I don't know what I can do," Dr. Seraphin said.

"We need to find a suspect in those files still in E Building."

"I don't how much use I can be. As I told you, I was the assistant deputy superintendent. By 1956, I no longer had direct contact with any patients."

"But you would know who to look for," Louis said.

She shook her head.

Louis leaned forward. "Dr. Seraphin, this guy isn't going to stop. We need some help."

She was quiet, looking at him. "All right," she said finally. "If you can get access to the files legally I could look at them and try to interpret the contents, perhaps tell you what *symptoms* to look for."

"I need more than that," Louis said. "I need you to give me some possible names."

Dr. Seraphin's chin tilted up in surprise. "That would be unethical," she said.

"I know," Louis said. "But isn't there some ethic about alerting the authorities when a patient poses a danger to others?"

"In a manner of speaking, but you're asking me to put dozens of people under the police spotlight simply because they once were patients, and for those who have managed to pull their lives together, it could be devastating."

"Just give us some names to check out," Louis said, hearing an urgency in his own voice. "I promise you if they don't look to be a suspect we won't even speak with them."

Dr. Seraphin was quiet, and he could not tell if she was growing irritated or contemplating his request. He tried something else.

"Look," he said, "right now, he's attracted to Hidden Lake. That's where he kills and that may be where he's still living. But when the place closes, he'll have no choice but to move on, and when that happens, we may never find him."

She moved a manicured hand through her cropped gray hair and glanced down the hall. Then she sighed.

"I need your word," Dr. Seraphin said, "that you will not contact any of these people until you are almost positive they could be your killer."

"You have it."

Dr. Seraphin sighed again. "I will have to refresh my memory," she said. "You said the E Building files were still there?"

"Yes."

"I will need to look through them."

"You'll come out there?"

Dr. Seraphin offered a half smile. "Unlike you, Mr. Kincaid, I have no qualms about E Building. It was my home for many years, too."

"When can you come?"

"I have to go to Milwaukee tomorrow for a seminar, but I will be back Wednesday," she said. "I have a place out on Wampler's Lake and was planning on taking a few days' rest there when I get back. I suppose I could meet you at Hidden Lake Thursday morning."

"That would be great," Louis said.

"I think it would be helpful if I were to see whatever information you have on the murders."

"You want to profile him?"

She nodded. "Exactly. Whatever you can provide will be useful."

"Thank you," Louis said, extending a hand.

Dr. Seraphin shook his hand slowly. "Now I have a request of you, Mr. Kincaid."

"Anything."

"No one is to know I'm coming back to Hidden Lake. I will meet only with you."

"I understand."

Dr. Seraphin turned toward her office. "I hope so," she said. Then she disappeared inside, the door closing softly behind her.

Chapter 26

The house was quiet. Louis waited just inside the door for a moment, listening for movement, but there was none. Phillip's second car, a small silver Ford, was not in the driveway and Louis had assumed either Phillip or Frances was out, but it seemed they both were. He was surprised. The last few times he had been in a room with both of them, they hadn't been able to look at each other. So maybe this was good.

Upstairs in his room, he pulled off his jacket and shoes, thinking about Dr. Seraphin.

He knew that what she was going to do was unethical and Louis wasn't sure that farther down the road their little trip back through those records wouldn't end up destroying an entire case against this guy. And he felt bad that he couldn't tell Dalum.

All the way home from Ann Arbor, Louis had thought about the Ardmore badge in his wallet, and he had to remind himself that some of the things he had

317

grown used to doing as a P.I. couldn't be done here. But then he remembered how Rebecca Gruber's thighs had looked, and how her insides had been torn up by someone jamming a piece of metal up her, and he knew he would go through with it, and that he would let Dr. Seraphin go through with it, too.

When he came back downstairs to the kitchen, he noticed a note next to the phone. It was from Phillip, a message that Joe had called. Louis picked up the phone and dialed her Miami number. It rang eight times before he heard her voice. But it was the answering machine.

"Hey, Joe," he said after the beep. "It's me. Just got back and got your message you called. Listen, I've got a lot going here right now and I still don't know when I'll be home. I've gotten involved in a case . . ."

He paused for a second, always struck with the weirdness of speaking into a machine.

"This case is a tough one," he went on. "I wish you were here so I could bounce some things off you, like we do sometimes. But anyway, if I get a chance, I'll call later."

Again, he paused, thinking he should say something else, but he didn't. He hung up the phone and went out to the living room, stretching out on the sofa, watching the shadows of an early darkness move across the ceiling. It occurred to him that he still might be here at Christmas. Joe would understand, because she knew how a case could crawl inside and eat at you until it was solved. But eleven-year old Ben would not. They had plans for the holidays.

Damn it. He wanted to wrap this up. And maybe with Dr. Seraphin's help, they could find the killer soon. But what about Claudia?

He had deliberately avoided giving Phillip any more details beyond the suggestion that maybe Claudia had been cremated in error. He hadn't told him about those cans of ashes. And he was thinking now that maybe it *was* better to bring him home an urn filled with the ashes of an unknown patient and let Phillip believe what he needed to so he could grieve in a way that wouldn't destroy the rest of his life.

But that was just another lie on top of a case filled with them, and before he did that, there was something he needed to do. He wanted to give Claudia one more chance to tell him where she was.

Louis went upstairs and pulled out Claudia's medical folder. He flipped it open. Her photo was right on top and he gave it a long look, hoping to see something new in her face that would help him know more about her. But there was nothing but those dark holes that were her eyes.

He took the folder back to the bed and spread it open, setting the picture up against the lamp on the nightstand. He started with dated treatment notes, hoping to find the periods of isolation Millie Reuben had told him about. But after Phillip had torn the file apart, Louis hadn't put it back together in any kind of order. Things were hard to find and he had to sort each piece of paper, trying to match it up with papers that looked similar or had the same headings.

The bedroom grew dark and he had gone through two Dr Peppers and a sandwich by the time he was able to figure out that the long gaps in any kind of treatments or medications must be the isolation periods. He wrote them down on a legal pad.

Claudia had been admitted to Hidden Lake in October of 1951, and had been put on Thorazine. But the records showed she had been taken off the drug almost immediately. There were no other treatments

it was Claudia's burn notation in 1959.

But how could something like that happen to both Millie and Claudia five years apart in a place that was supposed to be secure? How could a patient run wild and victimize women?

Louis leaned back against the head-board. Maybe the rapist wasn't a patient. Maybe he simply dressed like one so the women didn't know who he really was. Maybe he was an orderly, or worse, a doctor.

He reached over to take a drink of Dr Pepper and adjusted his glasses to keep reading.

Claudia was isolated again in the fall of 1961, and again in late 1963, both times for almost a year. There were no additional references to burns, but he had no reason to assume she couldn't have been raped and burned again during those times.

By late 1969, her treatments started to dwindle off to almost nothing. The doctor's remarks grew infrequent, almost like Claudia was no longer receiving any significant care. And he guessed by that time, the insulin had eaten away any functioning part of her brain. Then he read something that confirmed what he had been thinking:

Patient experiences long periods of depression, and at times appears catatonic and unresponsive to outside stimuli. Patient still hearing voices and no longer recognizes visitors.

Louis stared at the last line. Visitors?

He set that paper aside and started rifling through the others for something else. They kept track of visitors at prisons. Why wouldn't they do it at this place?

Here it was.

The first entry was December 1951, about two months after she was admitted. The visitor was Rodney DeFoe. There were probably fifteen other entries on this page that went up to early 1962, and Rodney DeFoe was on every line. It looked like he visited her a couple of times a year, mostly in the spring. No one else was on the visitors' log.

But there were ten more years of visitor logs to look at, and Louis started sifting through the papers, but he only found two for Claudia: April 1969 and the last entry, April 1972.

April 1972?

That didn't seem right. What had Phillip said?

It was right after my fortieth birthday. I went back to the hospital and they told me she had died there a year before.

Louis knew Phillip's birthday was December 18. And if he remembered right, Phillip was born in 1932, which meant his fortieth birthday was December of 1972. Dr. Seraphin had told him that Claudia died during a flu epidemic during the winter of '71–'72.

But this log listed a visit from Rodney in April of 1972, four or five months after Dr. Seraphin claimed Claudia was already dead.

Louis pulled off his glasses. Something was wrong. Or someone was mistaken. Memories — especially hard ones — could be unreliable, and Phillip was having a tough enough time with all this. Or maybe he himself was wrong about the year Phillip was born. Or maybe he wasn't remembering clearly what Dr. Seraphin had told him.

Claudia's death certificate. That would tell him.

He hadn't seen one in the file, but he searched again, careful to look at every piece of paper. But as he neared the bottom of the stack, he grew sure it wasn't in this file.

Why wasn't it? Becker's death certificate had been in his medical file, so why wasn't Claudia's?

He picked up the phone and called the Ardmore station. Chief Dalum wasn't in the office, but Louis left a message asking him to run down a copy of Claudia's death certificate. When the officer asked him for a date of death, Louis gave him 1972, but before he hung up, he added December 1971 as well.

Louis leaned back against the headboard, his gaze moving to the mirror and the twinkle of Christmas lights outside.

It pissed him off that he hadn't gotten her death certificate right off. If he had, this question — and maybe some other ones — might have been answered by now. There was so much in his head right now. Some things he *knew* — the fact that Claudia had been burned and possibly raped. But there was so much he *didn't* know — like had Claudia been murdered by the rapist?

If she had been murdered, why did Dr. Seraphin lie? And where the hell was Claudia's body?

Louis put the file back together, feeling a small wave of weariness. He slid off the bed and stuck Claudia's folder back in the dresser. She was a tough one to be around, like a black-sheep relative filled with so much need that it drained all the emotion of everyone around them. And every time he put her away, she left him with a faint sadness that took days to shake.

He checked his watch, wondering where Phillip was. It was almost nine now. Too late to expect Frances would be fixing anything for dinner. He headed downstairs to rummage up something. He had his head in the fridge when it hit him.

Maybe there wasn't a body.

He straightened.

If Claudia had been murdered, why not just put her mutilated body in a casket and drop it in the ground?

Louis closed the fridge.

But someone buried rocks. And he had the feeling that it wasn't as Dr. Seraphin had theorized: that Claudia had been cremated in error and some grave digger had buried a rock-filled coffin just to cover up his mistake.

There was no body to bury. But it was because Claudia had been murdered just like Sharon Stottlemyer. And just like Sharon, she had been left in a shallow grave somewhere out there — the cemetery, the woods, the apple orchards — never meant to be found.

It was a cover-up. Hidden Lake buried rocks not just to cover up Claudia's murder but to cover up the fact that they couldn't find her body. He could almost understand it, given the hospital's need to protect its reputation and the prominence of Claudia's family. Hidden Lake had faked Claudia's death certificate and then buried the rocks just in case anyone in the family ever came to visit.

And someone did. Rodney.

But that still didn't explain the visitors' log. No matter how Claudia died, why should there be any question about when?

Somebody was wrong. Or somebody was lying.

If Dr. Seraphin had been involved in the cover-up, there was no way she was going to tell him anything. There was no one at the hospital who could help now. Rodney DeFoe's name was on that visitors' log. And only Rodney could explain why he was visiting his sister who had supposedly died four months earlier.

The sound of a key in the front door made him look up, and Louis headed up the short staircase to greet Phillip and Frances. But Phillip was the only one on the landing and he turned to Louis slowly. He looked lost, and very alone. Louis didn't speak, waiting for Phillip to say something.

"She left me," Phillip said softly. "Fran went to her sister's in Brighton."

Louis put out a hand to Phillip's shoulder. "I'm sorry."

Phillip eased away from him and moved down the stairs to the living room. Louis followed him. It was dark, but Phillip didn't turn any lights on. He sank into a chair, his jacket still on, head bowed.

"Fran told me to take the time I needed and maybe when I'm finished, maybe then . . ."

Louis let his words hang, then glanced to the kitchen. "Can I fix you something to eat?"

"No," Phillip said. "Maybe a beer."

"Sure," Louis said.

"Grab yourself one, too. I want you to bring me up to date. You haven't told me anything in days."

Louis didn't reply. When he came back, he handed a beer to Phillip, then sat across from him on the sofa. The only light came from the kitchen and the room was full of shadows and the shimmering of tiny white Christmas lights winking behind the frosted windows.

Louis took a sip of his beer. He knew it was time to tell Phillip everything he had found out. But he searched now for the right place to start.

"I met a woman named Millie Reuben," Louis said finally. "She was in the same ward as Claudia in 1952."

Phillip was quiet, almost invisible in the deep chair.

"She told me Claudia spoke of you," Louis said.

Phillip took a drink and Louis heard him sigh with a sadness that reminded him of how he had felt when he closed Claudia's file a few minutes ago.

"Tell me more," Phillip said.

Louis did, taking him from Millie Reuben, the isolation periods, the insulin and shock therapies, the cremation cans, and eventually to the rapes, the burns, Sharon Stottlemyer's bones, and Rebecca Gruber's torture and murder.

And the longer Louis talked, the more he sensed Phillip was sinking deeper into himself. Louis finished up with what he was planning to do next — go through the E Building records to narrow down the hundreds of possible suspects.

"So you think . . ." Phillip whispered. "You think Claudia was murdered by this man?"

"I don't have any proof. Nothing I can use to make any accusations. But that's the way I'm leaning."

Phillip gave out a small sob, and his hand came over his face. Louis stared at the carpet, fingers tight on the bottle, his throat so dry he couldn't swallow. He had comforted many people before, men and women alike. But this was Phillip, his father in so many ways, and it seemed so strange to be the stronger one.

Louis rose and moved to him, kneeling down in front of the chair. "Phil," he said. "None of what happened to her was your fault."

Phil leaned forward, into him. Louis held him.

Chapter 27

By 11:30 the next morning, Louis was standing at the front door of the DeFoe house. He had rung the bell seven times and gotten no response. There was a black Jag XJ6 in the circular drive and he could see one light on inside the house, so he was sure someone was home. Where the hell were the servants? A monster place like this had to have a whole army of them.

He gave up on the bell and started in on the massive lion's-head door knocker. The sharp pounding sound it made on the heavy wood door echoed loudly in the portico.

No answer. But he was determined that the long drive to Grosse Pointe wasn't going to be for nothing. He pounded again.

Finally, the heavy door swung open.

"All right! All right! Who the hell —" Rodney drew up short at the sight of Louis. "You. What do you want?"

"I need to talk to you."

Rodney had a white apron tied around

his waist, one of those big things that professional chefs wore. His top lip was swollen with a crusted scar from where Phillip had decked him.

"I tried talking once already," Rodney said. "All it got me were two stitches inside my mouth. So, you here to take a swing at me, too?"

Louis shook his head. "I just need some answers."

"About what?"

"Your sister."

Rodney's eyes were wary. "I already told you this is none of your business."

"And I already told you I am not going to give up looking for her remains. Even if you do scare Phillip off with legal threats, you're still going to have to deal with me."

For a moment, Louis was sure Rodney was going to slam the door in his face. But then, Rodney just moved aside and nodded for him to come in. The heavy door closed behind them. The foyer was dark and drafty, not that much warmer than outside.

"Leave your coat there. No sense in you dripping all over the Oushak," Rodney said, flipping a hand toward a worn Oriental.

Louis glanced around and finally left his wet coat on a spindly chair. Rodney had gone down the hall toward a lighted room in the back of the house and Louis followed. Down another short hall and he emerged into a brightly lit kitchen. It was warm and fragrant with cooking smells.

Rodney's black velvet slippers made flapping sounds on the old black-and-white tile as he moved to the stove. He picked up a wooden spoon and began to stir something in a large copper pot. The kitchen was huge and, to Louis's eye, oddly old-fashioned looking, with an old porcelain sink, glass-windowed pantries, and a mammoth butcher-block island in the middle. The island was strewn with vegetables and bowls of fish, oysters, clams, and shrimp. There was a bottle of red wine and a delicate bubble-shaped wineglass.

Rodney set the spoon down and came over to the island. He picked up the glass and took a drink. As the glass came down, his eyes met Louis's.

"Do you like wine?" he asked.

Louis shrugged.

Rodney picked up the bottle. "This is a Pomerol . . . sixty-six Vieux-Chateau-Certan. Would you like some?"

Louis noticed the bottle was almost empty. "You go ahead."

Rodney smiled slightly. "Wise decision.

It's really too tannic and I brought it up out of the cellar much too early, I'm afraid." He poured the rest of the wine into his glass, spilling some on the wood block. Louis noticed there was another empty wine bottle over by the sink.

Rodney took a healthy drink. "Excuse me, it's time to add the tomatoes." He picked up a cutting board of sliced tomatoes and slid them into the copper pot.

"I'm making cioppino," he said, turning back to Louis. "It's an Italian fisherman's stew. Quite tasty. I got the recipe when I was living in Vernazza."

"You don't have someone to do that for you?" Louis asked.

"What, cook?" Rodney gave an odd grimace. "Mother fired the cook this week. She fired the maid, too. This has been . . . an ongoing problem. She has always hated having strangers in the house." Rodney went back to stirring. "Besides, I like to cook. It may be the only thing I really do well."

Louis slid onto a stool at the island. Rodney was, he realized now, if not drunk, then already well on his way. But maybe that wasn't all bad. When Rodney had shown up at Phillip's house, he had been sober and that had given him an edgy, threatening aura. But this man . . .

Louis had the feeling this was a man who became someone else when he drank, a man who could be manipulated to say things he didn't want to say.

"It smells good," Louis said.

Rodney pointed the wooden spoon at him, winked, and turned back to his stirring.

"Look, DeFoe," Louis said, "I want to ask you a question."

"And I will try my best to answer it. And please, if you are going to sit in my kitchen, I think you can call me Rodney."

"You loved your sister a lot, didn't you?" Louis said.

The spoon stopped for a moment; then Rodney resumed stirring. He didn't answer.

"I didn't think you did," Louis went on. "But then I found this visitors' log from Hidden Lake. Looks like you went to see your sister pretty regularly."

"Really?"

"Oh yeah. Couple times a year but every spring for sure. April, in particular, regular as clockwork. Just like the groundhog."

"February, dear boy. The rodent appears in February."

"In fact it was so regular you even

showed up after she was dead."

Rodney turned to stare at him. "Excuse me?"

Louis pulled a paper from his coat pocket. "This is the visitors' log. You went to see Claudia in April 1972."

Rodney just stood there, the spoon dripping on the tiles. Louis leaned over and spread the paper open on the butcher-block surface. Rodney peered down at it. Louis poked at the line with Rodney's name.

Rodney looked up at Louis. "Are you sure you wouldn't like a glass of wine?"

Louis tapped the paper again.

Rodney let out a huge sigh. "I was in Europe when I heard. I was not . . ." He paused, shaking his head. "My lifestyle had put me in the position of not having to face my problems. I had an infinite variety of pharmaceuticals at my disposal. And I tried them all."

He set the spoon down and picked up his wineglass. "By the time I emerged from my stupor and came home, it was spring. It was time to go see her. And I did."

"You went to the cemetery?" Louis asked.

Rodney nodded. "I looked at that little stone thing in the grass and I had the feeling that my sister had somehow slipped away while my back was turned." He took another drink of wine. "I went in to the hospital. I don't know, maybe I thought I could find out what happened to her. But it was too late."

Louis picked up the visitors' log, folded it, and put it in his pocket.

"Why didn't you pick up her remains when Hidden Lake called about relocating her?" Louis asked.

Rodney turned back to his stew. "Are you a religious man?" he asked.

"What?"

"Are you religious?"

"What's that got to do with anything?"

"Once, when I was in my thirties," Rodney said, "I ended up in Goa, India, this beautiful place with beaches, palm trees, great hotels, discos. Everything a dissipated trust fund baby could want."

He paused to shake in some pepper. "I met this woman there, an Indian woman. She tried to teach me about Hinduism, tried to get me to change my evil ways, I suppose. It worked, to a point. I stopped putting shit up my nose."

Louis was trying to decide how far to let this wander when Rodney spoke again. "Now what does this have to do with my

338

poor dead sister Claudia, you are asking yourself?"

"Yeah, in fact, I was."

"Well, while I was busy burning out my sinuses, something happened in my brain. Some of the religious stuff just sort of . . . stuck there." Rodney gave him an odd smile. "When I finally dragged my sorry ass home, I began to study it. Now, all these years later, I guess you could call me a born-again Hindu."

"I thought you were Catholic," Louis said.

"Mother is Catholic. I gave it up for Lent."

"You haven't answered my question," Louis said.

"I'm getting to it," Rodney said, not turning around. "Well, the thing is, Hindus have a rather different take on death. They believe that the body is unimportant, that the soul lives on to inhabit a new body."

"Reincarnation," Louis said.

Rodney nodded. "They also believe that when a loved one dies, if you grieve too much or too long, the negative energy keeps the soul from making its transition."

When Rodney turned back around, his watery eyes took a second or two to focus on Louis. "My sister's soul is gone. Neither she nor I have any use for her body," he said.

Louis stared hard at him for a long time. "You know something, Rodney?" he said, standing up. "That's the biggest crock of shit I've heard in years."

The barest smile came to Rodney's lips. "Well, then, perhaps you'll believe a simpler truth. Mother would not allow it. It's that Catholic thing, you know."

Rodney moved to pick up his wineglass but knocked it over. It fell to the tile floor, shattering. He shrugged and brushed the shards away with his velvet slipper. He swayed as he went to the cabinet and pulled down a new glass.

"Time for us to take a little trip to the cellar," Rodney said, turning to Louis. "Come with me, why don't you?"

Louis didn't want to go, but he didn't want Rodney falling down the steps. He followed him through a pantry and down a narrow stairway.

At the bottom, Louis paused. It was a large basement, with stone walls and a smooth concrete floor. It was dimly lit, very clean, and Louis could see the gargantuan bulk of an old furnace in the corner. There was one door in another corner, and Rodney led him to it.

Rodney held up a hand. "This is where I keep her," he whispered.

"What?"

Rodney pulled open the door.

Louis felt a rush of cool air, and his eyes picked up the glint of something, but it was too dark to make anything out.

A light came on. Wine . . . racks of bottles, floor to ceiling. Louis looked back. Rodney was standing at the doorway, his hand on a switch, a huge grin on his face.

"You should see your face," Rodney said. "You were so hoping she was in there, like that detective in *Psycho*, you really thought you were going to find that I was hiding away some decaying corpse."

Rodney was laughing as he moved past Louis into the wine cellar.

"Eeny, meeny, miney, mo, catch a Medoc by the toe," Rodney said, his finger traveling across the nearest row and stopping. He slipped a dusty bottle off the shelves and produced a corkscrew from his pocket. Holding the bottle between his knees, Rodney uncorked it, brought the bottle up to his mouth, and took a long drink.

Louis turned away, his eyes wandering out over the basement. Even down here, he could feel it. There was a disquieting aura about every part of this ugly old house, like nothing was in balance.

"I hate this house."

Louis turned. Rodney had come up behind him. He was leaning against the door of the wine cellar, gripping the bottle.

"It is a hateful house," Rodney said thickly.

Louis moved aside and Rodney came out into the basement. He stood there, swaying slightly, his eyes coming back to Louis but not really focusing on him.

"This is where it happened," he said, pointing at the concrete floor. "Right here. This is where my father shot himself."

Slowly, Rodney raised the bottle and began to pour out the wine. It fell in a thin stream, splashing on the concrete and over Rodney's slippers.

Rodney's voice wavered when he spoke. "I was eleven when it happened, away at Cranbrook. The director took me out into the hall and said I had to go home. No one would tell me what happened. Finally, Mother told me my father had a heart attack. She was lying, of course. But I didn't find out the truth until a week later when I heard the servants talking about having to clean up the mess in the basement."

Rodney shook his head slowly. "He's exiled, like Claudia. Buried in some cemetery way up near Port Huron instead of at St. Paul's. To this day, Mother still insists he died of a heart attack."

His eyes came up to Louis's face. "I don't have many memories of him, that's the hard part. The vacation house in Saugatuck, he took Claudia and me there in the summer, and I remember skipping rocks on the lake and him playing a ukelele on the porch."

Rodney sighed. "I suppose that's a better memory than Claudia had."

"Because she was so much younger?" Louis asked.

"No," Rodney said. "Because she was the one who found him. Found him lying here, dead. She was only five."

Louis looked back at the floor, watched the wine trickle into the drain.

"I believe that's when it started," Rodney said. "When she began to crack."

Louis was quiet.

"Mother never took her to any doctors," Rodney said. "Claudia grew up hearing Mother's lies about the heart attack, but having another completely different memory of her own."

"Let's go back upstairs," Louis said.

Rodney didn't move. "I thought when

she went to Hidden Lake, I thought maybe she would get the help she needed. I thought she would get better." Rodney's voice cracked, then dropped to a rasp. "Instead she got worse."

Louis thought about what he knew about the hospital. What he had read in Claudia's patient file about the drugs, treatments, and burns. A part of him thought Rodney should know about it, but it seemed cruel to tell him now. But what was more cruel? Letting him spend the rest of his life blaming himself, like Phillip?

"It's not your fault," Louis said.

"What do you mean?" Rodney said. "I turned my back on her. It's *all* my fault."

Louis pulled in a breath. "I need to tell you some other things, things that happened to her while she was in Hidden Lake."

Rodney took an unsteady step back, then stopped, his gaze coming up to Louis in slow motion. Louis tried to read the look, hoping to see some strength in Rodney's eyes.

"Tell me," Rodney said.

"Let's go back upstairs."

"Tell me."

Louis started with the treatments. Rodney stood perfectly still, arms at his side, listening. As Louis moved onto the rapes and the burns, Rodney's face started to change, the twisted look of disgust hardened to horror. Then, suddenly, anger.

Rodney spun away, throwing the bottle. It crashed somewhere in the darkness. Louis reached for him, but Rodney threw off his hand, bolting toward the wine cellar. But then he spun back.

"Get out!" he shouted.

"Rodney."

"Get the hell out of my house!" Rodney came to him, pointing to the stairs.

In the dim light, Louis could clearly see his face. Tears lined his cheeks. He was afraid to leave him like this.

"Get out. Get out now!" Rodney screamed.

Louis started to the stairs, then turned to look at Rodney. He had disappeared into the wine cellar. A second later, he came out carrying a bottle and the corkscrew. He walked to the center of the basement, then half fell to the floor. He sat there on the wet floor, then slowly began to wind the corkscrew down into the top of the bottle.

Louis watched him for a moment more, then went up the stairs.

Chapter 28

Louis sat in the Impala, motor running, heat on high. He had arrived at Hidden Lake at 7:45 to wait for Dr. Seraphin. Through the foggy windshield, he watched a couple of security officers coming across the grass. They wore black rain slickers and hats netted in plastic and they gave him a nod as they passed.

On the drive over, he had considered confronting Dr. Seraphin about his theory that Claudia had been murdered and the hospital had covered it up. But he knew she would only deny it and he would end up losing her as an ally. She was the only one who could get him suspects quickly. He had to keep her on his side — at least for now, until he had something concrete. Then maybe he could convince Rodney to go after her and Hidden Lake.

Headlights shimmered in the mist. They grew larger, then cut off as Dr. Seraphin's Volvo cruised to a stop next to him. Louis gave her a moment, then grabbed the envelope with the crime scene photos and an umbrella and got out.

Dr. Seraphin's driver threw open his door and walked around to the passenger door, popping open an enormous black umbrella. Dr. Seraphin stepped out under it and looked at Louis. Her hair was slightly softer — the tiny spikes lying almost flat. And she wasn't wearing her usual expensively tailored clothes. Instead, she wore a waist-length jacket of red leather and jeans with a razor-sharp crease.

"Good morning, Mr. Kincaid," she said.

"Good morning, Doctor." He had to struggle to keep his voice neutral.

Dr. Seraphin started across the grass toward E Building. Her driver kept a steady pace next to her, his thick hand holding the umbrella as his eyes were roaming the grounds. At first Louis thought he was taking in the creepiness of the asylum as most did when they saw it for the first time. But there was something else. He had a tight walk and the alert eyes of a cop or a security officer. Or, more likely, a bodyguard. Suddenly Louis was sure that's what he was. He wondered whom Dr. Seraphin felt she needed protection from. Muggers? An ex-husband? Former crazy patients? A murderer and rapist?

"Have you told anyone we're here?"

"No, ma'am," Louis said.

She dug into her purse, withdrew a small handkerchief, and patted the spray of rain from her face. Her eyes drifted over the buildings and he knew she had to be full of memories right now. It occurred to him that she probably lived with some pretty strange images, just as he did in some ways.

"It's not so pretty anymore," she said.

"Nothing like that nice postcard of yours," Louis said.

She pointed to the scrubby brush that fringed the far trees. "There used to be rows and rows of lilacs that were bright purple in the summer, and you could smell them from anywhere on the grounds." She sighed. "Well, let's get this over with."

As the red brick of E Building took shape in the mist, Dr. Seraphin paused. She was staring at the young security officer standing on the steps.

"You said no one would see me," she said.

"I can't do anything about him," Louis said. "We suspect the killer goes in and out of E Building, and we keep someone here all the time."

Dr. Seraphin did not move.

"He won't even care who you are, Doctor," Louis said.

She continued forward. Louis stepped ahead of her and pulled out the Ardmore badge, even though he and the guard knew each other by name.

"Good morning, Zeke," Louis said.

"Morning, Mr. Kincaid."

"We need to look around inside," Louis said.

Zeke unlocked the door and stepped aside. "You going to be here long?" he asked.

"A while," Louis said.

"Can I take a few minutes to go get some coffee? I've been out here in the cold for a while now."

"Sure," Louis said, glancing at Dr. Seraphin. "Go ahead."

Zeke handed him the keys. "If you leave before I get back, lock up and leave the keys with the guys over in the admin building."

Zeke walked off and Louis let Dr. Seraphin and her driver go in ahead. She stopped in the foyer, her shoulders rising and falling with a deep sigh.

"I should have warned you," Louis said. "The upstairs has been vandalized, too."

"It looks like the staff just abandoned it."

She shook her head and moved down the hall, her heeled black boots clicking on the terrazzo floor. Then she turned back to her driver.

"Oliver," she said, "why don't you check out the building while we do this?"

Oliver hesitated, either miffed to be asked to act as a security guard or because he didn't want to leave her. But he finally turned and started up the staircase, the same one Alice had taken Louis up.

Dr. Seraphin and Louis moved on to the records room and unlocked the door.

She stared at the stacks of boxes. "I had no idea there would be so many," she said softly.

"We think he may have raped as early as 1959, so we start there."

"And you're basing that on what this Millie Reuben told you?"

"Actually, no," Louis said. "We're basing it on Claudia DeFoe's file."

Dr. Seraphin's eyes swung to his face. "Claudia DeFoe? The woman whose remains are missing?"

"Yes," Louis said. "Millie Reuben told me about isolation periods and said that's when she was raped. Claudia was also isolated three times, the first in 1959. When she was returned to the general ward afterward, she was listed as having burn marks on her."

Dr. Seraphin studied him for a moment. "Tell me, were you able to determine why Miss DeFoe was put in isolation?"

"No," Louis said. "Maybe you can tell me why these women were isolated for months at a time."

Dr. Seraphin stiffened her jaw. "Did you drag me out here to question the way I practiced psychiatry three decades ago?"

Louis hesitated. "No, I'm sorry. I was just curious as to the reasoning at the time."

She relaxed some, but she still took her time answering. "There would have been two reasons," she said. "One would have been for safety. Certain people were isolated after an incident of violence against another patient or staff member."

"And the other reason?"

"It was something new I was trying with the patients suffering from severe depression," she said. "They were isolated in an effort to gain their total dependency. Once we had that, we treated them with various stimulation therapy."

"And drugs?"

"To keep them calm, yes."

"Sounds rather superficial."

"It was," Dr. Seraphin said. "But the idea was to try to teach the brain to process images and emotions differently, not unlike today's theories of positive thinking."

"Did you see any success in it?"

"Some," Dr. Seraphin said. "But we didn't know then that depression is a chronic chemical deficiency. Nowadays, very few need inpatient treatment and most live perfectly normal lives with Prozac and its sister drugs."

Dr. Seraphin fell quiet, but she didn't look away from him and he had the feeling there was something she had left unsaid and he thought he knew what it was.

"Doctor, you remember Claudia DeFoe, don't you?"

Dr. Seraphin drew a shallow breath. "Yes. I knew the name that first day you walked into my office. I'm sorry, but I couldn't really tell you anything then."

"Can you now?"

Dr. Seraphin looked up at him. "I will only tell you that if we had had the treatments then that we have now, I believe she would be living a normal, happy life."

Louis pushed the door open wider and Dr. Seraphin went inside the records room. Louis found an old stool in the hallway and brought it over. Dr. Seraphin dusted it with her hand before sitting down.

"Did you bring the police file?" Dr. Seraphin asked.

"Yes," Louis said, handing it to her.

She started looking through the reports and photos while Louis dug for the box labeled 1959.

"He has no respect for women," Dr. Seraphin said.

Louis dropped a box in the corner. "That's pretty obvious. Most sexual predators don't."

"Why do you think he burns his victims?"

Louis shoved aside another box. "Torture. I think he gets off on their pain."

"You think he gratifies himself while he burns them?"

"Probably."

"You're wrong," she said. "The burning is not sexual, despite the placement of it on the thighs. It's a brand."

"Like cattle?" Louis asked.

"Yes. It's his symbol of ownership, done after the rape."

Louis shoved a box to the side and looked at her. "So this guy rapes his victim, then while having an after-sex smoke, he makes his mark?"

Dr. Seraphin nodded, her head bent back over the reports. After a few more minutes of reading, she looked up again.

"You didn't tell me Rebecca Gruber was raped with an object."

"We don't know what it was."

"Did you find any semen?"

"No."

"Your man is impotent," Dr. Seraphin said.

Louis shook his head. "Millie Reuben said she was raped. She said she felt him."

"Millie Ruben's rape occurred in the sixties when the man was young and healthy. And he didn't kill her," Dr. Seraphin said. "He's changed since then. He's grown angrier over the years and if he's become impotent recently, his anger is magnified by his inability to perform."

"You see anything else that will help?" he asked.

"Your killer is a man who probably held no job, had little or no contact with his family, someone who came to Hidden Lake at a young, impressionable age."

"Stereotypical profile," Louis said.

"You've done some profiling?"

"A little."

"When did you say this Stottlemyer girl was killed?"

"A little over a year ago."

"Just about when the news that the hospital would be torn down made the papers."

"You think that's why he came back?"

"Yes," Dr. Seraphin said. "He has made the prodigal journey home, Mr. Kincaid. Like we all we do when we are feeling a little lost."

Louis was quiet, his gaze drifting back to the stacks of boxes.

"You're still very young," Dr. Seraphin said. "Perhaps you can't quite relate to that need to return to something you associate with security."

"Don't be so sure."

She was watching him as he moved boxes. He could feel her eyes on his back.

"Tell me," she said. "Where did you grow up?"

"Here and there," Louis said. He finally saw the box for 1959. It had two more on top of it.

"That doesn't sound very stable," she said. "And as children, we do need stability. That's how our image of home is formed, be it good or bad."

Louis pulled out the 1959 box and slid it to the center of the floor.

"How do you remember your childhood?" she asked. "Good or bad?"

"With all due respect, Doctor," Louis said, "that's none of your business."

She sat very still, watching him, and for a moment, he felt they were in some kind of standoff and that she was debating whether to get pissed off and leave. But she smiled instead.

"My apologies for prying."

"Apology accepted."

He took the lid off the box and dropped to his knees. The box was stuffed with manila folders, some of the names handwritten, some typed, most so faded he had to pull out his glasses to read the tabs.

"One thing, Mr. Kincaid," Dr. Seraphin said. "No matter how you remember your childhood, you can change that. Any time you want."

"You can't change what happened in the past."

"I didn't say that," Dr. Seraphin said. "But you can change *how* you remember it."

"If you change how you remember it, then it's no longer accurate now, is it?"

She smiled again, a smaller one. "Who's to say it isn't? It's your memory."

He pulled out a file and held it out to her. Dr. Seraphin accepted it and flipped through the pages, then set it aside. He handed her a second and a third, glancing up at the door for the driver, wondering what he was doing.

"I have a name for you," Dr. Seraphin said suddenly. "Do you want to write them down?"

"Yes," he said, pulling a small notebook from his pocket.

"Michael Boyd."

Louis wrote the name down. "Any record of him burning or torturing anyone?"

"No, but he may not have done those things early on."

"Anything else?"

"You asked for suspects, Mr. Kincaid, not their history."

"I need a little something more."

Dr. Seraphin looked annoyed with him, but she answered. "He came in at age fourteen. Raped his baby sister with a pencil."

Louis started to write again, his pen pausing over the paper at the image her words gave him. Then he went back to pulling files.

Ten minutes later, she spoke again. "Stanley Veemer. Killed his mother at age fifteen, then set the house on fire."

He kept handing her files, occasionally taking time to read some of them himself. But he didn't know where to look to find their crimes or the reason for their commitment, and most of it was foreign to him.

She was quiet for a long time after that, the stack of nonsuspects growing so tall it tipped toward the boxes, then spilled. It occurred to Louis how pissed Alice would be if she knew they were here, looking at this stuff and making a mess.

They finished with 1959 well into the next hour and started on 1958. He could hear the rainy wind whipping at the windows and suddenly the lights started to flicker. He looked up.

Dr. Seraphin laughed softly. "Can it get any more dramatic?"

Louis slid the box to her and stood up, stepping out into the hall. The corridor was lit only by the faint gray light from outside, the pale walls alive with the thrashing shadows of branches outside.

"I have another," Dr. Seraphin called out.

Louis went back inside the room and picked up his notepad off the box.

"Buddy Ives," Dr. Seraphin said. "Came in at age eighteen. Sexually assaulted his grandmother, then killed her."

"Why didn't a guy like that end up in prison? Why here in a hospital?"

"Up until the eighties, Michigan had a law that said if a defendant pleaded insanity, it was up to the prosecution to prove he wasn't," Dr. Seraphin explained.

Louis started to question her, but then he remembered something like that from his prelaw classes. It was a crazy law, asking the state to prove sanity in a man who acted insane by the very nature of his crimes.

"I remember that," Louis said. "It was almost impossible to prove back then. People didn't want to think a man who committed the worst of crimes could be as normal as they were, so it was easy to label him as insane."

"Yes."

"But still," Louis said, "why here? Why not in a state mental hospital?"

"Those grew full very quickly. We absorbed the overflow," Dr. Seraphin said. "Of course, with a financial supplement from the state."

"Must have been a nice extra income."

"It was never enough," she said, looking down at the folder in her hand. Louis sensed she was tiring.

"How much longer you want to go?" Louis asked.

"Let's go one more year."

Louis found the next box and they started again. His hands were growing stiff from the cold. He glanced up at her. Her face was expressionless, and he wondered what she was feeling right now, suddenly thrust back into the lives of those she knew in the most intimate of ways, lives that were lost and empty and unsalvageable.

"Earl Moos," she said. "He was committed by his family," she said. "He spoke of fantasies of rape and torture."

"Did he ever follow through?"

"Not to my knowledge. He was here until 1969, and would be about . . . fifty-eight now."

A weak suspect, but Louis wrote down the name anyway. They finished up the folders for 1956 and Louis rose again to his feet, his knees creaking.

"Can you come back another time?" Louis asked.

"How do you know you won't get lucky and find your killer among the names I gave you?" she asked.

Louis stuck the notebook in his pocket. "I don't put much stock in luck, Doctor."

"No," she said. "I don't suppose you would."

He held the door for her. They paused in

the corridor. "Where's your driver?" Louis asked.

"He wouldn't leave the building," Dr. Seraphin said. "He's not far, I assure you. Why do you ask? Are you afraid your killer will get him?"

"This is no game, Doctor," Louis said. "The man has been inside this building and he is dangerous."

Dr. Seraphin's eyes swept over the graffiti-scarred walls and the shadowed doorways.

"I think we better go look for him," Louis said.

Chapter 29

They went to the front entrance first, but there was no sign of Oliver in the lobby or outside. Louis started back down the hall, Dr. Seraphin close behind. They were near the back of the ground floor when Louis stopped suddenly.

Smoke. A bare whiff of it in the cold air.

Louis put out a hand to keep Dr. Seraphin back. He moved forward slowly toward the room at the end of the hall. With a quick glance back at the doctor, he stepped inside.

Oliver was standing in the corner, a cigarette frozen in his hand.

"Jesus," Louis breathed.

A moment later, Dr. Seraphin was at his side. She stared into the room at Oliver.

"What are you doing?" she demanded.

"I just wanted a smoke, ma'am," he said. "It was too cold to go outside." Oliver had snuffed out the cigarette and was standing there like a boy caught in a dirty deed.

Dr. Seraphin gave Oliver a frown, but slowly her eyes began to wander over the

362

plastic tables and stainless steel countertops.

Louis realized the room looked cleaner than the last time he had been in it. He guessed that the state cops had searched the building after Rebecca Gruber was found. He noticed dark fingerprint powder smudges around the windowsills and door frames.

As he took a step into the room, something caught his eye in the faint light. It was a large can, and he knew it hadn't been here before.

He walked to it. It had been opened with a can opener, but the top was pushed down inside. He got out a pen and used the tip to lift it open.

The can was half-full of creamed corn, a large serving spoon stuck in it. Louis used the lid to turn it so he could read the label. Southern Michigan Food Supply. Hidden Lake Hospital.

"Doctor," Louis said, "any idea where this might have come from?"

Dr. Seraphin came up behind him. "The hospital kitchen, I would presume."

Louis pushed the lid back down to see if there was any stamping or embossing on top. There was none, and he grabbed an old paper towel from the floor and used it to lift the can up so he could see the bottom. In small print, stamped on the bottom, he saw a series of letters and numbers, and the date April 1987. Over a year ago.

"I'd bet there are a lot of these missing from the kitchen over the past few years," Louis said.

"The police didn't think to take that?" Dr. Seraphin asked.

Louis set the can down and stood up. "It wasn't here when they searched. I'd bet it's been here less than a day or two."

"But that young man, the guard we saw outside, missed it," Dr. Seraphin said.

"The guard isn't a cop. He has no idea what to look for," Louis said.

"Maybe the police don't either," Dr. Seraphin said. "If they knew what they were looking for, they'd be as convinced as you that the key to this man's existence is this building, and they'd have people here."

Louis was quiet, not wanting to tell the doctor she was right. There was a cold breeze drifting in from somewhere and Louis looked around for a new broken window. He found it near the back of the room. But he was surprised to see it wasn't broken but just lifted open. The steel grating on the outside was screwed to the bricks, but the screws were loose, easily removed and replaced by hand.

"He has a new entrance, too," Louis said.

"And again," Dr. Seraphin said, "the guard heard nothing, saw nothing."

She was right again. Once he told the state police about the corn and the open window, they would have no choice but to put cops out here twenty-four hours. And do hourly walk-throughs. Maybe they could somehow push this man back into the open and leave him with nowhere else to go. Then maybe, just maybe, he might make a mistake.

Louis made a mental note to make sure he went back around to this window to tighten the screws before he left. Better yet, he'd find a way to keep the grating permanently fastened. And when he could, he'd do that with all the windows and shut this bastard out of the hospital completely.

He turned to see that Dr. Seraphin and Oliver had left the room. He followed them, deeper down the hall. He was trying to place where he was, and he realized they were near the narrow caged staircase that led to the upper floors.

"Do you smell that?" Dr. Seraphin asked.

Louis stopped, inhaling. It was urine. And not stale. And there was something else far more putrid.

Dr. Seraphin pushed open a plain white door.

It was a small bathroom. The white walls were splashed with spray-painted red graffiti and pentagrams. The floor was littered with soiled toilet paper, beer cans, and cigarette butts. The toilet was full of yellow water and feces.

"I find this man fascinating," Dr. Seraphin said, walking away from Louis. "He moves about this building with extreme comfort, despite the constant presence of the guards, the workers, and the staff."

"Is he smart?" Louis asked. "Or just gutsy?"

"He is neither," she said. "It's just that he operates with a logic you cannot. He sees this as his world and he moves with such ease and confidence in it I'm sure he feels he's invisible to everyone else."

"Explain," Louis said.

She shook her head, and he sensed she was annoyed at his ignorance.

"I need any help I can get, Doctor," Louis said, trying to be patient.

"His feeling of invisibility started when

he was very young," she said. "Either he was ignored and grew up believing he was in some way invisible to his parents or he was abused, which forces a child to wish he were invisible to prevent further harm."

"If he thinks he's invisible, why doesn't he just walk in the front door, right past the guard?" Louis said.

Dr. Seraphin smiled at his question. "You're thinking too literally. His belief is far more abstract. Because he's learned to behave in ways that keep him invisible, he will not do anything to change that."

Louis didn't want to admit to her he wasn't following. There was something else in his head, and he tried to push it away but the images kept playing.

A foster home, the last one before he had come to live with Phillip and Frances. That two-story brick house on Strathmoor, owned by Moe and the woman with the brassy red hair.

A closet. Small. Dark. And thick with the smells of dirty clothes and urine-stained sheets from the bunk bed under his that belonged to a tiny, brown-skinned boy whose name Louis couldn't remember.

There was a rope tied to the inside doorknob of the closet, and Louis was holding the rope with both fists to keep the door from being opened from the outside.

But he could hear Moe looking for them. Hear him throwing things and shouting for the little boy to come out and take his whipping for peeing the bed.

And Louis was holding the rope with all his might, but the door jerked open, ripping the rope from Louis's hands, and Moe's big body stood over them, a silhouette against the sunlit bedroom window, his kinky black hair a raging explosion around his head.

Moe jerked the little boy from the closet and threw him onto the lower bunk, and Moe's hand started coming back in long, vicious strokes, the leather snapping every time it hit skin.

And Louis remembered cowering back against the clothing and sheets, knees against his chest, eyes closed, praying Moe would not see him. Praying that just for once, he could be invisible.

"Mr. Kincaid."

He looked at Dr. Seraphin. "What?"

"Let's go on and see what else this man left us," she said.

Louis followed her farther down the hall. Ahead of him on his right, he saw the green door with PASSAGE 12 stenciled on it. Only now, a strip of yellow tape was strung across it.

Louis stepped to it quickly.

The yellow tape had MICHIGAN STATE POLICE stamped on it and hung loosely from the metal door frame. The frame had been pried away from the wall and the door had been forced open. It was now ajar and Louis pushed it inward, opening it the rest of the way.

The slim light illuminated dirty yellow tile walls and a concrete ramp that sloped downward. Once level, the floor turned to a gray tile that disappeared into the darkness ten or twelve feet deeper in.

"Where does this go?" he asked.

Dr. Seraphin was standing a few feet behind and she didn't come to the door. "It's a tunnel, Mr. Kincaid. There's a network of them connecting the buildings. We used them in the wintertime to transport food, supplies, patients, whatever we needed to."

He looked at her, stunned. "Why didn't you tell me about these before?"

"Excuse me?"

His voice grew sharper than he intended, but he couldn't help it. "This man gets in and out of these buildings like a ghost and you didn't think to mention there are tunnels here?"

"As you can see," she said, motioning to the pried door frame, "this door was not

369

accessible to anyone before the police opened it. It was sealed in the late seventies because the tunnels had been declared unsafe. And we didn't have the money to repair them."

Louis stepped down the ramp and looked at the inside of the door. There was no handle there, either. Only a thick, steel latch that had once been welded to the frame. It was not something that could have been easily removed by someone without tools, and now that it had been opened, the door no longer closed flush.

Louis shoved the door all the way open to gain as much light as possible and started down the ramp.

The air grew cold with a dirty dampness that made it hard to breathe. He could hear water dripping, see rusty streaks on the walls.

Louis stopped. *Damn it.* He needed a flashlight. He needed backup, too. He had no business going down here alone.

He started to turn back when something ahead caught his eye — a splash of gray in the faint shifting light. He went forward a few more feet. The darkness came down around him, and he felt his heart quicken as his eyes adjusted. Then it came into focus.

A cinder-block wall.

He moved to it, running his hand over the cold blocks from one end to the other. The wall filled the width and height of the narrow tunnel.

He pushed on it, but it didn't give. Then he shoved forward on individual blocks, making sure none of them was loose. It was solid. Louis dusted his hands on his jeans and backed away, still looking around. The side walls looked intact, and the ceiling was water stained but in one piece, a string of electrical sockets still in place. There were no other entrances. He walked back to the ramp.

Dr. Seraphin stood near the door, arms crossed. She looked amused.

"You should have told me it was bricked off," Louis said.

"And what good would it have done?" she asked. "You still would have gone down there to see for yourself."

He pulled the door closed as far as it would come. He couldn't believe the state police hadn't sealed it back up. The killer could easily smash away a few of the blocks, giving him access to other tunnels to hide in.

"Are all the buildings connected by these tunnels?" he asked Dr. Seraphin.

She nodded.

"Are they all bricked off like this?" he asked.

"Yes."

"Is there any way into the tunnels other than from the buildings?"

Dr. Seraphin had her hand on her chin, one finger pressed into her cheek. "Your mind is interesting. There's always another question to be answered, isn't there?"

"Yes, ma'am. And you haven't answered it."

"No, the only entrances are from the buildings," she said. She ran a hand over her cropped gray hair. "Mr. Kincaid, if you have no more need of me, I really need to get going."

Louis's eyes went to Oliver standing vigil behind her. "Thanks for your time, Doctor."

She smiled slightly, picking up on his irritation with her. She headed back down the hall toward the entrance, Oliver trailing.

He waited until they had left; then he backtracked to the records room. He picked up the police case files for Rebecca Gruber and Sharon Stottlemeyer, then paused.

The folders of the four men Dr. Seraphin had singled out were sitting alone near the stool. He already had their names in his notebook, but he needed more information. History, addresses, relatives, release dates. Anything that could help him find them.

Taking the files was illegal. But no more illegal than what Dr. Seraphin had already done. And he would never be able to reveal how he got the names anyway.

He picked up the four folders and his umbrella. Tucking the folders in his jacket, he went outside.

There was no sign of Zeke, the security guard. He'd been gone for more than two hours. Probably still on break in the administration building. Louis hurried to his car, dumped the folders in the backseat, and trotted to the administration building.

He stopped inside the door to shake the water from the umbrella. He needed to call the state police to tell them about the corn can and to convince them to come back and weld the tunnel doors closed.

There was a small room off the lobby that the security guards had commandeered as their break room, and when Louis went to the door, there were two guards sitting at a table sharing a thermos of coffee. He put in a call to the state police. The guy who took his message promised it would get to the right person, but as he hung up the phone Louis doubted it would. He made a mental note to call Dalum and tell him to put on some pressure.

Louis turned to the two guards at the table.

"You guys seen Zeke?" Louis asked.

"He was here about an hour ago when I came in," one of the men said. "I think he went back out."

Louis pulled Zeke's keys from his pocket. He was about to hand them over to the guard when the thought hit him. It could take days for the state police to get back down here to close the tunnels back up. The killer could have already found his way back in. Maybe the guy was down there now. And if they acted quickly, they could have him trapped.

Louis pocketed the keys and went back outside. At the Impala, he grabbed a flashlight he had stowed in the trunk yesterday and the diagram of the hospital grounds from the backseat.

Then he popped the glove box and took out his Glock. He hooked it on his belt and started off toward the nearest building.

Chapter 30

He was only going to check to make sure the cinder-block walls in the tunnels had not been compromised. That was all.

It was logical that the administration building would be connected to the tunnels, so that is where he would begin.

He didn't tell anyone what he was doing. He just walked the ground floor, looking for steel doors with no handles. Finally, he found one, painted green like the one in E Building, with PASSAGE 2 stenciled on it. Also like the one in E Building, it had been pried open and had yellow tape on it.

Louis pulled it open, flicked on his flashlight, and went down the sloping ramp. The tunnel had the same damp smell as the other one, and about twenty feet in Louis came to an intact cinder-block wall. Making sure it was secure, he backtracked. At the back of the building, he found a second tunnel door marked PASSAGE 1. It, too, was taped and securely bricked off. After he was positive there were no other tunnel entries in the building, Louis went outside.

He unfolded Spera's map and pulled a pen from his jacket. He made marks on the administration building outline where he had found the tunnel doors, numbering them 1 and 2.

There were seventeen buildings on the map. He looked around, trying to get the lay of the grounds. To his right was a large red brick dormitory-like building. The map identified it as Employee Housing. He decided he would start there and work his way around the grounds counterclockwise.

Luckily, the keys on the big ring Zeke had given him were all marked. He unlocked the main door and went in. Like most of the buildings, it had already been stripped inside by the salvage crews, the doors, office furniture, and anything of even remote value carted away. Louis noticed all the windows were secure as he made his way through the first floor of the large, L-shaped dormitory.

Finally, at the back north end, he found a steel door stenciled PASSAGE 3, pried open with the yellow tape lying on the floor. He shouldered the door open and went down the slope, flicking on the flashlight. About twenty feet in, he came to the cinder-block wall. No sign that it had been compromised.

After searching the rest of the building, he was confident there was only one tunnel door. He marked the door "3" on the map and went back out the front, locking up behind him.

To the east was a small plain building that the map said was the police and fire headquarters. A quick tour told him there were no tunnel doors in it. He found the same thing true of the small one-story cafeteria behind the housing building, but it was connected to the dormitory by a walkway, so he suspected the employees hadn't needed a tunnel to go back and forth for meals.

He headed north, toward the commissary. It was another small one-story building, but it was made of wood and looked to be much newer than the red brick buildings. Inside, the shelves and counters were bare. There were no other doors except the one he had entered.

Outside again, he trudged across the ice-crusted grass, heading north toward the mammoth, spired infirmary. He couldn't remember if he had seen any of the numbered passage doors when he had been down in the mortuary before. He didn't really want to go back in there, but he had no choice.

Unlocking the double front doors, he entered the gloom of the old infirmary's lobby. Down in the basement, he went slowly along the tiled corridor, searching for passage doors. Finally, he spotted the telltale heavy steel door. It was stenciled PASSAGE 9. That meant there had to be others in here. He found the cinder-block secure and came back out.

It took him a good half hour to find passage 8, which was also blocked off. It was so dark in the maze of basement corridors, he had to use his flashlight. Finally, he found himself in front of the door with MORTUARY stenciled on the glass. He went in, his footsteps echoing loudly in his ears as he ran the flashlight beam over the empty rooms.

The light came to a stop on the plain door. The columbarium. He hesitated. He knew Spera had taken all the cremation cans out, but he couldn't remember if there were any doors in the small room or not. He took a deep breath and pushed the door open.

The flashlight beam swept over the room. He forced himself to check every corner, trying not to look at the small sandlike mounds that dotted the empty shelves. He backed out, exhaling.

Back in the main corridor, he was almost to the staircase when his flashlight picked up a spot of bright yellow. A tail of crime scene tape. It led him down a narrow short hallway to an open steel door. Passage 7. He had almost missed it.

He went down the tunnel slope. The concrete floor was puddled and he could hear the drip of water somewhere. He swung the beam up over the walls and saw water seeping in from the low ceiling where the light fixtures once hung. Finally, about twenty feet in, the gray block wall emerged from the gloom. Louis moved the beam over it to make sure it was in place and quickly retraced his steps.

Outside, he paused on the portico to take in a deep breath of cold air and mark the three passages. He was facing south and could see the commissary and beyond that, the back of the dormitory.

The passage from the dormitory had faced due north. But it didn't connect with the commissary. So where did that tunnel go? Did it span the entire width of the compound and connect to the basement of the infirmary? That would make it maybe a half mile long.

His eyes traveled over the grounds, over the buildings with their empty windows looking back at him, and the realization hit him.

There were a hundred and eighty acres here, and there could be miles of these tunnels going in every direction, some of them possibly running under buildings with no exits. If he missed just one door, the whole security of the compound could be compromised. He had to be careful and do this right.

The power plant was next — a huge brick box with its towering smokestack thrusting two hundred feet into the gray sky. He went through the front door and the warren of offices, emerging into what he assumed had been a main boiler room once. It was a drafty, cavernous place with steel girders above and a dirty tile floor below. A bank of large windows fed the place with gray light that revealed six sets of gigantic turbines.

He spotted a door on the far wall of gauges and switches and went to it. The door led down a hall that dead-ended at a steel door. Passage 5. He confirmed that it was blocked off. Twenty minutes later, he emerged from the power plant, marking off passages 4, 5, and 6.

It was the same in the next three buildings he went in — the men's and women's wards and a huge decrepit building identified on the map only as D Ward. By the time he finished his tour of the laundry and the kitchen, he was able to check off passages 10 through 17. All had been yellow-taped by the state police and all were solidly walled off.

It was nearly two by the time he made it to L Building on the far western edge of the compound. His teeth were chattering and his hands numb as he stood outside, holding the map. L Building, the map indicated, was Occupational Therapy.

The inside was a mess. Old metal desks and file cabinets. Ramps, handrailed stairsteps, and padded wooden tables. Battered wheelchairs and a pile of old crutches. But it was all organized in a way that made Louis believe that this was where the salvage crew had set up some kind of holding area for their work. His suspicion was confirmed when he spotted a box of tools on a counter emblazoned with VASQUEZ SALVAGE.

He began his tour of the ground floor. He forced himself to go slow, his flashlight beam moving over the piles of junk and down the dark hallways. Finally, he found passage 18. It was blocked off.

He kept searching but didn't find any

other doors. Standing in an empty hallway, he pulled out the map. Something didn't seem right. All the other buildings had been connected to each other — except for the store and police headquarters — but they weren't used by patients. By that logic, the occupational therapy building *should* be connected to M Building next door, which the map said was Physical Therapy. There had to be another passage in here somewhere.

But where the hell was it? He had been through this building twice now. Maybe his theory was wrong. Maybe he was just cold, tired, and getting impatient.

Pocketing the map, he went back to the entrance and started over. He was about to give up when he saw a stack of doors leaning against a corner in a dark hallway. He went to the stack and shone the flashlight behind the doors.

The steel door was there.

Shit . . .

Setting the flashlight down, Louis began moving the heavy doors. He was sweating by the time passage 19 was revealed. The door was shut. No tape. The state cops had missed it.

He glanced around, looking for something to pry the door open with; then he remembered the tools and went back to get a crowbar.

It took him a good half hour to get the door open. The hinges were rusted and he could barely get it ajar. But it was enough to slip through. Wiping his face, he clicked on the flashlight and entered the gloom of the tunnel.

A putrid smell made him put a hand over his mouth. He was halfway down the slope when his shoe hit something soft and he skidded down. He threw out a hand to brace his fall and swung the light back.

Fuck . . .

A dead rat, writhing with maggots. He had stepped in it. Swallowing hard, he stood up. Directing the flashlight beam ahead, he moved on.

Twenty feet . . . thirty feet . . . how far had he gone?

It was so dark he couldn't see anything but the thin path made by the flashlight. He had a sense of being closed in, like this tunnel wasn't very wide or high. But he wasn't sure.

Where the hell was the cinder-block wall?

Forty . . . fifty feet?

His footsteps echoed in his ears, close, as if someone were walking directly behind him.

Something gray up ahead.

Louis let out a breath. Cinder block. He moved forward to make sure it was intact. But as he swung his flashlight to the left, it fell away into blackness.

Jesus. This wasn't a wall. It was a turn. The tunnel didn't end; it turned south.

He trained the beam into the bend. It disappeared, the light falling off into nothingness.

He swung the light back toward the direction he had come from. Black. But at least he knew there was a door back there.

Then he heard it. A steady *thud-thud* sound. Thud-*thud* . . . thud-*thud*, getting louder, louder. It took him a moment to realize it was his own pulse pounding in his ears.

He squinted into the darkness ahead. He could go get help. Or he could go forward and make sure the tunnel was secure at the other end.

What time is it?

He flicked the beam up to his wristwatch. Three. Why did it feel as if he had been down here for hours?

Go, Kincaid . . . go on, get this over with and get out of here.

Training the flashlight ahead, he moved forward.

The walls . . . old tiles . . . yellow and stained with rivulets of dark brown liquid. Steam pipes above, laid out like sinew and bones. Twenty more feet . . . thirty . . . forty.

He kept the flashlight beam low, concentrating it on the floor, forcing himself to watch the tips of his shoes as he walked.

Something ahead. A dull glint. The flashlight beam jumped in his hand, then steadied. A door at the top of a gently sloping ramp. Another steel door.

It had a handle. He gave it a pull. Nothing. The door didn't move. He set the flashlight on the floor and grabbing the handle with both hands, he pulled again.

Nothing.

He staggered backward, wiping a hand across his face. Pulling in a deep breath, he grabbed the handle again and pulled hard. It gave way and opened with a loud scrape. Dust and a dim light flooded the tunnel. He grabbed the flashlight and squeezed through the opening.

For a second or two, Louis just stood there, hands on knees, eyes closed. Then he straightened and looked around. He was in a large ground-floor room. As his breathing slowed, things came into focus: shelves . . . rows and rows of them. It looked like a storage room of some kind. A low-slanting light was coming through the grated windows, but it was too weak for him to make out details. He turned the flashlight up over the shelves. They were empty, but he could make out the faded label on the nearest one: CONDIMENTS. He moved the light down the long rows of shelving and picked out other labels: FLOUR. SUGAR.

The warehouse . . . he remembered now seeing it on the map. He unfolded the map. Yes . . . a large building in the far southwestern corner of the compound. He had to be in the warehouse.

He walked slowly through the rows of shelves. There were cans on some of the shelves, he saw now, large dusty cans. He stopped and turned one around. The blue label said STEWED TOMATOES. And it had the distinctive lettering he had seen before: SOUTHERN MICHIGAN FOOD SUPPLIERS.

So this was where he got his food. But how did he get in and out? Was that tunnel he had just come through somehow connected all the way back to E Building?

He found his way to the front entrance and flipped the lock, going out into the cold air. He stood on the frozen grass, looking north to the physical therapy building. He turned to his right and in dim light, he could just make out the spires of the infirmary far off in the northeast. He couldn't see E Building, but he knew it was there, just behind the infirmary, out on the farthest corner of the compound.

How in the hell did this guy get all the way from there to here without being detected?

There was only one answer. Somehow the tunnels were connected, despite the cinder-block walls. There was an entrance somewhere, and he had missed it.

He was too tired and too cold to go back and look again — alone. He locked the warehouse door and pulling up the collar of his jacket, started back across the compound.

As he was walking past the back entrance of the administration building, one of the guards he had seen earlier emerged.

"Hey," Louis called out, "you seen Zeke?"

"Nah. He probably left already. His shift was over at three." The man hurried off to his car.

Louis hesitated, then set off for E Building. He hadn't gone in there on his search for the tunnels, but he couldn't remember if he had locked it when he and

Dr. Seraphin left earlier. Zeke was probably still waiting for him there to return the keys.

Hunched into his jacket, Louis cut a quick diagonal across the compound, passing the infirmary entrance and turning left to E Building.

Sure enough, he had left the door unlocked. He went into the lobby. It was dark inside and icy cold.

"Zeke?" Louis called out. "You in here?"

No answer.

"Hey, Zeke!"

His voice echoed and died. Louis turned to go back out the door. The beam of the flashlight picked up a spot of color on the floor.

Blood. Louis dropped to one knee, touching a finger to the stain on the terrazzo floor. It was wet, but cool to the touch. And there was more. Trailing toward the staircase, small smears that looked brushed on the terrazzo like paint. On the bottom step, a larger, thicker streak.

Louis drew his Glock and moved the flashlight beam over the steps of the dim stairwell. The blood grew darker and heavier as the steps went up, and Louis followed the path, pressing himself against the wall to avoid stepping in it.

"Zeke!" he shouted.

His voice hung unanswered in the cold air. He reached the second-floor landing. The door was ajar, the edge covered in bloody fingerprints where someone had pulled it open. The floor was puddled and smeared with splashes of red.

"Zeke!" Louis screamed.

Nothing.

Louis stepped out onto the second floor, spinning first right, then left. The blood trail went left, down the hall, long, crimson streaks along the floor, like a body was being dragged. But there was so much blood, Louis knew the body had still been bleeding, the person still alive, when it was moved.

He stayed near the wall, listening for any noise, his eyes following the blood almost to the end of the hall. Then the bloody path took a sharp right turn to a closed door. The plate on the door read THERAPY. Under that, there was a slot for another plate, but it was empty.

Louis stood stiff against the door frame, slowly reaching down to try the knob. When he touched it, the door eased open and Louis stepped away from it, leveling the gun.

He heard nothing and after a few seconds, he stole a look inside.

The room was no more than ten by ten feet. The faded yellow walls were defaced with red and black graffiti. There was no furniture.

Zeke was propped up against the far wall. His chin was on his chest, his light hair wet with blood, arms limp at his side, legs spread out in front of him. His navy blue uniform was shiny with blood.

Louis stepped inside, checking behind the door, then spinning back to Zeke. He dropped to one knee and put a hand to Zeke's forehead to tilt his head back.

Louis swallowed back a small gag.

Zeke's throat was slashed, the skin ripped and ragged, like it had been torn apart with short angry strokes.

Louis drew back and pulled in a breath to calm the rising bile and anger. Then he stood quickly and reached for the door, his head spinning.

The man might still be inside E Building somewhere, but Louis wasn't sure whether to search now or leave Zeke here while he went back to the administration building to call the police.

Damn it.

Why had this happened? Why wasn't he halfway down the hall, going after this guy already?

The radio. Zeke's radio. Louis started to reach down to Zeke's belt, but his eyes caught a bright streak of red on the wall above Zeke's head.

It was mixed in with the other graffiti, but Louis could see now it was fresh, still dripping, and written in blood.

One word: BITCH. And a bloody handprint.

Chapter 31

The rain had turned to snow by the time the state police arrived. The dark blue patrol cars in the parking lot looked as if they had been sprinkled with powdered sugar. A few uniforms stood rigid at doorways, others darted in and out of buildings, scrambling to find some trace of Zeke's killer.

Louis stood just inside the door to E Building, hands in his pockets, watching the snowfall. Down the hall, troopers were scouring the rooms and he could hear them opening and closing doors. Another trooper stood on the landing between the first and second floors, arms crossed, posture stiff. Louis could hear a clamor of voices, footsteps, and radio transmissions coming from upstairs.

He stepped outside, staying under the portico. He saw a black van coming across the grass and guessed it was the medical examiner or coroner. Behind it was an unmarked state car with a light on the dash.

Louis looked out across the grounds. They could send a hundred men and he doubted they would find the killer. He thought about the four files in his car, and he knew he should turn them over. But it was going to be impossible to justify having them and harder yet to tell the state police how he got the patients' names in the first place.

The door opened and a man pushed out. Tall, bulky, his face ruddy from too many Michigan winters, his hair a golden brush cut on a square head. He wore a navy peacoat, a gold badge on the front, the buttons pulling across a wide chest.

"You Louis Kincaid?"

"Yes," Louis said.

The man sniffed from the cold and gave him a hard stare. "I'm Detective Bloom, State Police. They tell me you're a private detective. You got some paper?"

Louis wondered who had told this man he was a P.I. He had hoped the Ardmore P.D. badge would get him by these questions. Maybe it still would.

Louis showed him the badge. "I am a P.I., but I'm working with the Ardmore police."

Bloom looked at the badge, snorting softly. "Some hick chief handing you a piece of tin doesn't make you a cop here. You got a P.I. license?"

"In Florida."

"What the hell are you doing here?"

"I'm trying to locate a former patient for a friend, that's all."

The detective reached inside his coat and pulled out a notebook, flipping it open with one hand. "What's the patient's name?"

Louis looked at him. He didn't want to give anyone Claudia's name, but he knew they had to check him out, and that would mean going back as far as they could. He had no idea what they'd find, or what might still be on record for him in Michigan.

"Claudia DeFoe."

Bloom wrote it down. "Your address here and in Florida, your middle name, and your Social Security number, Kincaid."

Louis gave him the information, his eyes drifting across the grounds. He saw a white police car in the distance and wondered if it was Dalum.

"Why were you in this building?" Bloom asked.

Louis kept his eyes on the parking lot. This was going to get messy real quick. "I was helping Chief Dalum investigate the murder of Rebecca Gruber and —"

"I thought you were looking for this DeFoe woman."

"It started out that way, but then Chief Dalum asked me to assist him with —"

"I told Dalum to let us handle it."

"It's his town," Louis said. "He's protective of it. He was just trying to help."

Two men from the county van came up the steps with a gurney and a body bag, and Louis and Bloom stepped aside to let them pass.

"We don't need his help," Bloom said. "Or yours. Did it occur to you that maybe by sneaking around out here, you set this guy off and you got that guard killed?"

Louis tightened his jaw, biting back his first reply. Bloom was partly right. But he hadn't been the one to set the killer off. Louis believed it might have been Dr. Seraphin whom the killer was calling a bitch. And he knew he needed to tell Bloom that. But there was no way to say it and not lose Dr. Seraphin as an ally.

"You fucking amateurs," Bloom said.

"Look," Louis said, "when Rebecca Gruber was murdered, you guys made a big show out of coming out here and working the scene. But despite the fact that this place is enclosed by a fence, and the victim was an on-duty employee, and the killer likely lives out here somewhere, you left *no one* here for surveillance or to protect the remaining employees."

"Now I got some private dick telling me how to run my investigation," Bloom said.

"You didn't even seal the tunnels back off," Louis snapped.

"They're all walled up, you dumb shit."

"Well, you missed one. At least."

"You been down there?"

"Yeah."

"I oughta bust you for that."

"Go ahead."

The door banged open and three uniforms came out. Bloom grabbed Louis's arm and pulled him off the steps and onto the grass. The snow was growing heavier and Louis jerked up the collar of his jacket.

"You carrying a gun, Kincaid?"

He *was* carrying a concealed weapon, and he knew Michigan was supposed to recognize his Florida permit. But Bloom seemed like the kind of guy who had his own way of doing things.

Bloom noticed Louis's hesitation and thrust out his hand.

"Let me see it," he said.

Louis reached under his jacket and withdrew the Glock, holding it out to Bloom by the trigger guard.

Bloom took it, then held out his other hand. "Now your Florida P.I. license and CCW permit."

Louis dug them out his wallet and handed them to Bloom. Bloom eyed them both, then looked up.

"Okay, P.I.," he said. "Tell me what you know about this case."

Louis blew out a breath. "The chief and I think it's an ex-patient, probably come home to make some kind of statement about the place closing."

"What makes you think that?"

"All three victims were killed here and left here."

"You're so smart, why bury one and leave the other girl above ground where we can find her?"

"He didn't bury Rebecca Gruber because he couldn't," Louis said. "The cemetery had security posted. He had to take her somewhere else."

"Still could've buried her."

"Maybe he didn't have time," Louis said. "Maybe the ground was too hard. Maybe he just didn't care if we found her."

"Why kill the guard at all?" Bloom asked. "You think the guard saw him?"

"No. No one sees this guy. He thinks he's invisible. He killed him because he wanted attention."

Bloom took a long look around the grounds. "And you think this guy lives out here somewhere?"

"Yeah, I do," Louis said. "Look at the stuff he left in this building — a cigarette, a can of corn. He used the toilet. And I have one more thing for you. The warehouse."

Louis pointed to the far southwest corner of the grounds. "That's where he took the food from. It has two exits to tunnels. One of them is not bricked off and leads to the men's ward."

"And are the tunnels in the men's ward bricked off?"

"Yeah," Louis said. "But there are other tunnels that go completely under some of the buildings."

"So, what's your point?"

"That there has to be another entrance to the tunnels somewhere," Louis said, "something that connects underneath and allows him to get to the warehouse unnoticed. We're just not seeing it."

"*You're* not seeing it," Bloom said, "because it isn't there. We searched every entrance. Maybe the man gets into the warehouse through a goddamn window, Kincaid."

Louis's thoughts were rushed and he couldn't shut up. "Have you checked the basements? Maybe there's a hidden entrance to the tunnels. Maybe that's how he gets in and out."

"We checked. When they added the tunnels, they ran them down off the first floors 'cause the basements were such a mess. Except for the mortuary, all the basements were closed off. Concrete walls and broken pipes. Nothing there."

"Then where does he keep his supplies?" Louis asked. "Where's the can opener? Where's the rest of the cans he's hoarded away? And *where* do you think he killed Rebecca Gruber?"

"I don't know. Maybe he lives in a farmhouse on the other side of the trees," Bloom snapped. "He's not a mole."

"Don't be so sure."

Bloom snickered. "Well, I'll tell you what, P.I. You wanna see surveillance out here, you're going to see it. But he won't. We'll be hidden all over this place. If he even farts, we'll hear him."

"What about the employees?"

"They're out of here. As of right now."

"They have to finish closing up," Louis said.

"After we catch this guy, they can

finish," Bloom said. "For now, everyone's out of here. And that goes for you, too. You can pin that Ardmore badge on your forehead if you want but it's not going to get you access in here. You got that?"

Louis drew in a tight breath, knowing Bloom was right. Pulling everyone out and sitting in the shadows waiting for the killer to make a move was the smartest thing to do. But Louis wondered what the killer would do when he saw the place deserted and he had no more potential victims around.

And there was still Dr. Seraphin.

She needed to know what had happened here today, what was written on the wall. And she needed to know that it was obvious this man was someone who had a special attachment to his former doctor. A violent one.

Once she knew all that, maybe she would be willing to approach the state police with the same information she had given him. He had to give her that chance before telling Bloom they had already been through the files.

Bloom called to a uniform standing nearby and the man came over, looking at them from under the snow-covered brim of a garrison cap.

"Officer, I'd like you to take Kincaid here back to the station in Adrian."

"Yes, sir."

"Are you arresting me?" Louis asked.

"Let's just say we're going to keep an eye on you while we check you out."

"Aw, Jesus."

Bloom handed the officer the Glock. "Lock this up and don't give it back until he shows you an airline ticket to Florida."

Bloom walked away, and Louis looked at the officer. His face was set, shoulders stiff. Louis spun and started walking toward the parking lot. The cop followed, silent, always staying a few feet behind him. When they reached the cluster of patrol cars, Louis hesitated and the cop motioned to one, finally stepping ahead of him. Then he opened the back door and held it for Louis.

The ride was a long, silent journey through a misty white landscape, south on Highway 223. As they drove into Adrian, Louis stared out the window. The place looked a little like Dexter, the town where he had found Millie Reuben. He saw a sign telling him it was the county seat for Lenawee County, and before they got to the state substation, they passed a beautiful old red brick courthouse with gold arches and a flag high atop a white spire.

The car pulled to a slippery stop and the officer opened his door for him. Louis was led inside a building that looked like one of the smaller buildings at Hidden Lake, two stories of brick with long rectangle windows. Once inside, the officer passed him off to another uniform, who gave him to a man in a suit who asked for Louis's ID. Louis handed it to him, and was then told to sit in a hallway on a hard bench.

He doubted they would offer him a ride back to Hidden Lake and he finally got up, found a pay phone, and called Chief Dalum to come get him. As he hung up, it occurred to him that he should call Dr. Seraphin, too.

He dug her card from his pocket. A clerk at her Ann Arbor office answered, so he left a message for the doctor to call him at Phillip's tonight, then changed his mind and gave her Dalum's office number. He reminded the clerk again how urgent it was that he talk to Dr. Seraphin tonight. Then he walked outside and stood on the steps.

He could see the courthouse from here. His mind drifted back to the bloody hall in E Building and the word *bitch* written on the wall above Zeke's head. And he couldn't help but wonder if Seraphin knew who had written it.

He thought about the way she had profiled the killer so quickly, and he had no idea if that came from experience or a subconscious — or even conscious — memory. But why would she hide his identity? Embarrassment that she couldn't — or didn't — help him?

That was crazy. She was a doctor. And she was doing all she could to help, including breaking doctor-patient confidentiality.

A siren caught his attention and he watched a Lenawee County Sheriff's car pull away from the courthouse.

Something else hit him.

Hidden Lake was in Lenawee County, and courthouses had planning and zoning records, and even blueprints for structures. He glanced back at the doors to the state police substation. In the hall stood the trooper who had taken his ID. Louis went back inside.

The officer saw him coming and held out the cards. "You're free to go. But Detective Bloom wanted me to give you a message."

"Yeah, what?" Louis asked.

"He said to tell you you'll get the gun

back when you leave the state, and not to come around the hospital again or one of the surveillance officers just might shoot you by mistake."

"He can't keep my gun."

"I'm just the messenger." The officer walked away.

Louis stuffed the cards back in his wallet and pushed back out the front doors, heading toward the Lenawee County Courthouse.

Inside, he found the planning and zoning department, and waited behind three people filing construction permits. The office was small and overly warm, and he pulled off his jacket. Twenty minutes later, he was at the counter and facing a plump woman with yellow curls and jingle-bell earrings that tinkled when she moved.

"Can you get me the blueprints or building plans for Hidden Lake Hospital?" he asked.

"The insane asylum over near Ardmore?"

"Yes."

"Well, I don't know. Got a Sidwell number for me?"

"A what?"

"Got a parcel identification number?"

"No."

She turned away from him. "You're

lucky I got some holiday spirit here," she said over her shoulder. "Lucky, too, I know where that nuthouse is."

With a jingle of her earrings, she opened a large bound book and started flipping pages. After a few minutes, she disappeared into a back room.

Louis wandered over to the wall and absently read the notices, sometimes glancing out the window at the snow. He wondered if he would be able get back to Plymouth tonight. He could stay with Dalum again, but it was going to be hard not to share with him what he and Seraphin had done. But how was he going to track these four suspects down without the chief's help?

"Sir?"

He turned. The clerk was spreading the large blueprints on the countertop and Louis walked quickly to her.

"These are the blue lines," she said. "But all we have is from 1948 to the present."

"That's fine," Louis said.

She left him and Louis stared at the top one. It took him a few seconds to figure out it was a construction plan for one of the newer buildings — the commissary. It clearly showed there were no tunnel entrances in the store and that it was built over the top of an existing tunnel. He had been right.

The next paper outlined the plans for another building, erected in 1959. M Building, the physical therapy building in the southeastern corner, directly opposite from E. This blue line showed only the tunnel entrances and then dotted lines that faded to nothing as they moved farther away from the building under construction.

Same with the next and the next, plans for buildings constructed in the sixties. Not one diagram of the original structures, and not one that showed all the tunnels.

Damn it.

"You done?" the clerk called. "We're closing now."

He pushed the papers toward her. "Yeah."

She frowned. "Look, mister, it isn't my fault we don't have what you want."

"I'm sorry. Didn't mean to snap."

Louis left the office and headed back toward the state police building. He stayed outside, huddled against the cold, watching for Dalum's Ardmore cruiser.

The sun had faded, leaving a dark gray glow to the sky, and for a few seconds, Louis just watched the street. After a few minutes, twinkly white lights in sagging garlands on the streetlamps popped on. And from somewhere in the air, he could hear a tinny rendition of "I'll Be Home for Christmas."

He thought about Zeke and realized he didn't even know the guy's last name. Or if he had a family. He thought about Frances, sitting at her sister's house in Brighton. And he thought about the photo of Claudia DeFoe on his nightstand.

But mostly, he thought about Joe, curled up on her sofa, a mug of coffee in her hand, a cat at her feet. He thought of Joe and he knew he wasn't going to be home any time soon. He turned the collar of his jacket up against the cold, watching the snow sifting down from the quickly darkening sky.

Chapter 32

When Dalum picked up Louis at the Adrian Police Station, he relayed a message from Dr. Seraphin's office: The doctor had gone to her weekend cottage on Wampler's Lake and if Louis needed to see her immediately, he should come there.

Dalum dropped Louis back at Hidden Lake and after fighting their way back onto the property to get the Impala, Louis immediately headed to the lake. But after three drive-bys along the street Seraphin had given him, he had to stop at Jerry's Pub to get directions, where the bartender looked at the address Louis had scribbled on a paper and said, "Oh yeah, that's the old Beuller place."

It was easy to see why he had missed it. Dr. Seraphin's "weekend cottage" was set far back from the road and hidden behind large evergreens. There was an iron gate barring the driveway. The gate looked new, Louis thought, as he pulled up to the intercom.

The doctor herself answered, and the

gate slid back. He drove up the driveway and parked next to the Volvo.

It was dark, nearly seven, and still snowing. But thanks to several well-placed floodlights, he could see the house clearly. It was a large, two-story wood-frame home, probably built in the forties, and very different from the gleaming new minimanses that surrounded it. Far from a cottage, the "old Bueller place" had that carefully cultivated shabby look that whispered *old money.*

Louis was surprised when Oliver opened the door. "The doctor is in the den," he said.

Louis came in. He heard a click and a beep and turned to see Oliver locking the door and resetting an alarm. Louis followed him through a dimly lit living room and down a hallway. The den was all wood and glowing lamps with a fire crackling in a stone fireplace. An antlered deer head on the far wall loomed over the room, next to an antique gun case that held a couple of shotguns.

When Dr. Seraphin saw him, she set aside her book, shrugged off a red plaid throw, and stood up from her chair.

She was wearing what looked to Louis like a plain gray sweatsuit, but as she came toward him, he guessed it was probably cashmere.

"Good Lord, you look half frozen. Can I get you a drink?" she asked, taking off her gold-rimmed bifocals to let them dangle by a gold chain.

"No, thanks."

"You don't mind if I have one then." She went to a small table that held a variety of bottles. "Please, take off your coat and make yourself comfortable."

Louis didn't move. He waited as she fixed her drink, looking out the large windows. The backyard was fully illuminated by floodlights, revealing a couple of snow-covered Adirondack chairs on the deck and a white expanse that tapered down to the black lake. In the distance, Louis could make out a boathouse. It looked old and like it was ready to fall away into the lake.

Dr. Seraphin came up behind him. "I really need to do something about that boathouse," she said. "I don't even have a boat and it's such an eyesore."

Louis turned to her.

"Now, what was so urgent that you had to see me tonight?" Dr. Seraphin asked, drink in hand.

"A security guard was murdered in E Building today," Louis said.

Dr. Seraphin's face and shoulders sagged. She went to the sofa and sat down on the edge, clutching her glass in both hands, looking at the carpet.

"The killer slit his throat, then wrote *bitch* on the wall with his blood."

"Good God," she whispered, looking up at him. "But he killed a man this time. It's obviously a message of some kind, a way to get attention."

"Whose attention, Doctor?" Louis asked.

She stared at him.

"The guard was stabbed in the lobby, but then whoever did it took the trouble to drag the body upstairs and into an office before he slit his throat — into *your* old office, I'd bet."

Louis watched her face for a reaction. But there was just a bland sadness that seemed forced.

"It's your attention he's trying to get," Louis said. "Why?"

She set her glass on a table before she looked back at him.

"I don't know," she said.

"Well, you're a target now, Doctor, so you damn well better try to figure it out."

He could see a hint of displeasure flick across her face. But he didn't care. He was tired. Tired of hitting dead ends, tired of

411

chasing ghosts. A man had died tonight and he couldn't get it out of his head that somehow he had been responsible.

"You need to go to the police," Louis said.

She stood up. "Impossible."

"You need to tell them what you know, tell them about the files we pulled."

She was shaking her head. "I can't do that. I won't do that. I have a reputation to protect."

"Screw your reputation, damn it."

A couple seconds of silence ticked off before she spoke. "You are obviously under a lot of stress, Mr. Kincaid. I can't imagine it is easy for you right now, being caught in the middle of all this."

She went back to the bar. Louis heard the clink of ice cubes. His head was throbbing, probably from not eating all day. He shut his eyes briefly. When he opened them, Dr. Seraphin was standing in front of him holding out a glass.

"It's brandy," she said. "Take it."

He took the glass. The brandy burned a trail down his throat and hit his empty stomach like a hard punch.

"Please sit down," she said.

He perched on the edge of the sofa, his back to the fireplace, across from the chair where she had been reading. The book was open, facing down on the ottoman. He could read the title: *The Divided Self* by R.D. Laing.

"I want to help, Mr. Kincaid," Dr. Seraphin said, sitting back down.

"Then go to the police with what you know."

"I am the head of the state psychiatric association. Do you have any idea what will happen to me if they find out I breached confidentiality?"

"Look," Louis said, "when this guy is caught, there will be a trial. You will have to testify."

"You promised me —"

"There is no way I can keep you out of it now."

Her expression didn't change, but Louis could see the slow rise of anger reddening her cheeks.

"No," she said firmly.

Louis took a quick swig of the brandy and banged the glass down. He reached inside his jacket, pulled out four file folders, and tossed them on the ottoman next to the book.

"Then pick one, damn it. Tell me where to start."

Her eyes went from the folders up to his

face. "You had no authority to take those out of the hospital."

"So sue me."

For a moment she didn't move. A log fell in the fireplace with a sharp crack. Dr. Seraphin reached down and gathered up the files. She looked through each one slowly, then set them in her lap.

"I don't know," she said. "It could be any of these men, it could be someone we didn't even find."

Louis rubbed the bridge of his nose. His head was killing him.

"All right," Dr. Seraphin said. "I won't go to the police, but I will help you. I *want* to help you. I will advise you all I can. Find these four men, find out what they are doing now, find out who is functional and who is not. Maybe then I can narrow it down."

She held out the files, but Louis didn't take them. "And I'll go back over things tonight," she said. "I'll try to remember any others who seem to fit. Believe me, I want this man caught as much as you."

Dr. Seraphin was still holding the folders. After a moment, she set them on the ottoman and sat back in her chair, considering him carefully.

"Are you all right, Mr. Kincaid?" she asked.

"A headache, that's all."

She nodded. "Not sleeping well either, I would imagine." When he didn't say anything, she added, "I could write you a prescription for something."

"I hate pills. But thanks anyway."

"Another brandy then?"

"No, thanks," he said, even though he wanted one badly.

It was quiet. For a moment, just one, he wanted to close his eyes and give himself over to the silence, anything to stop the whirl of thoughts in his head. The warmth of the fire on his back was lulling. He didn't even realize he had closed his eyes until she spoke again.

"It's not your fault," she said.

He looked at her. "Excuse me?"

"The guard who died. It's not your fault."

He had a hard time not looking away.

"But it's quite natural for you to believe so," she went on. "When we are under stress, our reality can become distorted. We can lose our sense of what is true and what is not."

"I'm fine," Louis said.

She tilted her head, a bare hint of a smile tipping her lips. The amusement of an older woman for a young man? The sympathy of a doctor for . . . what? Louis couldn't read it at all.

"Take the past, for example," Dr. Seraphin went on. "We all see it through a prism of distortion. Whether it is an experience we wish to hold on to or a childhood that we need to believe existed — or didn't exist. We all abdicate reality to some degree to survive."

Dr. Seraphin's gold earrings caught the light as she shifted in her chair.

"Your past, Mr. Kincaid, would you call it happy?" she asked.

He almost said it, almost said, "Fuck you, lady."

Instead, he waved a hand toward the sofa. "Should I lay down now?" he asked.

She smiled, the lines in her powdered face suddenly rising into high relief. "I only ask to make a point," she said. "Understand a person's past reality and you might get a grip on his present one." She nodded to the four file folders. "As I said, tell me who these men are now and I will try to tell you if one of them is a killer."

Louis leaned forward and gathered up the folders. They both rose. For a moment, Louis just stood there looking at Dr. Seraphin. He was thinking of something Dan Dalum had said on their ride back to

Hidden Lake, that if the murderer was a former mental patient, and if they caught him, there was a good chance the man would go right back into an institution instead of prison.

Louis tapped the folders lightly on the palm of his hand. "Just tell me this much," he said. "Is this guy nuts or not?"

"That's not a word I use," she said.

"Okay, is he insane?"

Dr. Seraphin hesitated, then reached down and picked up the book she had been reading when Louis came in.

"Take this," she said, holding out the book. "Maybe it will help you understand."

"Understand what?"

"Life after death, a death of the mind, if you will."

Louis didn't really want the book, but she seemed to need to believe he did. So he took it.

"I read it in 1959 when it first came out. I had already been at Hidden Lake for ten years, but it forced me to reconsider how I viewed my patients," she said, nodding to the book. "Dr. Laing believed that madness should be viewed from the inside, and that it was possible to understand the insane by entering their world, relating to them, conversing with them."

Louis found himself thinking suddenly of Charlie.

"Psychiatry is a very conservative science, and Laing was seen as a quite a radical." She paused. "Strange, isn't it, that we doctors would consider compassion radical?"

"Yeah, real strange," Louis said. He wanted to get out of here, get away from her double talk, just go back to Dalum's lumpy fold-out sofa and crash.

He heard a sound behind him and turned to see Oliver standing by the door.

"Oliver will show you out," Dr. Seraphin said. "Drive carefully, Mr. Kincaid. The road out of here is very bad."

Chapter 33

Louis heard the bell over the door at the Sand Lake Inn tinkle again and turned. But it wasn't Doug Delp, so he went back to his beer. He had called Delp about thirty minutes ago, after he left Dr. Seraphin, and damn near ordered him to meet him at the Sand Lake Inn as soon as possible. He was grateful to find the restaurant was still open, but he had gotten lucky. They were holding a Christmas party for a group of local workers. The place was noisy, filled with holiday sounds and laughter.

Louis pushed aside the plate with its half-eaten burger and signaled the waitress for another beer. He had a passing thought that it would be his third beer, but he was staying with Dalum tonight and the drive was short. He'd be okay.

The door again.

Delp came through it this time, lugging his scarred briefcase. He was dusted with snow, the tip of his nose red. Louis picked up his beer bottle and walked quickly to him, taking him right back out the door to the Impala. Delp looked at the car.

"We're talking out here?" he asked.

Louis opened the passenger door. "Get in."

Delp slipped inside. Louis got in the driver's side and started the engine to warm up the car. Then he reached in the backseat and grabbed the four hospital files of Seraphin's suspects.

He tossed them in Delp's lap. "I need some help finding these guys."

Delp looked down; then his fingers went slowly to the file tabs, and he read each name slowly. His eyes jumped back to Louis. "These are suspects in the murders?"

Louis was silent, staring at him. The outside lights of the inn were bright and the shadow of the falling snow was like a ghostly leopard crawling across Delp's face.

"Answer me, Kincaid. These are suspects?"

"Yes."

Delp's eyes narrowed. "Why are you asking me to do this? Why not just get the cops to track these guys down?"

"They can't know where I got the names from."

Delp flipped open the top folder. He

read a few lines, then looked back up, a slow smile on his lips. "These are medical files. You stole these from E Building, didn't you?"

Louis didn't answer.

Delp had a full grin now. "Dude, I didn't think you had it in you. I'm impressed."

"Can you do this or not?" Louis asked.

Delp slapped the folder closed. "Hell yeah, I can do it. However, there are a few things I haven't heard yet."

"Like what's in for you?"

"Exactly."

"I can't pay you. Do it as a public service."

Delp laughed. "Not in my nature, Kincaid. Nothing is free in our world, you know that."

Louis was quiet. Delp's smile faded, the boyish sparkle in his eyes dying with it. He suddenly looked older, his face clouded with those moving shadows.

"You know better than anyone that everything has a price," Delp said softly.

"Don't start that shit, Delp."

Laughter rose up around the car and they both turned to watch a young couple stagger by the Impala. When they were gone, Delp spoke.

"There's a few other reporters hanging

around here now. Guys that have heard about Rebecca, the bones, and now this security guard."

"So?"

"But they don't know this former patient angle," he went on. "They don't know you were so desperate for answers you dug up Donald Lee Becker. And they don't know Claudia DeFoe's coffin was empty."

"You can have it all. Except Claudia. You leave out Claudia, I'll tell you about Millie."

"Who's Millie?"

Louis gave him a shake of his head. "When I have your word."

"Okay," Delp said. "Unless Claudia turns out to be a victim of this killer, then no deal on her. I told you that already."

"All right. Get your pad out and write down those names and whatever else you need from the files to get started. I can't let you have the folders."

Delp reached inside his jacket, grabbed a pencil and a notebook. He stuck a penlight in his teeth, opened the folder, and started writing.

Louis remembered the beer in his hand and he took a drink, watching the people go in and out of the restaurant.

"One more thing, Kincaid," Delp said.

"What?"

422

"I want to interview you."

"No way."

"I can make you famous."

"I don't want to be famous. Finish your notes."

Delp turned in his seat, the penlight in his hand pointed at Louis.

"I'm using your name with or without talking to you. It would make a much better story if I had your insights."

Louis shook his head.

Delp shifted the folders and reached to his feet to open his briefcase. After a few seconds, he came up with a tattered old magazine, already flagged to a certain page. Louis could see the cover. *Criminal Pursuits Magazine*. And he knew what story Delp was about to read.

" 'Kincaid, a twenty-seven-year-old un-licensed private investigator,' " Delp started, " 'refused to comment on his role in the capture of the Paint it Black serial killer, even after Lee County Sheriff Lance Mobley publically blasted him for his interference in the investigation. It is reported that Kincaid, an ex–police officer who left Michigan law enforcement a few years earlier under a black of cloud of sus-picion —' "

"Shut up."

Delp waved the magazine. "Is this the image you want?"

"I don't want any image."

"Well, you got one. You chase killers. Ordinary people love reading that shit. You can let crap like this sit out there or you can let me tell them what kind of man you really are."

Louis turned to the driver's window, trying to keep his breathing even. He was furious and he tried to figure out why, but things weren't making sense right now.

"I'm going to write it anyway," Delp said. "Not just when I do this story, but later in a full-fledged profile. With or without an interview."

When Louis still said nothing, Delp added, "I'll do you right, Kincaid. I swear."

"Goddammit, Delp," Louis said. "I'll do your interview, but you're going to do this my way or everything's off."

Delp hesitated, then nodded. "Okay." He went back to taking notes from the medical folders.

Louis turned to the window. The car was hot now, the vent still blowing strong. The snow had stopped and the floodlight was bright white against a solid black sky. He tried to turn his thoughts back to Joe, and

424

her smile and the feel of her body against his, but he couldn't.

The magazine article had taken him somewhere else. Somewhere back, deep into the northern Michigan pines. He was hearing the crack of a sniper's bullet, seeing blood spreading across the collar of a baby-blue uniform as he held his partner, Ollie, in his arms. And he was feeling the cold on the back of his neck as he stood over the body of the first man he had ever killed.

"Done here, man," Delp said.

Louis looked at Delp. "When will you know something?"

"Day after tomorrow maybe," Delp said, stacking the folders and tossing them in the backseat. He slipped his notebook back inside his coat, then reached for the door.

Louis caught his arm. "When you get back to me, you're going to tell me everything you find out, you got that?"

"I got it."

"And you breathe even a hint of this to anyone, I swear, Delp, they won't find you till spring."

Delp laughed as he pushed open the door. "Funny, Kincaid. Real funny."

Delp got out and Louis watched him walk to his Civic. Man, this was probably as low as he had ever gone, asking a reporter like Delp for help while experienced police officers fumbled around in the dark. And he tried to figure out why he had done it. He could have walked away from all of this as late as this morning and left Dr. Seraphin and Detective Bloom to figure it all out. If he'd done that, he'd be home by now, sitting on his porch, listening to the pounding of the waves, and drinking a beer, waiting for Joe's car to pull into his drive.

Florida and everything he had there had never seemed so far away.

Chapter 34

Louis was still asleep when Dee Dalum came into the guest room, gently shook him awake, and handed him the phone. He struggled to sit up as he took it.

"Yeah?" he managed.

"Louis, it's Phil." A pause. "Are you coming home today?"

Louis could see a gray morning light seeping out from behind the drapes and he could smell coffee brewing.

"I don't know, Phil," he said. "There's a lot going on here now and —"

"You aren't even staying here anymore, Louis."

Louis swung his feet over the bed to the floor. "I know. I was going to drive back last night but the roads were bad."

There was a long pause on Phillip's end. "I need you home. I need to talk to you."

"All right, Phil. I'll be there as soon as I can."

It took Louis three hours to make it back to Plymouth. The freeway was plowed, but all other roads were iced over, and twice he had almost lost the car into a ditch. He pulled up in the driveway tense and tired, flexing his hands, cramped from gripping the wheel.

The front door was locked. He dug back in his jacket pocket for his keys. The wind was bitter and his fingers were so cold he was struggling to separate the keys when the door swung open. Phillip stood there, dressed in a blue sweater and old slacks. He stepped back to let Louis inside.

As Louis wiggled out of his jacket, he thought about asking if Frances had come back, but he knew she probably hadn't. It was a little after 10:00 a.m. and the house was empty of any of her usual scents.

"How was the drive?" Phillip asked, taking his coat.

"Dangerous," Louis said.

Phillip said nothing and Louis headed to the kitchen to look for something to eat. It hit him how sharp his comment about the drive probably sounded, and he knew he was just tired. He hadn't slept well at Dalum's last night. Thinking about Delp and having to ask him for help. Thinking about what Dr. Seraphin had said. But none of that was any reason to snap at Phillip.

Louis turned to apologize, but Phillip interrupted him. "So, what's going on out there?"

Louis opened a cupboard and pulled down a box of Cheerios and some sugar. "We had another murder. A security guard."

"Yes, I saw something in the *Free Press*. That's terrible."

Louis grabbed the milk and was pouring it on the Cheerios when Phillip spoke again.

"Have you found any connection to Claudia?"

"Not to the killer, no," Louis said.

"To what then?"

"What do you mean, to what? I don't have any more information on Claudia than I had two days ago," Louis said. "And it's kind of hard to deal with her with everything else that's going on there."

"Hard to deal with her?"

Louis was pushing the Cheerios around with a spoon and he stopped. There was a tinge of annoyance in Phillip's question, and Louis bit back his first response, letting his irritation fade before he spoke.

"There aren't many leads for her, Phillip," Louis said evenly. "Right now, we have to catch this guy and maybe when we do, he'll tell us more. I don't know."

"But isn't there someone else you can talk to?" Phillip asked. "Aren't there more people out there like that Millie woman? More patients who knew her?"

Louis faced him. "Yeah. I can do that. I can go get all kinds of stories about Claudia. How she looked. What drugs she was given. All the horrible things she went through."

Phillip stared at him and Louis could see the anguish in his face, and he knew he shouldn't say one more word because he could hear the edge to his voice and one more word might be one too many. But they poured out anyway.

"Is that what you want, Phillip?" Louis asked. "More guilt?"

"No," Phillip said. "I have plenty of that."

Louis turned back to his cereal, but he just stared at it, working his way toward an apology he didn't want to give. Maybe Phillip needed to hear that remark. Maybe he needed to know just how pathetic he had become, hanging on to some kind of romantic dream that he could never get back, throwing his life away for a ghost.

"But that *is* why I asked you to come here," Phillip said. "I didn't expect you to get involved in another case."

Louis closed his eyes, his chest so tight he couldn't breathe. He didn't want to fight with Phillip. He didn't want to fight with anyone.

"If you want to quit all this, I understand," Phillip said.

"I don't want to quit."

"You sound like it."

Louis started stirring the cereal in slow circles.

"If you want to talk, Louis," Phillip said, "we can go down to the basement. Grab a beer, eat some nuts. You know. We can talk, like we used to do."

And the words were on his lips before he thought about them, and he heard them come out, but he couldn't believe they were his.

"We never talked, Phillip," Louis said.

"That's not true," he said. "I remember . . ."

Louis faced him. "I got lots of fatherly advice. I got nice clothes. And a damn good education. But we never talked."

Phillip's shoulders drew stiff, hurt coloring his face. It was a look Louis had never seen before. But it didn't stop the rush of emotion, and before he could stop himself, he was talking again.

"Did it ever occur to you why that coach

in high school wanted me on the basketball team?" Louis asked.

"Well, I —"

"Or why I didn't go to the prom?"

Phillip was just staring.

"Or why I ran away so many times? Or what I might have wanted to eat at Christmas?"

"Louis —"

"Did it ever occur to you that I might want something like greens or hot skillet corn bread or smoked turkey legs or anything that might be southern?" Louis stopped for a moment, trying to even his voice. "Or black?"

Now Phillip knew what he was talking about and his expression changed from confusion to indignation. Louis saw something else there — pity.

"I thought it was best for you to forget what happened to you before you came here," Phillip said.

"Forget?" Louis asked.

"Yes."

"Forget what happened to me, Phil, or forget what I was?"

"You talk like I tried to make you white," Phillip said.

"Maybe you did."

Phillip took a step back, and Louis

thought he was going to leave the kitchen, but he didn't.

"When they brought you here, Louis, you were eight years old," Phillip said. "You had marks and bruises. And I didn't care what color of skin those marks were on. I only wanted to make them go away."

Louis could feel the pounding of his heart. But he had no words now. His throat was too tight and the emotions suddenly too strong. He knew none of this was meant for Phillip. It was something else. And it was *about* someone else. A different white man in a straw hat, and a face that no matter how hard Louis tried to bring into focus, remained a blur.

Suddenly Phillip was gone and Louis was alone in the kitchen. And for almost a full minute, he didn't move. Then he sank into a chair at the table and put his head in his hands. He needed to apologize and he would. In a minute. But right now he didn't want to move. Right now, it was all he could do to control the waterfall of images and memories. Keep them inside and steady. And God, he needed to be steady right now.

Phillip came back into the kitchen and Louis forced himself to look up. Phillip was holding something out to him. Photographs.

"These were taken the night before you arrived here. Do you want to see them?" Phillip asked. "Do you want to see what I saw?"

"Yes."

"Are you sure?"

"Yes."

Phillip set them on the table. They were Polaroids. Three of them. Probably taken by Children's Service.

The first. His scrawny light brown back, splotched with the kind of bruises that came from being smacked.

The second. His butt. The skin colored a deep, bronzy red, some of the welts so big they looked like giant, bloody blisters. And on his upper thighs, ragged lacerations from where the buckle of the belt had sliced into his skin.

He sifted to the third picture. His face. Small, dirty, the lip split, his black hair uncombed and speckled with dirt.

But it was the eyes that pulled at his heart. A strange shade of smoky gray, wide with a beseeching stare. Desperate eyes in a tiny face, like something, someone, trapped behind a mask fighting to get out.

Louis stared at the writing on the wide white border. *Louis W. Kincaid. Age 8. December 1967. Detroit, Michigan.*

He remembered that December. And that house he had been in before coming here. He remembered Moe. And the man before Moe. But what he couldn't remember anymore was his first seven years in Mississippi. He used to be able to grab a few images. His mother in a blue dress. His older sister and her bright red lipstick. His brother . . . doing something near a river. And they were the good images.

But even those were fading.

His eyes drifted back to the photographs. God, he didn't want these to be the only things left.

"I'm losing it," he whispered. He looked up at Phillip. "The good part of my past. I'm losing it and I don't know how to stop it."

Phillip lowered himself into a chair. He reached over and put a hand around the back of Louis's neck and pulled him closer.

Chapter 35

Delp called late the next day. He had tracked down the four men from Dr. Seraphin's patient files. He was able to confirm that Earl Moos was living with his brother and hadn't left California for the last ten years. Stanley Veemer was doing time in an Ohio prison for manslaughter. And Michael Boyd had died of a drug overdose five years ago.

Louis picked up a file. That left only Buddy Ives.

Delp hadn't been able to find out much about the guy, just that he had been in and out of jail and worked a series of menial jobs since being discharged from Hidden Lake seventeen years ago. Delp was able to offer up one lead: Ives's last known address in Detroit, compliments of a parole officer.

Louis opened Ives's file to refresh his memory. Ives had sexually assaulted, then killed his grandmother, with whom he had been living at the time. Dr. Seraphin had explained to Louis that under Michigan law at the time, the prosecution had to

436

prove Ives *wasn't* insane. They failed, and instead of rotting in prison, Ives was sent to Hidden Lake.

Ives had been eighteen when he went in. He was thirty-two when he was released in 1973. That made him forty-eight now. Still young enough to have raped and murdered Rebecca Gruber and Sharon Stottlemyer.

Louis pulled a small picture out of the file. It showed a twenty-something man with messy sparse hair over a high forehead, eyes the color of dirty winter ice, and a cold sliver-moon mouth hiding in a bank of whiskers.

Louis closed the file. It was time to go find Buddy Ives.

The address turned out to be in northwest Detroit on Mansfield, a street hard by the CXS tracks. As Louis got out of the Impala, he could hear the tire-hum of the Jeffries Freeway nearby.

In its day it had been a nice house, with a big wraparound porch, the kind where people sat in swings, swatting mosquitoes and nodding to neighbors. Now there were trash cans on the porch, towers of yellowed newspapers, and a mud-caked blue recycling bin filled with beer bottles. There were five rusting mailboxes nailed near the door.

The doorbell looked broken, so Louis

opened the sagging screen door and pounded on the door. Nothing. He pounded again, then stepped to the window, trying to see something between the iron security bars and the dirt smears. There was a faded red sign in the lower corner: ROOM FOR RENT. SEE MAURY APT. 1.

Then the door opened with a loud scrape and a man poked his head out. Louis immediately saw the look — that mix of fear and false bravado that surfaced on the faces of older white guys when they saw a strange black man.

Louis had the Ardmore badge out before he took a step toward the man. "I'm with the police. I need to talk to you."

The guy's eyed flicked to the badge and up to Louis's eyes. "How I know that's real?" He had retreated behind the sagging screen like it could offer some protection.

Louis took a breath. "It's real."

The man was in his early sixties, his scrawny, scabbed arms hanging from the sleeveless white T-shirt, his face mottled with whiskers and spots.

"I'm looking for a man named Buddy Ives," Louis said.

"Don't know him."

"Are you Maury?"

"Yeah. I'm the owner here."

"Ives was living here as of 1986. Think hard."

The man shook his head. "I said I don't know him."

Louis pulled Ives's picture from his coat pocket and held it out. "Think harder."

The man stared at Louis for a moment, then let his eyes flick to the photo before they came back to Louis's face. "Ives . . . okay, yeah, he was here. But he ain't now."

"When did he leave?"

"Well, it was hot, I remember that, 'cause he was bitching at me to fix his AC and I told him I wasn't gonna do shit until he paid his rent. He wouldn't leave, so I let just let him sweat his balls off up there until he couldn't take it anymore and just left one night."

"You have any idea where he went?"

"He didn't say and I didn't care."

Louis stuck the photo back in his coat. "What can you tell me about him?"

"He was a dirtbag."

"How about being a little more specific."

"He drank and did drugs. That's dirtbag enough in my book."

"How long did he live here?"

The man had to think about that one. " 'Bout two years?"

"Did he have a job?"

"Yeah, at first. That's the only reason I

rented to him. He showed me a pay stub from Uniroyal. But it didn't last long. He was in jail once or twice, too, I remember."

"What else do you remember?" Louis asked.

"He was real sick once." The old man folded his scarred arms over his chest against the cold. "Don't know what was wrong with him but it was bad, real bad. I called the amblance but he wouldn't go. Just laid there and screamed that nobody was gonna stick him in a hospital. He almost died up there. It was nuts. . . ."

Louis had to ask. "Was he?"

"Was he what?"

"Nuts. Was Ives nuts?"

The man's skinny shoulders hunched up. "How the hell should I know? Lots of guys come through here that are a little off in the head, but if they keep quiet and pay their rent I don't ask." He shrugged again. "Ives didn't seem any more nuts than anybody else."

"What about visitors?"

"What? Women? Nah, never saw him with one." The man's eyes shot up to Louis's face. "Wait, there was one time. I remember one time he did bring some woman back here."

"You remember anything about it?"

"Hell yes," the old man said. "I was down here watching Carson and heard them go up the stairs, her laughing and all liquored up. Then I heard some yelling and figured they was just having a good time. Next thing I know, she comes flying down the stairs."

"What happened?" Louis asked.

"I went out to the hall and she was screaming and holding on to her dress that was all ripped up. Her face was bleeding. But she was mad and cussing up the stairs to wheres he was standing."

He stopped, shaking his head. Louis waited.

"I didn't want to get in the middle of that one, so I was glad when she just ran out the door. Never heard a woman use language like that, yelling that he . . ."

The old man paused, looking suddenly at Louis.

"Yelling what?"

"She was yelling that he couldn't . . . not . . . you know, couldn't get a woodie."

Louis stared at him.

The man stared back. "You know, a hard-on, a stiffy, a —"

"I know," Louis said. "Could I see his room?"

"Huh? What for? I had to throw everything out and repaint the whole place when the guy left. I got somebody new in there now."

"Did Ives leave anything?"

"Yeah, a mess. Garbage, needles on the damn floor, and shit on the walls."

Louis was about to ask another question but he paused. "He put shit on the walls?"

"Not just shit . . . *shit*. Like real shit. And he didn't just put it there, he wrote with it."

"Wrote what?"

"He wrote 'fuck you, Maury' with his damn handprint next to it."

The man's face colored and Louis knew it was from anger, not embarrassment.

"He must have been nuts. Anyone that would do that is nuts, right?"

"Probably," Louis said. "Thanks. You've been helpful."

Louis started back to the Impala.

"Hey, you catch the crazy bastard, tell him he owes me money!" Maury yelled from the porch.

Louis's mind was locked on Buddy Ives as he drove. Now that he was sure Ives had been the one to leave the bloody handprint in E Building, he knew there was no choice. He had to turn Ives's name over to Bloom.

He stopped for a traffic light and looked up. Where the hell was he? His brain had been so locked on Ives, he had driven fifteen minutes in the opposite direction from the freeway back to Plymouth.

He looked for a sign on the desolate street of liquor stores and vacant shops. Something familiar loomed in the corner of his vision. Through the swipe of the wipers, the image became clearer — a red brick building. It was boarded up and covered with graffiti, but a trace of its old elegance lingered in the slate mansard roof and the twin clock towers.

Suddenly, he knew exactly where he was. He was at the intersection of Grand River and Greenfield, staring at the old Montgomery Ward department store. Across the street was another decaying hulk — the old Federal store.

He stared at the sad buildings as a memory came clicking into high relief. There used to be a Kresges next to "Monkey Wards" and he had shoplifted candy there once.

A horn blared behind, startling him. He drove on across Grand River. Two blocks down, he made a sharp right turn.

It was a residential area of brick colonials and bungalows with bare old maples arching high overhead. He drove slowly down the deserted street, staring at the homes. So many were boarded up, a few burned out or with foreclosure windows on them. Everything looked alien to him, yet oddly familiar.

He passed a hulking red brick school enclosed in a high chain-link fence.

Jesus. He could remember. John Burns Elementary. He could remember sitting mute in a classroom and a fight on the playground.

He drove on. Then, there it was on the bent street sign: STRATHMOOR. He turned left and inched the Impala forward. He stopped. Leaning forward on the steering wheel, he stared out the windshield.

It was the house. That much he was sure of. A red brick place with a steep-pitched roof and two gargantuan evergreens guarding the front door.

It was the evergreens that he recognized. He remembered going up the snow-covered walk and how they blotted out the sun as he went between them.

Things were coming back to him now, things he had thought long lost in the shadows of his boy-brain. The long bus ride from Mississippi sitting next to a strange woman. Now he knew she was from social services, but then she had been just a fat white woman who smelled of the tuna sandwiches she ate.

Another woman's face swam into his head. Black, thin. A distant aunt . . . the person the white woman left him with. He remembered that tired black face and all the kids in her house and how she yelled at them. And how she took him by the shoulders and told him she didn't have enough for him, too.

Then . . .

Just a blur of houses. Three, four? Other houses and other faces who didn't have enough. That's when he started to run away. They kept finding him and bringing him to other houses.

Until they brought him to Strathmoor.

The memories from this house had always swirled thick and black in his boy-brain and chased him into adulthood. But until this moment, he had never known they were real.

Louis stared at the red brick house. A car came ambling down the street toward him. The deep *thud-thucka-thud* of music grew, pounding in his ears as the car drew abreast. The car passed, the fading music a dirge for a dying neighborhood.

Louis put the car in gear and drove away.

Chapter 36

Shells of burned buildings and evergreens that hid the sun followed him into his dreams that night. And when the sun falling on his face woke him, for a moment he didn't know where he was.

He dressed quickly in the quiet house and went downstairs. There was a note from Phillip on the kitchen table saying he had gone out and not to expect him back for dinner. He had left a fresh pot of coffee.

The sun was bright in a cloudless sky, and he had to wear sunglasses to see as he drove back to Hidden Lake. He pulled off to the side of the road as he drew near so the troopers at the gate wouldn't hassle him.

He cracked the window for some fresh air and, for a few minutes, he sat watching the two uniforms move in and around the entrance.

Yesterday, after he returned from Detroit, he called Detective Bloom and arranged to meet him here. His intent was to offer up Buddy Ives as a suspect. He knew he should have turned over all four names right after Zeke was killed. But he had been trying to protect Dr. Seraphin.

There was no way he could do that now unless he took the fall himself. And he had decided that was exactly what he would do: tell Bloom that he alone had found the names in the E Building files. Dr. Seraphin had a lot to lose. All he would get was slap on the wrist and a trip out of state again.

Louis got out of the Impala and was halfway to the security booth when one of the troopers spotted him and started over.

"Took you long enough," the trooper said.

"What?"

"We called an hour ago," the trooper said. "That crazy guy is back again."

"Who?" Louis asked.

"Charlie, the Fairy Queen."

"He's inside?"

"Yeah," the trooper said. "This is the third time in two days we caught him here. First time we ran him off. He was back three hours later. Second time, we turned him over to Chief Dalum. But he's back again."

Louis suppressed a sigh. "Where is he?"

"Sitting on the steps of the admin building. He's fucking up the surveillance, man. He ever shows up at night, some-body's going to shoot him."

"Can I go in and get him?"

"Yeah. The guys inside have just let him sit there so they don't blow their cover. I'll radio them you're coming in."

"Thanks." Louis started back toward his car, then turned. "Hey, I'm supposed to meet Detective Bloom here. If he shows up, tell him I'll be back."

"Will do."

Louis eased the Impala through the gates and to the front of the administration building. The place looked deserted, the ground a rolling ocean of white. Louis's eyes flicked up to the dark windows and he wondered how many cops were up there, wondered if there were rifles trained on him right now.

He saw Charlie huddled on the top step. Charlie saw him, too, but he didn't move. Louis had to park and get out, again feeling a dozen eyes on his back.

Louis stopped at the bottom of the steps. "We need to go home, Charlie," he said.

"This is my home."

"Not anymore. Don't you live with Miss Alice now?"

"I can't. I can't leave until the apple babies come."

"You *can* leave. You have a new home. C'mon, I'll take you back to Alice's house."

"Not until the apple babies come."

Louis looked around the grounds, then back at Charlie. He remembered something Dr. Seraphin had said at her lake house the other night, that madness should be viewed from the inside. He had tried reading the book she had given him, but it was dense going. The only thing he had gotten out of Laing's ideas was the notion that you could "converse" with the insane by trying to enter their world empathetically.

"Charlie, I got an idea," Louis said. "We'll go buy all the apple babies you want. Where do we get them?"

"I don't know."

"Let's go look."

Charlie's head came up quickly. "Do you know where they are now?"

"I bet we can find them."

Charlie stood up, pulling at the dangling wool straps of his multicolored hat. Once in the Impala, Charlie was quiet, sitting on the edge of the seat, eyes focused forward, hands on the dash.

Louis pulled out onto the highway and gave the trooper a final wave. Bloom's car was nowhere in sight.

449

"Do you have music?" Charlie asked.

Louis turned on the radio. It was tuned to a rock-and-roll station, and Charlie just stared at the dials, his head tilted toward the speaker. It was something by UB40, "Red, Red Wine." An easy song with repetitious lyrics and he could tell Charlie recognized it. He even started singing softly.

"You know that song?" Louis asked.

"Yeah."

Louis let him sing, glad his mind was off the apple babies. But then the song ended and "Candle in the Wind" came on. Charlie didn't seem to know that one.

"Do you have those things with music on them?"

"Tapes? I don't know. Look in the glove box."

Charlie opened the glove box and took out the two cassette tapes Phil kept in there. Louis had no idea what was on them; then it occurred to him Charlie might not be able to read anyway.

"What song are you looking for, Charlie?"

"Emma got to come feed ya."

"What?"

Charlie was staring at the tapes, and he started to sing again. It was low and slow and he was jerking his shoulders up and

450

down to the staccato beat in his head.

"Boomp, boomp, boompa pa boomp . . . boom . . . boom . . . boom."

"In-A-Gadda-Da-Vida?" Louis asked.

"Emmagottacomefeedthebaby," Charlie sang. "Donchaknow that I love you? Donchaknow that I'm blue?"

Louis laughed.

"That's an old song. How did you ever learn that?"

"I was born with it in my head."

"Born with it?"

"Just like the lights. Emma got to come feed the baby . . . Emma got to come feed the baby."

Louis knew this was no memory of Hidden Lake. And he couldn't help but take it a few steps further, suddenly seeing Charlie as a toddler, wandering through some psychedelic blacklight apartment, breathing in marijuana or eating pills from the top of a coffee table while his parents were passed out somewhere.

"Do you know Emma got to come feed me?" Charlie asked.

"Yeah."

Charlie started singing again, and in between verses, he looked back at Louis. "If you know it, then sing it."

"I don't sing, Charlie."

"Why not? And woncha sing with me and be my band . . ."

Charlie was into his music now, his whole body swaying back and forth as his voice grew deeper and hoarser, like he was trying to imitate something or someone he had seen, and suddenly he didn't sound like the same man.

Louis glanced at him, then sang part of a line, and Charlie looked at him, grinning. And they continued to sing for another mile, the car filled with twisted lyrics and sour notes.

"Stop!" Charlie yelled suddenly.

Louis hit the brakes and the Impala slid, then caught on the asphalt, coming to a jerky stop. Charlie was out of the car in a second, running back along the road. Louis caught up with him in a snowy driveway at a wide, metal gate.

Charlie pushed on the gate, and when it wouldn't give, he started to climb over it. Louis pulled him back down.

"Charlie," he said, "what's wrong? What's the matter?"

"This is where the apple babies are!" Charlie shouted. "This is where they come from."

There was a wood sign stuck on the ground: SHADY TRAIL APPLE ORCHARD &

CIDER MILL. CLOSED DECEMBER–JUNE.

Louis wasn't sure what the hell to do. But something in his gut told him to just keep going, just ask questions.

"Charlie," Louis said, "what are apple babies?"

Charlie was standing knee-deep in a snowdrift. "They're apple babies and they bring them to the hospital! They bring them in baskets."

"Can I make them?"

Charlie looked at him, confused. "What?"

"Are they dolls or something? Can I make them?"

"No, no. Only the ladies can make them."

"I can cook," Louis said.

"They're not cooked, Mr. Kincaid," Charlie said. "They grow."

"On trees?"

Charlie hung his head and moved away from him slowly, like he was giving up.

It hit Louis how weird it was that Charlie was the one getting frustrated with *his* inability to understand. Louis came closer, making an effort to keep his voice normal. "Charlie, what do the apple babies look like?"

Charlie's hands were curled around the gate, the tips of his fingers red. "I've never seen one."

"But you saw the baskets?"

Charlie nodded. "The baskets come in trucks."

"Like an apple truck?"

"Yes. It has apples on it."

"Do you eat the apple babies?"

"No. That would hurt."

"Hurt who?"

"The apple babies."

Charlie's face was raw, his eyes teary, and all the laughter that had been in him during the song was gone. It was freezing out here, the wind a brisk wash across the open farmland, and Louis knew he should take Charlie back to the car. But he didn't want anything to distract him. Not yet.

"Charlie, are the apple babies real?" Louis asked.

Charlie looked at him. "Real? Of course they are real. They're changeling babies. But they're not sick. They get taken away because they're perfect. The sick ones are left so the perfect ones can go away."

Louis studied him, trying to remember everything he had said about apple babies and the Shakespeare book and the baskets. "Is that why you came here, because you were sick?"

"Yes."

454

"And when you came, an apple baby was taken away?"

"I was a changeling child. I told you that."

Louis touched his arm, and Charlie turned to look at him.

"Charlie, how do you know there was a baby in the apple basket?"

"I heard it cry."

"Like you heard the graves cry?" Louis asked.

"Babies don't cry at the graves. Only girls."

Louis ran a hand over his face, sniffing from the cold. Charlie seemed unfazed, his gaze moving back to the bare trees.

"Charlie," Louis said, "will you come to the cemetery with me? Will you show me exactly where you hear them?"

"Okay."

Louis took his arm and led him back to the Impala. Charlie glanced back at the orchard as they climbed inside, but he seemed calm now, almost as if he couldn't remember why they were here. The two-lane highway was empty, and Louis pulled away from the snowy shoulder and did a U-turn, heading back east to Hidden Lake.

He let Charlie go first, prepared to follow him wherever he went. Spera's equipment still sat at the corners, and there were some open empty graves. Donald Lee Becker's was one of them, his concrete liner sitting in a frozen pool of black ice.

Louis watched for movement in the trees, wondering if there were troopers posted out here. But he doubted it. It was too open, with no place to hide, and it was too exposed to the weather. Not likely the killer could bring any more victims here.

Charlie headed to the middle of the cemetery. To their left was a row of trees behind which Louis could just make out the spires of the Hidden Lake infirmary. To their right, more trees that dwindled off into open farmland and orchards, and far ahead of them, up near where they had found Sharon Stottlemyer, more trees and thick brush.

"Where are you going, Charlie?" Louis called.

Charlie just pointed to the north end. He paused where they had found Sharon Stottlemyer's remains. The shallow grave had been carefully excavated. It didn't look like the other graves, and Charlie seemed to notice it was different, but he said nothing. He just moved on toward the back of the cemetery. Then he stepped into the brush and reached for a tree limb.

"Charlie, what are you doing?"

"Climbing the tree. This is where I hear them."

Charlie scaled it easily, his thin body squeezing through the branches and finding a perch about ten feet off the ground.

Then he sat and waited.

After a few minutes, Louis spoke. "Do you hear anything?"

"No."

Louis looked around. The only sound he could hear was the whistle of the wind in the trees. From back here, in the brush beyond the north boundary of the cemetery, he could clearly see the iron fence surrounding the back perimeter of Hidden Lake. He could see part of E Building through the naked branches and above its roof, the spires of the infirmary just beyond. He knew there had to be cops stationed up in E Building, and he wondered if they could see him right now.

"Can I come down now?" Charlie asked.

"In a minute," Louis said. He stepped farther into the brush. It was sharp and tore against his jeans as he crunched through it. He came to some small trees and pushed through them, glancing back to check on Charlie.

"Anything?"

"No," Charlie called back.

Louis went a few more steps, and the trees suddenly stopped. There was an area of brush that had been tamped down, like someone had walked on it. But he could see the brush was loose, like it had been carefully positioned. He knelt to push it aside but drew back, pricked by thorns. He pulled at the brush. Suddenly, his hand hit something hard.

Metal.

He was standing on a platform of some kind. Old, red-brown with rust. It looked like a door set in the ground.

"Charlie!" Louis called. "Come here."

Louis started yanking at the remaining brush. When Charlie saw what he was doing, he knelt to help. In a few minutes, they had cleared away a ten-foot area.

There were two metal doors, about eight feet wide, embedded in the ground. One hinge had rusted off, leaving one of the heavy doors slanting downward slightly. Nearby, coming straight out of the ground, was a pipe that looked it might have had controls or a lever on it at one time, but it was broken off now.

"Charlie, stand on that side over here and grab the edge," Louis said.

Together they lifted the slanting door,

letting it fall backward with a spray of snow.

Louis looked down inside. He could see the bottom of the hole, down to another iron platform. But that wasn't all that was down there. Louis could also see the beginnings of a tunnel.

"This is where the bodies come out," Charlie said.

Louis looked up at him. "You knew about this?"

Charlie looked at him from the other side of the hole, frowning at the sharpness in Louis's voice.

"Not anymore. It's closed now," he said softly.

Louis looked back into the hole, holding his frustration. It was his own damn fault. If he had spent more time talking to Charlie instead of dismissing him as crazy he would have found this sooner.

Louis stood up. "Charlie, I need you to do something. Go back to the car. There's a flashlight in the glove compartment. Bring it to me. Can you do that?"

Charlie nodded and ran off. Louis knelt by the door's edge, dropping his head into the hole. There was a rusted mechanism on the bottom platform that looked like some kind of hydraulic or pulley-type lift.

Louis stood and looked west. This hole was directly in line with the back of the infirmary. He looked back at the rusted doors. This had to be connected to the mortuary in the bottom of the infirmary. It made sense that there would be a direct way to transport the dead from there to the cemetery. Most likely, a casket would be loaded on a gurney in the mortuary and wheeled through a tunnel to here, where a lift was used to bring it up for burial. It made sense, too, that this would be a tunnel dedicated only to this grim task so patients and staff didn't have to see the dead. It probably ran under E Building, unconnected to the main tunnel system.

Surely they had bricked this one off, too. But if not, it was a perfect conduit for the killer that allowed him to enter the tunnels through the cemetery, outside the scope of the police surveillance.

Charlie was back with the flashlight and Louis clicked it on to check the battery. It was strong. Then he shone it down the hole.

Ten feet to the bottom, he estimated. The flashlight beam picked up the rusted workings of the lift. It looked to have enough places to grab on to so he could get back out.

"Are you going down there?" Charlie asked.

"Just for a second," Louis said.

"Don't go."

"I'll be right back."

Louis stuck his flashlight in his belt, sat down on the door rim, and grabbed the edge of the other door. Sliding off the ground, he let himself hang for a second, then dropped to the bottom.

He hit with a clang of metal, sending a stinging through his ankles that forced him to catch the wall to keep from falling. Afraid the crash had echoed through the tunnel, he grabbed his flashlight and pointed it into the darkness. The beam stretched on, fading to a whisper of light, then nothing.

Louis took a few steps, sweeping the beam over the floor as he walked. Concrete, with patches of ice. Leaves. Mud. Dead flies. Roaches. The ice had turned to water now, black and murky.

It was cold, the air thick with a mustiness that almost made him gag, and he had the awful thought that the liquid at his feet was seeping grave water, probably all around him, dripping down the walls and from the ceiling.

"Mr. Kincaid?"

"I'm okay, Charlie."

Shit. He should have counted his steps, but he'd been too busy looking around. Too busy keeping his heartbeats under control. But he knew he'd gone at least twenty feet and had not seen a cinderblock wall.

"Mr. Kincaid?"

Charlie's voice sounded like a child's, high and hollow off the concrete walls. Louis turned quickly, looking back. He could still see the shaft of sunlight back at the entrance of the tunnel.

"Charlie, can you hear me?" he called out.

"Yes . . . yes, I can!"

Louis ran the flashlight beam slowly over the walls. He could hear a dripping sound and smell rotting earth. A heaviness filled his chest.

This was where it had happened.

This was where Rebecca Gruber had been tortured and murdered. It had been her screams, her crying that Charlie, sitting in his tree, had heard.

He swung the flashlight beam into the darkness. The killer was down here somewhere, probably right now. If he didn't already know his home had been invaded, he would soon. And no way was Louis leaving this opening unguarded. He had to go get help.

He went back to the shaft and looked up. Charlie was still there, peering down.

"You coming out now?" Charlie asked.

"Yeah," Louis said, clicking off the flashlight and slipping it into his belt.

He grabbed hold of a piece of metal screwed lengthwise into the concrete wall, jerking on it to make sure it was steady. Sticking a foot on one of the lower rails of the lift, he stepped up. The lower rail crumbled into dust.

"Damn it," he said.

He tried the corner, where the thin bars came together, but it was already loose, and his weight crushed it to the floor.

He stepped back and looked up. It was more than ten feet up to the top, he saw now, maybe close to fifteen. No way could he reach the middle bar, not even if he jumped. He took the flashlight back out and steadied it on the rails. They were all broken and rusted through. No. Not broken. They were all unscrewed deliberately. Some were even missing.

He turned and looked down the tunnel. This man didn't want anyone coming down here and getting back out.

Louis went a few feet back into the

tunnel. There had to be something sturdy enough to stand on, something the killer used to get up. If he could just get part way, he could reach that middle bar and swing his legs up to the edge or reach Charlie's hand. But he didn't see anything he could use.

"Mr. Kincaid?"

"I'm all right, Charlie."

He came back to the shaft. He saw a single metal post, three feet high, welded to the corner of the platform. Clicking off the flashlight, he stuck it back in his belt.

"Charlie, I'm going to try to climb up," Louis said. "Reach down and grab my hand and pull, okay?"

"Okay!" Charlie leaned over and extended his arm down as far as he could. Louis brought up his foot and was able to get it up on the post. His fingers found another thin piece of metal close by, the gap between it and the wall so small he could barely get his fingertips between them.

He eased his way up, most of his weight balanced on the sharp tip of the narrow post. He leaned inward to grab the middle bar but still couldn't reach it. Charlie's outstretched hand was a good three feet above him. He had to get higher.

He knew if he jumped and missed the

bar, he'd fall back to the floor. But he had to try. He made a leap, catching the bar with both hands, his fingers immediately sliding on the crusty film. But he did a quick pull-up, and grabbed it again, a stronger hold this time. The bar was like ice, and the rust like sandpaper under his fingers.

He could see Charlie's fingers frantically waving overhead.

He swung his legs up, missed and swung again. His heels caught the rim. The bar snapped. He fell back to the bottom of the hole.

The fall knocked the breath out of him, and for several seconds, even the darkness was spinning.

"Mr. Kincaid!"

Louis shook his head. "Damn it," he hissed, trying to get up. "Son of a bitch . . ."

"Mr. Kincaid!"

He looked up. Charlie's face was blur far above him. He struggled to his feet.

"Charlie, you're going to have to go get help." The fall had knocked the wind out of him and he could barely pull in enough air to talk. "Can you run back to the hospital?"

"Yes."

"Can you get to the gate, where the policemen are?"

"Yes."

"I need you to do that for me," Louis said. "Right now. I need you to run as fast as you can and bring the policeman at the gate back here. Right here."

"Okay."

Louis pulled in a shallow breath. "Don't go inside the hospital. Don't climb the fence and don't try to find any policeman inside the fence. Go right to the gate."

"Okay."

Louis stared up at him, afraid he didn't understand. "Okay," Louis said, "tell me, where are you going to go?"

"To the gate. To get the policeman."

"All right," Louis said. "Go. Now."

Charlie took off and Louis reached back for the flashlight. It was gone. His eyes swept the concrete floor and finally he saw it. He picked it up and flicked it on, training the beam into the dark tunnel.

His chest and left shoulder were throbbing from the fall. He felt dizzy and slid down to the floor, sitting there, trying to get some air back into his lungs. And when he could breathe, he looked up at the bright blue sky.

It seemed very far away.

Chapter 37

Thirty-five minutes. A damn long thirty-five minutes.

Louis leaned against the wall, staring at the sky. He had heard nothing from above. No Charlie. No footsteps. No sirens. No voices.

It was well after three now and what little warmth the sun had provided all afternoon was long gone and the sky was turning a smoky gray. In another two hours, it would be dark.

He looked back at the lift. He had broken every slat and even pulled a post from the wall in his attempts to climb it again. His knuckles were bleeding and he had ripped his jeans along the shin in a second fall. The cold was seeping into his shoes and down his collar.

He stared down into the tunnel.

Charlie should have been back by now. Unless the troopers had just put him in a squad car and called Dalum to pick him up again. Maybe if Dalum did, Charlie would tell him about the tunnel.

Maybe.

He looked back up. Well, he could stand here and stare at the sky or go find something that he could use to climb up with.

Louis turned on the flashlight and shone it ahead of him into the darkness. He took three deep breaths before he started walking, but this time he tried to count his steps, and he guessed he had gone thirty feet when he stopped to listen for sounds.

Dripping water and a lingering echo of something. His footsteps? His heart?

He moved on, the darkness suffocating, the only light coming from the sweep of the flashlight beam as it jerked around the cave of concrete.

Ten, twenty feet more, and he wondered if he had crossed under the iron fence that formed the eastern boundary of the Hidden Lake grounds.

Then the light picked up something new. Doors. Large, heavy, and made of rusted metal. They were wide open, pushed back against the walls.

There would be no cinder-block walls in this tunnel, Louis suddenly knew. These doors were the barrier to the outside. He bent and examined the sides, looking for a latch or a lock. There was none. Then he pulled on them. Neither was easy to move, both too rusty and old, their bottoms resting heavily on the floor.

The flashlight beam picked up something else. Long scraping arcs across the concrete floor where it looked like the doors had been forced open and closed many times. He was about to turn away and move on, when the light caught something on the door.

Paint, maybe. Or even blood . . .

A scrawl that looked like a handprint. And it came to him in an instant. The old man in Detroit, Maury. Buddy Ives's landlord said Ives had put the same mark on his apartment wall. But there was something else, too.

Louis stared at the handprint.

The same mark had been on Dr. Seraphin's old office wall in E Building, near Zeke's head. He remembered seeing it now next to the word *bitch.*

Ives was their killer. Louis had no doubt now. The teenager who had raped and killed his grandmother, raped Millie Reuben, and killed Sharon Stottlemyer and Rebecca Gruber, was living here.

He had been right. Dr. Seraphin had been right.

He shone the flashlight ahead of him, the beam lasering through the darkness. He knew he shouldn't go any deeper into the tunnel. But if Ives was living down here, there had to be something down here *he* used to climb out with. And it couldn't be much farther. Ives would want to keep it handy, in case he needed to make a quick exit.

A few more feet. He'd still be close enough to hear the doors close if Ives somehow came back behind him.

He moved on. The water was all over the floor now, a black rivulet that ran downhill with the subtle slope of the floor. He was starting to hear other things, too. The scratch of little feet. Faint knocking noises behind the wall, like some trapped animal. And the trickle of water moving in pipes he couldn't see.

Then suddenly the beam of light lost the wall, disappearing into an expanse of darkness to his left. It took a second for him to realize it was another tunnel, branching off in a T from the tunnel he was in.

He tried to clear his head, reorient himself, and get a bead on his direction. If the tunnel he was in now ran east-west from the cemetery to the mortuary, that meant this new one ran due south. Maybe this was Ives's other exit.

He swung the flashlight beam into the darkness to his left. But this south tunnel could lead anywhere, and he was damned sure he didn't want to end up under the hospital in a maze of darkness.

He would go straight ahead, keep heading to the mortuary. It wasn't much comfort, but at least he would know which building he was near then. Maybe some cop would hear him.

Shit, maybe some cop would *shoot* him, thinking he was Ives.

Louis walked on, the water at his feet turning to a slimy sludge of mold. Then he started hearing something else. The pitter of something alive and moving, and a few steps later, he saw it and he froze. The rat froze too, its eyes glowing red in the flashlight beam. Then it was gone.

He waited until his heart slowed; then he went a few more steps.

The beam picked up something gray ahead. A cinder-block wall. He hurried to it, and sticking the flashlight under his arm, he ran his hands over it. All the blocks were in place, solid and unyielding. He even gave it a kick to make sure.

"Fuck," he whispered.

The screech came out of nowhere, long and lingering, the sound slashing through the tunnel.

At first he thought it was a woman

screaming. And it seemed to come from somewhere in front of him, maybe on the other side of the wall. But then he knew it was the scrape of metal on concrete. And it came from behind him.

He spun and ran back, the flashlight jerking over the walls, the sound of his breath rushing in his ears. Twenty feet. Ten. Five. But he still couldn't see the doors.

Then suddenly the light hit metal and he ran right into them.

Closed. They were closed.

He spun backward, trying to hold his breath, trying to hear something. But he heard nothing. Ives was gone. Probably out through the lift entrance. He would have no reason to stay down here now. Ives knew more cops would come. He was probably crawling out onto the grass this second. And by the time Charlie brought anyone here — if he brought anyone here — Ives could be out of the state.

Damn it! Son of a bitch!

Louis almost threw the flashlight, but he stopped himself. He pulled in a thick breath and looked back at the doors. He hadn't seen a lock. But there was no handle either. His fingers groped along the edges, but the doors were tight and flat

472

against each other. He knelt, feeling every-where, looking at every corner, and looking again, even checking the bottom for some way to get his fingers under it. Nothing.

Okay. Think.

Again, he ran his hands over the doors, but there was nothing. Finally, he stood back and shone the light down on his palms. They were stained with rust, dirt, and blood from where he had reopened the tears in the knuckles. He realized his hands were growing numb. And suddenly, he felt something else. A nub of fear, deep in his gut.

Stop this. There has to be something down here you can use.

Cans of food. Some form of furniture. A blanket . . . he could use a blanket right now. Or a fucking exit.

Wait . . . there is another exit. You saw it in the warehouse. It was somewhere south . . . you can find it.

He went back to the T-intersection and turned south. A few feet into the new tunnel the concrete walls and floor changed to that same ugly tile he had seen in his short walk in the E Building tunnel. He knew he was definitely inside the fence now, but he couldn't gauge what building he might be near.

473

He swung the flashlight up to the ceiling. There was a single line of electrical sockets, most empty but with a few bare bulbs still in place. But he didn't see any switches and the lights were probably disconnected anyway.

There was less water now, but more rats. The scratching and scampering were almost constant, and every once in a while the light would catch one as it moved along the edge of the wall. He started keeping the beam at waist level, not wanting to see them.

Then he started spotting trash.

Large, open cans of corn, peas, and soup, the edges of the tins crusted with mold and crawling with roaches. Then the smell of urine, and he lowered the beam to the floor, knowing what he was going to see, but needing to look anyway.

Feces. Little piles. Dried. Some fresh. A trail of them.

Louis put a hand out to the wall to steady himself, fighting the gag in his throat. He wanted to close his eyes, but he knew if he did, he'd lose his stomach.

He forced his feet forward, one step at a time, and kept moving until the smell faded. The corridor was clear for a while longer, filled with just tiny pieces of garbage and an occasional dead mouse.

He realized he had stopped counting his steps and he wondered how far he'd come and he found himself looking up, as if he could somehow see through the ceiling and earth and figure out what building he was under.

He moved on, following the jump of the flashlight beam. The sound of the rats and water was still in his ears, and he realized he was growing used to it, beginning to think of it as normal.

Then he came to another intersection.

This time the tunnels went in both directions, and he had three new paths he could take.

He walked straight ahead, counting on some weird feeling that it might be right. Maybe fifty more feet, another intersection. Again splitting in four directions.

He had a sudden strange image of Hansel and Gretel leaving bread crumbs along their trail. He reached inside his jacket, grabbed a felt-tip pen, and used it to mark an X on the tile wall with an arrow pointing back toward the way he had come.

He heard a soft shriek, something like a frightened animal might make, and he turned quickly, scanning the tunnel. He waited, unsure what it had been.

Now another shriek. Stronger. Closer. Human.

He spun back, unable to tell the direction, his mind suddenly electrified with a dozen thoughts that were coming too fast. Was it a woman?

Then a third, this one a full scream.

Oh, Jesus. It was a woman.

Where was she? Was she alone? She had to be alone. Ives had left, hadn't he? Why else close the doors? Why lock himself out?

She had to be alone. Had to be tied up or just lost. And he had to find her.

Then another scream, this one piercing, and it was echoing all around him. He took a step down one of the side tunnels, listening, but still there was no sense of direction. He was about to shout back at her, but she screamed again — a long, agonizing scream that ricocheted through the dark tunnels and seemed to go on forever until it was absorbed by the darkness.

Then . . . laughter? Yes, just a trickle of it, so quick and unexpected that when it was gone he wasn't sure he had heard it.

Ives. He hadn't left the tunnels. He was down here with a woman and he was hurting her.

Louis started to call to her but he

stopped himself. Shouting would alert Ives that he was here. But Ives already knew that, didn't he? But what if he didn't? What if Louis called to her and Ives panicked and killed her? Then came looking for him?

Jesus. Think, Louis. Think.

Another scream, a ragged, piercing one. Louis stepped to his right, drawn to that tunnel, and he moved down it.

More screams, a rush of them, each one louder and more wretched. Louis quickened his step, the light jumping, his ears following the echos. But there was still nothing to see. Nothing.

Until suddenly another cinder-block wall. As sturdy and solid as the one by the mortuary.

Louis spun back.

Where the hell was she?

He trained the light into the tunnel, the beam stretching long and deep into the blackness.

Where the hell was he?

Chapter 38

He couldn't remember ever being so cold. The noises were all different now, the walls alive with scratching, like they were filled with a million rats he couldn't see. And water seemed to ooze from the tile.

The flashlight was off now to save the battery. As he stood in the darkness leaning against the wall, he tried not to think about the dampness between his toes or what was dripping on his head.

The screaming had stopped an hour ago.

He wanted to know what time it was. He clicked on the flashlight. It was after 7:00 p.m. Dark outside now. He turned off the flashlight.

He slid slowly down the wall, hoping the floor was dry. It was, but it was cold. He sat anyway, drawing his knees up and leaning his forehead against them.

He heard the squeak of a rat, but he didn't move. It struck him how weird that was. Four hours in here and suddenly rats were nothing. But maybe they'd always been nothing. Maybe now he knew rats better than he knew the smell of clean sheets fresh from Frances's dryer.

Mississippi had rats. They had been all over the junkyard and the dump. And sometimes they'd crept up to the house, looking for something better maybe. Something fresher to eat. Or flesh to gnaw at.

You bit again, Louis?

Yes, ma'am.

You been playing in the dump?

No, ma'am.

Louis lifted his head, not liking this memory, trying to focus on something to clear it away, but there was nothing to see. He knew he should get up, knew he should keep walking because it would help his mind work. But he was going to give himself a few more minutes.

Our childhood, be it good or bad, makes us what we are, Mr. Kincaid.

"Well, Doc, you might be right about that."

Shit. Now he was talking to himself. But maybe that wasn't so bad either. Talking kept the mind alert.

A scream came from the darkness, but unlike the others, it was weak and pitiful. It kicked at his heart, and he found himself on his feet, moving again down the tunnel, pushing into the blackness.

The scream came again, louder now, and laced with whimpering and words. He could make out words now. Real words.

"*Please* . . . please stop . . . please don't hurt me anymore . . ."

He started running.

"Oh God! God, help me. I want to die!"

An intersection again. The corners marked with his pen, but it didn't matter now. The screams were all that mattered, and he could hear her close now. He was close.

"Help me! Help me!"

She had to be right ahead. He slowed his steps, turning on the flashlight, sweeping it across the floor. He was afraid Ives would see him coming, but he needed to see where he was.

But then it was quiet again.

"Are you there?" he called. "Tell me where you are!"

A muffled sob, fading whimpers, and the sound of something being dragged. Ahead. They were up ahead. He moved forward. He had gone on almost fifty feet when he realized he hadn't heard another sound.

He stopped, silence filling his ears. He pulled in some air to steady himself, and kept going, his eyes watching the beam on the concrete floor. It was clean here. Just roaches running along the edge of the wall.

Then the beam caught something wet and dark.

Blood was pooled at his feet. More blood streaked the floor ahead, disappearing into the darkness. And on the wall, about three feet up, scrawled in blood the word BITCH. And the handprint again.

He spun to the darkness. "You fucking bastard!" he shouted. "Where the hell are you?"

His words hung in the damp air until the tunnel sucked them up. He looked back at the blood, holding the flashlight steady on it. Then he knelt, feeling a strange urge to touch it. Still warm.

His eyes jerked to the smear of blood across the floor and he rose quickly, following it. Ives was dragging her, and she was still bleeding, leaving the floor streaked red and wet. It went on and on, across an intersection.

Why wasn't he hearing anything? Where were they?

The smears were fading but he moved forward, straining to see some drop or smudge that told him he was still going in the right direction. But suddenly, the blood trail was gone.

He looked up. In front of him was another cinder-block wall.

It had been quiet for a while now. Last time he had checked his watch it was 8:10. He guessed that was an hour ago. But he didn't check now. He needed to save the light.

He was sitting on the cold floor again. He felt something on his hands and he wiped them on his jeans, staring again down the tunnel.

His mind had started to drift the last few minutes. Back to things he hadn't thought about in years. He knew what it was, knew what isolation did to people. He had seen it in jails and prisons and in this hospital.

"Get up, get up," he whispered.

But he didn't. He worked his head back to Ives and the handprint he slapped on walls and the word BITCH he had painted just for Dr. Seraphin.

Why did he hate her so much? Because she was a woman? Because she had been his doctor? Because she hadn't been able to help him?

Her words came back to him.

Your man is impotent. In the sixties he was young and healthy. . . . He's changed since then . . . grown angrier and if he's become impotent recently his anger is magnified by his inability to perform. . . . a man who lost the last few years, no job, no contact with his family . . . who came to Hidden Lake at a young, impressionable age.

"Nice profile, Doctor," Louis said. "You nailed him."

Louis let his own words echo, trying to find the rest of it, knowing something else was there that he wasn't getting. Then it came to him.

"You nailed him because you knew all along who he was, didn't you?" he said.

Louis lowered his head, fingers on the bridge of his nose, something else in his head now.

"You knew he was a rapist then," he said. "You knew what he did in here and you kept it a secret and then, years later, you released him into the world."

Louis didn't move, his mind filled with Millie Reuben's strange story and the vacant look in Claudia DeFoe's eyes, and he tried to imagine them tied to a bed, Buddy Ives standing at the foot of it, a cigarette in his fingers, smoke curling from his lips. The image started to crystalize into something else, as more of Seraphin's words came back to him.

Something new I was trying with the patients . . . isolating them to gain their dependency . . . we treated them with various stimuli.

Louis shut his eyes, trying to make sense of his thoughts, knowing that what he was thinking was so crazy it had to be impossible, but he didn't think it was.

Something new I was trying . . .

Was it possible it had been some kind of therapy? A physical kind that involved sexual pain and pleasure? Acted out in rapes that Dr. Seraphin not only knew about, but arranged and condoned?

God. He was right. He knew he was.

Louis pushed himself to his feet, taking a second to steady himself, surprised his legs were so cramped and weak. But the idea about Seraphin gave him a surge of energy and he wanted to use it to move, afraid that if he stayed on the ground much longer, he wouldn't get up. He moved forward in the darkness.

There was something that came in total darkness, he thought. An unsettling kind of awareness that allowed people to hear even the faintest sound. Like a rat breathing. Or the grass growing. Or a heart beating in a tunnel a hundred feet away. Like the heart in that Edgar Allan Poe story . . . the heart under the floor that beat and beat and beat.

His body was trembling with a cold he couldn't feel anymore. Sometimes he thought the numbness was death setting in and he'd put a hand over his heart to make sure it was still beating.

No more walking now. He was too cold. He was on the floor, his legs drawn in, his hands shoved into his armpits.

In the last few hours, the screams had come and gone. He had been trying to keep track of them, but he had lost count a long time ago, sometimes wondering in the quiet whether he had heard them at all.

He had lost an hour or more somewhere. Part of him thought he had slept it away, but he didn't think he could sleep, although he knew he should. Sleep was essential to alertness. That's what they taught in the police academy. Cops needed to stay alert or they died.

He rested his head back against the wall, watching the darkness shift from gray to black to sometimes even flashes of white, when he blinked.

His partner Ollie had died. But it wasn't because he wasn't alert. It was because the bullet had been an inch high, hitting him above the vest in the neck. He hadn't been able to save Ollie, couldn't stop the blood pouring from his neck.

Louis glanced at his feet, watching a rat. It stopped and he could make out its eyes, like they could somehow find a reflection of light where there was none. Louis moved his feet and the rat ran off.

Get up. Get up and walk. You're drifting. You're back to things you haven't thought about for years. You'll freeze to death if you sit here. And she'll die. The woman will die.

She was already dead. Like Ollie was. Like Zeke was. And Rebecca Gruber. He had done nothing for them, just like he had done nothing for Phillip, except be ungrateful and give him grief. And just like he had done nothing for Kyla.

Get rid of it. I don't want to screw up my life.

Are you sure she had an abortion, Louis?

What if she didn't? What if you have a kid out there and its mother is too ashamed of you to tell the kid about you?

No, don't go there. Not now. Not with this. Think about anything but this.

Louis struggled to his feet, and started to walk. He turned on the flashlight, using the little sliver of light to provide some sense of reality. But the light was growing weak, and he clicked it off.

You're no better than him.

That man you keep in the drawer in your bedroom. That picture you keep of that white man who wasn't there for you. That man ran out on his son, ran out on you. But you are no better. No better than the man who slept with your mother and then walked away, ashamed of his black woman and his black child.

Something hard grabbed at his gut and he felt his whole body tighten. He stopped walking.

Don't you cry, boy. Don't you cry or I'll whip you twice as hard and twice as long.

He was seeing things now, seeing that old picture of himself as a boy, the one Phillip had given him at the kitchen table.

Then you stay in that closet, you sorry little bastard. Stay there until you starve for all I care.

Louis pressed the heel of his palm to his forehead.

It was after 1:00 a.m. He had no idea where he was now, if he was anywhere near the lift entrance. He had walked everywhere, met with cinder-block walls or more tunnels. He could no longer remember the layout of the hospital or what the map looked like that Spera had given him.

487

One thing was clear right now. He might die in here. Slip into a coma and freeze to death. And it struck him how sad that was. No one wanted to die, but wasn't there something about some professions, some lives, that dictated a person should die in a dignified fashion? Soldiers . . . cops.

Not that he even *was* a cop now.

He reached back and pulled his wallet out his pocket, flipping it open to the Ardmore P.D. badge. He wanted to look at it, but he didn't want to waste the light. So he ran his fingers over the embossing.

Not the Detroit badge he once wanted.

Not the Miami-Dade badge he could have had.

Joe . . .

My God. Joe.

For an instant, he could see her. Hear her. Touch her. Then she was gone, her face fading as quickly as it had come. He was going to die and he had never told her things. Never told her that one thing.

He lifted the wallet back to his face, his numb fingers clumsily flipping the plastic sleeves to find her picture, but he couldn't remember which was hers and he couldn't see them, not even if he held it right in front of his eyes.

He groped in the dark for the flashlight,

struggling to angle it toward the open wallet. He clicked it on.

Nothing happened. The batteries were dead.

Chapter 39

Somewhere in the darkness, a baby was crying. It wasn't an angry cry so much as an exhausted one, the tiny voice breaking with each gulp of air, like babies did when they still had hope someone would come to them.

No. Not a baby. It was the woman.

He knew that. She was dying now. He could hear it in her voice, feel it in the air because the air was so cold.

Ives had abandoned her, leaving her alone in the darkness to die. Leaving them both to die.

The crying stopped. He waited, hoping he would hear it again but praying he didn't, praying now that she would die so she wouldn't hurt anymore. So he couldn't hear her anymore.

What time was it? He took out his pocketknife and started picking at the watch's crystal, thinking if he could pry it off he could *feel* the hands and know. It would be the only thing he might be able to know.

Images were playing on the dark screen of his mind, images of what Ives had done to her. Ripping out her insides with some piece of metal. Then burning her. He could smell the cigarette smoke now, too. Sometimes it was just around the corner. Other times, it was a faint whiff that disappeared as quick as it had come, like the smoke had inside E Building.

He went back to working the crystal. Finally it popped free, and he heard it hit the concrete floor. Carefully, he put his fingers on the exposed watch face, trying to feel the hands without moving them. But his fingers were numb, so he blew on them a few times before trying again.

Two-twenty. In the morning?

He put the pocketknife away and he started to walk. He walked slowly now because without the flashlight, he couldn't see where he was going. He walked slowly now because he knew she wouldn't be there. He didn't call to her. His throat was raw from his own shouts that were never answered.

The echoing whimpers grew softer, like a baby crying itself out before sleep.

Like an apple baby . . .

Louis stopped. Where had that come from? The apple babies weren't down here.

They were in orchards and cider mills and baskets that were taken away in apple trucks. *Right, Charlie, right.*

The crying sounded now like it was underwater and he closed his eyes again, wishing her dead. Wishing the baby dead.

"Stop!" he screamed.

Silence. It settled around him like a thick black blanket. And he welcomed it.

He pressed his forehead against the cold tile. He was losing it. He had to stay focused. But on what?

Ives . . . Seraphin. *Stay with what you know is real.*

But what did he know? Everything was one black tangle in his mind. What did he *know?*

That Seraphin knew Ives raped patients. No, more than that, she let it happen. She condoned it.

Why? Why? Think! Therapy . . . she was using rape as some perverse sexual therapy?

The tile was cold and wet beneath his forehead, but he didn't lift his head. Didn't even open his eyes because it was almost like he could see now with them closed.

Ives . . . Seraphin.

Why did she give him those other three suspects?

492

Why did she let Ives leave Hidden Lake? Why did she set a rapist free?

A sound. Whimpering. He opened his eyes. No, it was his mind playing tricks. There was no crying anymore.

He shut his eyes. *Stay focused on what is real!*

Babies . . . they were real. Charlie had seen one, and he believed him.

Women patients locked away in isolation. Why? Pregnant from the rapes? Charlie saw babies. But where did the babies go? Maybe they weren't normal because of all the drugs. Maybe they were aborted, their remains cremated and abandoned with all the others in the mortuary? Or . . . or taken away in baskets so no one would see?

Claudia?

She had been isolated. Did she have a baby? Where was it? Where was Claudia?

In the dark, her face came to him, the face in the photograph from her patient file. Claudia's face came to him and it was as real as his own thoughts.

His fingers were shaking as he touched the tiny hands on the watch face. Three . . . and six. Three-thirty? He stuck his hands back under his armpits. He hadn't moved in the last hour. He was still huddled on the floor, knees pulled in against the cold. He couldn't feel his feet anymore.

It was so quiet now. No crying, no sounds at all.

No one was coming.

He took the pen from his pocket and felt along on the tile for a smooth spot.

What to write? And to who?

He had things he needed to say, things he had never said. To Phillip. And Kyla. To his sister and his brother. To a little boy named Ben. To Mel and to Sam Dodie and to Jesse . . . Jesse. God, he couldn't even remember his last name.

His fingers were so cold he could barely grip the pen. And worse, he was starting to feel sleepy.

Stay awake . . .

He turned back to the wall, uncapping the pen.

He didn't know what to say to *her.*

They never had to say much to each other. And it didn't seem right now, especially now, to write something Joe would know was fake. There was something about her that kept him strong and he didn't want *not* to be strong here. It was important what he wrote to her now. It would be what she would remember after all else was gone.

He turned slowly, his fingers finding the wall. He tried to spit on it but he had no saliva, so he just wiped it with his sleeve. Then in slow, careful strokes, he moved the pen across the tile.

J O E

He set the pen on the floor and closed his eyes.

Screaming. His eyes jerked open and he struggled to get up, bracing himself on the wall and wincing at the pain in his frozen feet.

No, not a scream. It was a scraping sound. He started down the tunnel toward the sound, limping, swaying from wall to wall. Another scrape, louder now.

It was the doors. Had to be the doors.

He tried to go faster, but each step sent stabs of pain shooting up his legs. The tunnel seemed to be growing colder. He hit an intersection and kept going. And then, suddenly, the air started to change. There was something different in it now, something colder and sharper.

More water. And the crunch of glass under his feet. No, ice.

And the air. It was cold. So fucking cold.

And so . . . so fresh. He kept following it.

He stopped. In the black void ahead, he could see something. He squinted, afraid his mind was deceiving him again.

There was something there. A glimmer of gray . . . a faint cast of light and he knew what it was. The doors. The metal doors were open and the air he was feeling was coming from the opening by the lift.

The doors were open.

He stumbled to them, pressing his hands against the rusty surface. Then he felt his way along the concrete wall, his feet slipping on the water, the air getting colder and clearer.

The lift came into view, blue in the shaft of moonlight. A shadowy iron square, frosted with ice, shimmering at the end of the tunnel.

And next to it, a ladder.

He staggered to it. He fell off the first step of the ladder and he had to concentrate to make his foot stay on the rung. He grabbed the sides and pulled himself up, first one step, then another. And finally he was aboveground.

He threw himself off the ladder, hitting a thick layer of crusty snow, and he wanted to just lie there, but he didn't, and he crawled a few feet, then pushed his body up onto all fours, gulping in the air. He stayed that way for a long time, afraid to open his eyes, afraid it was all a dream. His hands grew cold in the snow.

Slowly, he rose to his knees and looked out at the cemetery.

Everything was iced over, silvery white under a generous moon, all of it still and unmoving and pure. And it was beautiful.

Chapter 40

The light was pale pink, the morning rising as if it were coming from a deep sleep. Even the voices seemed hushed, and the footsteps in the snow were a soft steady crunch, like something brittle and fragile was breaking under the ground.

Louis stood wrapped in a blanket, someone else's shoes on his feet, gloves on his hands. His body still trembled, but the cold was gone, leaving nothing inside. He watched the police work, watched as they disappeared in and out of the hole in the ground like roaches scrambling from the light.

Chief Dalum stood nearby, silent now, long ago giving up trying to urge Louis to go to the hospital. Louis had asked about Charlie, but Dalum hadn't known anything. Didn't know where Charlie was or why he hadn't delivered the message.

"Bloom is here," Dalum said suddenly.

Louis looked toward the cemetery entrance. Detective Bloom was hurrying toward them, his face red and wrinkled from sleep, his coat open, shirt half tucked in. Another man struggled to keep up with him, talking quickly as they both made long strides across the snow.

Bloom stopped at Louis, silencing the other cop with a wave of his hand. Louis looked at him for a moment, then away.

"What the hell were you thinking going down there?" Bloom asked.

Louis stared at the hole in the ground, pulling the blanket tighter. He heard Dalum say something to Bloom, and then the two walked away. Bloom came back a few minutes later, head down, and he blew out an apologetic breath.

"You need to see a doctor," Bloom said.

"When they find her."

Bloom glanced at the hole. "We have someone working on the electricity now. If she's down there, they'll find her."

"She *is* there," Louis snapped.

"Wasn't what I meant, Kincaid. Any idea who it was?"

"No."

A uniform waved at Bloom. "Lights are on down there," he called. "At least in some places."

Bloom gave him a nod, then looked back at Louis. "You warm enough?"

Louis ignored him.

Bloom motioned toward the hole. "You feel like showing us anything?"

Louis didn't move. Bloom waited for an answer, but Louis couldn't give him one, couldn't even take a step toward the hole. There was a part of him that knew how that looked, that it looked weak and frightened, but he just couldn't do it.

"Look," Bloom said, "I'll have one of my officers drive you back to Adrian."

"No."

"What the hell do you want me to do with you then?"

"Just leave me alone."

"If you won't see a doctor, then I need a statement and I need it quick. Anything you can tell us might help catch this guy."

"He's gone."

"How do you know that?"

Louis spun to him. "Because I fucking know. And I know what's behind all this, too. I know what they were doing here and why they were doing it and why they had to hide it."

"What the hell are you talking about?"

Louis almost said it. Almost told him about the babies and the experiments, about Ives and Seraphin, but something stopped him. It was a small, instantaneous flash of clarity that he knew he should listen to. If he told him what he knew, Bloom would think he was crazy, really crazy.

But there was one thing he could tell him. "His name is Buddy Ives," Louis said. "He was a patient here."

"I guess you just fucking know that, too?"

"His handprint is on the damn door down there — just like the one he left on the E Building wall."

Bloom fell quiet, his gaze drifting back to the lift. He let the silence fill the moment, and Louis finally looked away from him.

"I guess we owe you and Charlie an apology," Bloom said.

"You've seen Charlie?" Louis asked.

"Yeah," Bloom said, his voice edged with embarrassment. "When he showed up at the security gate yesterday afternoon my officer arrested him."

"*Arrested* him?"

Bloom's hand came up. "We told him three times to stay off the grounds. We had no choice."

"You stupid son of a bitch."

"Hold it right there, Kincaid."

"Was the cop fucking deaf?" Louis said.

Bloom put a hand on Louis's chest, but Louis pushed it off, losing the blanket as he stepped into Bloom. Bloom grabbed Louis's arm and tried to turn him, but Louis twisted away and his arm came back to take a swing, but he never made it. He was pushed down into the snow, a dozen hands keeping him there. He jerked back, trying to push himself up, but he had no strength, and he finally went limp under their pressure.

Bloom's mouth came down to his ear. "Please," he said firmly. "Don't do this. Let us help you."

Louis lowered his head, taking a moment to close his eyes and calm himself. Then he gave Bloom a nod and the hands left his back. Bloom and Dalum helped him to his feet. Louis wiped his face and stared at the ground, trying to sort his thoughts, but he couldn't. Things still didn't seem right.

A cop handed him the blanket and Louis took it and put it around him. He just looked at the snow, his mind almost as frozen as his body.

A radio went off somewhere close by and Louis thought he caught something about a girl and he was at the edge of the hole before Bloom. Two uniforms and a man in a CSU jacket stood at the bottom.

"We found a body," one of them called up. "It's bad."

Louis stared at the man, anxious to know more but afraid of what it might be. Afraid the woman he heard dying was Alice. Or even Dr. Seraphin.

"What did she look like?" he asked.

The crime scene investigator glanced at Bloom for permission to answer and Bloom gave him a nod.

"Twenty — maybe," the man said. "Long brown hair, hundred ten, hundred fifteen pounds."

Louis stared down at the man's face, seeing the emptiness in it as he went on, talking about things Louis had to concentrate on to understand.

"She was nude, beaten some, then burned, maybe with a cigarette, and it looked like someone tried to dig out her insides, Detective."

Louis turned and walked away, stopping ten or fifteen feet away from the hole. He could feel his mind shutting down, filling itself with a cottony darkness.

After a few seconds, Bloom came up behind him. "You ready to leave now, Kincaid?"

"Yes."

"Stay at the station house until I get there. If you want a doctor, have the officer call one. We'll take care of it."

Louis nodded and headed toward the gates of the cemetery.

Charlie was in a cell, sitting on a single bunk, his back to the wall. It looked like a temporary holding cell, but it was locked, officers working nearby, phones ringing and computers clicking.

A cop unlocked the door, swung it open, and left. When Charlie didn't move, Louis stepped to the cell.

"You can come out now, Charlie," Louis said.

Charlie looked up at him, then down, embarrassed. "Is Miss Alice here?"

"No," Louis said. "But she's coming to pick you up."

"I'll wait here. It's cold out there."

"Can I come in and wait with you?" Louis asked.

Charlie didn't answer, but he scooted over on the bunk. Louis went in and sat down next to him. He was still shivering a little, but he wore a Michigan State Police sweatshirt now, given to him after he had taken a shower in the cops' locker room.

He had stayed in the shower almost thirty minutes, feeling the hot water burn his skin, standing there, eyes closed, hoping the heat and water would somehow wash away the stench of the tunnel and everything else, but knowing somewhere inside that nothing would ever wash it off.

Charlie was staring at the cops, his breaths slow and heavy.

"I messed up," he said finally.

"We both did."

Charlie glanced at him, holding the look a long time before he spoke. "They told me you got stuck in the hole."

"Yes."

"Were you down there a long time?"

"Yes."

"Was it dark?"

"Yes."

"Were you scared?"

Louis didn't answer. Charlie drew his feet to the edge of the bunk and wrapped his arms around his knees.

"Did you see them?" Charlie asked.

"See who?"

"Those things that come in the dark."

"Yes," Louis said. "I saw things."

"Did you see the apple babies?"

"I heard them."

Charlie lowered his head to his knees and was quiet for a long time. "They're not coming back, are they?"

"No," Louis said quietly.

Charlie lifted his head and pulled his

knees closer to his chest, watching the stir of activity in the office.

"You don't need the apple babies to make a new home somewhere, Charlie," Louis said. "You have everything you need to do that by yourself."

They sat silent, only the ringing of phones and murmur of voices in their ears. Charlie seemed to be thinking about what Louis had just said. Then Charlie looked at him, his eyes clear and focused.

" 'I had a dream,' " he said softly. " 'I had a dream past the wit of man to say what dream it was. Man is but an ass if he go about to expound this dream.' "

"That's from your book," Louis said.

Charlie nodded. "Do you know what it means?"

Louis let out a long breath. "Yes, I do."

Detective Bloom stood behind his desk, collar open, tie loose, his eyes fogged with fatigue or maybe disbelief, Louis wasn't sure. Dalum stood off to the right, and another detective Louis didn't know stood to the left.

All three were digesting what he had just told them, which had been everything he knew about this whole case. The rapes, dating back to Claudia and including

Millie Reuben, and both of them being burned with cigarettes. How they had dug up Donald Lee Becker. Louis then went on to betray Dr. Seraphin, explaining how she came to E Building and picked out suspects. How Ives had been one of those suspects.

And then he had wrapped it up with his theory of how Dr. Seraphin had for some reason condoned or arranged the rapes, and that there had been babies conceived — Charlie's apple babies — and those babies were aborted or later killed because of deformities and were now in rusty cans in John Spera's tent.

Louis waited, watching their faces, knowing with every word how insane it sounded to three seasoned cops, but he didn't care. He knew it was true.

Bloom looked at Chief Dalum. "Maybe you should take Kincaid back to your house, Dan."

Dalum looked at Louis, trying to work some sympathy into his face, but Louis was seeing only incredulity.

"I know how crazy it seems," Louis said. "But I can take you to Millie Reuben. She'll tell you. She may even be able to identify Ives as her rapist."

"No."

"Then take me to Dr. Seraphin's lake house," Louis said, stepping forward. "Confront her on all this. Ask her about our trip to E Building and how she picked Ives out and why she let him do what he did."

Again, they were quiet. Louis felt a slow shiver make its way across his shoulders as he waited for an answer, some sign that they would take this one step further.

"Do your damn job," Louis said. "Just ask her some questions. She knows everything."

"All right," Bloom said. "I'll go out there."

"I want to go with you."

"Jesus Christ," Bloom said. "Give me a break here, Kincaid. You're in no shape to go anywhere."

"I can help you. I know what to ask, how to handle her."

Bloom gave a heavy sigh and he looked to Dalum, then back at Louis. "All right, but you keep your mouth shut unless I need you to open it. We clear?"

"Yeah."

Bloom picked his coat up off the chair, his head moving in a slow, impatient shake.

"I want my gun," Louis said. "Give it back to me."

Bloom was pulling the black overcoat on his shoulders. "Not today, Kincaid. You see yourself a doctor first and we'll talk about that."

Louis rubbed his face, fighting the urge to argue, knowing he wouldn't win. He turned and left the office, walking stiffly through the halls and pushing out the front doors.

Everything was gray and muted and cold. He stood on the steps for a few minutes, then walked down to the sidewalk, head bent, hands in his pockets.

The door opened behind him and he looked back to see Chief Dalum come out, but he turned away from him, not wanting a lecture. Or sympathy. Or pity.

"Louis," Dalum said.

When Louis didn't answer him, Dalum came up next to him and stood quietly for a second before speaking. "I want you to know, I believe most of what you said in there."

Louis stared at the ground.

"Something else, too," Dalum said. "The state has no death certificate on file for Claudia DeFoe."

Louis could not answer. There was something in his head that couldn't grasp what Dalum was telling him. Couldn't figure out what to do with the information. God, what was wrong with him?

He felt Dalum's hand on his shoulder. "It's time for you to go home," he said. "You need to be with family right now."

Louis's eyes were drawn to a state cruiser pulling from the parking lot. It stopped in front of the station, and Bloom honked the horn for him.

Louis faced Dalum, reaching slowly into his pocket and withdrawing his wallet. He flipped it open and took out the Ardmore badge.

"Thanks for everything, Dan," Louis said.

Dalum took the badge and Louis walked away from him, toward the blue cruiser.

Chapter 41

Oliver opened the door of the lake house and stood there, one hand still on the door to block their entry. Bloom held open his coat so Oliver could see the badge.

"We'd like to see Dr. Seraphin."

Oliver's chin dipped in a quick nod and he walked away, leaving the door open as he disappeared down the hall. Louis and Bloom made their way to the living room. Louis was drawn to the fireplace and moved to it, holding out his hands. Bloom went to a window.

"Lake's not frozen over yet," Bloom said.

Louis didn't answer.

"Pretty isolated area for a woman who might be in danger from a crazy man," Bloom added, turning back to Louis.

"I think the man who let us in is her bodyguard," Louis said. "My guess is she's had him for years."

"Why?"

"Because she knew Ives might come after her someday."

Bloom looked at Louis, his face wrinkled

with the same doubt as it had shown in his office. Louis let it go, edging closer to the fire. He heard footsteps coming back down the hall, then Oliver's voice.

"The doctor will see you in the den."

Dr. Seraphin was standing near the glass doors that led out to the snow-covered deck, a glass of white wine in her hand. Behind her, the lake moved with an icy slowness, almost blending into the smoke-colored afternoon sky.

Her eyes went to Louis and stayed there. She seemed to sense something was different and her face reflected first a glimmer of curiosity, then changed to a mask of defiance. Maybe anger.

"Good afternoon, Officers," she said.

Bloom introduced himself, flashed a badge Dr. Seraphin did not look at, and started speaking slowly, first telling her about Ives, the latest victim whose name was still unknown, and the cemetery tunnel, then adding a few words about Louis's being trapped in it.

"I had forgotten about that tunnel," she said softly. "How long were you trapped, Mr. Kincaid?"

"Over twelve hours."

Seraphin showed no expression. "How terrible for you."

"Yeah."

Bloom moved forward. "Doctor, I need to ask you a few questions about Buddy Ives."

"I'm afraid that's confidential."

"Well, now," Bloom said, "if what Kincaid told me about you visiting E Building is true, I don't see how you can hide behind confidentiality now."

Her gaze finally swung to Bloom. "What do you mean?"

"Kincaid tells me you two went through the patient files last week and you picked him out four suspects, Doctor. Ives included."

"That's absurd."

"What?" Louis said.

Bloom threw a hand toward Louis, then gathered a breath. "How about we ask your bodyguard, Doctor?"

"My what?" Dr. Seraphin asked.

"That big fellow that answered the door."

"Oliver is my driver and personal assistant. Nothing more."

"How about we ask anyway?"

Dr. Seraphin set her glass down and walked to the door, calling softly for Oliver. He was there in a second, his bulk filling the frame, his beefy face expressionless.

"Oliver," Bloom said, "did you and

Dr. Seraphin visit Hidden Lake last week?"

"No."

"Anytime in the last month?"

"No."

"Anytime in the last year?"

"I have never been to Hidden Lake Hospital," Oliver said.

Louis lowered his head, working hard at staying level. He should have expected this. Seraphin would never have made that visit without first making sure she could deny it later.

"Tell me, Oliver," Bloom said. "What's your job here?"

"I am a driver and an assistant."

Louis watched Bloom, worried he was buying all of this crap. Damn it. He had to figure out a way to get to Seraphin. Make her admit something.

"Why would I need a bodyguard?" Seraphin asked.

"Kincaid thinks Buddy Ives is after you," Bloom said, "that you're the ultimate victim, so to speak."

She was unfazed. "Why would this patient want to hurt me?"

"Because of the rapes," Louis said.

Her face gave a little, her upper lip moving with a tiny tremor, but Louis knew

514

Bloom hadn't seen it. His head was down to his notebook.

"Rapes?" Dr. Seraphin asked.

"Ives raped at will for over two decades," Louis said. "While he was in your hospital, while he was under your control, while his victims were in isolation."

Bloom quickly stepped in. "Kincaid, let me handle this."

Seraphin's eyes shifted to Louis. "Detective, have you had Mr. Kincaid examined since his experience in the tunnel?"

Louis moved forward and Bloom caught his arm, holding tight. "Hang on there, Kincaid."

Bloom looked to Seraphin. "How about we just get a statement from you on this rape thing, Doctor? Just for the record?"

"This is abominable," she said. "If Ives managed to hurt anyone while he was in-stitutionalized, I had no knowledge of it."

"He raped Millie Reuben," Louis said.

"Who is she?"

"A former patient. I talked to her. She remembers everything."

"I'm sure she does," Seraphin said. "In her own way."

Louis felt everything starting to slip from under him; Seraphin was studying him; then she shook her head, pulling gently on the sleeve of her sweater.

"Detective Bloom, you're wasting my time and yours and you're only furthering Mr. Kincaid's trauma by letting him pursue these ridiculous thoughts," she said.

"Trauma?" Louis said.

"Yes," she said. "You're not a stupid man, Mr. Kincaid. You have training. You know what fear and isolation do to the mind. Certainly you recognize you're irrational right now."

"I know exactly what I'm saying," Louis said.

She looked at Bloom, a sad smile on her lips.

Bloom closed his small notebook. "I do have one more question, Doctor. How could you release a man like Ives?"

"I was not at Hidden Lake when he was released," Seraphin said. "And even if I had been, there was probably little else I could have done."

Bloom looked at Seraphin, tapping his notebook on his hand. Then he turned to Louis. "Come on, Kincaid."

"No," Louis said. He faced Seraphin. "I can prove you were there in E Building. I can find someone who saw you. Your fingerprints will be on the files. And when we find Ives, he'll tell us what you did inside that place."

"I hope you do catch him."

"Kincaid. Let's go now," Bloom said.

Louis stared at Seraphin. Bloom pulled at his arm, but Louis shrugged it off.

"You need to deal with what happened to you," Seraphin said. "I can help you."

"I don't need your help," Louis said.

Louis turned away from her and pushed past Bloom. He heard Bloom say something to her, but he wasn't sure what it was and didn't care.

He was standing outside in the driveway, trying to sort his thoughts, when Bloom came out the door.

"She's lying, Detective," Louis said.

"Maybe, maybe not," Bloom said. "But if she *did* allow Ives to rape whoever he wanted when he wanted, why would he hate her so much?"

Louis glanced back at the house, then at the ground, a jab of panic working its way through his chest. Suddenly it felt as if his whole body were shutting down, that even the simplest thought — like the way home — was hard to bring into focus.

"I don't know," Louis said.

Chapter 42

He felt as if he were back in the tunnels staring at a cinder-block wall. Dead-ended. Blocked. Nowhere to go. And with this small echo of a voice in his head whispering that maybe he was seeing things that weren't really there.

The farmland was a blur. After Bloom had dropped him off, he had picked up the Impala and just started driving, heading out into the cornfields away from Adrian.

He realized suddenly he was speeding and eased off the pedal.

He wasn't crazy. Angry, and fighting to stay awake, but not crazy. Something bad had been going on at Hidden Lake and Seraphin was behind it. But no one believed him and he had no proof. Millie Reuben's word wasn't going to convince Bloom. But who else was there who knew the truth?

The wind was gusting hard, sending dervishes of snow spinning across the road. The Impala fishtailed and Louis hit the brake. The car skidded to a stop on the empty road. Nothing around him but beaten-down cornstalks and just beyond a barbed-wire fence, the remnants of a listing gray-plank barn.

Louis sat there, hands gripping the wheel. An old windmill groaned in the wind.

Who *else* knew the truth?

Rodney.

He had been to see Claudia regularly. That much he could prove with the visitors' log. Rodney might have seen something, remembered something she did. Or the way she looked. Might have seen her pregnant.

There was a tractor path just ahead. Louis pulled the car into it, turned around, and headed back the way he had come. At least he had a plan now — detour back to Plymouth to pick up Claudia's file and then go to Grosse Pointe.

Frances's car wasn't in the drive when he pulled up to the house. Louis was glad; he didn't really want to face Phillip right now. Inside, he didn't even stop to take off his coat. He found Claudia's file in his room and was starting back downstairs when he heard the door. He hesitated, then went down.

Phillip was hanging up his coat in the hall closet and looked up.

"You coming or going?" Phillip asked.

"Going," Louis said. "I'll be back later."

Phillip shut the closet door. He wanted to say something. Louis could see it in the way Phillip's hand lingered on the closet knob, blocking Louis's path to the front door. Louis felt a stab of guilt for the way he had left things the last time they had spoken. But he knew he was in no frame of mind to fix it right now.

"You look terrible, Louis," Phillip said.

For a second, Louis thought about telling him about the tunnels. "I'm all right," he said.

The wounded look on Phillip's face made Louis suddenly feel as if he were ten years old again. "Phillip, don't worry about me," Louis said.

"I'm thinking you should go home," Phillip said.

"What?"

"I want you to let this go, forget about it."

Louis shifted the folder to under his arm. "Can you?"

Phillip hesitated, then nodded slowly.

Louis looked off toward the dark kitchen, then back. "I don't want to leave you here alone, Phillip. What about Frances?"

"That's between us. You can't fix that, Louis."

The sadness was etched in Phillip's face, and Louis knew it wasn't about Claudia. It was about Frances and what Phillip might have destroyed.

"I have to go somewhere," Louis said.

Phillip's eyes held his for a moment, and then he stepped aside.

It was dark by the time Louis pulled into the drive at the mansion on Provencal Road. There were no cars in the circular drive, but the old leaded windows glowed gold in the cold night.

A maid answered. She told Louis that Rodney wasn't in but was expected back shortly. Louis told her he'd wait and pushed his way into the foyer before she could stop him.

The maid led him to the same library where he had first met Rodney. There was no welcoming fire burning, and the room was illuminated by only one table lamp. Louis sat in a wing chair by the dead hearth. A good twenty minutes, maybe a half hour passed. Finally, he got up and switched on two other lamps. The old house seemed to breathe around him, exhaling a cold vapor into the still air.

"Can I help you?"

Louis leaned forward to peer around the

wing chair. It was Eloise DeFoe. She was wearing a fur coat, holding it around her like a blanket against the cold. Her mouth was a slash of red in her small white face.

Louis rose. Her expression shifted. "You're that police person," she said.

"Investigator," Louis said. "I'm waiting for your son."

She pulled off her black leather gloves, then shrugged out of her coat, leaving it on a chair. "I can't tell you when Rodney might be home," she said. "He's very un-reliable."

"I'll wait," Louis said. He sat back down in the wing chair.

"I can't imagine why you need to talk to him," she said. "Perhaps I can save you some time? What is it you need?"

There was something about her stance, her ramrod posture, that told Louis she wanted him out of here.

Louis stood up. "I need to know more about your daughter Claudia."

Eloise Defoe just stared at him.

"Why didn't you ever visit her at Hidden Lake, Mrs. DeFoe?"

"My daughter was ill," Eloise said. "The doctors advised me that it was best to leave her alone so she could heal."

Before Louis could reply, there was a

sound out in the foyer. A man's voice and then, a few seconds later, Rodney DeFoe was standing in the doorway. He was wearing a handsome camel cashmere overcoat and a bright red scarf hanging loosely around his neck. He looked harried and, Louis noted, disoriented.

Rodney's eyes found Louis's face. "Well, look who's here, Columbo."

Eloise DeFoe's eyes swept over her son as he came into the room, and Louis picked up the scent of her disdain — and, from Rodney, the smell of alcohol. Rodney ignored them both, heading toward the table of glasses and bottles. The room was quiet as he poured himself a drink.

"Rodney, we need to talk," Louis said.

Rodney didn't turn around, but Louis could see him raise the glass and take a big drink.

"I said we need to talk," Louis said.

Rodney turned. "Really? And what other filth have you come to tell me? Telling me she was raped wasn't enough? You want to see me *lose* it again?"

Eloise came forward. "Raped? Who was raped?"

Rodney's eyes drifted to his mother, then to Louis. "Go ahead, tell her."

Louis was silent.

"Tell her, damn it," Rodney said.

"Who was raped?" Eloise demanded.

"Claudia!" Rodney shouted. "Claudia was raped. Your daughter Claudia was raped! In that place!"

Rodney turned away, slamming the drink down.

Eloise stared at his back. "That's impossible," she said finally. "I would have been informed."

Rodney spun around. "Informed? You think they would have *told* us something like that?" His face crumbled. "Jesus, if I had known . . . I could have . . ."

Louis took a step toward him. "Rodney, I have questions —"

Rodney closed his eyes and shook his head.

"You visited Claudia —" Louis said.

"You visited her?" Eloise interrupted.

Louis ignored her. "Rodney —"

Eloise pushed her way to Rodney, grabbing his arm. "You went there?"

"Yes, I went there," Rodney said. "I went there to see her."

"But I told you —"

"I don't care, Mother. Go ahead, cut me off, throw me out. I just don't care anymore."

Louis pulled the picture of Claudia from

the patient file and walked to Rodney, holding it under his nose. "You don't care?"

For a long time, Rodney didn't move. Then his hand came out and he took the picture. It shook slightly as he stared at it.

When he looked at Louis, there were tears in his eyes. "She was beautiful," he said. "Not like this."

"Rodney, listen to me," Louis said. "In all the times you saw Claudia, did you ever notice if she was pregnant? Did she ever say anything about it?"

"Pregnant?" Eloise said.

Rodney just stared at Louis, the picture of Claudia still in his hand.

"Think, try to remember," Louis said. "Did she ever talk about being pregnant? Did she ever mention a baby?"

Eloise was at Louis's side. "I won't listen to this anymore. I won't listen to you talk about my daughter like this anymore," she said. "Get out of my house before I call —"

"Shut up!" Rodney shouted.

Eloise drew back. "How dare you raise your voice to me," she said.

"Shut up! Shut up!" Rodney shouted again.

"Rodney, don't —"

"Don't what? Don't tell, Mother? Well,

fuck that. Fuck you! I've had it! I can't do this anymore!"

Rodney's face was red, sweat beading on his forehead. When his eyes came back to Louis they glistened with rage, and for a moment Louis thought of the way Charlie's eyes had looked when they locked him in the cell.

"Claudia *was* pregnant," Rodney said. "She was pregnant when she went into Hidden Lake."

Louis was stunned into silence as his mind struggled to accept what he had just heard — and what it meant. He looked from Rodney to Eloise, but neither was going to say anything.

"Phillip?" he asked.

Rodney nodded.

It was so quiet Louis could hear the soft tick of the sleet on the windows. He had a vague sense of Eloise DeFoe moving away. Rodney's eyes shifted as he watched his mother go to the sofa and sit down.

Louis turned toward her. "Did you know? Is that why you sent Claudia away?"

"No," Eloise said firmly. "I didn't know until the hospital called me months later. I sent her away because it was the only way I could control her."

"You sent her away because you were

afraid she was just like Father," Rodney said.

Louis could see it in her face, see that Rodney was right, that Eloise DeFoe was ashamed of her own daughter's mental illness.

Louis turned back to Rodney. "Tell me what happened that night."

Rodney pulled in a deep breath and sat down in the chair. "Claudia was going to run off with Phillip." His eyes went to Eloise. "But *she* found out and locked Claudia up in her room."

His eyes were locked on his mother. "I should have gone to her," he whispered. "I heard her crying and screaming, but I just stayed down here like a fucking coward. I stayed down here, sitting right here in this same chair with my drink."

He was silent for a moment. "I think I passed out. All I remember is it was quiet. The next thing I remember was some strange guy shaking me and telling me Claudia had slit her wrists in the bathtub. I ran outside and she was strapped on this thing and they were putting her in the ambulance and she looked . . ." He took in a slow breath. "She looked . . ."

Rodney put a hand over his face. The shoulders of the camel coat began to move as he cried.

Louis saw something on the floor by Rodney's feet. It was the photo of Claudia, crumpled into a wad. He looked back at Rodney, but he couldn't muster much pity for him. He was a weak man who believed the world turned only in rhythm to his own needs. And even now, it was still about him.

Louis looked back at Eloise. "You were the one who found her and called the police?"

Eloise nodded, her mouth set in a hard line. "I went up to check on her when I realized I hadn't heard any sound from her room. I went up there, but she wasn't in her bedroom. I went to her bathroom and that's where I found her. She had taken a razor blade and cut her wrists."

Louis looked back at Rodney. He was staring at his mother with anguished eyes.

"Claudia was very ill," Eloise said. "I couldn't control her. I had no choice but to send her to Hidden Lake for her own safety."

"What happened to the baby?" Louis asked.

Eloise just sat there.

"You're Catholic. You wouldn't have allowed it to be aborted," Louis said. "What happened to the baby?"

Eloise didn't blink as she met his eyes. "I signed adoption papers. I did what was necessary. I don't know what happened after that."

"Who arranged it?"

"The hospital."

"Dr. Seraphin?"

She was quiet. But the answer was there in her face, in the shock that Louis knew the name.

"I think you should leave," Eloise said.

Louis picked up the crumpled photograph of Claudia and put it in his pocket. He left, pausing outside to dig the car keys out of his jacket. The door opened behind him, but he didn't turn.

"Wait!"

Louis glanced back. Rodney was coming toward him. Louis ignored him, opening the Impala's door and getting in. Rodney grabbed the door before Louis could shut it. He looked down at Louis with reddened eyes.

"Tell Phillip I'm sorry," he said.

Louis jerked the door closed. He started the car, revving the engine, and Rodney stepped away. As Louis headed down Provencal Road, he looked up at the rearview mirror. Rodney was still standing there in the driveway.

★ ★ ★

"Silent Night" was playing softly, emerging strained and tinny sounding from the old radio and fading away into the shadows of the basement. Louis sat at the bar, a warm beer in front of him. He was waiting for Phillip to get out of the shower and he'd been down here maybe fifteen minutes, sometimes rolling a walnut between his fingers as a way to pass the time. And a way to keep from looking at himself in the mirror.

He had caught a glimpse of himself when he first sat down and hadn't liked what he had seen. He looked older, and defeated, the shadows in his face hard. Even his eyes were a deeper shade of gray like there was something opaque behind them now.

He heard the water cut off, and the rushing sound in the pipes above his head faded to a drip. He rolled the walnut across the bar, watching it flop end over end until it came to a stop next to the bowl. When he heard Phillip's footsteps on the stairs, he drew a breath and took a drink.

Phillip wore a red-and-green striped sweater and black slacks, his wet hair slicked back. Louis waited while he grabbed a beer from behind the bar and settled onto a bar stool.

"Are you going to tell me you're leaving?" Phillip asked.

"No," Louis said.

Phillip looked down, turned his bottle slowly. "So what is it then?"

"Claudia was pregnant when she was sent to Hidden Lake."

Phillip said nothing, didn't move except for a slight slump of his shoulders.

"She had the baby and it was put up for adoption by her mother," Louis said.

Still Phillip didn't speak or look up. Louis let the silence lengthen. He picked up the walnut and set it back in the bowl, catching another glimpse of his face in the mirror. Then his eyes moved to Phillip's face. Phillip's eyes were closed.

"Rodney knew," Louis said. "Says he's sorry."

Phillip finally looked up. "Sorry?"

Louis nodded.

"He takes my child and he's sorry?"

Louis again nodded, not knowing what else to say. Phillip drew a breath so deep and hard that Louis could hear it, and it seemed to bring some rigidity back to Phillip's posture.

"Can we find this child?" Phillip asked.

"I don't know," Louis said. "It depends on how it was done. If they left a paperwork trail. If it was even legal."

"It wasn't legal. It couldn't be. I never signed anything."

"I know. But it's real easy to cover something like this up. Falsify the mother's name. Fake a birth certificate. A shady attorney."

Phillip touched his arm. "Will you try?"

"I don't know," Louis said.

Phillip looked away, his mind suddenly on something else, and Louis was grateful he didn't ask more about finding the child. He wanted to help Phillip, and he knew that if it were his child, he'd want to find it. But there was something else to finish first.

"The child would be thirty-six, Louis," Phillip said.

"I know."

"Did you ask if it was a boy or girl?"

"No," Louis said. "I'm sorry."

"It's all right," Phillip said. "It's all right."

Phillip slid off the bar stool and started back up the stairs. Louis watched him, surprised at the sudden change in his face — and his step. It was resolve or acceptance, or maybe a mix of both.

"Phillip," Louis said, "where are you going?"

"To see Frances," he said. "This is something I need to talk over with her."

"Don't you think it will make her even angrier?"

"I don't know," Phillip said. "I just know I need to talk with her."

"Jesus, Phil," Louis said, "aren't *you* angry?"

"Of course I am," Phillip said. "But I don't have to stay that way. You've given me something I never thought I'd have. You've put everything into focus for me."

"Wait a minute," Louis said. "What are you going to tell this kid when you find him or her?"

"I'm going to say 'I'm your father,' " Phillip said. " 'And I made a mistake.' "

Phillip disappeared up the steps and Louis turned back to the bar. He didn't understand how Phillip could be happy about confronting a long-lost, grown-up child when it would be so painful and hard. He didn't understand how Phillip could ever expect Frances to accept this on top of everything else. And he didn't understand why Phillip wasn't furious.

He should be. Not only at Eloise DeFoe

and Rodney, but at Seraphin and everything she had done to Claudia.

Claudia . . . something was coming back to him, something Charlie had said about the apple babies, and suddenly he knew that what he thought in the tunnels was only half right.

Claudia and Phillip's baby . . . that was what had started it all. Someone had probably paid good money to Seraphin for that baby. And that was what had given her the idea.

Use women patients for breeding. Use Ives to impregnate them. A scheme to create healthy, white infants that Seraphin could adopt out to wealthy couples.

Seraphin's voice came back to him:

The hospital had so little funding, so money was always a problem. . . . I was instrumental in correcting many deficiencies.

Those long periods of isolation. It wasn't therapy or to punish patients; it was to keep the pregnancies secret. Then the newborns were removed from the hospital in baskets, driven away in fruit trucks.

Babies . . . conceived by a rapist, sold to the highest bidders so Dr. Seraphin could keep her programs in place. Buy new equipment. Make a career.

Proof. He still had no real proof. There

was nothing to connect Seraphin directly to Ives.

Louis stared at his reflection in the mirror, something clicking in his brain. He slid off the stool and went quickly upstairs to his bedroom. It took him a moment to find the patient file for Buddy Ives. He grabbed his glasses off the nightstand and began flipping through the files.

He found the notation he was looking for: Ives had been put in "temporary isolation" at least five times. He was about to pull out Claudia's file to compare the dates when something on Ives's form caught his eye.

He stared at the bottom of the form at the signature right above the typed line ATTENDING PHYSICIAN.

Dr. Rose Seraphin.

Louis pulled out other forms. She had signed them all. He slapped the file shut. Seraphin had told him she had stopped seeing patients after being promoted to assistant deputy superintendent. So why the hell was her name on every piece of paper in Buddy Ives's file?

His eyes swung to the phone. He searched his wallet for Seraphin's lake house number and dialed.

Oliver answered. Louis was polite when

he asked for her. After a few minutes, Seraphin's voice came on the line.

"Good evening, Mr. Kincaid," she said. "Have you called to shout at me again?"

He took a breath, working hard on sounding contrite. "No," he said. "I called to apologize."

"I appreciate that."

"I also called for something else," he said.

"Yes?"

"I need some help."

She was quiet for a moment. "What kind of help?"

"Personal," he said, lowering his voice, trying now to sound pathetic. "I lost it down there, Doctor."

She said nothing.

"It scared me," he said. "Scared the shit out of me."

"And you want a session?"

"Yes."

Again, a pause. "I'm closing up the lake house in the morning," she said. "If you want to see me, you'll have to come here."

"Thank you."

"Tonight."

"I'll see you around seven."

"I'll be waiting, Mr. Kincaid."

Chapter 43

It was snowing hard by the time he started up the hill toward Seraphin's house. He had gone only twenty feet when the Impala lost traction and stopped. He tried again but the tires spun and the car went nowhere.

"Shit," he muttered. He looked out the windshield at the huge wet flakes caught in the headlight beams. Far up the hill, between the bare trees, he could see the front of the house in the glare of the floodlights. No choice. He had to walk the rest of the way or risk getting stuck here all night.

He got out and trudged up the hill. The driveway looked like it had been plowed recently, but there was at least a foot of fresh snow covering it now.

Seraphin's Volvo was parked to the left of the front door. Louis went up and knocked. Oliver opened the door immediately, wearing his usual black suit.

"The doctor's waiting for you in the den," he said. His face was red from cold or exertion. There was a mound of Vuitton luggage behind him.

"I can find my way," Louis said.

Oliver gave him a cold stare, then hoisted up two bags and headed outside to the car.

Seraphin was behind a desk, sorting through some papers, when Louis came into the den. She looked up and gave him a curt smile as she continued putting papers in a briefcase.

"Please, make yourself comfortable, Mr. Kincaid. I'm just finishing up here."

Louis slipped out of his jacket and took a chair. He noticed two Vuitton duffels on the floor next to the desk.

"So, where are you going?" Louis asked.

"Florida," she said. "I have a condo on Hobe Sound." She smiled again. "I just can't tolerate the cold the way I used to. The price one pays for getting old, I suppose."

Louis had to grit his teeth at the small talk. "Yeah."

Seraphin snapped the briefcase closed and set it on the floor near the duffels. She came forward, pushing up the sleeves of her beige sweater as she took the chair opposite him. "Now," she said. "What exactly is wrong?"

"I was hoping you could tell me," Louis said.

"Have you ever been in therapy before?"

"No," he said.

"Well, there's nothing to be nervous about."

"I'm not nervous."

"Do you always sit on the edge of a chair like that?"

Louis hesitated, then sat back, draping his hands over the chair's arms. "Is this better?"

She allowed her smile to widen. Then she, too, sat back in her chair. "You said something happened to you while you were in the tunnels," she said.

He nodded.

"That you were scared."

He nodded again.

"Can you tell me why you felt scared?"

"You mean besides the fact I was locked down there with a crazed, insane murderer?"

Seraphin somehow managed to keep her expression neutral. She picked a speck of lint off her beige skirt. Her eyes came back to Louis's face and stayed there, waiting.

Louis let out a long breath. "I heard things," he said finally. He waited, seeing a new spark of interest in her eyes.

"Go on," she said.

"I heard things and I don't know if they were real."

"What did you *think* you heard?"

"Babies . . . babies crying."

There was a quick flash of something across her face. Louis was sure he had seen it.

"Why do you think you heard babies?" Seraphin asked.

"Why do *you* think I heard babies, Doctor?"

She uncrossed her legs and sat up straighter in the chair. "I would guess it was your guilt," she said.

"What do I have to feel guilty about?"

"That you couldn't save that poor woman. I would guess that it was her cries you heard in your imagination."

Louis shook his head slowly. "No. It was babies."

She tilted her head as she looked at him. "Do you have any children of your own, Mr. Kincaid?"

"This isn't about me."

"Of course it is."

Louis sat forward in his chair. "I know what you did. I know you used Buddy Ives to impregnate patients and that you sold the babies. You isolated the women and then shipped their babies out in apple baskets. For money."

Seraphin didn't move.

"How much did you make, Doctor?" Louis pressed. "Enough to build a new infirmary? Enough to pay off the nurses? Enough to get appointed to the state board?"

Louis stopped. He couldn't believe it. Seraphin was smiling.

"That's quite a story," she said. "You believe it's real, don't you?"

He could feel the balance shifting back to her, but he wasn't going to let it happen. "I know Claudia DeFoe was real," he said. "And I know she was pregnant when she came to Hidden Lake."

A small crack in Seraphin's smile.

"Rodney DeFoe told me everything," Louis said. "And Claudia's mother told me she signed adoption papers. You took her baby and sold it. That's how you got the idea for all this."

Seraphin rose slowly, walking a slow, deliberate circle. "You've taken this one tragic incident and made it into this preposterous black market baby conspiracy."

"So I'm right," Louis said.

"Right?" she asked.

"About the babies."

"You seem to need me to confirm something you already know."

541

"Just tell me, damn it. Am I right?"

Seraphin hesitated. "Did you read that book by Dr. Laing I gave you? He identified a state called ontological insecurity. It means lacking a sense of selfhood and personal identity."

"I know who I am," Louis said.

She studied him for a moment. "But your experience in the tunnel may have altered that. Dr. Laing said that when people are in a threatening situation from which there is no physical escape they can dissociate — their mental self splits from their body and what they experience is like a dream."

"I read part of that damn book," Louis said. "He also said being threatened can make your thinking extra sharp."

Another small smile, as cold as the air. "Then you have nothing to worry about."

She was still putting it back on him. Making him believe he already had the answers to his questions. But he didn't.

"Where is Claudia DeFoe?" he asked.

She stared at him. It was a cool, long look that he could read nothing into. For several seconds, neither spoke. Then a sound behind Louis made Seraphin's eyes swing up.

"Yes, Oliver?"

"The snow is getting worse. We have to

542

get going, Doctor, or we won't make it out of here," he said.

"Right," she said. "Take those bags and finish loading the car. I will be along shortly."

Oliver picked up the two duffels sitting by the desk and left.

Seraphin looked back at Louis. "I'm afraid our time is up, Mr. Kincaid."

She turned off the nearest lamp, then went to her desk and picked up her briefcase.

Louis stood up. "Where is Claudia DeFoe?"

Seraphin was at the doors leading to the deck. She gave them a hard tug to make sure they were locked. She turned to him.

"Dead," she said. She switched off the floodlight. The backyard went black. She looked at him.

Louis didn't move.

"You're not going to leave until you hear this, are you?" she asked.

"No."

"Claudia committed suicide," Seraphin said. "She got out one night and just walked into the lake."

"How do you know it was suicide?"

Seraphin paused, seeing the look on Louis's face. "She left a note for Rodney," she said. "I have it in my office in Ann Arbor. I'll show it to you."

"Why didn't you just tell the family the truth?"

"You know their history. It would have been cruel. And there would have been other . . . repercussions."

Louis sat back in the chair. He understood what she was saying. And he wanted to believe her about the way Claudia died. But . . .

"What happened to her remains?" he asked.

Seraphin sighed, taking a moment to answer. "She was cremated by mistake. You can find her remains in the columbarium. There are small numbers imprinted on the tops of the cans. It was done as a precaution in case the labels were lost. Look for number 926. There is a file somewhere in E Building that holds the cremation log. You'll find her name there."

She held up her hands as if she wanted to say something else, but then she just dropped them to her sides. "I probably should have told you all this a long time ago, but I was hoping to spare everyone," she said softly. "I'm so sorry."

He was quiet. Unmoving. In the reflected light from the desk lamp,

Seraphin's face looked suddenly old and deflated. The hardness that always seemed to be there was gone.

Louis picked up his coat off the chair.

"Good-bye, Mr. Kincaid," she said.

He left the den. Out in the foyer, he paused to put on his coat. There were still three large suitcases sitting next to the open front door and a trail of wet footprints leading outside.

Leaving the door ajar, Louis stepped out into the snow. The Volvo was parked to the left of the entrance. There were two suitcases sitting back near the closed trunk. Louis turned up his collar and started back down the hill.

The snow was up to his calves and he walked slowly, his mind locked now on Claudia and her baby. He had his truth now. Claudia was dead. He had his truth now about the baby — from Eloise DeFoe and now Seraphin. But that was all that seemed real. Everything else that had happened at Hidden Lake might as well be a damn dream for all the chance he had of proving it.

And Ives . . .

Where the hell was he?

Seraphin was afraid of Ives. She was smart to be leaving.

Louis stopped.

The suitcases sitting by the Volvo. Something weird about that. They were covered with snow, like they'd been sitting there a long time. And the trunk was closed. Why would Oliver leave them in the snow to get ruined?

Forget it, Kincaid. Go home. Get some sleep.

But something felt wrong. *Shit, just go back and check.*

Louis turned and trudged back up the hill. In the glare of the floodlights, he could see that the front door was closed now, but the suitcases were still sitting by the truck untouched, a heavy layer of snow on top now. Where the hell was Oliver?

Louis went to the back of the Volvo. The snow was tamped down, but the impression was half filled with a fresh cover. Louis stood, looking into the trees, his ears attuned to any sound. But there was only the soft hiss of the falling snow.

He walked to the driver's door, jerked it open and found the latch to pop the trunk. He went back and threw the truck open.

Oliver lay facedown across the suitcases. There was a huge jagged hole ripped in his neck. The blood had soaked through his collar and onto the suitcases below.

Louis drew back, scanning the nearby trees.

Shit. Ives was here.

His eyes shot to the closed front door. Ives was inside.

Louis pulled up Oliver's jacket, searching the body for a gun. Nothing. He needed a weapon . . . something. Rolling the body onto its side, Louis pulled out a suitcase, tossing it to the snow, looking for something he could use. There was a large black kit and he tore it open.

A tire iron. He grabbed it and ran to the front door.

Chapter 44

He pushed against the door. It was locked. He bumped against it with his shoulder, but the door didn't give. He pounded on it with the tire iron.

"Dr. Seraphin!" he shouted.

He heard nothing from inside.

The windows. There were two, one on each side of the doors, but their wood shutters were closed and padlocked.

He stepped back to the door, his eyes on the brass door handle. He'd break it off. He started slamming at the handle with the tire iron, smashing it with vicious swings. The wood splintered and the brass started to bend and finally pulled loose from the door. But the lock wouldn't give.

"Dr. Seraphin!" he yelled again.

He changed angles, jamming the tire iron into the crevice between the lock and the jamb, trying to snap the lock off. The door start to rattle, but still something was holding the lock in place.

He stepped back and kicked at it with the flat of his foot. It shuddered but didn't open, and he kicked it again, and a third time, and finally on the forth, it popped open, slamming back against the wall.

"Dr. Seraphin!"

The house was dark. The living room, the hall, all the lights were off and still he heard no voices. No screams. And he wondered if he was too late. The den. She would still have been in the den.

The door at the end of the hall was closed and he shoved it open, bracing himself in the doorway for anything or anyone, but the room was empty.

And cold.

The sliding glass doors were wide open, snow swirling and dancing on the rush of wind. On the floor, near the doors, lay a long thin tool with a rusty handle and a spray of sharp prongs on the other end. The prongs were wet with blood.

He scanned the rest of the room. An overturned table, shards of glass from a broken lamp, bunched-up area rugs, and blood . . . lots of it, tracked across the floor to the deck outside.

Louis stepped quickly to the doors, flipping on the back floodlight. The entire yard and dock exploded in a wash of white light and it was so bright against the snow

Louis had to blink to bring everything into focus.

Blood.

Red footprints and long, bloody drag marks stretching across the snowy deck and down the sloping yard.

Ives had taken her with him. But why? Where did he think he could go?

Louis squinted into the yard.

The boathouse. Ives would think it held a boat, a way to escape and a way to take Seraphin with him so he could finish her later.

Louis took a step outside, then turned back to the room.

The gun case.

He smashed the front glass with the tire iron, jerking out the closest shotgun, a long-barreled twelve-gauge. He cracked it open. It was not loaded.

He tried the other one. Empty. He reached for the small drawer at the bottom of the gun case. It was locked and it took only one hard jam of the tire iron to split it open.

Fuck! No shells.

He grabbed the twelve-gauge. He had to hope that Ives would see the gun and believe it was loaded and surrender.

Louis started to the deck, then spotted a

phone on the desk. It would take at least thirty seconds to call, but he knew he had to. He punched in the Ardmore station number, left a rushed message with the dispatcher, then headed out into the deck.

The cold air was a sudden burn against the rush of adrenaline surging through him. The snow was deepening, up to his ankles now. As he walked he searched the yard, looking to the shadows for movement, but there was nothing. Just the track of red in the snow leading down to the boathouse.

The narrow door to the boathouse was unlocked and he threw it open, taking a second to back off, waiting for a possible shot, even though he knew Ives didn't use a gun. But still he waited, and coming from inside, he heard a soft, pained whimpering, and the hiss of a man's voice.

Louis stepped inside, the floodlight spraying in around him, painting the rugged wooden walls with a gray light.

The boathouse was long, the beamed roof about ten or twelve feet high, strung with ropes, hooks, and pulleys. Along the outside walls was a narrow wooden walkway, braced by a thin weathered rail. And between them was the black opaque surface of the lake.

It took a second for Louis to see Ives, but slowly his body began to take shape in the shadows. Ives was pressed into the corner at the far end of the boathouse. His head was covered in a black wool cap, long hanks of dark hair snaking from it, a spray of whiskers darkening his jaw. His slender body billowed with the bulk of a filthy old parka.

Ives held a long knife in one hand, his other wrapped around Seraphin's neck. She was clinging to his arm, her fingers pressed into the sleeve of the parka. The front of her beige skirt was soaked with blood.

For a second it was still, then sounds began to register. Ives's ragged, desperate breaths. Seraphin's whimpers. His own pounding heartbeat.

Louis pointed the shotgun. "Let her go."

Ives brought the knife down, thrusting it into her abdomen. Seraphin screamed, her body going limp, the scream quickly turning to a wet gasp.

Dear God.

Louis quickly moved closer, the shotgun leveled, hoping to force Ives into a decision. But Ives didn't seem to even be aware Louis was there. Didn't seem to recognize the gun as anything that could hurt him.

"Ives!" Louis shouted. "Listen to me."

Ives looked up, looking toward Louis but not at him. His face was strangely calm, his eyes small empty holes that were searching but seeing nothing.

Then he unexpectedly flipped the knife to the hand that held Seraphin and Louis thought he was going to cut her throat. But Ives ignored Seraphin and the knife, focused on his empty hand.

"Ives!"

Ives reached down and touched Seraphin's skirt, then pressed his fingers deep into the shredded fabric, into the wound.

Jesus.

Then he jerked his hand free, and brought it to himself, rubbing the blood on his crotch with frenzied strokes. Whispers now. Grunts. Hisses. Groans, as if there were some animal inside him fighting to get out.

Louis moved closer, watching for some sign Ives would defend himself or lunge at him, but Ives had reached back to Seraphin to get more blood. She was unconscious. Or dead.

"Ives!"

Finally Ives looked at him, his wild pupils still for just a second. Louis lifted the shotgun and aimed it at Ives's forehead.

"Let her drop."

Ives hurled himself sideways. Louis reached for him — both of them — but they were gone, crashing through the rotted railing and hitting the thin ice with a splintering splash. Ives disappeared underwater, taking Seraphin with him.

Louis leaned over the railing, stunned, his eyes searching the surface. For several seconds he saw nothing but the swirl of ice and black water. Then Ives's head broke through, frantic, spinning, spraying water. And he still had Seraphin in his grasp, holding her now by the hair. Her eyes were open but Louis couldn't tell if she was alive.

Ives struggled to stand in the waist-deep water and when he got his footing, he started to trudge away toward the open lake, dragging Seraphin behind him.

No. No.

He couldn't let Ives just swim away, but he couldn't go in the water after him. If he did, he would have to overpower Ives and do it quickly. And he realized in that instant that it might be for nothing. That Seraphin could already be dead. That Ives would freeze out in the lake anyway. And then he knew it was none of that. He was afraid to go into the water. Afraid he couldn't take Ives. Afraid he would die.

He jumped.

The water stabbed at his body, pushing the air from his lungs, and he gasped, his heart throwing itself into a furious hammer. *Move. Move!*

He forced his legs forward. Ives was only a few feet away, weighed down by the heavy parka and Seraphin. Louis lunged, grabbed the parka's collar, and Ives spun, one hand still gripping Seraphin, the other flailing the knife. He started stabbing at Louis, thrusting up and down. Louis tried to use the shotgun butt as a weapon, but he couldn't get in a solid hit.

Damn the gun. He tossed it to the water and grabbed Ives's jacket with both fists, jerking him above the water and slamming his back against a piling so hard Ives let out a groan. But the knife came up and started on a downward thrust. Louis caught Ives's wrist, keeping the knife high in the air, using his body weight to slam him harder against the piling.

Louis saw panic in Ives's eyes.

Ives let go of Seraphin. The water started to take her away. Louis's eyes flicked to her, and Ives's fist came in hard, smashing into Louis's temple. Before

Louis could react, he was hit again.

Louis threw all his strength into dislodging the knife, slamming Ives's hand against the piling. But the bastard didn't let go, like he was feeling none of it.

Louis tried to rip Ives's fingers from the knife handle, twisting them backward. The snap of bone and Ives let out a bellow, dropping the knife. Louis lunged for it before it sank. Ives slumped against the piling.

Louis could barely stand up. He needed to get out of the water. He started slogging toward a small wooden ladder on the other side of the walkway. His frozen fingers touched wood, but he couldn't grip the rung.

An arm came around his neck, grappling at him, pulling at his jacket, almost taking him underwater, and Louis knew if he went under now, he would not come back up.

He spun, grabbed Ives behind the neck, and jerked him forward, chest to chest, so close he could feel Ives's panicked breaths. Louis stuck the knife into his belly.

Ives jerked. Gasped.

Louis stabbed him again. And again.

Ives let out a rasp and his body went limp and he fell against Louis, the knife still in his gut, the water around Louis's hand suddenly warm.

A thick stillness settled over them. No sound except the lapping of the water against the pilings. Louis draped one arm over the ladder rung, afraid he was going to pass out. Ives's body started to drift away, the back of the parka ballooning with enough air to keep him afloat.

Louis didn't want to think. Couldn't think. He just needed to get out of the icy water that was eating away at his legs and chest and head.

The knife . . . where? Then he remembered. It was still in Ives's body. Louis looked out to the opening leading out to the lake. Ives's body had disappeared.

He was shivering so hard he could barely hold on to the ladder rung. Willing every muscle to work, he started to pull himself up. His feet fumbled to find the rung, his legs burned. But suddenly he was there, flat on his belly on the wood.

He knew he couldn't stay there. He struggled to his knees, then his feet. Stumbling from the boathouse, he trudged through the snow, the floodlight like acid in his eyes, the air so thick and so cold he felt like he had to push his way through it.

He went down. Hands. Knees. Snow in his nose. Icy water in his lungs.

Louis lifted his head. His legs. He couldn't feel his legs. But he could feel his heart. Beating.

Jesus. Jesus. God, help me. I can't think. I can't feel. I can't move.

Things were going black. But from somewhere he heard a sound. A sound he knew.

Sirens.

Chapter 45

"What happened?"

For a moment, Louis couldn't reply. Then he pulled the blanket tighter around his shivering body. Dalum was waiting, looking down at him with pleading eyes, like he needed someone to make him feel that what he was thinking wasn't crazy.

Louis spoke, but nothing came out. His throat was raw or frozen and he cleared it. "I killed Ives," he said.

"Out there?"

Louis nodded and he heard himself saying something about Seraphin and he was watching Dalum's face as the words stumbled out. Then another face came into focus. Detective Bloom. And then Louis could see uniforms, hear other voices.

Bloom was talking now, face close, but his words were making no sense.

"Stop," Louis whispered. "Stop. Speak slower."

"You're saying Buddy Ives killed Dr. Seraphin and you killed him in a struggle?"

Louis nodded. He realized he was only half dressed, wearing a dry T-shirt and socks. Two pairs. And he was only now starting to feel the warmth from the fireplace. He looked at it, wanting to move closer, but he couldn't manage the strength.

"Who killed the man in the Volvo trunk?" Bloom asked.

"Ives."

Bloom was quiet. Everyone was quiet. It was a deafening kind of silence, filled with questions and doubt.

"Ives is out there," Louis said. "Go find him."

"The lake may ice over by the time they float up," Bloom said. "If that's the case, we won't find them until spring."

Louis coughed, tasting water, feeling as if the muscles in his stomach were ripping apart, and he brought a fist to his mouth to stifle a second cough. His eye caught the lower end of a pair of uniform pants as they walked by. The cop's feet were bare.

"Kincaid," Bloom said.

"What?"

"I need some answers here. How do I know you didn't go off the deep end and kill this Oliver guy? Or the doctor? Or that you didn't murder Buddy Ives in cold blood?"

"You don't," Louis said.

"Then what do you expect me to do?"

"I don't know."

Dalum's voice came back. "Detective, right now he needs a doctor. Let me take him over to the hospital."

Bloom stood up. He said something to Dalum that Louis couldn't hear; then he was gone. A few minutes later, he heard the squeak of a gurney and he was being helped up. He tried to keep the blanket around him, but the edges kept slipping from his fingers and he felt as if he were dropping off into a sleepy fog.

He was flat on his back, faces above him. Then the air was cold, the sky dark. A bump as they hefted him off the porch. Snow settling on his face. He could see sleeves. Patches. The red and white of the EMTs. The blue and gold of the state police.

"Dan?" he called.

"I'm right here," Dalum said.

Two full days by the fire and still his feet felt cold. Most of his whole body felt cold, but it was his feet that bothered him the most. He hadn't lost any toes to frostbite. Had no permanent damage to his muscles. Or bones. The two ugly bruises on the side of his face would go away, too.

He slumped lower in the chair, easing his stockinged feet closer to the fireplace. He pulled the afghan over the MSU sweatshirt, and closed his eyes, listening to the perky voice of Jane Pauley on the *Today Show* as she told the ladies how to make Christmas ornaments out of egg noodles.

Phillip was on his way to Brighton to pick up Frances. Louis had overheard him on the phone last night, telling Frances that Louis had been through a rough time, killed a man, and almost drowned, and that Frances should come home and spend some time with him before he went back to Florida. She had agreed.

Detective Bloom had called last night. He still couldn't find any bodies and the lake was starting to ice over, making the divers' search dangerous. He said it might be spring before they found them. Asked Louis if he'd stay in Michigan for a few more days at least. Louis said he would. Until Friday. His flight left at two.

Louis glanced over at the phone. John Spera had called an hour ago to tell him he had gone through all the cremation cans. He had found a can with the number 926 on the top. There was no label, Spera had told him. Short of finding the cremation file in E Building there was no real way to prove it held Claudia's remains. Louis told Spera to keep the can in a safe place until he could come and pick it up.

Louis muted the television, thinking about Claudia, how there was nothing to mark her existence except numbers. First that sad stone marker in the cemetery, then Spera's tags, and now this. At least he had the ashes to offer Phillip. He hadn't decided yet if he was going to tell him what Seraphin said about Claudia committing suicide.

Louis heard the hum of a car motor, close like it was in the driveway. But it was too soon for Phillip to be back. A few seconds later, he heard boots crunching in the snow, then the doorbell. He debated whether to answer it. His feet still prickled with every step, and the muscles along his back and legs were bruised and tight.

Again, the doorbell.

He pushed up out of the chair and hobbled toward the door. The bell had rung two more times by the time Louis opened the door.

Rodney stood on the porch, his camel overcoat buttoned all the way up, his gloved hand about to ring the doorbell again. Instead, he slowly removed his sunglasses.

"Good morning," Rodney said.

"What are you doing here?" Louis asked.

"I've come to see Phillip. Is he here?"

"No," Louis said.

For a second, Louis thought about telling Rodney about the ashes. But it didn't seem like the right thing to do before Phillip knew.

"Do you know when he'll be back?" Rodney asked.

Louis shook his head.

Rodney hesitated, like he wasn't sure what to do or say. Then he nodded stiffly and turned. Louis started to close the door.

"Wait."

Rodney had turned back. For a moment, he just stood there, looking at Louis, his face drawn with sadness. Louis waited, his hand on the door.

"I've made a mess of most of my life," Rodney said. "A mess of others' lives, too, I'm afraid."

Louis didn't say a word.

"I was wondering if you might take a drive with me."

"To where?"

Rodney fought to keep his eyes steady. "Saugatuck."

Chapter 46

Rodney kept the black Jaguar at a steady clip, dodging the eighteen-wheelers and slow Chevys on I-94. Louis sat silent in the passenger seat, his minding racing ahead to Saugatuck.

I've made a mess of most of my life. A mess of others' lives, too, I'm afraid. I was wondering if you might take a drive with me.

To where?

Saugatuck.

Why?

That's where she is.

Rodney hadn't said much since they started out. And even though Louis had a million questions he needed to ask, only one seemed important right now.

"What is she like?" he asked finally.

Rodney didn't take his eyes off the road. "I see her once a week. Sometimes she's almost normal, like you or me or anyone. Then there are the days I have come to call her otherworld times. And then are the bad days when I can't see anything behind her eyes at all." He glanced at Louis. "Do you understand what I mean?"

Louis nodded, looking back out the windshield. The traffic slowed as they neared Jackson. For a long time, neither said anything.

"You despise me, don't you?" Rodney said.

Louis didn't answer. He let the silence lengthen before he finally spoke. "Just tell me one thing. Why are you doing this? What, your guilt finally get to you? You expect Phillip to forgive you?"

"No," Rodney said quietly.

"Then why now after all these years?"

Rodney seemed to be thinking for a moment. "The night they took Claudia away . . . I've spent my whole life trying to find ways to forget that night. Did a damn good job until you showed up."

He glanced at Louis and looked back to the road. "But when you came to the house Monday, something my mother said to you made me remember something. It was like it had always been there in the back of my memory, but like I said, I didn't really *want* to remember."

When Rodney spoke again, his voice had an edge.

"Mother said that when she went upstairs, Claudia wasn't in her bedroom and that she found her in the bathroom with her wrists slit."

"So?"

Rodney was shaking his head. "But that wasn't possible because Mother had locked Claudia in her room and Claudia's bathroom wasn't attached to her room. Claudia couldn't have been in her own bathroom."

"I don't follow," Louis said.

"I think my mother locked Claudia in *her* bedroom. That's where I remember Claudia being when the police came, in Mother's bathroom."

Rodney was quiet for a moment.

"I saw the bathroom after," Rodney said. "The maid was there, with her bucket and rag wiping down the walls and the tub, and . . . Mother always hated messes."

"Rodney —"

"Let me finish. I'm trying to tell you I didn't see it then but I do now. Claudia didn't slash her own wrists. Mother cut her."

Louis looked away.

"She must have drugged her," Rodney said. "God knows there was always enough Valium in the house. She drugged her, then held her down and cut her."

Louis remembered what Millie Reuben had said, about Claudia having no memory of cutting herself. *She used to cry all night. I never heard someone cry so much.*

"I never believed Claudia," Rodney said softly. "She always said she didn't cut herself. But I didn't believe her. I didn't believe her because I always just thought she was . . . damaged."

"Damaged?" Louis said.

"She was the one who found Father." Rodney glanced at him. "I already told you that, didn't I?"

"Yes."

For a second, Louis thought about telling Rodney to pull over. He looked too distressed to drive. But Rodney's hands were steady on the wheel.

"Why did you go through the whole charade of the death and burial? Why not just take your sister out of there?" Louis asked.

"It was mostly because of Phillip. Dr. Seraphin had red-flagged Claudia's file to prevent anyone from visiting her."

"Why?"

"Because of the baby. Seraphin was afraid if Phillip saw Claudia, he would figure things out. When Phillip came back to see Claudia, Seraphin panicked and told Phillip she had died. Right after that, she called me and said I had to get Claudia out of there."

"Why bury the rocks?"

"Seraphin said we needed something Phillip could see, something real. So she gave him a grave to visit."

"How'd she get away with it?"

"She had the power, especially in E Building, because no one really cared what went on there. She told everyone Claudia had had died of the flu. She had patients do the burial."

"And you went along with all this."

"I wasn't going to let Mother put Claudia in another one of those places. So I took her to Saugatuck. Mother never went there so she never knew. She still doesn't."

"You can't keep her to yourself anymore," Louis said.

Rodney nodded. "I know."

Most of Saugatuck's shops and restaurants were shuttered for the winter. There were only a few old boats left in the harbor, and on the street, snowdrifts were heaped against listing fences normally meant to hold back the sands.

Rodney headed away from town on the road that rimmed Lake Michigan. No cars. No people. The beautiful homes overlooking the lake were shuttered, their lawns covered with pristine blankets of white. Far off across the huge gray expanse of Lake Michigan, a freighter sat poised like a toy against the blue wall of sky.

The Jaguar slowed. Louis looked up at the house. He remembered Phillip's description of the house as an old stone fortress. But it was really a modest place compared to its neighbors, outdated and softened by the embrace of a veranda. The driveway was freshly plowed and there was a green car parked by the front door.

Rodney pulled in behind it and turned off the engine. "This was our old summer house. Claudia and I both loved this place. I think this was the only place we were happy when we were kids."

"Rodney, do you know where Claudia's child is?" Louis asked.

"I wish the hell I did," Rodney said softly.

He sat staring at the stone house for a moment, then opened the car door. Louis followed him up onto the porch. Rodney unlocked the front door and they went in.

A black woman with a lilting accent

greeted Rodney by name and took their coats. Rodney introduced her as Enid Lewis, a nurse who had been taking care of Claudia for the last fifteen years.

"How is she today, Enid?" Rodney asked.

"Good. We're playing poker."

"Poker?"

"I taught her. We play for shells. Is that okay?"

"Of course."

Enid led them deeper into the house. Louis had a sense of old slip-covered chairs, overflowing bookcases, and walls of framed photographs. They passed through a living room with a stone fireplace. There was a model of a clipper ship on the mantel surrounded by shells and twisting pieces of driftwood. The placed smelled of pine furniture polish and something good cooking.

The wood floor creaked as they made their way to a room in the back of the house. The sun streamed in from a wall of windows falling on old white wicker furniture softened with blue cushions.

She was sitting at a table in the corner. Her head was down as she shuffled cards and the sun fell on her long pale hair.

"Claudia, your brother's here," Enid said, going forward.

Her head came up and Louis saw her face.

He knew she was in her fifties now, and those years were there in the lines in her face, the softening of her jaw, and the silvery streaks in her hair. Other things were there, too, in the faraway gaze of her eyes and the odd, broken-bird angle at which she held her head. But then her eyes found Rodney and she smiled and suddenly Louis saw everything that Phillip had seen thirty-five years ago.

Rodney went to her and bent to kiss her cheek.

"Did you bring me cherries?" she asked.

"I told you, Claudie, they're not in season yet. Soon," Rodney said gently.

"Ah . . . winter. I forgot," she said.

Rodney turned and gestured to Louis. "I've brought a friend."

Caramel-brown eyes. "Hello," she said.

Louis came forward. "Hello, Claudia. I'm Louis."

"Are you a friend of my brother?" she asked. Her love for Rodney was there in every part of her face.

"Yes," Louis said. He nodded toward the chair opposite her. "Can I sit down?"

"Only if you let me win." She smiled up at

Enid, who was hovering near the windows.

"Be careful. She cheats," Enid said.

Louis sat down. Claudia starting dealing the cards. Her moves were deliberate and slow. Louis picked up his five cards.

"You forgot to ante," Claudia said.

"Sorry." Louis moved a shell to the middle of the wicker table.

Claudia fanned her cards and looked over at Louis. "Go ahead," she said.

Louis didn't even look at his cards before he moved two shells to the center. Claudia did the same and looked at him expectantly.

"How many?"

"What?"

"Cards," she said eagerly.

"Oh . . . two," Louis said, setting two cards down. He picked up the new cards she dealt.

"I'll take five," she said. She took five cards but didn't lay any down.

"Claudia, can I ask you some questions?" Louis began.

She nodded, intent on trying to fan all the cards.

"I have a friend who knows you," Louis said. "Do you remember someone named Phillip?"

She looked up. "Phillip," she said softly.

"Do you remember him?"

A cloud passed over her face. "Gold leaves," she said.

Louis glanced over at Rodney, who lowered his head.

"Gold leaves . . . silver ring," Claudia said. "Phillip gave me a silver ring." She looked up at Enid. "What happened to that ring?"

"I don't know, dear," Enid said.

Claudia's gaze drifted to the window. Louis wasn't going to press it, but suddenly Claudia began to hum. Then the words came and she sang softly.

"A boy and girl, they can kiss
  good-bye,
and run down the hillside together.
But a man and woman, their hearts
  can cry
forever and ever
Though oceans may sever.
True be my true love . . ."

She smiled at Louis. "We danced."

Louis nodded. "I know. Phillip told me."

"Phillip is here?"

"No," Louis said. "Would you like to see him sometime?"

"Oh yes."

Louis looked up at Rodney. He had his eyes shut. Enid was watching Claudia carefully. When Louis looked back at Claudia, her eyes had gone blank. Then she went back to arranging the cards. Her hands were small and she was having trouble holding all the cards. Louis caught a glimpse of a white scar on her left wrist.

"I think it was your turn," Claudia said.

Louis pushed two more shells to the middle of the table. She did the same.

"You're supposed to lay your cards down now," she said.

Louis fanned them out. He had a pair of jacks.

Claudia smiled and set her ten cards down. "Two pair," she said. She gathered in the shells.

"Claudia, do you remember a baby?" Louis asked.

"Baby?" She was picking up the cards and didn't look up.

"Yes. You went to the hospital. Do you remember a baby?"

Her expression was suddenly harder, but Louis couldn't tell if it was from a memory or because she was concentrating on shuffling the cards.

"I heard it crying," she said, her delicate fingers struggling with the cards. "The baby was crying. I heard it but I never saw it."

Her eyes shot up to Louis. "They took it away. Where is the baby?"

Louis hesitated. "Someone is loving it," he said.

She nodded slowly.

Enid was hovering and Louis motioned her back with his eyes.

Claudia let the cards fall to the table. She covered her face with her hands. "The second one hurt," she whispered.

"What?" Louis said.

"The baby. The second one hurt so bad."

Louis heard the sharp intake of Rodney's breath, but he kept his eyes locked on Claudia.

"Claudia," Louis said gently, "do you remember being in the hospital?"

Her hands remained on her face but she nodded.

"Do you remember anything that happened to you there?"

"A dark room," Claudia said. "And a doctor with hands like ice."

Seraphin, Louis thought. "Do you remember a man?" he pressed.

"That's enough," Rodney said, stepping forward.

Claudia's hands fell. Her eyes were dry but anxious. "A man?" She shook her head.

Thank God. Seraphin had doped her up enough so she couldn't remember Ives. Only Millie carried that nightmare.

Millie . . .

"Claudia, do you remember Millie?"

"Millie? Millie? We ran to the apple orchard." Claudia's face softened. "Millie was my friend."

Louis was relieved to see the distress draining from Claudia's face.

"Would you like to see Millie maybe?" he asked.

She nodded, smiling. Then she looked down, seemingly noticing the cards for the first time. "Do you want to play again?" she asked.

Louis looked up at Rodney. His face was ashen. He turned away. Louis moved a shell to the middle of the table.

"Your deal," he said.

Claudia's smile widened and she gathered up the cards. Enid came forward to pick up the ones that had fallen on the floor.

Louis leaned back in his chair, watching Enid's gentle ministrations. He was watching Claudia, too, wondering how someone could have so much taken away — a lover, a baby, a life — and still endure. He was watching her and thinking about being in the tunnel and listening to that woman scream as she died. He was watching Claudia and thinking how envious he was of the peace he saw in her face.

She was dealing again. This time she gave herself two cards and dealt him ten. She set the rest of the deck in the middle of the table.

"Your move, Louis," she said.

"I don't know what to do," he said.

"It's easy," she said. "You hang on to the ones you want to keep and throw away all the rest."

The caramel-colored eyes held his for a moment. Louis started laying down his cards.

Chapter 47

It was late when Phillip returned home from Brighton. Frances had come with him. There had been no chance to talk to him alone until Frances had gone to bed. Louis waited until Phillip went outside for a smoke and followed him.

The moment seemed right. He told him about Claudia.

Phillip listened quietly, then asked one question. *When can I see her?*

We'll go first thing tomorrow, Phil.

It had been an emotional morning. Phil had waited until breakfast to tell Frances. Louis slipped off to the living room, wanting to listen, knowing he shouldn't. But he had watched.

They were seated at the kitchen table, Phil's hand over Frances's. Louis saw Frances's shoulders stiffen, then slump forward as Phil spoke. A few seconds later, she rose quickly from her chair and left the room, walking by Louis, jaw set, tears in her eyes.

But she had been at the front door when

they left. Phillip was too lost in what lay ahead to see the look on his wife's face as they pulled out of the drive, but Louis could see it. She was scared.

They needed to make a side trip on the way to Saugatuck, Louis told Phillip. Just before leaving the house, Alice had called, asking Louis to come out to say good-bye. She told him she and Charlie would be at the hospital where she was packing up her office. Louis had tried to brush it off, saying it was a long drive, knowing Phillip was anxious to get to Saugatuck, but then Charlie came on the phone.

I have a Christmas present for you, Mr. Kincaid.

Louis told Charlie he would be there about ten. On the way, they had passed a mall and Louis had the thought he should take Charlie a present, too, and he had just the right one in mind.

Louis found a music store and was halfway to the checkout with Iron Butterfly's *In-A-Gadda-Da-Vida* tape when it occurred to him Charlie didn't need, or probably want, the real version.

Louis put the Iron Butterfly back and wandered to the classical section. It was right in front: Felix Mendelssohn's *A Midsummer Night's Dream*, the complete score from the ballet. Louis added a Walkman and three sets of batteries and paid five dollars to have it wrapped.

There was one car in the Hidden Lake parking lot. It belonged to Alice. There were no police cars. No security. Just a monstrosity of a crane, the wrecking ball hanging motionless against the blue sky. A few bulldozers sat nearby, waiting to be put into action.

Louis put the car in Park and glanced over to the passenger seat. Phillip was bent forward, looking up at the administration building.

"I've been to the cemetery many times," Phil said. "But I haven't been inside the gates for fifteen years. If you don't mind, I'll wait here."

Louis left the Impala running and hurried up to the door, Charlie's present in his hand. The building seemed even emptier than before, no security officers roaming the halls, no voices. Up on the second floor, Charlie was sitting on the nurse's desk, head bent over a comic book. He wore a cherry-red sweatshirt and what looked to be brand-new jeans.

"Hi, Charlie," Louis said.

Charlie's head came up and he slipped

off the desk quickly, his eyes moving to the silver box in Louis's hand. He shifted his weight, trying to hold back a smile.

Louis was about to hand it to him when Chief Dalum came down the hall from Alice's office. She was right behind him. Both were in sweatshirts and jeans. Alice wore red Christmas ornament earrings.

"I didn't see your car outside," Louis said, extending a hand to Dalum.

Dalum took his hand, holding it a second longer than he needed to, tighter than he needed to. "Alice called me and said you'd be stopping by. I wanted to say good-bye," Dalum said.

"Thanks for coming."

"So, when you heading home?"

"Tomorrow."

Dalum tilted his head toward the parking lot. "Who's that with you?"

"My foster father. We're on our way to see Claudia DeFoe."

Dalum raised an eyebrow. "So you found her? Alive?"

"Yes," Louis said. "Last thing I expected."

"Was it?"

Louis held his look for a second. "I don't know what I expected."

"Best way to be," Dalum said. "For a cop."

Louis was quiet, trying to think of a quick way to thank Dalum for everything he had done. Thank him for sitting by his side the other night in the Ardmore Hospital. And for not saying a word for three hours. And for the warm fire in his house later. And the bowl of Campbell's chicken noodle soup on his nightstand at one in the morning.

"I'll stay in touch," Louis said.

"Send me a postcard," Dalum said. "One of those ones with the sexy babes in bikinis."

"Will do."

Charlie was waiting, eyes still on the silver package in Louis's hand. Louis held it out. "Merry Christmas, Charlie."

Charlie took it slowly, his long fingers picking at the bow as if it were the petals of a delicate flower.

"Just rip it open," Louis said.

Charlie did, letting the paper and box lid drop to the floor. He stared at the tissue paper, then looked up at Louis, confused.

Louis reached in and pulled out the Walkman and headphones, and set them on Charlie's head. Charlie still didn't seem to understand. Louis slapped the Walkman in Charlie's hand and hit the Play button.

Charlie's eyes widened and his right

hand moved to the side of his head, cupping the earphones. Louis held the cassette cover in front of his face. Charlie smiled, somehow knowing what it was.

Alice stepped up, reaching for Louis's hand, not in a handshake, but in an embrace, both hands over his. "Thank you," she said. "For his gift, and for what you did."

Louis was quiet, watching Charlie. Charlie was swaying to a tune no one else could hear, and at that moment he looked like some kid on the beach in Florida oblivious to everything and everyone else.

Louis looked back at Alice. "Do you have a job lined up?"

"Not right away," Alice said. "I have some savings. Maybe I'll look after the first of the year. There's a shortage of us, you know. Nurses."

Louis glanced at Charlie again. "I need to say good-bye now."

Alice waved her hand to get Charlie's attention, and he looked up, pulled the headphones down to his neck, and grabbed a box wrapped in red paper from behind the desk. He came to Louis and held it out.

"Merry Christmas."

Louis took the box, peeled off the paper, and lifted the top. It was a hat. Knitted wool, with a red and yellow zigzag pattern and two long chin ties with red tassels on each end.

"I tried to tell him," Alice said softly, "that you live in Florida and you don't need a hat."

"It's a helluva hat," Charlie said.

Louis laughed. "Yes, it is."

"It'll keep your head warm."

"Yes, it will."

Louis took a deep breath, trying to decide how he wanted to say good-bye to Charlie, but Charlie made the decision for him.

He stuck out his hand, fingers spread. "Good-bye, Mr. Kincaid."

Louis shook his hand, held it for a moment, then grabbed Charlie around the neck for a quick hug. Charlie drew back, cheeks red.

"Men shake hands," Charlie said.

"Friends hug."

"Okay."

Louis said good-bye again to Alice and Chief Dalum, and he tucked the wool hat under his arm and started down the steps. He paused at the first landing, stopped by something he couldn't see, slowed by an image he tried to bring into focus.

It was of a woman sitting on steps similar to these, her three children at her feet, an uneasy husband standing in the shadows, watching. Louis glanced up at the second floor, then moved on, pushing open the doors and walking back into the early morning sun. He stopped short on the walk, drawing a quick breath.

Parked next to Alice's car was a state police cruiser. Detective Bloom stood leaning against it, arms crossed, eyes in a squint, his badge glinting the same yellow gold as his hair.

Louis walked to him. Bloom stayed against the fender, watching him, waiting.

"We identified the victim from the tunnel," he said as Louis came near. "A sixteen-year-old girl. Her family has a farm nearby."

Louis was quiet.

"Nothing's come out of the lake yet," Bloom went on. "My divers are exhausted. We're calling it off for a few weeks, see if something floats up."

Bloom was staring at him, and Louis had the sense that he was testing him for some kind of reaction.

"And we identified that tool in Seraphin's house," Bloom said. "It was an old obstetrical instrument called a quadruple dilator. Made in the 1800s. It disappeared from one of the hospital showcases about a year ago."

Louis remembered the prongs on the end, and he could see how it must have worked. He knew it wasn't a random choice of weapons for Ives. He had taken a tool specifically designed to destroy a woman's sexuality.

Seraphin's words came back to him: *Your man is impotent. He's grown angrier over the years, an anger magnified by his inability to perform.*

An image came to him of Ives standing in the corner of the boathouse, rubbing Seraphin's blood on his pants, desperately trying to arouse himself.

"Jesus," Louis whispered.

"What?" Bloom asked.

"You asked me before why Ives hated his doctor. Why did he hate someone who let him live out his rape fantasies?"

"Yeah. So?"

"Seraphin may have been cruel, but she was a doctor. She would not have released Ives back into the world without somehow making sure he was no longer dangerous. She castrated him."

Bloom's eyes narrowed as he tried to picture it. "More bullshit," he said. "And who gives a damn anyway?"

"You should," Louis said.

"All I care about is finding those two bodies, putting them in the ground, and stamping this one closed," Bloom said. He nodded toward the administration building. "And I'll be glad when they knock this damn place down and we can forget it was even here."

A gust blew up behind them, sweeping the dry snow up in a sudden eddy. Louis blinked against the wind as he looked at the red brick buildings.

"I need to get on the road," Louis said.

"I'd like you to stay in Michigan a few weeks."

"No," Louis said. "I'm going home."

"I still got questions," Bloom said.

"I gave you a five-page statement."

"One that reads like a horror novel. One with no ending."

Louis didn't answer.

Bloom shook his head, lips tight; then he turned and yanked open the passenger door to the cruiser, bending inside. When he came up, he had Louis's Glock in his hand.

Bloom thrust it out. Louis accepted it and started away.

"Hey."

Louis turned back to Bloom.

"I'm going to be calling you in Florida."

"You do that."

Louis got in the Impala and shifted into Reverse. He hit the brake, his gaze going back to the administration building, then to the bulldozer sitting nearby.

"I'd like to make one more stop," Louis said, looking at Phillip. "Do you mind?"

Phillip gave him a slow nod. "Whatever you need to do, Louis."

Chapter 48

The car was quiet except for the scratching noise coming from the backseat. Louis looked in the rearview mirror. Doug Delp had his head down and was scribbling in his notebook.

Louis looked back at the road. He didn't know if he could trust Delp. But he did know now that he could trust his own instincts. And his instincts were telling him that there was a story that needed to be told about Hidden Lake and that Delp was the only one who could do it.

Phillip was sitting silent in the passenger seat. He had agreed to let Delp write the story, but only after Louis had convinced him that Hidden Lake needed to be exposed and that Delp would be sensitive to Phillip's privacy. But Louis hadn't told Delp that Claudia was alive. Or that she and Phillip had a child.

He planned to. But he wanted to make sure he got something from Delp in return.

As they drove through the endless cornfields, Louis continued to tell Delp everything he knew about Hidden Lake. Ives, Seraphin, the rapes, it all came spilling out of him.

When Louis got to the part about being locked in the tunnels, he paused, his eyes trained on the road. After a moment, he went on, his voice as steady as he could manage. He started to talk about hearing the girl's screams and stopped again.

Louis's eyes flicked up to the rearview mirror. Delp was looking at him, waiting for more.

"You want to come back to that part?" Delp asked.

"Yeah."

Louis glanced over at Phillip. There was a sadness in his expression, like hearing the story had made him regret what he had put Louis through.

Louis used the rest of the drive to finish the story, pausing only once, when he got to what had happened in the boathouse. Delp was still writing when Louis turned onto the lakeshore road. Then his head shot up, his eyes swinging left, to the gray lake.

"Where are we?" Delp asked.

"Be quiet."

Louis turned into the drive and parked behind Enid's car and the black Jag. He

591

looked at Phillip. Phillip was sitting back, shoulders stiff, eyes unblinking. His hands were clasped together in his lap. Louis waited for him to move. Or breathe.

The front door to the house opened and Rodney came out, stuffing his hands in the pockets of his slacks. Phillip pushed open the car door and slipped out, hesitating a moment before he walked to the porch.

Rodney said something, then stuck out a hand. Phillip did not take it. Rodney spoke again; then the two of them walked inside the house.

Delp leaned on the front seat. "What's going on? Who is that guy? What the hell are we doing here?"

"Shut up."

Louis sat watching the house, glancing down at his watch. One minute, two . . . five.

He opened the car door and got out. "Stay here, Delp."

Louis shut the door on Delp's protests. He walked to the porch and opened the front door, slipping inside. He closed the door quietly and stood for a moment in the foyer.

It was quiet. Louis heard a sound and looked to the living room on his left. Enid and Rodney were sitting across from each other, stiff on their chairs.

Whispers. Coming from the sunroom at the back of the house. Claudia's soft voice. Phillip's softer answer. But he couldn't hear anything that was being said.

Louis bowed his head. *I shouldn't be here.*

He turned and left, closing the door behind him.

Delp was standing by the Impala, a cigarette in his shivering hand. He tossed it to the ground as Louis came near.

"Claudia DeFoe is in that house, isn't she?" Delp said.

"Yes," Louis said, looking back to the house.

"You're not going to let me in there, are you?"

"Not yet."

Delp paused. "Quid pro quo," he said.

"That's right," Louis said.

Delp's eyes went to the house. "What do I have to do?"

"You're good at finding things, Delp," Louis said. "There's someone I want you to find for Phillip."

Chapter 49

He looked out the wet windows. The American Airlines jet was sitting in the cold rain. The waiting area was crowded with snowbirds, college students, and irritable children off to their first trip to Disney World.

"Looks like you're finally boarding," Phillip said.

Louis checked his watch. "I should be home by four."

Phillip nodded, drawing a tired breath, his gaze moving to the tarmac and an incoming flight. Louis watched him, seeing the same pensive look that had been there since the drive back from Saugatuck yesterday. Phillip wasn't sad so much as solemn, like he realized one door had closed but another was standing open. The old resoluteness was there in his eyes, too. At least now Phillip *knew*. And Louis could see that he was going to deal with it.

Frances . . .

Louis didn't know about her. There had

been no time to really talk. He would write her when he got home.

There had not been much time to talk to Phillip, either. But now he had time, if only ten minutes.

Your move, Louis.

"Phil," Louis said, "I owe you an apology."

Phillip turned to him.

"I was wrong."

"About what?"

"That night in the kitchen. I was having trouble dealing with things," Louis said. "It was getting to me and I took it out on you."

"I didn't see what it was doing to you," Phillip said.

The final boarding call came for his flight.

"I need . . ." Louis began.

Phillip waited.

"I never told you," Louis said. "I never thanked you."

"For what?"

Louis shook his head slowly. "Everything."

The ticket agent was looking at them. Louis picked up his duffel bag and faced Phillip. Before he could say anything, Phillip pulled him close and held him.

"I love you, son."

"I know."

Chapter 50

His suitcase was unpacked. But he hadn't stopped there. He had swept the sand out of the cottage and cleaned out the refrigerator, tossing out the withered lettuce and old cartons of Chinese takeout.

Then he had turned his sights on the bookcase in the living room. He dusted all the books and CDs, then cleaned the four items on the top shelf — an old puka bead necklace, a tiny human skull, two picture frames, and a shiny black stone.

The necklace had belonged to a missing girl. The skull, from some unknown infant, had washed up on his beach after the hurricane. The sepia-toned photograph was of his mother, Lila. The other frame held a quote from Winston Churchill given to him by the widow of a dead cop. The black stone was a snowflake obsidian, a gift from his partner Ollie.

Each was a piece from his past, mementos from people whose lives had touched his for an instant before they were gone.

He carefully wiped the dust from the obsidian, remembering what Ollie had said. *It is the stone of purity, Louis, that balances the mind and the spirit.*

He set the stone down next to the baby skull, then reached into his suitcase and withdrew a small box. He took out the woolly hat Charlie had given him, folded it into a square, and set it on the shelf. Then he turned to survey the cottage. One last thing to do.

In the bedroom, he stripped the rumpled sheets from the bed and remade it with fresh white ones. He took his time, smoothing the wrinkles and positioning the two pillows. Then he cranked open the jalousie windows and the sea-tang breeze poured in.

Back in the living room, he paused to sort through the mail that had accumulated while he had been gone. Bills, junk, nothing that couldn't wait. There was a postcard showing an old fort in St. Augustine. Louis turned it over and smiled as he read Ben's boyish scrawl. He stuck the card under a refrigerator magnet.

He got a Heineken out of the refrigerator. Then he uncorked the bottle of cabernet that he had picked up at Bailey's Market on the drive in from the airport.

He didn't like red wine, but she did.

Pouring a full glass, he took the wine and the beer out to the porch. He set the glass down on the table and lowered himself into the lounge chair.

The sun was starting its descent into the gulf, but it was maybe eighty degrees. Still, he sat there, wearing a heavy sweatshirt, his arms crossed over his chest.

He couldn't seem to get warm.

It would pass. He knew that. He knew other things now, too. He knew that Delp would tell the story and help Phillip start the search for his child. He knew that Phillip and Frances had to find their own way. He hoped it was back to each other.

He knew that he couldn't wait to see Ben next week when he got home from St. Augustine. He knew he would be going fishing this month with Sam Dodie and that they wouldn't catch anything. He knew he would meet his friend Mel Landeta for a beer at O'Sullivan's. He knew there would always be a bottle of Remy Martin for him on the shelf at Roberta Tatum's store and a table for him at Timmy's Nook.

He knew, after three years of denial, he wasn't going back to Michigan or any-where else. It was hard to put down roots in the Florida sand, and the things that survived here did so with only the greatest grit and determination.

But he had done it. This was his home now.

The lowering sun hit him full in the face and he laid his head back and closed his eyes.

He knew he was happy.

The crunch of gravel made him open his eyes. A red Bronco was pulling into his drive. He didn't move. He just sat there and watched as Joe got out.

Everything was warm, rendered red gold by the generous sun, and the moment was still, unmoving, more real than anything had ever been in his life. And she was beautiful.

About the Author

P. J. Parrish has worked as a newspaper reporter and editor, arts reviewer, blackjack dealer, and personnel director in a Mississippi casino. The Edgar-nominated author currently resides in Southhaven, Mississippi, and Fort Lauderdale, Florida, and is married with three children, three grandchildren and five cats. P. J. Parrish is currently at work on the next Louis Kincaid thriller. Please visit the author's Web site at www.pjparrish.com.